"Does money appeal to you?"
Carol Grahame asked Dr. Brade.

"It's the only thing that does."

"How much would it cost to open a medical office in Charlesville, where I live?"

"I think $2,000 would do it."

"The day we're married I'll turn over $2,000 to you."

"And how will I live?" Brade asked.

"I'll pay you $500 a month until you're on your feet. Through my connections you'll meet the kind of people you need to know. The rest will be up to you."

"I can take care of the rest," he said, thinking, *It might even be enjoyable. . . .*

"One more thing," Carol said, with no special emphasis. "This is a paper marriage. It has no other implications. Is that clear?"

SPENCER BRADE, M.D.
was originally published by
Doubleday & Comp

Books by Frank G. Slaughter

Published by POCKET BOOKS

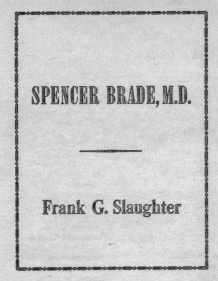

SPENCER BRADE, M.D.

Frank G. Slaughter

A POCKET BOOK EDITION published by
Simon & Schuster of Canada, Ltd. • Markham, Ontario, Canada
Registered User of the Trademark

SPENCER BRADE, M.D.

Doubleday edition published 1942

POCKET BOOK edition published July, 1953
16th printing .... June, 1976

This POCKET BOOK edition includes every word contained
in the original, higher-priced edition. It is printed from
brand-new plates made from completely reset, clear, easy-
to-read type. POCKET BOOK editions are published by
POCKET BOOKS, a division of Simon & Schuster of Canada,
Ltd., 330 Steelcase Road, Markham, Ontario L3R 2M1.
Trademarks registered in Canada and other countries.

ISBN: 0-671-80610-6.

Printed in Canada.

CHAPTER I

He stood in smiling content before the door of the Surgical Building that bore his name in small neat letters. Tomorrow there would be a second line on the ground-glass panel. The legend would read:

SPENCER BRADE, M.D.
Assistant Professor of Surgery

Eventually it would, in the natural course of events, be changed to Professor of Surgery. Meantime the ambition which had, ten short years before, seemed so unattainable was on the eve of achievement. None of his whilom classmates would have believed it of the gay-hearted, charming, rather fastidious young medical student who, however, had never let his car, his extensive wardrobe, his social connections, and the other elegances of existence natural to him interfere with thorough and honest work in the science to which he had devoted himself.

He would not have believed it of himself. Nevertheless, that hope had been implicit in his heart when, with his class, he had heard old "Paddy" Ryan deliver his annual message of advice to the young graduates in a quavering voice that still echoed through the clinics of Europe and America as the voice of high purpose and sure authority, commanding the respect of medical scientists the world over.

That snappy car of Spencer Brade's was gone now, together

with many other embellishments of extravagant living. The Brade taste for luxury had been curbed since the bad years of the early thirties had wiped out the family fortune and thrown young Spencer upon his own resources, except for a meager remnant of inheritance which he presently went through with pleasure if not profit, and upon which he looked back with no more than a normally healthy regret. They had not hit him too hard, those deprivations. His was a buoyant nature, and, like most buoyant natures, undulant also, with hollows of depression between the crests when things went wrong.

There had been little to discourage him in his medical course. Blessed with an apprehensive mind, a retentive memory, and the precious knack of insulating his brain from outer contacts while working, he had come through with ease and distinction. Nobody wins a Lakeview diploma without effort. But the hard way was not too hard for Spencer Brade. The laboratory work, doing blood counts in the middle of the night, sewing up drunken Negroes in the accident room, setting fractures under the white glare of the emergency light—all had been part of the game, necessary steps in the grind that transformed the raw and awkward intern into the finished surgeon. Becoming resident surgeon had been the first important advance; seeing his name heading the list of appointments as instructor in surgery four years after graduation, still another. Now would come the triumph which all ambitious youngsters throughout the great clinic coveted; tomorrow at the graduating exercises his name would be read out as an assistant to the great Dr. Robert Powers.

Only a man who had grown up at Lakeview could know what it really meant to be a teacher there, only one whose very fiber had absorbed the traditions, the customs, that distinguished it from all the thousands of other hospitals throughout the country. It wasn't simply a hospital, Lakeview. It was a fiery pillar, a beacon of everything that was best, everything that was most serviceable, altruistic, uncompromising, in medicine and surgery. No one who had not walked its worn tiled halls for years could realize that. No one who had not sat for hours on the rickety chairs in its lecture rooms, who had not seen the sunrise shine in the front door of the emergency room on a Sunday morning while he labored to finish the accident toll, the broken bodies from automobile crash-ups, the clean slash of razor wounds, the black eyes and broken jaws from fights in dingy barrooms, who had not been through that rigorous mill and loved it and come back for more, could ever know what it meant to feel on his shoulders the burden and pride of carrying the banner, of keeping the Lakeview standard the high and shining thing it represented to profession and public throughout the country.

He turned a corner past the tiny hospital post office which was closed now, for it was after five, past the new research wing whose donor would be revealed at tomorrow's exercises, and entered the broad lobby where humans were dwarfed by the benign marble Christ towering a story and a half upward into the skylighted rotunda. It was a symbol, that statue, of what the hospital meant to broken and suffering and hoping humanity.

"Any calls for me, Miss Wythe?" he asked the gray-haired receptionist at the information desk beside the switchboard.

"Nothing at all, Dr. Brade."

He nodded. "Going to the exercises tomorrow?"

"Haven't missed a Lakeview graduation in fifteen years," she said. "I'll be there to hear your good news. It will be a popular appointment, Dr. Brade."

Spencer Brade smiled. It must be on the hospital grapevine, he thought.

In the hallway he met a former classmate, Mark Travers. He had never specially liked Travers, although he respected him. With all the money in the world back of him, Travers had been a faithful, plodding, thorough though unimaginative worker. The broad, sober face above the stocky shoulders now wore an expression of discomfort, as if its owner would rather not have encountered Spen just then. Surely it was not because he was jealous of the other's coming promotion. Travers' had never been the petty type of mind. Spen said pleasantly:

"Hello, Travers."

"Oh, hello, Brade." There was a pause. "Haven't you forgotten your umbrella? It's coming down heavy."

"Got a rainproof epidermis," said Spen cheerfully. "I like the rain."

Travers seemed to be trying to bring himself to further speech. Spen waited, eying him curiously.

"Well, good luck, Brade," he said hollowly. "I've always said you were the best man in the class. Better than I am, a lot."

"Phooey! But it's nice of you to say it, Travers. So long."

3

He *is* jealous, thought Spen, and trying to show himself he's not. Devil of a queer way to congratulate a fellow!

He made a run for a streetcar which took him within a block of home. He had nothing to do until ten o'clock when Flick Fleming, who was on early duty, was throwing a beer party in his honor. Meantime he was restless with happiness. He needed exercise, something to work off his surplus energy. He'd have a drink, get into a raincoat, and go for a long walk. He wanted to get to open country where he could stretch his legs and lungs and breathe the warm, sweet air of the May night.

Another car line took him to a distant suburb where he got out. As he passed through a lane of straggling hovels he recognized the neighborhood. He had once sat for hours in one of those dingy habitations, waiting for the addition of still another black-eyed bambino to the teeming brood of an Italian popcorn vendor. Open fields appeared on either side of him. Presently he came to a concrete road, rising to a bridge under which a stream swept in muddy and turbulent spate. He strolled up the arc and leaned over, finding a response to his inner unrest in the plunge and seethe of the water beneath.

A car slid up back of him, almost to the abutment, and stopped. From its long gray lines and the quiet purr of the engine he judged it to be of an expensive make. The lights went off, leaving only the pin-point red of the fender lights. Neckers, probably; fugitives from the country club a mile or so away. Let 'em neck. They wouldn't disturb him. And he certainly had no intention of bothering them.

The car door opened and a slight figure stepped out into the rain, which had now moderated to a mediocre sort of drizzle. It was a girl. She seemed to be looking about her uncertainly. Spen kept still. He was sure that she had not noticed him. She picked her way carefully down the bank and took a path that led upstream. Though he could not be sure, the interested observer thought that she carried some small object in one hand, while with the other she held her long coat against the marauding wind.

Curiosity beset him. What kind of place was this for a rendezvous? Was there a boathouse or a dwelling place up there, where a lover awaited her coming? He moved along the parapet, the better to watch her.

The girl emerged from a clump of willows, half curtaining an abruptly sloping point, and felt her way forward with careful

4

feet. Then first it came to him with a shock that she might be going to throw herself into the torrent. He shouted.

What happened so swiftly thereafter he could not clearly make out. But there was a cry; she seemed to be throwing something outward, and then she slipped down the declivity and was being borne toward him in the strong current.

An extreme and positive distaste took possession of Spencer Brade's mental processes. He could see no valid reason for risking a life of which he thought well for a stranger who was probably a lunatic or a damned hysterical fool, at best. Thus far this was good, solid, logical thinking. Deeper down lay an instinct which imperatively forbade his standing passive and letting a woman drown.

In two or three seconds while the flood had possession of her Brade did some, cool, rapid reasoning. If he plunged over the rail into the full onset of the flood the chances were that, even if he got a grip on her, both of them would be battered into insensibility. But twenty rods downstream there was a sharp bend to the left, against which the current piled before swerving to its channel. If he knew anything of the course of water under pressure, a floating object, assuming that it floated that long, would veer shoreward there before being hurled onward.

He ran down the bridge, vaulted the rail, and made a dash for the vantage point. Straining his eyes upcurrent, he could at first see nothing. Perhaps her clothing might have caught on some rock or submerged log. Then he saw a dark blue object roll and rise almost at his feet. Seizing a stoutly rooted shore willow, he threw himself forward and caught the skirt of the long coat.

To drag his salvage up on the bank was no great effort. He stretched her on the ground and made a cursory examination. She was breathing, but there was a rattle suggesting that some water had found its way into her lungs. A discolored area over her right temple testified to her having struck some obstacle in her headlong descent.

Concussion, he diagnosed, and probably not severe, for her breathing was regular and even. She'd be okay in a little bit if the exposure and the water in her lungs didn't make trouble. Once again he lifted her to his shoulder and made his way up the bank. She was still unconscious when he placed her in the seat of the car, but her breathing was better; the rattle seemed

5

fainter. How serious her condition was, he could not tell, but one thing was sure: she must be taken somewhere for prompt treatment. He slid under the wheel and started the motor, heading back for the city, steadying her inert body when he ran over a bump or stopped at a crossroad. Once she moved a little and moaned, but her eyes did not open.

The logical thing would be to take her to the Lakeview Hospital. But Flick Fleming would be on duty in the emergency room, he thought wryly. It would be a long time before Flick stopped kidding him about "making them swim back." And, besides, something about his charge touched his sympathies unprofessionally. She looked so young and helpless. And there was an air of mystery or uncertainty about the whole business that troubled him. Suppose he did bring her in and turned in his report? It would be interpreted as attempted suicide, a police matter. But was it that? He was not so certain. Maybe his shout had startled her into losing her foothold on the slippery bank.

Moreover, on the evidence of her car and her clothes, she was rich. What the newspapers would do with a queer case like that would be plenty! It might start a scandal which would mess life up for her incalculably. He reached his decision, though with dubious reflections upon what he would be letting himself in for if she died on his hands; he would take her home with him and look after her there.

His apartment on the first floor consisted of a small living room, a bedroom, and a kitchenette. He carried the girl in through the back door so as not to attract attention. He felt the pulse as he laid her down. It was strong and full. She was firmly built, tanned, probably athletic; she ought to be okay with a night's sleep.

Methodically, as if he were stripping any other patient half dead with coma, he peeled off her wet garments. Her skin was blue from exposure as he wrapped her in a robe of woolly toweling and began to massage her arms and legs through the rough texture of the robe. Color appeared faintly in her cheeks, a sign that her circulation was overcoming the effects of exposure and the blow she had sustained. She moaned once as he slapped her cheeks briskly, and her eyelids half lifted, then dropped shut once more. From the almost empty bottle he brought a tumbler of whiskey, pried open her lips, and poured the liberal drink down her throat. She gulped it automatically, and he poured another drink and repeated the procedure. That would be enough stimulant for her now, and also enough of a sedative to make her drowsy for a while. Carefully he covered her with blankets, leaving little exposed but her nose and a few strands of coppery-gold hair against the pillow.

In the bathroom he quickly stripped and stepped under the shower. When he came out, wearing pajamas and a bathrobe and filled with a sense of well-being from a brisk toweling, he saw that the girl had moved until she was lying on her side, with one shapely arm beneath her head. He took what remained in the bottle to dull somewhat the discomfort on the studio couch in the living room.

Adventures were his dish, he thought with satisfaction as he lay down on the couch and pulled up the cover. He could imagine how Flick would whistle when he recounted for him the evening's measure of excitement. It wasn't every day that he went out for a walk in the rain and wound up with an incognito in his apartment.

CHAPTER II

EARLY light was seeping through his living-room window when Spencer Brade, who had slept with one ear on a hair-trigger, heard sounds from the bedroom.

"Lie quiet," he called. "I'll be right in."

His guest made no reply. She had propped herself on one elbow and was staring at the door when he entered.

"How do you feel?" he asked.

"I hardly know yet." The softly slurred terminals and lazy inflection marked her as Southern. Her dark eyes were troubled. She sank slowly back, gazing at the ceiling.

"Any pain?"

"Stiffness. All over my body."

"Naturally. You got thoroughly bumped."

"Who undressed me?"

"I did."

Her regard moved slowly to her face. She shivered. "Did anything happen?"

"Plenty happened. Don't have it on your mind."

"You know what I mean," she said somberly. "Did anything happen to me—here—in your bed?"

"Oh, that!" He laughed, and the tensity of her expression relaxed. "I'm a physician," he said. "That's why you're in my bed. No other reason in the world."

Her fingers, long and slim, lightly explored the bandage on her head.

"Did you put this on?"

"Yes. Let it alone."

She studied her hands. "I'm filthy."

"There wasn't time to clean you up last night. You can have a bath when you feel up to it. This afternoon, perhaps."

She thought a moment. "You're not married," she pronounced.

"How do you arrive at that?"

"There's no feeling of a woman in the place. Not even a servant."

"Can't afford luxuries," he answered lightly.

"You don't mind having to give them up?"

"How do you know I had to give them up?"

"That robe you're wearing," she explained. "It's Balthazar Specialty silk, isn't it? That's luxury."

"Clever," he said. Rather an extraordinary person, he thought, to indulge in deductions about his being rich or poor in such conditions.

"My head feels buzzy," she complained.

"Rest will help that. Look. It's not yet seven o'clock. You'd better go back to sleep. I have to go out. About ten o'clock or so I'll be back and get you some breakfast, and you'll feel better. Meanwhile I'll fix you something to go on with."

He went into the bathroom and returned with the pentobarbital capsule which she swallowed obediently.

"That'll hold you for three or four hours," he said. "By the way, Miss Grahame, I'm Dr. Spencer Brade."

"How did you know my name?" she asked abruptly.

"From your car registration."

"What else do you know about me?"

8

"Nothing. . . . Well, of course, that you're twenty-one and live in Charlesville, Georgia."

"Do you know Charlesville?"

"Never been there in my life."

"Is my car wrecked?"

"No. Why should it be?"

"I don't know. I'm still a little vague."

"Don't try to think. Lie back, now, and go to sleep. The bathroom is down the hall to your right. But be very careful if you get up. You may find yourself wobbly."

"Concussion?" she asked.

"Never mind. I'll do the diagnosing on this case. All you have to do is obey orders."

Their conversation was resumed at ten-thirty over coffee, rolls and marmalade. She sat in his biggest chair with the Balthazar robe over his spare and well-worn suit of pajamas.

"Where are my clothes?" was her first question.

"I took them over to the cleaner's. At the risk of my cherished reputation. Back at eleven. That's the theory. More likely, two-thirty."

"Am I a prisoner till then?"

"You could send and get some other clothes if it's anything immediate."

"It isn't." Her face was somber again.

"Then, as your physician, I advise you to lean back in that chair while I wash up the dishes."

"I suppose I ought to help. But I'm really not much good."

"You're not supposed to be. Not after that crack on the head."

"I mean at all. For anything."

"Oh well! Perhaps you haven't had to be."

She heard him whistling over his work in the tiny kitchen. Soon he reappeared, carefully drying a last spoon with the cloth. She managed to achieve a smile as she turned her head toward him.

"Do you know how you strike me, Dr. Spencer Brade?"

"Favorably, I hope. You're my first home patient."

"As being extraordinarily happy." She spoke the words with a queer sort of envious admiration.

"Not a bad guess."

"It's more than happiness, though. There's excitement in it. It's more like—what's the word I want?—elation."

9

"A good word. It'll do nicely."

"Is it a girl? I hope it's a girl."

"No. No girl in the picture."

"But it must be something *very* good."

"Purely on the professional side. But you're right. A very observant young lady."

"Is it a secret?"

He guessed shrewdly that she was interested in him as a means of keeping her mind off herself, and this he approved. "Not a bit," he replied. "It's of only personal and technical interest, though. Since you've laid yourself open to it, here goes."

In light, half-humorous terms, tempered to the lay mind, he sketched the outline of his years: his boyhood in the Kentucky bluegrass, a pleasant and not academically unprofitable four years at Princeton, the definite leaning toward surgery which had brought him to Lakeview, the comparative hardships of his student years, mitigated by his excited absorption in the work, his hopes, and the long-cherished ambition, to be so soon fulfilled.

"I was born with a silver spoon in my mouth, and I end up with a surgeon's knife in my hand. Of course I'd like to have both, but I'd take the scalpel every time. Thus ends our little saga, with the faculty meeting tonight to appoint our hero assistant professor of surgery."

"That's awfully good for a man as young as you, isn't it?" she asked.

"It's next to the last chapter of a *Horatio Alger*," he admitted with a smile. "From pampered playbody to penny-pinching pedagogue in ten easy years."

"What was the stimulus?"

"Money, or rather lack of it. Dad lost his dough, so little Spencer had to get down and dig."

"Ever yearn for the good old days?"

He looked at her quizzically. "Why ask that?"

"Do you?"

"We-ell, you don't have everything and then suddenly nothing without some regrets."

"I wonder if you're not really better off for the loss."

"Maybe so; maybe I wouldn't be a teacher now."

"You love it, don't you?"

10

"More than anything else in the world." And then as if a little ashamed of the fervor of the admission: "It's a lot more satisfactory than private practice."

"Not as much money in it, though, is there?"

"No. But enough. Tonight's boost will fatten up the little old pay envelope too. So, you see, it's really a pretty swell world from my point of view."

She seemed to consider this carefully. "Is that why you were so good to me?" she asked presently. "To pay off your debt to a generous world?"

"Not so much that. You were more or less thrown at my head, you know."

"But you might have taken me to a hospital and dumped me there. Isn't that the usual procedure?"

"And the police might have asked you troublesome questions."

"The police!" She seemed to shrivel. (She's been having experience with them, he thought.)

"Well, you didn't drive your car out there at midnight to do an exhibition swan dive with all your clothes on in a raging flood, I suppose."

"What *do* you suppose?" she asked slowly.

"That's beside the question. The police theory would be that you were trying to commit suicide."

"I wasn't."

His brows went up. "No? Accident?"

"You don't believe me."

"No," he said equably.

"Why?"

"Because you don't believe yourself. You're just trying to make yourself believe yourself."

"Oh, please don't be smarty with me," she besought. "I'm confused enough, as it is." She rose, walked over to the window, stared out into the sunshine, then resumed her seat with her elbow on knees. "I don't know," she said. "And that is the truth."

"It might be at that," he allowed.

"I went to throw something away. And when I'd done it, a wave of sick rage went through me like poison. I hated everything: myself, my life, that whole world that you think is so swell. . . . And then I was in the water. . . . And then I was sorry."

11

"All right," he said. "That's that. Call it an accident. But don't do it again."

"I won't. It's a promise."

"I'm going to have a bath now. Want a morning paper?"

She shook her head. "I'd rather just rest."

She heard his whistling above the thud and splash of the noisily filling tub; heard too, the impact of the outer door, pushed back against the wall, and thought it might be her returned suit. A hearty voice said:

"Spenny, you damn lazy swine! Why don't you get up in the morning?"

A spare form and keen reddish face thrust past the shielding portiere. The voice continued:

"Won't answer the phone. Don't show up at—Jee-miny!" The visitor had discovered Carol Grahame.

"Did you want to see Dr. Brade?" she asked composedly.

The newcomer's eyes were globules of amazement. He had come into the room, but he now began to back up in the manner of a puppy suddenly confronted by the presence of an insect of unknown but suspect possibilities.

"Excuse *me!*" he said in weak accents. "I didn't know he had a wom—I d-d-d-didn't know—"

"It doesn't matter. Dr. Brade is taking a bath."

"Of course," said the man and blushed a fiery crimson. "I didn't mean *that,*" he gasped, evidently feeling worse and worse.

The splashing stopped. The intruder looked uncertainly at the girl.

"Dr. Brade," she called. "There's a friend of yours here."

"Hey? What? Who?"

"It's me, Spen. Flick Fleming," the man said meekly.

"Well, what the hell——? Come in here."

"Excuse me," mumbled the caller. Still backing, as if from royalty, or in fear of an attack upon an undefended rear, he disappeared around the corner.

Spencer Brade interrupted the process of toweling himself to demand: "What do you think you're doing here at this hour?"

"Sorry, old man, and all that. I'd never have butted in if I'd known."

"Known what?"

"That you had a girl here. So that's why you ditched us on the party. I don't blame you."

12

"Have you got eyes in your fool head?"

"I'll say I have!" returned his friend with animation. "And is the lady easy on 'em! Jee-miny! What a face. You're a fool for luck, Spen."

"Hand me that shirt back of you and come to earth. If you weren't such an unbelievable ass you'd have noticed her bandaged head.

"Now that you mention it. Oh-h-h-h!" Enlightment was slowly dawning. "A patient?" he said. "Is that the idea?"

"What a mind!" Brade admired. "Leaps to its unerring conclusion with all the swiftness and precision of a pregnant cow. Now go back and entertain her while I dress."

He thrust the visitor in the hall and called, "Miss Grahame, this is Dr. Foster Fleming. Treat him gently. He isn't as weak in the mind as you might think."

She smiled at the perturbed young man and said, "Sit down, Dr. Fleming. Shall I go out while you talk to Dr. Brade? Is it private?"

"Not at all. Merely a message." To his friend, entering, he said, "Powsie wants to see you in his office at twelve, Spen."

"I'll be there. Thanks."

"His notification," Fleming explained to her. "He's on his way up. Doesn't have to work half as hard as a deserving guy like me, and what does he get for it? Everything."

"You're a liar," said Brade. "I work while you sleep."

"To catch up after you've fallen behind. Then he not only catches up on the rest of us, but he goes out in front."

"What he's trying to impress on you, Miss Grahame, is that I'm a genius. Far be it from me to deny it."

"Aren't you pretty good yourself?" the girl asked Fleming with a smile.

"Laborious; laborious," he grunted. "An old faithful plug."

"Hard work is his pet form of bragging," Brade said.

"Nobody'll ever say that of you, my boy," retorted his friend.

"Stop quarreling and give me a cigarette, somebody," said the girl. Both young men sprang as if galvanized.

She lay back in the chair, at ease, her feet crossed, her figure small and slim and suave as revealed beneath the light silk robe, her eyes smiling. It was borne in upon Spencer Brade that his caller's fervor of admiration was justified. Even with the bandage throwing her face out of proportion, she was an

13

undeniably seductive young person. Fleming was speaking again.

"Why do you leave your receiver off the hook, Spen? Afraid of being inter—Oh lord! There I go again!"

Carol Grahame laughed aloud. "If you mean that I spent the night here, I did. But I was unconscious most of the time."

Brade sensed in her manner a sardonic hardihood, of which he had caught faint intimations earlier. Maybe she wasn't as girlishly innocent as she looked.

"Well, I've been trying to get him all morning. No answer. What's the idea, Spen?" said Fleming.

"Petty resentment on the part of the telephone company," returned the tenant negligently. "Bills payable on the tenth. Or else."

"Oh!" said the girl. "What's the——? Where is the telephone company?"

Brade's face stiffened. "No thank you," he said. "I'm getting out soon anyway."

"You could regard it as part of my fee, couldn't you?" she asked.

"No fee."

"I don't like that," she protested. "Am I a charity patient?"

"Medical rules."

"We're not allowed to practice for money," Fleming explained.

Brade got up. "Too much talk," he pronounced. "My patient is getting tired."

"I'm sorry," said the other young doctor. He rose also.

"No; it's done me good. Cheered me up," the girl said alertly.

"You'd better lie down for awhile," prescribed Brade. "There's milk and crackers in the icebox. Won't hurt you to go light on eating. Sleep if you can. When I get back we'll see what's next."

Hardly were the two men in the hallway when Fleming opened up.

"Where'd you get her, Spen?"

Brade gave a modified outline of the night's adventures, with the accident angle.

"Where does she live?"

"Down Georgia way."

"Oh! Not a Baltimorean. Where's she staying?"

"To tell the truth, I forgot to ask her."

"She must be rich."

"I didn't ask her that either. Where do you get your slant?"

"Something about her. Her easy, confident way, I expect."

"Probably you're right. She hasn't volunteered much about herself."

"Mystery *and* beauty, huh? Look out, boy!"

"You're the stricken eagle, Flick. Look out, yourself."

The other sighed volcanically. "I haven't seen anything like that since last time I was in love," he declared. "Well, good luck, Spenny. Kiss Old Powsie on the brow for me and tell him if he's got any more fat jobs that you know a worthy young man who only asks a chance to get on in the world."

Carol Grahame, asleep in the chair, stirred, stretched, and opened her eyes. Someone was moving around in the bedroom.

"Is that you, Dr. Brade?" she called.

He came out and stood, staring at her without speaking. His eyes were hot and shrunken in a haggard face. He passed in front of her to throw open the window, and she caught a whiff of liquor in the air. Sitting down opposite her, he reached mechanically for her pulse.

"How do you feel?" he asked in the tones of an automaton.

CHAPTER III

ENTERING Dr. Robert Powers' office, Spencer Brade was at once struck by the great surgeon's appearance of perturbation and uncertainty.

"Sit down, Brade," he said. "I'm afraid I have bad news for you."

Brade knew with cold certainty what the answer would be before he put the question. "The appointment?"

15

"Yes. I'm sorry."

"Who gets it?"

"Mark Travers."

"Travers! Good God Almighty! How does Travers rate it?"

"Travers is an industrious worker, a sound reliable man." Old Powsie spoke without conviction.

"Is that the reason? Wait a minute. You don't have to answer." Suspicion and wrath were rising within the visitor. "I saw old Perley Travers mousing around the campus yesterday. *He's* the mysterious millionaire that gave us the research laboratory. *That's* the reason."

The department chief walked over to the window and gazed out at the new structure as if to fortify himself. "The announcement of the gift will be made this evening," he said.

"Jobs for sale. At Lakeview! Christ!"

"You're forgetting yourself, Brade." said Dr. Powers sharply.

"I've got a hell of a lot more to forget," came the savage retort. "Ten years of hard work and silly hopes. And Mark Travers lands the job. If that isn't a sellout, what is it?"

"I don't like it any better than you do," said the older man. "But there are other considerations that you may not have thought of."

He pointed them out. Hospitals, he said, great clinics, are like people. They need money to run on, to keep up their work. Their duty is partly to uphold necessary traditions, the things they represent, to set up and maintain medical standards for the guidance of others; partly to provide treatment, furnish skilled hands and eyes to carry diseased bodies through illness, or comfort them until death relieved their distress. To do all this takes money.

Everywhere endowments had shrunken; investments were not earning the high interest rates they had been returning when they were made. Hospitals, medical schools, even the richest foundations, were grasping at straws to keep themselves going, to be able to provide the clinical material that was vital if the students were to have the experience from which they learned their craft.

"It's a bigger thing than your career or mine, my boy." he said compassionately.

"It must be," said Brade with unappeased bitterness, "when an institution like Lakeview will sacrifice principle and fair play for it."

16

Old Powsie sighed. "I can't blame you for taking this hard. It's a setback. But it's not permanent. Your chance will come."

"Not here."

"Why not here? This is your place. This is your career."

"Not any more. Not good enough. It'll do for Travers and his kind. Not for me."

The small, wide-set, calm eyes regarded him intently. Queer, thought Spencer Brade uncomfortably, how impressive that pudgy little man could make himself at will.

"You consider that Lakeview is no longer good enough for you? Did I understand you correctly?"

"That's it."

"Now I shall have to tell you something about yourself which I might otherwise have left unsaid, Brade. I have watched your development since your last year in school. You are a brilliant student. You are gifted with great manual dexterity and assurance; you're born to be a surgeon. But there is another side to this, and there Mark Travers is your superior. I should never have selected him over you, as you know. But since you presume speaking contemptuously of him, it is as well that you should know wherein you, yourself fall short. You do not stand up to disappointments. When you missed the Arline Corcoran award by a hair, you sulked and thought yourself defrauded. There have been times when your work has slumped below its best—oh, only temporarily, I know. You always came back. There have been intervals, I think, when you were having too good a time, drinking too much, also."

"It never pulled down my standing," said the other defiantly.

"Standing isn't all. Natural ability isn't all. To reach the top in achievement and service—and that is what I have hoped for you—there must be character."

"Thank you, Dr. Powers." He knew in his heart that he was making a poor face of it, trying to find refuge in sarcasm, but his hurt pride drove him. "I have an idea that I'll be able to get along with what character I have in what I'm after from now on."

"And what is that?"

"Cash. Hard cash. There's nothing else worth working your head off for. The Travers deal——"

"One moment, sir! There was no deal. I will not permit you to use that word."

"Oh, all right! Appointment, then. The Travers appointment

proves my point, doesn't it? What I tried to get by hard work and at least a reasonable amount of ability—you admit that—was bought and delivered to him in the open market. Okay. I'm out to cash in on my M.D."

"Young man," said Powsie, "I'm not going to preach to you. But have you stopped to think what the degree of M.D. commits you to morally? What it means?"

"I know what it means to me now. M.D.: Money Doctor. Big-Money Brade; that's me."

"Where do you think you will end up with those standards?"

"In a rich and fashionable practice. Oh, I'll be ethical; ethical as all hell! I'll put up a swell front. You've got to, to impress the right people. Look at Eaves-Smith. Look at Falconer and what he's done already for himself in Philadelphia."

"I wouldn't have either of them as an orderly," said the other contemptuously.

"Well, if you're through with me, sir, I think I'll go out and get drunk."

"You're taking this like a spoiled child, Brade," said Powsie. "Nevertheless, I think—I hope—you're going to snap out of it. You're too good a man to throw yourself away, chasing a cheap success." He held out a pudgy hand. "Good luck and returning sanity to you," he said with somewhat melancholy smile. "When that day of recovery arrives come back to us."

In pursuance of his avowed purpose, Spencer Brade stopped at two bars before he remembered about his patient. He couldn't go back to her drunk. He would get her into shape, land her wherever she wanted to go, and then take suitable measures to forget, for the time anyway, the bitterest day of his life.

Something of this must have shown in his face as he stood beside the girl and put his mechanical query to her, feeling for her pulse. She drew away her wrist.

"I'm all right," she answered. "But you're not. What's happened to you?"

"Nothing."

"You can't tell me that. You look like a different person. And it's no improvement. What's the answer?"

"Why should I bother you with my troubles?" he said sullenly.

She was studying him, her expression alert and intent. "I've got a hunch," she said deliberately, "that we're two people in a

18

jam. Isn't there just a possibility that we might be useful to each other?"

"I don't know how," he began. But her manner, purposeful rather than sympathetic, impressed him. "Oh well," he yielded. "I spilled a lot of blah to you about myself this morning, so you may as well have the sequel. The whole thing was phony. I didn't get the appointment. Another bright dream gone to hell. Let's have a drink on it."

"You've had a drink, haven't you?"

"I've had two. And I'm going to have ten more. Or maybe twenty."

"Then our talk can wait."

"This thing is way beyond any talk. What should you and I talk about?"

"I might have a proposition for you."

"Uh-*huh!* Not a little touch of abortion perhaps?"

She winced. "How could you tell I was that way?" she demanded, caught off guard.

"Couldn't. Not medically. Deductive psychology. When a good-looking young gal in a five-thousand-dollar car trips and falls into a midnight flood, it's usually a case of *cherchez l'homme.* But I'm not professionally interested in abortion. Not yet, anyway. Of course I may get around to it later."

"Neither am I interested in it. I couldn't bear the thought of it. I'd feel unclean all my life."

"What is your little proposition, then?"

She surveyed him with doubt. "Are you sure you're in shape to consider it? It's important."

"Give me two minutes."

He went into the bathroom. When he reappeared she was seated at the cleared table. She motioned him to the seat opposite.

(Cool hand, he thought, I'd better watch my step with this female birdling.)

He said, "I've taken a shot of caffeine. Now let's have it."

Leaning forward, she set her elbow on the table and cupped her chin in her hand, scrutinizing him from somber and calculating eyes.

"Hold it," he said. "I'd like to have a picture of you like that. How would I title it, though? Messalina? Cassandra? Or Scarlett O'Hara?"

She shook her head. "I'm not acting a part."

"Back to reality. I'm waiting."

With unswerving gaze she asked, "Would you consider marrying me?"

He smiled. "Very flattering. But why pick me? Not a sudden and fatal infatuation, I suppose."

"No infatuations at all," she returned composedly. "As a matter of personal preference I'm not sure but what I like your little red friend better."

"Flick Fleming? Why not try him, then?"

"If I'm any judge of faces, he has too much character," was the cool reply. "I doubt if he'd do it."

"Oh! A physiognomist," commented Brade, not too well pleased. "Thanks for the gratifying comparison. I daresay you're right."

"Or if he did," she went on, "it might be from another motive that would bring about complications. He might fall in love with me. You won't."

"How can you tell that?"

"You're much too wrapped up in yourself, I think."

"More flattery. You're almost fulsome, my dear. Go ahead. What's the inducement?"

"Money. Does it appeal to you?"

"It's the only thing that does."

"Then I'd like to know more fully what happened this morning to make such a change in you."

He told her, in such detail as he considered necessary for a clear picture.

"You're through here, then?" she assumed.

"Definitely and absolutely. I'd see the whole lot in hell before——"

"What is your plan? What would you do if you could?"

"Pocket surgery. Settle into a rich community and operate on their purses. I'm all through with ideals. They get you nowhere."

"There's no idealism in my offer. How much would it cost to open a medical office in Charlesville, where I live?"

He did some quick figuring on the back of an envelope. "Two thousand dollars would do it in bang-up style."

"The day we're married I'll turn over to you two thousand dollars."

"That's all very well for a start. But how am I to live?"

"I'll obligate myself legally to pay you five hundred dollars a

20

month until you're on your feet. Give me a list of your local debts and they'll be settled. Through my connections at home you'll meet the kind of people you need to know. The rest will be up to you."

"I can take care of the rest," he assured her.

"When the time comes a divorce can be arranged without too much scandal. Meantime, we're on a purely business basis. How much time do you want to make up you mind?"

He stared at her, aghast. "My God!" he said. "And you're only twenty-one years old."

"I've aged a good deal in the last month," she said quietly.

"Any other strings on this?"

She reflected. "I take you to be a gentleman by birth and upbringing. My family has always maintained certain standards, social and professional. And I don't want a husband who will let me down."

"Show me the money and I'll live up to it."

"Then it's a bargain?"

"You've bought yourself a husband. Body, boots, and britches; lock, stock, and barrel; hook, line, bob, and sinker, with principles, ethics, and my immortal soul thrown in. Do you smell brimstone, Miss Mephistopheles? When do we have our child?"

"Don't!" she said.

"Sorry," he said. "I won't ask any more irrelevant questions."

She made an effort at self-mastery. "It's quite all right," she said. "You've a right to know about me. Only—I'm not quite up to it yet."

"Of course not," he said in quick contribution. "I'm not shining as a physician any more than as a fiancé. But I should like to know when we're to be married."

"Would day after tomorrow be too soon?"

"Not for me. Let's have a drink on it."

She relaxed, smiling faintly. "Make mine a martini."

Presently they were touching glasses.

"Sometime," she said, "if this goes through, I'd like to come back and see Lakeview. I've always been interested in medical things. I even thought once I'd like to be a doctor."

"A hen medic? You? With that face? You'd break up the class."

"I've taken a sort of amateur nursing course," she went on,

21

ignoring the rather crass compliment. "It's in my blood, I expect. Allston King was my great-uncle."

"The orthopedist? I take off my hat to him. He made a lot of money."

"He did a lot of good," she retorted hotly. "When he was dying people that he'd helped came and prayed outside the hospital."

"I'd rather they'd pay me than pray for me," he said.

Again her chin dropped into her curved hand. "Are you really as hard and cheap as that? Or are you posing to yourself because you've been so badly hurt?"

The martini, on top of the previous drinks, was distilling a not too subtle heat through his nerves. "Never mind me," he said in a changed tone. "Let's consider us. What d'you say, we have another drink and go out somewhere to dinner and then come back here? Did you ever give any thought to the trial-marriage theory? I believe there's something in it."

She finished her cocktail and set it down before answering him.

"This," she said with no special emphasis, "is a paper marriage. It has no other implications whatsoever. Is that clear?"

"Clear—and cold," he said. "Quite right. You make the terms. I take 'em. Here's to Dr. and Mrs. Spencer Brade."

She got up. "I'm going now. You can call me at the Belvedere if you change your mind. I'll probably write you some details tonight."

He helped her on with her coat. "Shan't I drive you down? No? Very well. Good luck. And, Carol, I'm sorry about this, if that helps any."

"Don't be," she answered quietly. "I'm doing quite well for myself and, I hope, not too badly for you."

"I'll take the risk," he said.

CHAPTER IV

HER LETTER came by the early mail. Before opening it Spencer Brade studied curiously the writing on the envelope. It was small, firm, even. Not the hand of a flighty girl who would fall for any easy seduction. He shut his eyes, the better to recall her face. Beautiful? Impressionable? Flick Fleming had thought so. It was not really beauty, though; not in the technical and classic sense. He doubted whether the face would withstand the test of critical analysis. But that didn't matter. There was both warmth and character in it, mirth, too, he thought, though the occasion had not given much play to that; potentialities of passion, also, in the slow, shadowed eyes and the generous mouth; strength in the set of the chin and the fine modeling of the brow. For so young a girl she had shown unexpected poise. Incongruously he felt a sense of pathos in that.

He brewed his tea, made his toast, and sat down to a leisurely consideration of the letter.

This will be easier to write than to tell. For background, imagine a childhood without parents—both of mine died while I was a baby—surrounded by a strict and overanxious guardianship, a very maidenish maiden aunt who started by spoiling me and ended by jailing me. There was plenty of money: the Grahame Mills. You will hear more about them later.

At seventeen, when I was still very young for my age, I had an escapade with a boy a year older than myself. It was quite idyllically innocent and callow; hardly more than nervous handholding and a hasty kiss good night. But the boy was Irish, "not of our set," and Yankee Irish at that. You know what that means in a close-bound Southern circle. Still, nothing very ghastly would have come of it, I suppose, if Phillip had not helped himself from his employer's till to buy me a birthday present. His poor, hysterical mother told the police all about it, and my name was in the police-court-report headlines. You can imagine the kind of sickly romance the reporters would make of it. I have had a horror of newspaper publicity ever since. So I owe you a special debt of gratitude for shielding me from it in this case.

Aunt Candy (Miss Candace Grahame, and you will know plenty of her before you're through) went into panic, and I went into the convent. Vacation times I was chaperoned within an inch of my life. I might as well have been living in an iron lung. At twenty-one I went on strike. Even then, with money at my own command, I was too repressed to assert myself openly. An invitation from a convent mate for a cruise on their yacht gave me an opening. I fixed up some letters for Sara Marvel to mail from South American ports and struck out for freedom. Miami Beach appealed to me because I didn't know anyone there. I registered at the best hotel, picked up some perfectly respectable women acquaintances, and began to see life. You have probably seen Tony d'Zaril's name in the social columns. [The reader pursed his lips into a silent whistle.] He called himself a count. Probably he was. He owned to twenty-nine years and was certainly all of that. I suppose I ought to hate him, but I don't. He was a sunny creature, as irresponsible as a thistlebird. We had a lot of fun together. If I had been deeply in love with him—but that doesn't matter now. We were married by a justice of the peace.

Tony wanted it kept secret for a few months. Some story about a small inheritance from his family in the Balkans, on condition of his not marrying until he was thirty. It was all right with me. The secrecy rather appealed to my undimmed sense of adventure. I don't think I felt very much married, anyway; just footloose and free and gay. We bought a car—that is, I did—and rambled around, having a grand time. The the police caught up with Tony in Washington. It was something about money. He swore to me he had not been dishonest. I daresay he hadn't, by his standards. I got him out of it, and it was hushed up. While he was at his lawyer's a very polite and hideous young man from the legation called on me and told me, with many expressions of regret, that there was an earlier wife somewhere in eastern Europe. When Tony came in he denied everything and challenged the ugly young man to a duel. But the ugly young man, always very polite, had documents. Then they murmured a while in their language and Tony broke down and wept and raved and threatened to kill himself and finally said that he would go back to Sofia, or wherever it was, and get a divorce and marry me all over again. I tried to give him some money to go on with, but he wouldn't take it. He said he hadn't married me for my money but because he was in love with me, and he was going to make me believe it. It didn't make any difference then. It was all over for me. I wouldn't marry him if he did come back, though I was sure he wouldn't.

For a time I thought I was very unhappy. Then I began to wonder why I wasn't more unhappy. Then I began to wonder about something else. It was all new to me, the way I felt, and at first I didn't even suspect. Some way it hadn't occurred to my mind that this could happen to me. For a woman almost three months married, I was still right innocent. I came here to Baltimore to find out. When the tests showed my condition I was appalled. It didn't seem fair. Naturally I thought of an operation. But I found I couldn't do it. If I did I'd never feel clean again inside. A man can't understand that, perhaps; not even a doctor. So there is my story. If you want more of it I will answer any questions that you have a right to ask.

One more thing. I did not set out to kill myself. I meant to throw away my rings, wedding and engagement, that he gave me. They were probably phony anyway. Then something came over me: a kind of a rage. And then I was in the water. I am not really that kind of a coward. I am glad you pulled me out. Now that you know the facts, if you still want to go through with it, I'll do my best to see that you're not sorry for your bargain.

CAROL

It was a good letter, Brade decided; straightforward, intelligent, and courageous. It told him what he had a right to know. The rest he would find out as occasion offered. He was still pondering when Fleming came in. The redhead was vehement.

"Of all the lousy, stinkin' deals! The dirty, dollar-chasing, low-down bast——"

"Skip it, Flick."

"I could swallow it all, except Old Powsie. How he could——"

"Powsie was on a spot."

"You're going to stick here and ram it into their guts, aren't you?"

Brade shook his head. "No. I know when I'm licked. I'm quitting."

The other's face gloomed over. "Aw, come on, Spenny! That isn't like you. Don't let 'em put it over you like that. What are you going to do?"

"Get married."

"Get *what?* Married! Jee-miny! What on?"

"The lady's money."

"You? You're a goddamn liar. You wouldn't do that."

"I wouldn't have, day before yesterday. I'm going to, tomorrow. And you're helping me."

"As how?"

"Best man."

"Like hell I am!"

Brade grinned at him. "Wait till you hear who the bride is."

"I don't need to hear. I know. It's that face-lifted, hand-raddled, rich old hag of a Francey widow that's been chasing you round like a she-cat in the heat. Why, Spen, she's forty, if she's a day. I'll see you in hell before I stooge for you in that sellout."

"Wrong gal, my boy."

Fleming clawed at his ear. "Then it's that little blonde social worker, Emmy Harvey. She's all right, I guess; I wouldn't say a thing against her except she hasn't got the sense a goose was hatched with. And she'll prove it if she marries a ten-dollar-a-month guy with no prospects."

"Another bad guess," said Brade calmly. "It's Carol Grahame. The girl you saw here yesterday."

"You're crazy! Batty! Noodle-socked! Why, you don't even know her. Unless you were putting one over me about the accident and my first suspicions were right. But she doesn't look that kind. Was that all hooey about the accident?"

"No. It was straight. So is she. Case of love at first sight."

"It might be, at that, on your part," conceded the visitor. "But what about her?"

"Thanks, and nuts to you."

"Oh, I'll admit you've got something. You're no movie glammerboy, but there's a kind of to-hell-with-it-all air about you that seems to snare the gals. Now, take that widow——"

"Skip the widow."

The analyst continued his survey. "You're a smooth talker; great for bedside manner. Your clothes always look like the best in Fifth Avenue with the gloss slightly frayed off; just enough to be interesting. And you act as though you expected things always to come your way but wouldn't give one good goddamn if they didn't. Yes; there's sure something about you."

"Skip me also. Are you going to see me through?"

"Sure, I will. But I'd rather trade places with you."

"She'd get a better man," said his friend, suddenly grave. "Well, we've got some preliminaries to look after."

"Leave 'em to me. I'm bossing this show. Lend me your buzzer till I make a clean sweep of my whiskers, and I'll go down and hold conference with the bride."

Left alone, Brade considered his resources. He had seven dollars and fifty cents cash and about fifty dollars left in his bank account. Allow twenty-five for traveling expenses to Charlesville; say fifteen more to carry him over until he could leave. That would leave him enough for a handsome gesture. He ordered ten dollars' worth of white roses delivered at the hotel in the morning, telephoned the presser to fix up his four suits, and went out to blow himself to a four-dollar necktie and a white carnation. The best man, returning, found him writing letters.

"Eleven o'clock at that City Hall," he announced. "I'm the bride's adopted brother. We'll meet you there."

"Right."

"And, say, Spenny."

"Well? Spill it."

"How's about cash money? I could spare you fifty."

"What would you hock? Your microscope? No, old lad. I'm all right that way."

"Okay. Eleven, sharp. Bureau anteroom on the third floor. Don't take a farewell bachelor drink and be late."

The calendar on the wall of the waiting room showed Friday, June 4. The clock stood at eleven twenty-seven. Dr. Foster Fleming fidgeted and sweated in his chair. Carol Grahame, fresh and cool as a lily, looked out at the window. In another corner a young couple were quarreling while an older woman tried tearfully to make peace. The girl's contours left no room for doubt that she needed a wedding ring.

"How much longer do we wait?" asked Carol.

"He must have got in a jam somewhere," said her companion uneasily. "Damn his fool soul!" he added with fervor.

"In fifteen minutes," said the girl, calmly regarding the clock, "I shall be out of this, and probably well out of it."

"Give him a break," begged Fleming. "That clock's three minutes fast."

"He may have decided to call it off, don't you think?" She was still placid.

"No; I don't think," he retorted feebly.

"Telephone for Dr. Fleming," a voice announced. "Telephone for——"

But he was already out of the room. In two minutes he was back, grinning.

"It's all right. He's been delayed. He'll be right along."

"In fifteen—no, fourteen minutes?" asked the girl implacably.

(Startled, he thought, for all she looks so soft and silky, that gal is nobody's woolly lamb.)

"I didn't find out what's keeping him," he said. "There was a wop on the phone. He didn't do much but splutter." The horrid thought had come across him that maybe Spenny had liquored up for the occasion. If that was it he'd beat the damn fool's head off!

"My train leaves at one-five," she said. *My* train; not *our* train, he observed.

"Look," he said imploringly, "there's other trains. You wouldn't want to get into a fight would you? I'm awfully strong. And you don't get out of this building except over my dead body."

She smiled at him. "I like loyalty," she said. "Well, he'd better have a good excuse."

"Oh, he will! He always has," said the friend incautiously.

Spencer Brade was in no self-excusatory mood when, at eleven thirty-five, he walked jauntily in. His freshly pressed blue reefer coat had a dust smear on it. His cuffs were soiled and rumpled, and there was a smudge across his forehead. He said, "Hi, Flick," to his attendant; then to his bride:

"Sorry. I got held up. Friday's luck."

"What the hell held you?" demanded Fleming.

Still growling, the other left to see if the clerk was ready for them. Carol glanced at the clock, and then at her groom. Her brows went up. Brade was annoyed.

"Do you want a written report?" he asked brusquely.

"I suppose you could have sent word," she said quietly. "It hasn't been pleasant for me."

"It isn't so easy to send word when you're working beneath a fallen wall."

"I see. But did you *have* to go?"

"No; I didn't have to. But you don't pass up that sort of thing when you're the only man available. There were two laborers pinned in. One of them would have died."

"I thought," she said imperturbably, "that from yesterday on you were out for the money and nothing else. Laborers can't be good paying patients, are they?"

"That isn't the point. I'm not asking you to understand."

"Perhaps I do, though, a little." She touched his hand lightly. "Thank you for the roses. It was a kind thought. Here's our friend, Flick back. You've been a terrible strain on his nerves." She eyed Brade queerly. "Suppose I'd sent word over the wire that unless you came at once I'd walk out on you."

"It wouldn't have made any difference. I couldn't walk out on *them.*"

"I feel better about marrying you," she said. "Let's get it over with."

The best man led them to a desk above which stood a sign, MARRIAGE LICENSES. The clerk wore a dark eyeshade and black sleeve holders. He reached for a blank form, not troubling to look up at them.

"Names?"

"Spencer Brade, M.D."

The clerk scribbled the name on the first line with a queer, nervous scrawl. He stood waiting.

"Carol Grahame," said the girl quietly.

"Ages?"

"Twenty-nine."

"Twenty-one."

"Born?"

"Logan, Kentucky."

"Charlesville, Georgia."

All other details were elicited and entered.

"Three dollars, please."

The money was paid and the license delivered.

"Thank you. Justice of the peace, three doors down."

The J.P. was fat and benign and had a quid of tobacco in his cheek. He spat into the cuspidor by his desk and took the license with one hand while he reached for a small black book with the other.

"You act as witness?" he asked Fleming. "Okey. We'll need another. Hey, Pearl," he called back over his shoulder. "Come here and witness."

The blonde stenographer came forward. The justice began reciting with the book open in his hand before she was halfway across the room.

"Join hands." He didn't look at the book in his hand as he spoke. "Do you"—he paused and looked at the license—"Carol Grahame, take this man to be your lawfully wedded husband?"

"Yes." Her answer was clear and crisp.

"Do you"—he glanced again at the license—"Spencer Brade, M.D., take this woman to be your lawfully wedded wife?"

"I do." He sounded to himself very businesslike. Well, why not? This was business, wasn't it?

"Then I pronounce you man and wife."

The fat man looked up expectantly. The blonde stenographer was smirking at them. Flick was grinning. Oh, of course! The final episode of a wedding. He bent over his newly acquired wife. She lifted her lips. They were cool and soft and not unfriendly. Flick looked hopeful. She nodded smilingly, and he kissed her. All was regular.

"My fee is five dollars," said the J.P., signing the certificate.

The witnesses signed after him. The groom paid with an uncomfortable thought for his dwindling pile.

Carol's car was outside. They bade Fleming good-by and got in.

"I've just about time to pick up my things and catch my train," she said. "I'm leaving this car to be gone over and shipped on."

"It will be a week at least before I can get away," he said.

She nodded. "That will be all right. I'll get Aunt Candy broken in on the idea of you. How are you off for money?" She put the question in the most matter-of-fact way. Nevertheless, he flushed.

"I can get by."

"You'd better let me leave you some."

"I'd rather not."

"Aren't you being oversensitive?"

"Possibly. You see, I've never been a gigolo before."

They were drawing in at the hotel now. She turned and

looked at him with a clear, level regard. "Spen," she said resolutely, "we can make this hard for one another or we can make it easy. There's no reason why we shouldn't have a decent sort of life, even though its only temporary. We're both decently bred people. If you hadn't been a gentleman I wouldn't have married you. You couldn't have been fitted into the scheme of life at home. Maybe that's snobbery. I can't help it. I wouldn't even want to. I won't pretend that I admire your ambition. But that's your affair. If you're out to make a lot of money, why, so are all successful businessmen. I expect it's all right. When you've come to be a success, if it will make you feel any better, you can pay me back what I've loaned you. But if you start out by feeling ashamed of being obligated it's going to mess up our lives pretty hopelessly, isn't it?"

She spoke with decision but at the same time with an undertone of appeal that moved him.

"You're right, of course," he said. "And it's clever and kind of you about putting it on the loan basis. I get what you're after; you're trying to salvage my self-respect. But if you don't mind, I'd rather not take the money by hand, though I expect it's childish of me. Send it to my bank. And, Carol, I think you're quite a fella."

She laughed. "That's better. Hold the thought. We'll do."

He waited while her luggage was loaded into a taxi and drove with her to the train. She gave him her hand at parting.

"I'll write you about the setup at Charlesville," she said. "Better wire me the day before you leave. Good luck."

At the bank next day he found a credit of twenty-three hundred dollars. Enough for the office equipment and to pay all his debts. She must have mailed it from the train. Very competent and businesslike of her, he thought, with more admiration than pleasure. It was like marrying a perfectly conducted trust fund.

Brade was walking through the hall, carrying his instruments from the room he had just vacated, when he met Dr. Powers coming out of his office. Powers looked depressed.

"Hello, Brade. Haven't changed your mind?"

"No, sir."

"I wish you would," said the other with the unmistakable note of sincerity. "I'd still like to have you stay on."

"I'm afraid I couldn't support a wife on the microscopical grubstake Lakeview pays."

31

"A wife?"

"Yes. I was married this morning. Mrs. Brade has money; a lot of it. Don't you want to congratulate me?"

"No," said Old Powsie. He shambled on, shaking his head regretfully.

CHAPTER V

THE TRAIN had been speeding through rough fields of young tobacco and cotton since Spencer Brade raised the window of the Pullman and looked out on the countryside. He was well down in the deep South; the heat that filtered in told him that. In an hour he would be in Charlesville, facing a new and uncertain life. That did not worry him; he possessed plenty of self-confidence, both professional and personal. But he was full of a healthy curiosity.

Carol's promised letter of information had been little more than a chart for the guidance of a newly wed husband. Now he took it out for a final reading.

I am not a good liar. I do not like deceit, even when it is necessary. It went all right with Aunt Candace. You and I met at a dance in Trenton five weeks ago and fell for each other. Both shot through the heart. Married in three days. Kept it quiet because of some minor family complications of yours. You can make those up.

(Handing me the old bag to hold, reflected Brade. Am I supposed to make up a family too? I could use Uncle Marsh. He's too senile to make any objections.)

Aunt Candace, he learned, might not take to him at once. He would be on trial with her. But she would be polite and considerate; she was always that. Look out for shrewd questions, though. She was sharp as a steel trap. Anything he

32

told her would be filed for reference in a tenacious memory. Their stories must hang together or there would be trouble. It would be as well for him to cultivate a courteously reticent habit for a time. He could be very busy and wrapped up in his work.

Charlesville, as Carol indicated it, sounded quite festive. Already she had been caught in a whirl of parties. There would be more to introduce him to local society. His name was up for membership in the country club and the Beauregard Club. Owen James was his sponsor. Owen was a sort of third cousin. Everybody in Charlesville who was anybody was more or less related. Carol hoped that he would like Owen, who had been a clergyman but had grown impatient with the arm's-length attitude of the slum folk with whom he dealt and had turned to medicine to get himself closer in touch.

(Not too good, thought Brade. Probably a "Christer.")

It was gay and young, that letter; even a little challenging. Between the lines he read a latent anxiety lest he fail to adjust himself to the Grahame way of life. She might have trusted him that far. After all, though, she hardly knew him.

She signed herself "Yours loyally, Carol." He liked that. It was not too much or too little. It pointed her intention to live up to the terms of their bargain and with a little friendliness thrown in. There was a P.S.

Aunt Candace does not know about my condition yet. We must talk that over.

He tore the letter into small pieces, crowded it through the window, and went into the washroom. He shaved carefully, shook out the new tropical-weight blue suit he had bought, and adjusted his tie with special care before the mirror. A pursy man, fanning himself with a folded newspaper, addressed him good-humoredly.

"Think pretty well of yourself, don't you, young fella!"

Brade grinned. "Well, is there anything seriously wrong with me?"

"I'd say not. Putting on the warpaint to knock 'em cold, huh? Making Charlesville?"

"Yes."

"What's your line?"

"Line? Oh! Medicine."

"Drug-supply house?"

"No. Practice."

"Uh-huh. Been there long?"

"Just starting."

The other whistled. "Charlesville's lousy with doctors. Hundred thousand population, and I'll bet a thousand of them can write M.D. after their names. So you'll be the thousand and oneth. Well, God help you! It's a good enough town in its way, I reckon. I make it six times a year, but I wouldn't live there if you gave me City Hall. Too damn snooty for my tastes. Oke-kay if you're in with the right folks. I wouldn't wonder but you might beat the game. You look like you belonged. What's your specialty?"

"Why I haven't any exactly. General surgery."

"That won't get you anywhere. Gotta have a trade-mark. It impresses folks."

"How do you know so much about it?" asked Brade, amused.

"I travel for a bunch of trade publications. One of 'em is medical. You think over what I told you. Specialize or starve. Maybe you'll starve, at that."

Back in his seat, Brade wondered why he had not thought of the point before. That fat perspirer was right. Specialization was a universal condition. You could beat it by making the right contacts, getting lined up with the right people. And concentrating. What specialty, though?

Surgery was all right. But anyone could claim to be a surgeon, and most of 'em did. Emphasize some branch of surgery in order to make himself stand out from the ruck? Fortunately he had been well trained in all departments: six months of neurological, six months of urology, a year of gynecology.

He pondered lovingly the nose-and-throat racket. Nothing else in medicine gave such easy returns for so little work. Take the deviated septum and the continually infected sinuses that were always having to be irregated and finally operated upon at four or five hundred a throw. And then there were the tonsils that were always needing to come out. And the nice infected ears that threatened to become infected mastoids and often did. It was certainly a soft graft, nose and throat.

Of course he might set himself up as a Jack-of-all-trades, snatching the tonsils and adenoids, treating Junior's sore toe one day, and delivering Sister Sadie's first baby the next. But

34

that was chicken feed, after all. That was the cheap and easy line for the catch-as-catch-can practitioner, the sloppy man without ambition or energy enough to keep up with the parade. There wasn't a lazy bone in Brade's body, he flattered himself. The last likelihood in the world was that he would let himself become careless and slipshod. Money he was determined to have, but he was quite willing to work honestly for it.

Gynecology called for more quality in a man's work, but it held out richer prospects. The Lord had been good to the gynecologists, he thought with cynicism that had been coloring his thoughts lately. Women spent more money on their bodies than men, externally and internally. Providence had loaded up the dear creatures with a lot of accessory organs that were always getting out of kilter, then tied them in with a nervous system that was geared to a hair-trigger, ready to go off any minute. Yes, the Lord must have been thinking affectionately of the gynecologists when he made women. There were fine, legitimate pickings in the department. As for the sharks, the handholders, the hypodermic givers, with their twaddle of hormones for this and hormones for that, female-kind was a veritable gold mine for them.

He had watched with contemptuous tolerance the tactics of high-priced specialists who called the fat women with bank-director husbands "dear lady" and listened to their symptoms with such flattering absorption. All right; if he must, he could show a technic as smooth as the smoothest of the expert hypocrites. He'd give the old hens shots for their pains and suspend their uteri with the best of them. It didn't make any difference that the shots and the operations wouldn't have much, if any, effect. They'd have something to talk about when the played bridge. And that was what counted. Soon, if he purred smoothly enough and made each one think he was vitally interested in her, perhaps just a little bit as an attractive woman as well as a patient, his name would be heard regularly, his praises sounded over the bridge tables. One patient satisfied meant three more knowing about him, maybe a lot more than that if there was a party and they progressed. Bridge was a great thing for the medical profession. He'd get out that paper he'd written on tumors of the ovary, brush it up a bit, and give it to the local medical society as soon as he could land himself on a program. That would get him off the mark in good shape and label him a gynecologist with his fellow M.D.s.

The train was slowing up now, crossing the broad, muddy river that skirted the city. Here and there Negroes fished despondently from battered rowboats. At the far end of the bridge a big building loomed up. It had many windows through which he could see men and women, more women than men bending over machines. Machines that spun cotton into thread, that wove thread into cloth. Cotton mills. He'd seen them before on a trip to Florida. Cotton mills where sweating humanity wove cloth to cover their ill-nourished bodies.

The train passed the tall building, and now there were small cottages, row on row, street after street, some little more than enlarged goods boxes, showing rear yards foul with rubbish, clothes strung across porches with sagged railings, children, bowlegged and potbellied from disease and malnutrition, here and there a woman, pale, her hair scraggly, her face molded into the mask that comes from years of work, of having babies, of poor food, of seeing her children develop tuberculosis and die coughing up the frothy surge of their own blood—they were not pretty sights, those houses. Brade guessed that they were profitable; vaguely he wondered whether any of Carol's money came from them. Well, that was her business, not his.

There would be plenty of opportunity for practice there. A modicum of that sort of charity work gave a new man a good name in the community. Those people in the cotton mill, those children with joints big with tuberculosis, with backs distorted by Pott's disease, were the ones who needed the surgical skill he possessed. He knew something of the kind of medicine they got. Pill peddling, quackery, babies delivered by midwives who didn't know enough to wash their hands. Castor oil for appendicitis, with the victim turning up at the hospital days later, his eyes hot with fever, his cheeks caved in, his pulse racing, his belly big with his own pus. Those people couldn't pay doctors, couldn't pay hospital bills, couldn't pay for white-tiled delivery rooms when the women's time came. And there wasn't anyone else to pay. The cities, sometimes the counties, did what they could, but the politicians are foxily loath about diverting funds that might save lives from their own pork-barrel projects. They cried about suffering, down-trodden humanity before elections but did damn little to ease that suffering once they got the necessary number of votes to put them in office. It was the same story everywhere. The rich man got rolled for his dough, but at least he got real treatment when there was something wrong with him. The poor man didn't have any dough so he didn't get anything.

The best you could do was only a drop in the bucket. You could cure rickets with sunlight and cod-liver oil; you could build up childish bodies and start bone forming again around tuberculous joints with well-done operations. Then the minute you let them go, back they slipped to too little food, to too much dirt, to the things that had caused the disease in the beginning. What good did treatment do when you were bucking the stone wall of an economic system that was based on exploiting people who had to take it because they had to live?

Hey! What kind of stuff was that for a young man starting a new life on sound, money-grabbing principles? He wasn't here to find flaws in the capitalistic system but to pick his meats out of it. There was no percentage in utopian thoughts about justice and things like that. Stick to practicalities. As a corrective to unprofitable idealism he stared at his shabby old topcoat on the back of the seat. Next season he'd have a brand-new one. Bought with incisions, with sutures, with pink little appendices that had never been inflamed, with ovarian cysts so small you couldn't see them. He'd do the work well, and he'd be paid well for it.

The train ground its teeth and stopped impatiently. Brade stepped out and looked around.

"Hello, darling!"

The voice was gay with welcome. He turned and beheld with new and startled eyes the woman from whom he had parted on defined business terms a fortnight earlier. This was his wife, this flowerlike girl with the supple grace of youth and vitality. His wife? Not in reality. His financial backer; his only visible means of support. That was what he had to keep steadily in mind for the present.

Some women flourish on pregnancy. Evidently Carol was one of that lucky sisterhood. From the crown of her pert hat, along the fluent lines of her fresh blue chambray frock, to the tips of her smart little white shoes, she was cool perfection. Setting a hand on each of his shoulders, she kissed him lightly.

"Did you have a rotten trip?" she asked. "Here's the red-cap. Come on."

She tucked her arm familiarly beneath his. Several people, he was aware, were looking their way with well-bred suppression of interest. Carol waved to one couple.

"He *is* real, you see," she called.

The Brade brain was working rapidly, but not too steadily. A new emotion was disturbing the mechanism. The gist of his troubled thinking was that relationships could and frequently did change, after marriage, though usually for the worse. Was there any reason why the Brade relationship should not alter for the better? Optimistically he could see none. It was a money deal now, but that was only a phase. When the debt was satisfied what was to prevent his approaching Carol Grahame— Carol Brade—as man to woman, as husband to wife? Therein was an added and keener—and more worthy—incentive for making money and making it quickly. The idol, Success, had more faces than one.

"You're looking quite wonderful," he said and meant it.

"Why not?" she returned lightly. "Haven't I got my husband back?" She was playing her role of happy bride to perfection. "Aunt Candy's waiting in the car."

"Is she in good humor?'

Carol laughed. "Like a tigress awaiting her prey."

The severe black limousine, parked beneath an oak tree, was occupied by a severe black figure, that of a pudgy little woman with lusterless hair, serene eyes, and a fresh skin. Brade guessed that she was somewhere on the far side of sixty and probably knew what illness was only by observation of weaker folk.

"Here he is, Auntie," Carol said.

"How do you do?" said Miss Grahame, giving him a firm, gloved hand. "Simon will take your trunk check. Get in. Did you have an uncomfortable trip?"

"Not too bad," he answered. "I'm a sound, reliable sleeper."

"I like sound, reliable people," she said.

(Thought Brade: She might as well tell me in so many words that I'm under suspicion.)

Carol came to the rescue with small talk, to which he contributed. As the aged Negro chauffeur sidled the car cautiously through the prosperous traffic, the newcomer took mental notes. Charlesville he judged to be typical of that part of the South. The big, low buildings in this quarter could be nothing else but tobacco warehouses. And close at hand were the supply stores, conveniently located to remind the farmers, when they sold their tobacco, that the expenses of last years's crop had not yet been paid. Main Street was lined with the usual clothing emporiums, five-and-tens, and drugstores. Over it all the sun presided with impartial warmth, making the cool breeze generated by the movement of the car specially welcome.

The car approached a tall new building through the ornate doors of which crowds of people passed.

"That's the new Medical Arts Building," Carol said. "Your future address."

"I should judge the medical profession does well here," Brade observed with relish.

Aunt Candace regarded him briefly and coldly. "Dr. Cannaday has his office at his residence," she stated.

Was there an inference that Dr. Cannaday would never have made a remark like Brade's?

"He's your family physician, isn't he?" he said.

"He is. He brought Carol into the world. He has always taken care of our medical needs. I can see no necessity for all the fancy signs in that building. Specialists! They're so set on making money, they can't think of anything else."

The hostility in her manner was making Carol uneasy. Her husband thought best to ignore it for the present. "Specialists have their place," he pointed out. "There is more to know now than in Dr. Cannaday's day. One person can't hope to cover everything. That's what justifies specializing."

"Are you a specialist?"

Brade made his first profession of faith. "Yes. Gynecological surgery. Diseases of women, you know."

Aunt Candace sniffed. "I *do* know, though you evidently think I don't. In my day a dollar bottle of Vegetable Compound took care of those things."

"Did you take it on Dr. Cannaday's advice?" asked Brade with apparent innocence.

"No; I didn't. He said it was damn quackery. But what doctor would treat you for a dollar? Would you?"

"It would be more like ten, I'm afraid."

"Hmph! I don't doubt it." She leaned forward. "Go around by way of the mill, Simon," she directed.

They left the center of town and approached a large building in the outer part of the city. It had much the appearance of the textile mill Brade had passed on the train coming in, but the

39

houses in the settlement were different. They were larger, neater, better kept. There was more space between, and most of them had tiny green lawns. Here and there a few bright-colored flowers stood in window boxes or in little beds beside the houses. Farther away he could see a large open space that was evidently a playground, for there were children noisily using the swings and slides.

"The Grahame Mills," Aunt Candace said. "Carol's father built them. The finest cotton mills in the South. Never had a strike, never been shut down in fifty years."

"The houses certainly look better than most I've seen," Brade said.

"My father was a good employer," said Carol with pride. "He looked after his people. I believe they call it paternalism now, and the high social thinkers all snoot it. The Grahame idea was that anyone who was good enough workman to be in the Grahame Mills deserved decent living conditions. He equipped that playground. There's a football field there and a baseball diamond."

"What's the large building in the rear?"

"The gymnasium. With a full-sized swimming pool."

"I'm beginning to get the picture," he said. "I'll bet you live in a patriarchal white house, with pillars and porticoes, set far back into shrubberies and trees, with a winding drive and horse-and-buggy gates so narrow that a car can hardly make them."

"Young man, did you come down here and look the place over before deciding to marry my niece?" demanded the aunt.

"Aunt Candy!" cried Carol, shocked and reddening.

"Well, here it is," said Aunt Candy imperturbably.

The car turned between heavy pillars of gray stone up a curving driveway. A broad expanse of green carpet covered the rising slope of a small hill. The drive wound upward to a large white house that sat serenely on the summit. Tall Doric columns supported the roof over the portico. Ivy and other climbing vines threatened to cover the entire front of the house. A fat colored woman in a white cap was standing by the front door.

Spencer Brade drew in a deep breath of nostalgia. This was the environment that he had known long before, different only in degree, not in kind, from his memories of bluegrass Kentucky before the Brade fortune vanished, leaving barely enough to provide for his medical education on the scale which he thought suitable. Carol was looking curiously at his somber face. He pulled himself together.

"All it needs is a darky chorus off stage and the family retainer with a tray of juleps," he said lightly.

"It is rather like a movie scene, isn't it?' Carol admitted. "They tried to get it for *Good-bye, Southern Girl*, but Aunt Candy threatened to return the first camera shot with a forty-five, so it fell through. Would you like a drink?"

"No. I'd like a bath."

"I'll show you your"—she caught herself—"our rooms." Brade thought that he saw Aunt Candace's eyes make one of their swift, unobtrusive shifts.

As the pair reached the stairhead Carol said, "Slip Number One. And I was the one to make it. You're good. She'd never suspect anything from you."

"She doesn't like me."

"Not yet. She wouldn't like anyone that married me, at first. The spinster's daughter, you know. I think you have your temper under very good control."

"I'm not going to take too much from her, though."

"No; I wouldn't want you to."

"Carol, is this her house or yours?"

She smiled. "Aren't you looking for unnecessary trouble? It's a joint ownership. Feel better?"

"Yes, I do. I shouldn't care to be on Aunt Candy's charity list."

She touched his lips with her fingers in light rebuke. "That's barred," she warned him.

There were a number of rooms giving on the high, airy hallway. She opened the next to the last door.

"This is yours. Your bath opens off on the right."

The bedroom was spacious, furnished with antiques and a soft-hued Chinese rug. The double bed with its tall, beautifully carved posts, was covered with a blue-and-white quilt, dated 1832.

"Luxury," he said appreciatively. "I could do with some luxury after ten years of Lakeview. Aren't you afraid of softening me up?"

"You're a good surgeon," she said seriously. "I'm relying on that."

"How do you know?"

"I talked with your friend Flick. And I've seen a letter that Dr. Powers wrote to one of our local men."

"Good old Powsie! What a farewell lecture he read me on the loft ideals and standards of the profession!"

She smiled at him. "Are you trying to impress me with your hard-boiledness?"

"Oh, I can still use ideals. They're a useful feeder for the practical side."

"It wasn't the practical side that made you late for our wedding," she reminded him.

"Anyone is liable to moments of weakness," he said flippantly.

"I wonder," she mused, "how you and Owen are going to get on?"

"Owen?"

"Owen James. I wrote you about him."

"Oh! The ex-preacher. Does he represent idealism to you?"

"Yes; I think he does. I wish he were more practical in some ways."

She crossed the room to pull wide the French windows which gave access to a small balcony overlooking the primly hedged garden. To the left was a small door.

"Where does that lead?" he asked.

"Into the corner room."

"Yours?"

"Yes."

He looked at it with more care. There was no lock. He opened it. On the other side was a brass bolt. He smiled at her

"New?"

She met his eyes. "No."

"What will Aunt Candace think?"

"She won't know."

"I shouldn't be too sure of that. She doesn't strike me as lacking perceptiveness. And some of these old maids have surprising intuitions in matters of sex."

Carol flushed angrily but said nothing. The husband felt a malicious satisfaction in baiting her.

"It's a good, stout bolt," he observed, examining it. "And of course you could always strengthen your defenses with barbed wire."

She said with a flash of temper which he found both amusing

and challenging, "Please to remember that I don't know you very well, Spen."

"And don't trust me at all," he supplemented.

She let that pass without reply.

"Perhaps you're right," he said.

This time the challenge was unmistakably his.

CHAPTER VI

THE TENTH FLOOR of the Medical Arts Building sprouted a new shingle:

SPENCER BRADE, M.D.
Consultation by Appointment

In that environment was established the medical conservatism and success of Charlesville. The rentals were high but were worth it. The newest recruit set about furnishing his setup in consonance with the dignified surroundings. He had given much thought to this important superficial matter and had consulted his wife, whose taste he knew to be reliable.

The waiting-room furniture upon which they decided was dark-stained and discreet; the rugs soft in tone. On the walls were hung only two pictures, rare colored etchings which Carol had brought down from Grahame Lodge: delicate eighteenth-century themes in cheerful colors. Her hand was manifest, also, in the very feminine, very chic dressing room for patients. The consultation room was small, quiet and intimate, inviting to confidences and suggesting helpfulness; the examining room a shining exemplar of up-to-dateness with the instruments glittering in the case by the sterilizer under the clear, yet modulated overhead light. Even the pads of the examining table were of extra thickness, calculated to keep the ailing person comfortable, to relieve the tension inevitable in the circumstances.

Five hundred dollars had gone into air conditioning. It brought the total well beyond two thousand dollars which Brade had figured. That could not be helped. Future patients would have to pay for it.

For supporting figure in this careful and costly stage setting he found a registered nurse who could take shorthand passably and type accurately. Miss May Garner was middle-aged, plain, pleasant-looking, gentle of hand and voice, and thoroughly competent. She helped to get away from that cold, professional touch felt almost universally in hospital clinics, often in dentistry establishments, and even in offices of the best doctors.

It was Dr. Brade's idea to create an atmosphere of personal interest and sympathy, calculated to soothe the jumpy nervous systems of the women patients. Viewed from the open door—and Miss Garner's instructions were to leave the door open as much as possible—the office gave just the impression sought by its presiding genius, a quietly, reservedly successful retreat where anxiety would be assuaged by kindliness and professional skill. Sound, legitimate showmanship. Brade thought, with sardonic amusement, that if the office could find voice it would murmur, "Dear lady."

When all was in order he sent out engraved announcements to physicians in the city and surrounding county, notifying them that Dr. Spencer Brade had opened offices in the Medical Arts Building, Charlesville; "Practice limited to Gynecology and Surgery." Then he sat down to wait and to simulate the appearance of industrious concentration.

Feelers were soon put out to him in the form of invitations to attend the meetings of several civic clubs. He accepted but held off from joining any until he could be certain just which group would be most advantageous to his professional designs. He got books on socialized medicine from the library and began studying them. Shortly after selecting his club he would casually mention something about state medicine and leave the impression that he was deeply interested in the subject. That bait should be enough to land him an invitation to speak. He would arraign government medicine in no uncertain terms, thereby probably getting his picture and sections from his talk published in the papers. It was a legitimate form of advertisement. He planned to take advantage of every such opportunity.

Next in order were the hospitals. He must get on the staffs of the two private institutions, perhaps of the City Hospital also. Here he expected that his connection with the Lakeview Center would help him; also, those letters from Dr. Powers, who evidently still hoped to save him as a brand from the burning flame of his own avowed ambitions.

The week after his announcements went out he was called on the telephone.

"Dr. Brade?"

"Yes."

"Dr. Tyre calling—Blanton Tyre."

"Oh yes, Dr. Tyre." Brade had heard of him. He was head of the successful Tyre Clinic there in the Medical Arts Building.

"Got your card," Tyre was saying. "How about coming up to see me? We're on the fifteenth floor, you know."

"Why, thank you," Brade said. "I'll be glad to come up. Are you busy now?"

"Not busy at all; not busy at all. I'll look for you." The receiver clicked in his ear.

Perhaps he'd be able to make some useful connections through Tyre, he thought, as he rode up on the elevator. He knew that the Tyre Clinic largely dominated the profession locally. Even so, he was surprised to find how much space it occupied. These fellows must have a gold mine was his thought when he entered the large waiting room, still half full of patients, although it was late in the afternoon. A trim, slim young secretary, with an impertinent, intelligent face, dark-lidded eyes, and a generously curved mouth, took his name and nodded.

"Dr. Tyre is expecting you."

As she applied herself to the telephone it struck him that she was quietly appraising him and that the appraisal was not wholly impersonal. He heard Tyre's rich tones attenuated on the wire.

"Sure. Bring him right in."

"This way, please, Dr. Brade." She moved briskly and lightly along the inner hallway, passing a dozen doors before she opened one and stood aside for him to enter.

A large, high-colored man, well rounded and well groomed, strode forward to greet him.

"Glad to see you, Dr. Brade. Glad to see you." Then, to the girl: "Oh, Kenny—Miss Mangan."

"Yes, Dr. Tyre?"

"Tell them at the hospital to turn over that osteo operation to young Barnes. It's hopeless, anyway," he added in explanation to the caller.

Brade began to formulate an estimate of the man. He was just a little excessive, his appearance too glossy, his manner too florid: the manner which comes with and advertises success; the manner perhaps, which helps to win success in a profession where superficialities count for so much and are so essentially of no account. The hand which warmly shook Brade's was large, muscular, and pinkly manicured. The cigar which was extended in the other hand was expensive, probably three for a dollar. The welcome-stranger effect was a thought overdone. It was meant to impress. But why should a Tyre wish to impress a tyro, Brade asked himself, rather pleased with his unspoken turn of phrase. He did not admire the type. But the cold logic to which he had committed himself told him that this was a man to pattern after.

Yes; this was the kind of outfit to be in. Here was the assurance of established success. The kind of patients who came here were able to pay and doubtless did pay well for the privilege. No piddling two-dollar practice in this layout.

"You've got a mighty fine wife, my boy," said his host heartily. "I know Carol and Miss Candace like my own kin. A mighty fine girl."

Brade murmured something courteously affirmative.

The big man puffed for a moment. "Limiting your practice to gynecology and surgery, I see."

"Yes."

"You may find it a little slow at first. Made any hospital connections yet?"

"No. I'd like to get some staff connections, if possible, without having to wait until fall."

"You won't have any trouble at all, none at all," Tyre assured him. "I hear that Dr. Powers of Lakeview says you're good. I'll take his word for it and pass it along. *And* if *I* vouch for you, you're on."

"I'd certainly appreciate it," Brade told him.

"Send in your applications right away. I'll see that they get through. Now about the City Hospital. You really ought to be on the staff out there. Does you no end of good, gives you a chance to show what's in you, and gives you some valuable publicity among the doctors." He leaned confidentially. "Here's

46

one thing I've learned: when you do surgery you've got to depend a lot on the medical men, the general practitioners, to send the patients to you. If you treat them right and get a good name with them you're set. Never act superior or imply that their judgment isn't just as good as your own. They like to feel that you are one of them, that you look at things from their viewpoint."

(I wonder if that included cutting them in on a little of the fee, thought the recipient of this gratuitous and valuable counsel.)

"Another thing that's important for a young man," the older man went on in a fatherly tone, "is to make the right social contacts. With the Grahame connection, you don't have anything to worry about there. I notice they passed you into the country club by special vote." Brade could see that his new friend was impressed. "Now about the City Hospital. What's your choice of department?"

"Gynecology. There ought to be more of an opening there, don't you think?"

"You're right," the older man agreed. "I've been thinking for some time that we ought to have a specially trained gynecologist in our own clinic. Of course I do pelvic surgery, but there's a lot of new stuff coming up nowadays, hormones and such. We might find a place for a comer in that line one of these days."

So that was why this smooth old bird was making up to him. It looked good. If he could get lined up with the Tyre Clinic early nothing could stop him. His cue now was to go carefully. Wouldn't do to seem to eager at first. He'd lay low, do a lot of hospital work, and show that he knew his stuff. Then when the time came to talk turkey he'd have a basis for negotiations.

"You've certainly got a fine setup here," he said. "How many are there of you?"

"Two besides myself. My son Castleman, who does our pediatrics, and Dr. Hewlett, our internist. We've a compact, smooth-working little group. Come and take a look."

He led the way to the end of the hall. The visitor was pleasantly surprised at the size of the laboratory they entered. Two white-clad technicians were busy at microscopes. The place was as completely outfitted as any medical-school laboratory he had ever seen. His respect for the Tyre group went up. These fellows believed in doing things right. Through the open door

47

of a small room marked METABOLISM he could see a couch and the latest in machines. A portable electrocardiograph stood just inside the door of a similar room beside the first. Across the laboratory was a closed door that was labeled PATHOLOGICAL LABORATORY.

"We do a large volume of laboratory work," Tyre was saying as they halted just inside the laboratory. "Patients nowadays expect to have laboratory work done. They look to get a lot for their money. Your success depends on giving 'em what they want. It all makes for better medicine."

They moved down the hall. Tyre opened another door paned in ground glass. This office was decorated with what at first appearance seemed nightmare taste. A photographic panel of Mother Goose illustrations ran around the wall halfway to the ceiling. There was a hobbyhorse beside the desk and several small chairs around a low table in the corner. It looked more like a child's playroom than office. Through the open door at the back the gurgle of a pleased infant could be heard.

"This is Castleman's office." Tyre beamed. "Novel idea, don't you think? Decorating it to suit the taste of his patients."

A tall blond young man, fast developing into a replica of the older Tyre, came in, followed by a young woman carrying a fat, naked infant.

"Hello, Dad," Castleman Tyre said. "I'll be with you in a minute."

"We'll give the young fellow his Schick test next week, Mrs. Shields," he told the mother and slapped the laughing infant on his broad plump back. "Can't have you getting sick on us, young fellow, now that you've started off so well." The mother went into an adjacent room. The junior physician turned to the visitors.

"Glad to know you, Brade," he said in answer to his father's introduction. "Been aiming to look you up. We owe you a grudge for stealing our prettiest girl right out from under our noses."

Brade smiled his acknowledgments. "Quite an organization you have," he said.

"We do pretty well," the other admitted. "Dad used to kid me about the decorations in here. They set us back three hundred, but they make a big hit with the mothers. And after all, it's the mothers that bring the patients in my specialty."

"Now, Castleman!" his elder reproved him. "You'll be giving

Dr. Brade the impression that we're in medicine for the money alone."

Castleman opened a door, and they passed through. Bookshelves, packed with textbooks and bound volumes of medical journals, lined the walls. There were several comfortable chairs and a reading lamp in the corner. Ash trays were conveniently located. The proprietors watched the stranger's appreciative glance travel about.

"We fixed this room up as a combination lounging room and library," explained the younger Tyre. "Also for general utility purposes." He moved over to a cabinet in the corner, lifted the top, and complete cellaret rose into view. There was even a bowl of ice, ready in the center of the nest of glasses and bottles.

"We usually manage to get together about this time for a drink," Blanton Tyre explained. "What will yours be, Brade?"

"Scotch and soda, please."

The whiskey was good. He didn't have to look at the bottle to know that only best was used here. A short, fat little man came in and mopped his brow. His naked scalp was glistening with sweat.

"I tell you, Blanton," he exploded into speech as he waddled to the cabinet and reached for a glass. "we've got to put in air conditioning. It's too hot in here to live."

"You're getting too fat, Carter," the surgeon returned. "I want you to meet Dr. Brade. Brade, this is Carter Hewlett, our internist."

Hewlett's pudgy hand was moist like his face. "Glad to know you, Doctor," he said. "Just passing through?"

"Dr. Brade married Carol Grahame," said Castleman Tyre.

"Oh! Of course, of course. Well, well! We'll have a drink on that."

Once more the young husband was impressed with the obvious importance accruing to him from his marriage. He was certainly getting the worth of his bargain—yet that was not the wholly satisfactory thought that it should have been. The bargain itself, was not too pleasant to think of. Well, he could justify himself and eliminate that feeling of cheapness by making good on his own, as he resolutely intended to do. He'd show Carol before he was through that he didn't come from the bargain basement.

Wait a minute, though! What was this about Carol? Why

should he want to prove himself to her? Better not let any thought of the personal side of their relationship intrude. That was beyond the bargain. Trouble lay in that direction. He must hold to his determination to think of her not as a wife, not as a woman, but as a partner in a deal.

Remember that, you fool, he adjured himself. You'd better get a bolt for the door of your thoughts.

Doctor-talk eddied back and forth as the drinks were consumed: Talk of operations, new medical discoveries, other innovations which might prove to be discoveries or perhaps only pretentious claims, estimates of fellow practioners, sometimes frank, sometimes obscure; opinions on vitamins, hormones, and the ductless glands. The name Owen James was mentioned.

"That chap's headed for trouble," predicted Hewlett.

"He's a medical Bolshevik," declared Castleman Tyre.

The senior Tyre's laughter boomed. "Why qualify it with 'medical?' "

The visitor rose. He had no intention of overstaying his welcome.

"It's been very pleasant," he said.

"Drop around any day," said Blanton Tyre. "You'll always find a drink, at least."

Brade thanked him, making a mental note to wait at least ten days, unless specifically invited again. With medical gogetters like this Tyre outfit, it was best to move slowly.

On the way out he passed the desk where sat the girl whom Tyre had called Kenny and then Miss Mangan. She looked up and smiled at him. There was something knowing and significant in that smile. He wouldn't wonder at all if Miss Kenny Mangan knew a lot of what went on in the Tyre Clinic.

In the next few days he spent some of his spare time driving the car, which he had bought on easy terms, through all parts of the city. He wanted to get a general idea of his new environment. Equipped with shrewd capacities of observation and analysis, he gradually built up the picture of an industrial-aristocratic town, not as bad as it might be; certainly not as good as it ought to be.

Broad paved streets pushed back the frontiers of red clay that threatened to intrude once more where scarcely a generation before it had held full sway. Dust swirled through the town with the hot breeze of summer, veiling the millowner's shiny limousine parked diagonally to the curb beside the mud-spattered flivver from the hinterland. In the new suburbs gracious homes were set well apart; in the older residential sections tall columns showed cracked and faded where paint had not replaced wear of age and diminishing fortunes.

A small creek, tributary to the river and now no more than a starveling dribble of slime, cut off the low-lying portion of the city. It was a physical check to social progress and change, a barrier more unassailable than any symbolic railroad tracks, separating the millowners from the millworkers, the rich from the poor, the culture of peace and stability and traditions from the raw stuff of primitive human wants. There the explorer's eye was arrested by a signboard, handmade and hand-printed, nailed to a scrawny tree.

Welcome
to
Hookworm Flats

Beyond rose a tall, gaunt building, efficiently adjusted by makeshift to the uses of a hospital, an evidence of progress. There was still plenty of room for reform in the surrounding block of small hovels, teeming with undernourished weaklings, who would grow older only to begin their apprenticeship to the stunting service of the mills. It was nobody's fault, perhaps. Strained economic conditions must be reflected in low wages. But some of these slums were a disgrace to any municipality.

Summing up his impressions, the newcomer estimated Charlesville to be a community which would be very gracious to its chosen, pretty callous to its unprivileged. In other words, a typical American city. At the close of his explorations he was glad to drive home to the spacious mansion which shut out all problems but that of his own status there.

CHAPTER VII

CAROL called to him from the garden as he got out of his new car.

"Go up and dress, Spen. We've got people for dinner."

"Who?"

"Sort of a family affair. Only half a dozen. You're going to be inspected for blemishes. Mind?"

"I'll be on my best marital behavior."

His cold bath made him feel fine. Coming down, he found Carol in the hall. In her filmy evening frock she looked like a radiant girl. Nobody would have believed that she was a wife, and pregnant, at that. Well, he reminded himself ruefully, she was neither so far as he was concerned.

"I like you in evening clothes, Spen," she said. "In the strict privacy of the family I'll admit that you aren't any professional beauty. But you do look like you were somebody."

"So I am," he replied lightly. "Carol Grahame's husband. I'm finding it very helpful."

"You'll get over feeling that way about it. Are you prepared to go through your paces? The Grand Inquisitress is here."

"Is that the formidable cousin?"

"Yes. Cousin Carrie Carskaddan. She's half Northerner, but otherwise there's nothing against her character except her temper."

A man somewhere between thirty-five and forty came up the steps. He was of medium size, with the build and light step of an athlete. His face rugged, seamed, and weary, was lighted by deep-set gray eyes of singular clarity. The lean chin and high cheekbones guaranteed firmness of character, but the mouth, mobile and sensitive, suggested both humor and tolerance. Not at all the professional "Christer" type, which Carol's casual outline had suggested.

"Oh, Owen!" Carol said happily and went to him with hands outstretched.

"Sorry I couldn't dress, Carol," he apologized. "Didn't have time. I've just left the clinic."

"You never do have time," she said. "Owen, this is Spen."

The two men shook hands.

"Where's Aunt Candy?" asked the newcomer.

"Out in the garden with the family dragon."

Owen James smiled. "Have you been forewarned about her?" he asked the husband.

"Not as much as I ought to be, I expect."

"I did tell Spen she was an old hellion," said Carol.

"She has always loved you," Owen James said.

(So have you, thought Spen, startled and impressed by something somber, brooding, that had betrayed itself in the other's manner of speech.)

"Yes; I suppose that's true," said Carol. "Though she'd never admit it. She's really an old dear, when you understand her."

"Just how old, nobody knows," put in Owen James. "Because she won't tell. My guess is eighty something. She lives in the horse-and-buggy age literally. Won't own a car or permit one on her place. Calls them devil's stink wagons. Drives around town in a brougham with two bay horses almost as old as she is and holds up Main Street traffic like a veteran's parade."

"The police are all afraid of her," chuckled Carol. "Go on, Owen."

"She had two ruling passions: running other people's lives for them and being an amateur vamp."

"At eighty?" said Spen incredulously.

"Not that kind of vamp. It's an old name for volunteer firemen. She's the Oldest Living. Has a badge, and a siren, and an alarm system in her house, and goes to all the three-alarm fires night or day."

"And she doesn't like doctors," added Carol. "An Atlanta surgeon once charged her a thousand dollars for cutting off an infected toe, and when he got the letter she wrote about it he wrote back and said he was sorry it hadn't been her head."

A high, clear voice from beyond the hedge announced:

"Disgraceful. That's what I call it. Disgraceful, underhanded, and suspicious. Marrying a man she'd never seen nor heard of until—Don't you dare shush *me*, Candace Grahame."

"That's you, Spen," said Carol with eyes of laughter.

"I should say it was you," he retorted. "You're the disgraceful, underhanded, and suspicious character. I'm only unseen and unheard of. Cousin Carrie's got something to learn."

"You'll never convince her of that," said Owen James.

There passed through the hedge gap, with Aunt Candace in attendance, an ancient and regal figure in cermonial black: tall, angular, and so straight that the gold-headed stick in the hand had rather the effect of a drum major's baton than a support. The neck was long and appeared longer because of the high white collar with whalebone blocking that engirdled it; the head small, and the features sharply sculptured as if from heavily feined marble. Small, very elegant glasses were perched high on a haughty nose. The apparition slashed at a bush with her cane.

"Needs trimming," she said. "What do those lazy niggers of yours do for their wages, Candy?"

"Didn't I say she was a dragon?" murmured Carol.

"St. George for Merrie England," breathed out Spen and marched forward to meet the foe, followed at a respectful distance by the other two.

"How do you do, Cousin Carrie?" he said politely.

Cousin Carrie conned him up and down as if he were some animal paraded for her inspection and possible purchase.

"And who are you, sir?"

"This is Spencer Brade," put in Aunt Candace. "You know Carol's husband."

"Oh-h-h-h-h!" There was a contemptuous uplift to the response. "You're the mysterious young doctor. I think less than nothing of doctors. Grasping crooks!"

"We must live," murmured Spen. He was rather enjoying this.

"At least you seem to be a gentleman," she conceded.

"What would you expect a member of your family to marry?" he inquired blandly.

"Though you can never tell from surface indications," she qualified. "I suppose it's no drawback to you that Carol is a rich woman."

54

"Not the slightest. Rather an advantage, don't you think?" he drawled.

"Mmp!" the old lady snorted. "Well, you needn't expect to lay hand on any of *my* money through your marriage."

A rueful expression wiped out the young man's amiable smile. "Why wasn't I warned?" he muttered. "Now I suppose it's too late."

"Well!" breathed Cousin Carrie in bewilderment. She returned to the assault. "And what kind of doctor might you be?"

"A good one, ma'am. Would you like to see my testimonials?"

"Don't be impertinent. What's your specialty?"

"Gynecological surgery. I'm a gynecologist."

She eyed him with disfavor. "Gynecologist," she grunted scornfully. "What's it in English?"

"Well, you might say a sort of lady's tailor," he drawled.

Carol giggled. Aunt Candace gasped. Cousin Carrie, with a slightly puzzled expression, began:

"Hey what's that? A lady's tail—— Waw-haw-haw-haw-haw!" She beat upon the earth with her cane, writhing in appreciation of the well-weathered pun. "Tchek-tchek-tchek! A lady's—— You're a vulgar and presuming young squirt. Candace, put this creature next to me at dinner. I want to see how far he'll go."

Carol and Owen dropped back with Spen.

"You're fast on your feet, Brade," chuckled Owen.

"I suspect I'll have to be with this family," said Spen, looking sidelong at his wife. "Any more like her, Carol?"

"No. The other three guests are quite harmless. You won't mind them at all. You're doing beautifully, Spen."

Throughout the meal Spen was kept on his toes, evading, blocking, and occasionally countering Cousin Carrie's barrage of questions and insinuations. As the coffee came on she said:

"Anyway, I know now why Carol married you."

The shock of it startled him into nervous laughter. Offended, the old lady glared at him.

"I was paying you a compliment, young man, if you did but know it."

"A highly appreciated one, Cousin Carrie," he assured her with a bow.

Only partly assuaged, she sniffed. "You acted like you saw a joke in it. Maybe you'll explain later."

(And if I should, he thought, what a riot there would be in this peaceful household!)

After the ladies had left, Owen James moved up beside him. Spen said:

"I understand you have a clinic of sorts here."

"Of sorts," agreed the other. "Come and look it over."

"That must be the place I saw when I was prowling around Hookworm Flats."

"It's the best we could do. The fire inspectors keep threatening to condemn us."

"Not much of a center for private practice, is it?"

"I haven't time for private practice. The other kind keeps me too busy."

"Charity work's all right in moderation," Spen said. "But I consider that medicine owes me a decent reward for what I know and do."

"Certainly. I understand that point of view, though I don't follow it. I suppose that primarily I'm a clergyman, and the medical side is nothing more than my approach. My personal slant on practice is that by helping people solve their problems of disease and health I can set them on the right track and help them heal their souls." He smiled. "Perhaps you don't believe in souls."

"I have troubles enough looking after their bodies," Spen said.

"Well, these mill people have a hard enough time keeping the two together and don't get too much help in it. Some interesting surgical problems come up from time to time," he added suggestively.

"Who does your surgery?"

Owen James frowned. "I do more of it than I ought. It isn't my métier. By the way, I'm getting a young man in who was in medical school with you—Felix Bernitz."

"Bernitz? Of course. But he's not a surgeon. He's a psychologist. Where did you get him?"

Before there was time for a reply the other guests closed in, and the talk became general.

When the men guests emerged into the drawing room Carol segregated Owen James.

"How did it go? About the clinic, I mean."

He hesitated before answering: "I doubt if he'd be interested."

"Why not?" she demanded.

"He's very ambitious. As he should be, of course. I'm not blaming him for that. He wants to make medicine pay his way. I should say the Tyre Clinic would be more in his line." He did not think it necessary or advisable to tell her that echoes of Spencer Brade's diatribe to Dr. Powers, wherein he proclaimed his cynical creed of pocket surgery, had reached Charlesville through a letter from a staff member.

"You don't think much of the Tyre Clinic," said Carol.

"It's very successful."

"Are you fencing with me, Owen dear?"

"After all, he's your husband."

"Because he's my husband he ought to be in there, helping," she said with conviction.

He smiled rather mournfully. "Are you going to sacrifice him to the family tradition?"

"Oh, sacrifice!" she retorted impatiently. "Owen, would you take him if he did offer to help?"

"I—don't—know."

"He isn't good enough?" There was a note of incredulity.

"Technically I'm sure he's very good. I'm not sure how he'd fit in. It's a difference of theory."

It was midnight before Cousin Carrie Carskaddan, always the last guest at any party, took her majestic leave. Carol said to her husband:

"Let's walk for a few minutes. It's so lovely and cool." They strolled down the curving drive. "Was it much of an ordeal?"

"No. They were all very nice to me. I like the old she-dragon."

"She's crazy about you. Spen do I show my condition?"

"Not a bit. You're looking wonderful."

She swept him a curtsy. "I'm feeling fine. Don't they say that's a bad sign?"

"Midwives' superstition."

"Aunt Candy looks at me so queerly at times. I wonder if she suspects."

"A young married woman is always under suspicion. How about telling her?"

"I hardly know why I haven't. Some lingering remnant of shame, I reckon."

"Shame? That's stupid."

"But it's such an absurd position," she fretted. "You—and I and the baby coming. And Tony gone out of my life."

"Would you want him back?"

"Not for a minute!"

He was glad to note that there was no regret in her tone. After a pause he said, "Your Aunt Candace doesn't look any more queerly at you than at me."

"No; she doesn't. I've noticed that too. I'll tell you what it is though. She doesn't approve of separate rooms."

"Neither do I."

She turned a startled gaze upon him and looked away. "What do you think of Owen James?"

"I've got to look out or I'll like that guy."

"Why shouldn't you like him? I want you to like him."

"He's in love with you. He can't look or speak without showing it."

"Poor Owen!" she said softly. "I never could live up to him."

"Why do they call him a Bolshevik?"

"Who does?"

"The Tyres."

"They would! He's been trying to get a cleanup of housing conditions in the mill districts on the ground that they're a menace to public health."

"Not the Grahame property, surely!"

"No. We look after our people. But some of our friends, who are also friends and patients of the Tyres, are bad landlords. Naturally they call Owen a Red because he threatens their profits. It's considered very bad taste, by the way, to mention these things when you're out."

Spen said reflectively, "Can't James do enough good in his clinic without butting into other people's economics?"

"He thinks not."

"I imagine he wasn't a brilliant success in private practice."

Carol laughed. "He had the makings of a great specialist. Half his women patients were in love with him. It almost drove the poor boy crazy."

"Were you?"

"I? No." A shade darkened the moonlit beauty of the face. "I wish I could have been. How much trouble I'd have saved myself! Aunt Candace always wanted me to marry him."

"That's pleasant news for a young husband!"

58

She did not respond to his light tone. "I wish you could help him with his clinic."

"And get all Our Best People down on me? The prospect terrifies me."

"I don't believe anything terrifies you, Spen."

"I'll admit I'm not specially timid. But I'm politic. Even so, I might find something down there to interest me."

"I'm sure you would." Carol threw out her arms, yawning unshamedly. "Oh, I *am* sleepy! I'm going up. Good night."

"Good night," he said. "I'll have one more smoke."

He had a drink also when he got into the house. Then, because he was restless and unsettled, he had another, a long and stiff one. There was no light to be seen beneath the communicating door when he entered his room. He tried it gently. As he expected, the bolt on the far side had been drawn. He tapped lightly. No answer, but he thought he heard a stir within. He tried again.

"Carol," he called.

"Well? What is it? What do you want?" The voice was startled and cold.

"Nothing," he said. "Sorry."

He turned away. A surge of rage passed through him. After it came the thought of Kenny Mangan's impudent face and upraised provocative eyes.

CHAPTER VIII

THE APPOINTMENT of Dr. Spencer Brade to the gynecological service of the City Hospital was not long delayed, thanks to the Tyre influence. Because most of the staff members took summer vacations, he soon found himself doing double and triple work among the charity patients. As his office demands were still light, this made the least difference. Meantime he welcomed the chance to show his fellow M.D.s how well he was qualified. All this he regarded as accumulative capital, the hard-earned increment of experience and opportunity and, more slow of acquisition, reputation. Somebody would pay for it later. He reconciled it with his creed of pocket surgery on this ground.

Notwithstanding his grim determination to turn everything to his eventual profit, he could not wholly immunize his emotions from the recurrent tragedies of the charity clinics: long lines of sweating, shamed, frightened humanity, waiting for shots that would control and perhaps cure their syphilis; the tortured bodies in the orthopedic department, lifting drawn, misshapen limbs; the pallid victims of undernourishment, exhibiting hands and arms scaly with the lesions of pellagra from diet of corn bread, fat meat, and molasses, a regimen which gave none of the vitamins so necessary to living.

Nor could he wholly close his mind to the economic implications, the deep-lying flaws of a system which left a formidable proportion of the populace underfed, underpaid, unable to pay for proper drug or medical service, or even to buy the necessary food for preventing deficiency diseases; helpless victims of the nerve pains of polyneuritis from lack of Vitamin B, unsightly examples of potbellies, the bowlegs, the contracted pelves from want of Vitamin D. He had read the facts of the sordid lives, the crowded quarters, the disease-spreading filth of those small mill workers' houses as he came into Charlesville on the train that morning back in June. He was reading now the same lesson in the faces of the people who came from those houses, the people who bowed over the spinning machines, watching the ever-repeating shuttling of the threads as cloth was woven, sweated for a livelihood that they never seemed quite able to attain.

He trained himself to shut off his mind from these ugly and unprofitable thoughts, just as he shut his eyes to the remnants of tonsils he saw remaining after some would-be surgeon had removed the rest of those too easily accessible organs together with twenty-five dollars from the pocket of some poor devil who believed he was getting a bargain. It was a bargain he would later regret when his sore throats kept up, when his rheumatic joints kept on swelling, when the murmur in his heart kept increasing, when he had to pay a real surgeon to clean up the messy job left behind, or was forced to join the mob at the charity clinic because his money was all gone. Sometimes he would curse silently when he saw smooth whiteness of a young woman's body scarred and distorted by the bungling surgery of a tyro who never should have been allowed to pick up a knife. Surgery that wasn't necessary, removing an innocent appendix, ovary, or tube for a pain that had its origin in constipation, for a backache that came from standing too many hours over a spinning machine, from too little fresh air, from too little recreation.

There were compensations. Devotion to his profession was deep in the grain of Spencer Brade. To whatever category of self-advantage he might choose to assign it, he was conscious of the selfless satisfaction of the worker whose task of salvage is the highest in the scope of human endeavor. To fight for a human life through hours of which every minute was a crisis; to restore the shattered mechanism of a body to efficacy—these were achievements which eluded his best attempts to adjust them to the dollar standard. It was payment in kind, the pathetic gratitude of the haggard young husband whose wife had almost died from a ruptured tubal pregnancy; the smile of the older woman, still eager for life, for whom he had removed the malignant tumor that was slowly draining her blood, her strength, and her hope. Sometimes it was an effort to recall himself to his new and practical principles after experiences like these.

"I've been a sap too long," Spen had said to Dr. Powers in the bitter gall of disillusionment, and the old man had answered sternly:

"Not long enough."

(Oh well, he now thought, I suppose I'll always be a softy in spots. But I'm not going to let it get in my way.)

Passing through the the main hall one afternoon, he caught a glimpse of a dark, keen-eyed face with a racially distinctive nose. Somehow it connected itself in his mind with Owen James. Of course! James had spoken to him of Felix Bernitz; Bernitz, who had been his classmate in medical school, had graduated almost as high as himself, and after a year interning in general medicine had dropped out of his ken. Five years since they had met.

"Hi, Bernie!"

"Hey? What? Oh, Spen Brade! Glad to see you. I heard you were here."

"I didn't know you were. Owen James started to tell me, I think."

"Yes. I'm working with him. Been away for three months taking some special courses, or I'd have been around to see you."

"What's your line?"

"Neurology and psychiatry."

Spen's pursed features expressed a graphic distaste. "You would pick 'em tough! Me, I'd rather have a boil than a neurotic on my neck."

"Somebody's got to look after 'em," Bernitz pointed out. "The average practitioner can't recognize mental or nervous trouble until it reaches the stage of a disease."

"When it may be too late."

"That's the damnable tragedy of mental cases," the other went on. "If doctors would train themselves to recognize these warning signs and turn their patients over to a trained psychiatrist there'd be a lot less beds in the insane asylums."

"You've got something there, Bernie. It's like I said. Most of us would rather have a boil. We don't want to be bothered with the problems of the neurotics and the hypochondriacs. We just give them one medicine or another and send them about their business, or we do unnecessary operations on them that make them worse."

Bernitz grinned. "First time I ever heard a surgeon admit that," he said. "You must be slipping. That really is the worst thing about the psychoneurotic—the fact that unscrupulous surgeons are always ready to operate on them. Give me a patient that's been operated on two or three times and I'll guarantee that nobody can cure her. And nine times out of ten the operation isn't necessary."

"Well, we surgeons have got to live. What about you Bernie? Where did you go when you left Baltimore? How did you happen to wind up here?"

"Well, that's a long story," the other said. "I went to the Psychopathological Institute in New York and had two years of psychiatry and neurology. Then I worked in the outpatient clinic of one of the medical schools up there. That's where I met Owen James. He was a great deal older than I, but we became friends. He persuaded me to come down here to Charlesville. Look out for that bird, Spen. He can make you do anything he wants."

"Not me!" said Spen vigorously.

"You'd like his shop, though. I work down there whenever I get a chance. Sort of a human-relations clinic," Bernitz explained. "We try to work out people's problems for them so they can take care of themselves with a little help."

"I thought the services of psychoanalyst were only available to the rich. Don't tell me you're bringing it to the millworkers."

"That's what we're trying to do. But we're not always successful. It's hard to adjust a patient to his environment when the environment doesn't provide enough for him to eat."

"I've always thought," Spen said thoughtfully, "that we ought to have some really sincere consulting psychologists in medicine. We all see cases who could be sent to one. A mental-disease specialist can't do the job satisfactorily——"

"Folks are sensitive too. They don't like to admit that they're consulting a psychiatrist. They feel that there's some disgrace attached to it, and you can't hardly blame them. You know how people shun a person with mental disease."

"We doctors are not much better," Spen said. "I know how I feel lost when I get a patient who isn't just right. I can't afford to take time to work the cases out and try to find the conflict. Half the cases we gynecologists see are in women who are not sexually compatible with their husbands. Nothing much you do for them will help any, if you don't clear up the whole basis of the trouble."

"That's what I'm after at the clinic. If I can make it work out among the poorer people I might get a psychology clinic started here for the middle and upper classes."

"Now you're talking sense," the other approved. "There ought to be money in that. Look at the fees these fake psychoanalysts get in New York for telling women what their dreams mean and that their husbands don't understand them."

Bernitz laughed. "Same old Brade, aren't you!" he said. "Always making cracks about medicine and money."

"This time I mean it. I'm out for the shiners, Bernie.

"Nuts!"

"All right," Spen said. "Come around and look at my elegant and air-conditioned office some day. The picture of a sucker trap: that'll convince you."

Bernitz shook his head. "I can't see you going commercial. Why, in medical school you were the biggest softy and idealist in the class."

"What about you, slipping a little loan to the class hardup and buying ice-cream cones for the kids in the orthopedic ward?"

"The difference," Bernitz explained, "is that nobody ever expects a Jew to be generous. There are a lot of doctors in town right now who would tell you that I work with Owen James for the advertising it gets me."

"They don't hold your race against you down here, do they?"

"Don't they!" He laughed shortly. "Just to the extent that I had one hell of a time getting privileges at the hospitals. Even now they won't let me on the staff of the City Hospital."

"They're probably afraid of you. You're too good. And a Jew who doesn't care for money would always be under suspicion. Or do you?"

Bernitz grinned. "Sure, I like money. So did my old man. Consequently I've got enough to coast along on. Look, Spen; I respect a businessman or a lawyer who's after every dollar. That's the measure of their success. A doctor is different. It's a bigger game."

"Nothing's a bigger game than success," Spen retorted. But he was conscious of an inner discomfort and exasperation. "I'll call you up and we'll lunch together pretty soon," he said, shaking hands. "It's swell to find you here."

(But why hadn't he asked Bernie to dine? Of course he knew why. That annoyed him further, because he was ashamed of it.)

At closing time several days later Spen descended to the lobby of the Medical Arts Building to find the place jammed by a sudden downpour. Near the drugstore entrance he noticed Castleman Tyre bending over his secretary, Kenny Mangan, in earnest talk. Not so good, he thought. He went back for raincoat and umbrella. When he returned the girl, alone now, was staring disconsolately out into the uproar. He went over to her.

"This *would* be the day I'd wear my new hat," she said. "Twelve eighty-seven, marked down."

"Where do you want to go?" Spen asked.

"Home. To Emboro. My bus station's two long wet blocks from here."

"*My* bus is across in that parking space," he said. "I'll be glad to take you."

She hesitated, then said enigmatically, "All right. But we'll

64

have to move quick. It's right nice of you," she added gratefully.

A minute later she was seated beside him in the runabout. The storm swelled to a cloudburst before they had more than turned off the main thoroughfare. Twice they barely escaped collision with cars which were driving blindly without lights.

"This is bad," Spen said. "Are you in a hurry to get home?"

"Not particularly."

"Then we'll pull in and ride it out at anchor."

"Okay by me," she said easily.

He eased the car into a boiling gutter and set the brake. His passenger turned on the interior light.

"Do you mind?" she asked.

Spen smiled at her. "Self-protection?" he asked.

"No. I want to straighten myself out. That wind knocked me cockeyed." She shifted the mirror and set herself to rights. "Gosh, what a flood!" she said as the car rocked under the impact.

"If you're in no hurry," Spen said, "why did you ask me to move quick back there in the lobby?"

"Fatty was coming back."

"Fatty?"

"Dr. Tyre, Jr. My respected boss. He'd gone for his car to take me home."

"And you didn't want him to?"

"What do *you* think?"

"What's the matter with Tyre?"

"Oh, nothing, I reckon." She added viciously, "They can't ring *me* up on their cash register."

"I see," said Spen, amused.

"Well forget it. I talk too much."

She did not have that impertinent nose and that firm little chin for nothing, Spen reflected. As she chatted on he sensed a certain shrewdness, mingled with good will, in her. She seemed a distinctly likable little person.

The storm was modifying its fury now.

"Let's get going," she suggested.

Branches and shrubbery, blown into the streets, kept their progress slow. His passenger said abruptly to Spen:

"Are you coming in with us?"

"Us?" he repeated in surprise. "Who?"

"The Tyre Clinic."

"Oh! I haven't been asked."

"You're going to be."

Spen felt a leap of exultation in his nerves. "You seem to be well informed."

"A secretary hears a lot of things. You'd be surprised."

"And tells them all?"

Miss Mangan addressed herself, "Is that a slap in the jaw for you, Kenny! And serves you right."

Spen was contrite. "I'm sorry," he said. "That was rotten of me. But I still don't understand why you should be telling me all this."

"I'm trying to even up. It was pretty decent of you to take me way out here.

"Bunk! Anybody would have done it."

"Maybe. And anybody else would have made a pass at the girl."

"Perhaps I'm slow," he suggested, amusement at her frankness arising in him again.

She regarded him with grave speculation. "No; I don't believe that's it at all. I think you're too square to go looking for immediate returns on a favor. That's something a girl appreciates. It's unusual."

"Yet you want to repay in another way," he pointed out.

"Why not? But I told you I talk too much. Not to every Tom, Dick 'n' Harry, though."

Less interested in her than in what she had opened up in the way of his prospects, Spen went on, "Are you pretty sure of what you said about the clinic?"

"Why else do you think old Tyre got you on the City Hospital staff?" she returned with uplifted brows.

"Oh, kindness of heart toward a young fellow starting out."

"Kindness of *what*? Blanton Tyre? Someone's been filling you with cold soup."

"Why did he bother, then?"

"To get a line on you. They've been checking on everything you do."

"Since you know the situation so well," he said lightly, "what's your advice in case they do ask me to join?"

"What's your angle?" she asked gravely. "What are you in this game for?"

"Money. All I can legitimately get out of it."

"Come on in," she said. "The water's fine."

66

They had now reached the suburb. "That apartment house on the corner," Kenny directed. "I've got a flat there with a friend. She's a nurse."

When he pulled to the curb, she did not get out at once but sat staring in front of her.

"Something on your mind?" he asked presently.

"Yes. You said I talked too much."

"I apologize."

"Never mind that. If any of this ever gets back to the clinic I'm ditched."

"You've no cause to worry there," he assured her.

She opened the car door. "Thank you," she said. "You're kind. There's one reason why I'd as soon you didn't come in with us."

"What is it?"

"You couldn't take me home in case of another storm. It wouldn't be ethical, you being my boss. Would it? Good night."

Her laughter, light and soft, hung in the air a split second before the angry wind snatched it away and merged it in the storm.

CHAPTER IX

CAROL had set the note of their association. Tactfully and with a minimum of friction she had developed a facile, light, sometimes bantering comradeship between them which could readily simulate marital affection when Aunt Candace or anyone else was present. It was rather like a well-grounded friendship between two men of the same household. From Spen's viewpoint the troublesome factor was that Carol was not a man but very much a woman and a most desirable one.

Did she realize this fact and its implications? Sometimes he angrily doubted it. A gay sort of intimacy formed her attitude, which she contrived to keep essentially impersonal. Couldn't she guess that his masculinity would not be permanently satisfied with that? Masculinity? Did she ever consider that angle? There was no sign of it. Of course her conduct was quite within the terms of their pact. But this made it no easier for him. The whole situation was unnatural. What did she think a fellow was? A monk?

There was another angle to consider. Pregnancy, as he knew, sometimes dulled or even temporarily eliminated the sexual appetites. Carol might be one of that considerable percentage of prospective mothers who could not bear a man near them while carrying a child. Perhaps later?

Not too pointedly and always giving it a half-playful slant, he once or twice tried to direct the talk to that subject. Carol exhibited an exasperatingly adroit elusiveness. She was not crass enough to remind him flatly of the marital bargain. But she side-stepped every attempt to get her to define her feeling. The nearest to a response that he got from her was a smiling, "I think we do very well as young marrieds, Spen. We're regarded as quite a model couple."

After a dinner party of rather curiously assorted couples, held at the country club, Carol, on the way home, shrewdly analyzed the various ménages: the fussy wife, the domineering husband, the overdemonstrative pair, the humorous quarrelers, the two who went their separate ways with perfect good will, and so on.

"Which kind of wife would you want me to be, Spen?" she asked lightly.

They had just entered the hallway of their home, and he stopped and looked at her to give his words full meaning.

"What would you say if I told you that I'd like you to be a one-hundred-per-cent wife?" he said.

"That isn't what I meant." Her voice had changed and chilled.

"It's what I mean."

Again she said and this time with a touch of her charming impatience, "Oh, Spen! I think we're doing quite well as we are."

"Well, I don't," he said boldly. "It's all very well for you to cast yourself for the role of virgin wife, but what about me?"

She colored. "Are you claiming that it's unfair?"

"It's absurd and humiliating. Bolted doors!"

"I've never meant to put any restrictions on you," she said with an effort. "If you feel that—if you want to—to——"

"What I want is you."

"I think you've been drinking too much, Spen."

"You think it's the liquor talking?" he said harshly. "Wrong! In case you're interested, I've felt that way about you ever since you met me that day at the train." His temper broke. "If I were half a man," he snapped, "I'd smash hell out of that door."

"And out of our agreement?" she said pointedly.

He paled with anger. "True, of course. Be a good little boy or your allowance will be stopped."

"You know that isn't what I meant."

"I don't know what else you could have meant," he retorted. "Thanks for the reminder. After this you won't need any bolt. You can feel perfectly safe from intrusion."

"You needn't be bitter about it."

"Quite right. I think I'll go back to the club and have a drink or two.

"Shan't I get you one from the sideboard?"

"No, thank you. It might stir me to indiscretion. Good night."

He got out the car again and drove back to the country club. After two drinks he looked at his watch. Not yet eleven o'clock. Going into a telephone booth, he called up a number. A voice that he did not recognize said:

"Miss Mangan? No; but she's right here. Ken! Kenny! Wanted on the phone."

"Hello," he said. "This is Dr. Brade, Spencer Brade."

"Oh," answered Kenny Mangan's cool voice with its undertone of being always faintly amused. "I was just going to bed."

"Don't do it. Come out and have a drink with me instead. I'll drive out and get you."

There was a pause. Then, "How many have you had?"

"Does it matter?"

"It might."

"Well, several. But I'm still Old Reliable."

"Ask me some other time," she said. "Good night—and thanks for calling me."

Spen swore: the hot, puerile oaths of frustration. He went back to the bar and ordered brandy and soda.

Breakfast in the Grahame household was a family affair. At seven-thirty precisely Aunt Candace appeared and took her place behind the superb silver coffee urn which was a family relic. The others were expected to be at hand promptly. This morning Carol was ten minutes late. Aunt Candace looked up from her paper.

"Good morning, Carol."

"Good morning, Aunt Candy. Has Spen finished already?"

"Your husband did not stop for breakfast," returned the old lady dryly.

"Oh, I remember! He had an early operation at the hospital."

"I hope," said Aunt Candace ominously, "that his hands are steadier this morning than his feet were last night."

The best Carol could do was, "I'm sorry if we woke you up coming in." It was, she felt, a pretty lame best.

"Not 'we,' " the old lady corrected. "He. You were in your bed. Alone. As usual."

The wife caught her breath. What was coming now? How much did this shrewd and quiet onlooker know? Or suspect?

"I wanted to come early," she said. "Spen went back to play some bridge."

"How long is this sort of thing going to continue? I'm waiting for an explanation, Carol."

Carol's chin went up. "I've nothing to explain. Ask Spen."

"You brought him into this house," her aunt reminded her.

"Does that make me responsibe for all his actions?"

"At least you might show some degree of interest in his behavior. I don't understand you lately, my dear."

Here, Carol perceived with sudden inspiration, was her opportunity. She plunged.

"Aunt Candy, I'm pregnant. I'm going to have a baby."

"How did you get that way?" the other shot at her.

"Why—why, by the usual method," answered Carol, taken aback and reddening.

"Not by keeping your bedroom door bolted," was the grim response. "That bolt is gathering rust."

"Well, that's why," returned the bride, still scarlet.

"Is it, indeed! I can't be expected to understand these things," she pursued calmly, "but it doesn't seem reasonable to me."

"He—Spen understands."

"Last night I was so disgusted that I was ready to tell you either you and your husband must leave this house or I would. But I'm not so certain he hasn't some sort of excuse. What sort of wife are you? Perhaps it's this that is turning him into a drunkard."

"That isn't fair. Spen isn't a drunkard."

"He's on his way to becoming one," insisted Miss Grahame relentlessly. "I've been keeping tabs on our house supply of liquor."

"You would!" said Carol contemptuously and, as she knew, most unfairly.

The deep-lined, plump old face opposite her quivered. "Are we quarreling, my child?" said the old lips painfully. "Are we parting?"

Carol ran around the table, dropped to her knees, and hugged the stubby form.

"Darling, I'm a beast! Forgive me. Nothing is going to come between us, not ever. Be patient with me. It's a little difficult right now. But it will all come out right."

Shortly before six that evening, Spen's car drove in. He came up the stairs, humming softly, entered his room, and went directly to his bathroom, leaving both doors open. Carol, following, heard the plunge and hiss of the water in the washbowl as he doused his face. She had to call twice before he heard her.

"Hello!" he called back. "Be right out."

He tossed the towel behind him as he came through the door, looking, as always, immaculate in spite of the heat.

"How do you feel?" she asked.

"Fine. Why not?" Plainly he was not going to admit anything about last night.

"Spen, I've told Aunt Candace."

"About last night? That's perfectly lovely! That makes everything——"

"Not about last night. About the baby."

"Not the whole story!"

"No. Just that I was going to have one."

"How did the acme of Southern Womanhood take it?"

"Spen! I wish you wouldn't."

"Sorry, Carol. I really think the old lady is a swell person, which is more than she thinks of me. It must have been a shock to her. She's so damned virginal."

"That's what *you* think," returned his wife, suppressing a desire to laugh. "You should have heard her on the topic of the bolted door."

"Oh! You touched on that too?"

"She's known all about it from the first. One doesn't have to tell her much."

"Obviously. What's our cue now?"

"Carry on as is. Of course she couldn't possibly suspect the truth about the baby."

Spen reflected. "It's just as well you told her your condition. Cannaday's your doctor, isn't he?"

"Yes. He's part of of the family tradition."

"I've met him. He seems to me pretty old school. Still, some of these older g.p.s. are pretty wise boys. I expect he's all right. I think I'd feel easier if he made a sort of an inspection just for safety."

"Spen," she said thoughtfully, "you can be a very nice person when you want to be."

"Oh, I have my points." He grinned. "As a medical man," he added.

She promised to arrange an appointment for the next morning. About noon she called her husband.

"Want to take an expectant mother to lunch?"

"I certainly do."

"Do you know the Green Bay Tree? Meet me there. One o'clock all right?"

It was a quiet, expensive little place not far off the business district. They found a table in an alcove. The headwaiter, recognizing Carol, came and was deferential. Spen ordered with care and discrimination.

"Nothing wrong, is there?" he asked when the waiter had left them.

"No. I'm fine, Dr. Cannaday says."

"Why this rendezvous, then? Not but what I'm delighted to have so charming a guest."

Carol gave him a friendly smile. "Shall I tell you something? I like to loll and talk at my meals. It can't be done at home. I love Aunt Candy dearly, but she is a damper on cozy conversation. Every dinner is a function.

"This certainly is a relief."

Carol stretched luxuriously and accepted a cigarette. "How is the practice coming?"

"Pretty well. Three operations already this week."

"Big ones?"

"One of them. The others were just day's-work stuff. Not

bad for the summer season, though, when I've been here so short a time."

"Spen, do you still feel the same way about medicine now that you've started in to practice?"

"How do you mean?"

"Well, about the business side of it?"

"The question of ideals or money?"

She nodded.

"Well," he said thoughtfully, "I don't exactly know. Being in practice has shown me that the men who get ahead are the ones who demand a good financial return for their work."

"How about Owen James? Don't you think there's a lot of truth in what he says?"

"James is the idealist type. I'm not sure how good he is professionally. It's dangerous to put any consideration above sound technic."

"Don't you think he does a lot of good?"

"I'm sure he does. And probably some harm. But we all do that."

"Have you been to his clinic yet?"

"No. I've been meaning to. Glad you reminded me."

"Watch out for Owen," she warned him smilingly. "He'll grab you and put you to work if he can. He has no conscience about making use of people for his beloved clinic."

"Has he made use of you?" Spen asked curiously.

"Not directly. I send him a small check once in a while for urgent cases."

"So I'm not the only medical gigolo on your list," he said, and before the words were in her ear, regretted his break.

Her face stiffened. "If there's any man in the world less a gigolo than Owen James, I haven't met him," she said deliberately.

(He thought: I wonder whether she'd defend me as hotly if I were attacked. Probably not. Why should she?)

"As we're on the subject," he said coldly, "let's talk business. I'd like to know where I stand."

"Aren't you satisfied with the business arrangement?" she asked, surprised.

"Oh, it's more than fair. It's generous. But how long does it last? That was left up in the air, wasn't it? When do you divorce me?"

"I hadn't given it much thought. Do you *want* a divorce?"

"No. But you do."

"Just where do you get that?"

He said impatiently, "You've made it plain enough that you've got no use for me as a husband. You're a woman, Carol; I suppose you're a normal one. You aren't going to live celibate all your life."

Her expression darkened. "But—divorce! It isn't so simple. If there were only two of us to be considered——"

"You mean your baby? He's adequately provided with a father and the name of Brade, isn't he?"

"Of course. It's Aunt Candace I'm thinking of. She's as stiff on the matter of divorce as any Roman Catholic."

"Let's be reasonable, Carol. Are her prejudices to control our lives?"

"No-o-o-o. Be honest with me, Spen; I've always been with you. Is there some reason why you want to be free? Is there someone else you want to marry? If that's it——"

"It isn't. There's absolutely no one."

"Then why bring up the question now?"

"As I told you, business. If, after your child is born, you plan to get from under and leave me on my own financially, that's perfectly all right. But I consider that I have a right to know where I stand."

Her face cleared. "Certainly you have. Name the time yourself. You're not straining my finances, you know, Spen. For our style of life I'm a rich woman."

"Just the same I'm going to pay back every damned cent," he said bleakly.

"That's as you see it." She had the instinctive wisdom not to argue the point. "From the practical standpoint you've been worth to me every cent you'll ever cost me if we continued the arrangement through our lives. But if it will make you more comfortable to strike a balance—isn't that what they call it?—it's quite all right with me."

"And meantime we go on with this anomalous marriage of ours indefinitely?"

"Not indefinitely. Long enough to fix up a plausible and decent divorce. I can get Aunt Candy used to the idea in time, I hope. But to rush into court or out to Reno as soon as Baby is born—don't you think that would be a little on the extreme side?"

He regarded her with reluctant admiration. "Sometimes,

Carol, I suspect you of having a lot of hard, cool common sense back of that innocent smile. I wish I could take the situation as calmly as you do."

"Think how much worse the situation was for me before you came into the picture."

"Naturally. I'd feel different, I suppose, if I were the baby's father."

With undisturbed composure she said, "It's a little late to consider that." Her eyes steadied in anxious inquiry upon him. "You're not going to hate the child, are you, Spen?"

"Do you want me to break down and say that I'm in love with you?" he demanded harshly. "That's the only possible reason why I should hate the baby you've conceived with another man."

"But——" she began helplessly, when he broke in again:

"Never mind. Love is outside the bargain. Business is safer as a topic. Let's get back to it. I've got news for you. Probably I'm going to be asked to join the Tyre Clinic."

"Spen! Already? They must think awfully well of you."

"They think awfully well of my connections." He smiled. "Meaning you."

"It can't be that alone."

"Oh, they know I'm competent. What do you think of it?"

"You won't be hampered too much by idealism there, at least."

"No; thank God!"

"Spen, what's the term for a double personality? The medical term?"

"You mean split personality? Schizophrenia."

"That's it. Did you ever diagnose yourself for that?"

He laughed. "Don't worry. I'm all of one pattern mentally. All of one purpose too. I'm going to be a damn good surgeon and I'm going to get damn well paid for it. Anything I do on the side, as for your friend James, perhaps, is a hobby, a luxury."

"Sure it isn't a salve?"

He spoke deliberately. "Carol, I think we'll do better if you leave my professional affairs strictly alone, as I shall henceforth leave our marital situation. Comprehended? as we say in French. It's time I got back to office hours. Just possibly there might be a patient there. Will you pardon me?"

"Certainly, Dr. Jekyll," said Carol. She smiled as she said it.

CHAPTER X

LIKE so many mill towns, Charlesville presents its contrast of luxury and misery in sharp juxtaposition. The gracious expanse of Grahame Lodge overlooks slums as grim, dreary, and unsanitary as the more sensational plague spots of Pittsburgh or Chicago. From the mansion's uppermost windows one might glimpse through the screen of treetops the fetid shacks of Hookworm Flats center of the worst slum district in the river bottoms Huddled hovels, stifling in summer, heatless in winter, and without normal decencies of sanitation at any time, pay a handsome return on ancient and respectable investment to some of the most Christian folk in the city.

Sometimes as he drove in at night Spencer Brade could catch the gleam of lights far below from a distant four-story frame edifice gaunt and shambling. which looked as if it might once have been turned to the uses of a cheap athletic-and-social club or perhaps of a dance hall with less respectable adjuncts on the upper floors This was now operating as a free or near-free hospital and clinic under the control of Dr. Owen James. Each time that Spen noticed that grotesquely peaked roof he reminded himself that he really ought to drop in and see James, if only on Carol's account. Then one evening Carol reminded him of it.

"Why haven't you been down to see Owen James?"

"Why. I hardly know. Too busy, I expect."

"Doing what?" She said with a smile.

"Practicing medicine. Making a living."

"There's plenty of medicine to be practiced down there."

"But not much of a living in it."

"I believe you're afraid," she taunted.

"Of what?"

"Owen. Afraid he'll catch you and corrupt your stern fiancial principles, as he's done with your friend, Dr. Bernitz, and a lot of the younger physicians."

"Wouldn't that be terrible!" Spen retorted lazily. They had finished dinner and were strolling through the garden.

"Come on. Take me down there now," teased Carol. "I dare you."

"What a slave driver I married!" mourned Spen. "Never a moment's rest. All right. I'll bring around the car."

They skirted the upper mill section to reach the winding road that followed the sluggish black surface of the creek. Black cypress knees projected from the water where the stream had overrun the swampland, covering it with a dark oily blanket. Long graybeards of Spanish moss hung from the trees and rustled faintly when a vagrant breeze stirred them a moment from their complacent slumber. The road crossed the bottom on a narrow iron bridge and wound back toward the huge glass-fronted buildings of another one of the textile mills.

Following his companion's guidance, Spen turned into a narrow, rutted driveway which dropped down to the steps of what struck him as a singularly unprepossessing entrance. A strong reek of antiseptics met them at the door. Inside new planks had patched the rotted floor; new stucco, not yet relieved with paint, gave a futuristic effect to the distempered walls. Several women were seated along the walls, on their faces the look of patient resignation that comes with poverty and with the dull knowledge that nothing better is in prospect.

At a battered desk an elderly nurse welcomed them. Her uniform was shabby and wrinkled, though spotlesss, and in her face past suffering and fortitude had etched lines of kindliness.

"It's Miss Gra—Mrs. Brade, isn't it?" she said, peering nearsightedly. "Dr. James will be so glad to see you. And your husband," she added as Carol presented Spen.

She dispatched an aged and decrepit orderly for James. He came back with Dr. Bernitz.

"I've heard Owen speak of you." Carol acknowledged Spen's introduction. "Where is he?"

"In the operating room. He's up against a tough case."

"What sort?" Spen asked interestedly.

"Stomach resection. He got Dr. Gamble in to do it. But Gamble's pretty old and slow. Owen's worried."

"Couldn't you help them out, Spen?" asked Carol quickly.

"You'd be lifting a load from Owen's mind," said the psychiatrist. "Old Gamble's, too, I think."

"Why, I might have a look," assented Spen cautiously.

"Take me along," said Carol. "Owen's been promising to let me see an operation."

"You wouldn't like this one," warned Bernitz. "It isn't going to be a bit pretty."

"I'm a hardy Norseman," said Carol. "Twenty dollars forfeit to the clinic if I go feminine on you and faint or anything."

"We could use that twenty," Bernitz replied. "Well, if it's all right with Spen——"

The husband nodded. All three went up to the operating room. It was small but well lighted. The chipped surface of the instrument cabinets and the sterilizers visible through the door of the smaller room beyond were scrupulously clean. Three people worked intently under the central light. Owen James, a frail elder, and a nurse.

"I brought Spen and Mrs. Brade," said Bernitz.

The clinic chief looked up. "Hello, Carol," he said. "Glad to see you, Brade. This is Dr. Gamble."

The old man on the right side of the table nodded.

"Go on with your work," said Spen. "We'll just watch."

The visiting pair climbed into the white-painted observation stand at the end of the room and seated themselves on the narrow bench. Spen studied the operating field with an appraising eye. It was a familiar scene to him, the white-covered table with its rectangle of sterile towels covering the edges of the incision, the orderly rows of instruments arranged on the nurse's table, the basin beside here in which sponges and packs were soaking in warm solution.

"We've found a sclerosing ulcer on the posterior wall of the duodenum," said Owen. "Dr. Gamble is hesitating whether to resect or do a short-circuiting operation."

"Is the ulcer active?"

Gamble answered. "Apparently so. He still has pain."

"Then you'll have to resect if you want to cure it," Spen said positively. That was elemenatry surgical knowledge; there was no need to quibble.

"Just what I was saying," said Owen.

Gamble did not speak. He lifted the stomach from its nest of warm gauze packs and felt once more the portion of the intestine where the ulceration lay. Even from where he sat Spen could see the induration, the area of hardness surrounding the lesion. He could see also that Gamble's movements were uncertain, not sure and easy as should be those of a surgeon tackling such a difficult operative procedure as a gastric resection. Every inept movement was like a red flag warning Spen's innate surgical sense that all was not as it should be.

Carol looked at him questioningly. Even her untrained eyes had seen the uncertainty in the operator's gestures. He shrugged his shoulders, but the concern in his eyes did not abate. Nothing is harder for a born surgeon than to stand by and see bungling work.

Gamble reached for a clamp and began to place it before clicking the ratcheted handle into place. His hand shook, and there were beads of sweat on his brow. Suddenly he looked up, eyes haggard.

"I can't do it," he burst out. His face was piteous. "I—I'm not up to it today." His hands fell to his side, and he stepped away from the table. "Isn't Dr. Brade a surgeon?" he appealed.

"A first-class one," said Bernitz.

Spen stared uncertainly at the shape on the table. How far would he be compromised if it became known that he had associated himself professionally with a man whom the very group he wanted to impress called a "medical Bolshevik?"

"Spen!" said Carol urgently. "The man's likely to die, isn't he?"

"He certainly is."

"Then——?" There was both challenge and appeal in the monosyllable.

"All right," he said. "Cover the field with a pack while I scrub."

Twelve minutes later, two to change clothes and ten to scrub his hands and arms, he thrust his gloved hands into the sleeves of a sterile gown and pushed the rubber fingers snugly on with a gauze sponge. It would be no easy job, he realized as soon as he examined the involved portion of duodenum with his trained fingers. The ulcer had apparently perforated backward toward the pancreas. There'd be plenty of inflammatory tissue back there, tissue that would be hard to dissect free. The easy way would be to do a gastroenterostomy, creating a new opening between the stomach and the small intestine, short-circuiting the food around the diseased area. But that was dodging the issue. That wouldn't cure the patient. And whatever else Spencer Brade might be, he was first of all a surgeon.

He reached for a clamp and began to free the lower border of the stomach, clamping off the blood vessels and securing them with strands of catgut tied tightly.

From her vantage point in the observation stand Carol felt a thrill at seeing the swift, sure movements of his hands. Gone now was the faint twinge of nausea that had assailed her as the first pungence of the antiseptic met her nose; the blood-stained draperies around the operative wound came within her vision. Here was a real drama, a skilled operator working his magic of curative surgery, removing the source of danger, bringing permanent healing to diseased tissue.

She lost all sense of time as she watched while step by step the operator freed the last six inches of the stomach and the first two of the small intestine. She flinched mentally when the heavy jaw clamp went across at each end of the area he was removing and the cautery bit its way across the stomach and intestine while the acrid pungence of the smoke penetrated even to where she was sitting. She marveled at the dexterity of fingers that could handle the slender curved needles so rapidly with either hand that each stitch was merely the gleam of light on the needle as it came through the stomach wall.

And finally when it was finished, when an opening had been made between the cut end of the stomach and the side of the small intestine, when the regular passage of the food had once more been insured and the disturbing influence of the ulcerated area removed, when the operative wound was safely closed with sutures tightly and securely tied by Brade's strong fingers, she felt as if she had been witnessing a miracle. The skill, the precision, the quiet assurance, gave her, for the first time, a sensation of pride in the man she had married. It was like watching a perfect machine, infused with humanity. Only—a new sensation stirring dimly within her was not such as one would feel for a machine.

Down in the office, after Dr. Gamble had left, mumbling thanks, Owen James said to his impromptu guest surgeon:

"That was a swell job, Brade. You got us out of a bad spot. Poor Gamble is too jittery for this work."

"Why do you have him, then?"

The other sighed. "We have to take what we can get when we pay nothing. Well, it's pleasant to see you here. I've been waiting for you to come around."

"Like a spider," said Carol, hooking her arm into his. "Own up, Spider. What are you after him for?"

"Not a thing in the world," protested the other. "She's always suspecting me of tricky intentions," he complained to Spen.

"She's got a mean nature," said Spen gravely. "I'm glad if I was able to help you, James."

"If I could find a man like you at call! I'm fishing for one. Lakeview man named Fleming. You must have known him."

"Flick Fleming?" cried Carol. "Why, he was best man at our wedding."

"Funny he didn't say anything about it in his letter."

"Oh, he never writes anything about anything," put in Spen. "He's the world's stingiest correspondent."

(Good old Flick! he thought privately. Afraid of giving the situation away. I hope he comes. . . . Or do I? Having Flick in a local medical organization which was manifestly headed for trouble might be awkward. Should he write a warning? No; no use. Flick ate trouble!)

"He hasn't reached any decision yet," said Owen.

"Could he afford to come here?" asked Spen, and something in his manner lowered the temperature of Carol's aroused admiration.

"Probably not," Owen admitted. "But he's interested in some of the things we're trying to do. So I'm hoping he'll come anyway."

"My bet is that he will," said Carol, adding, "if I'm any judge of people."

Was that a slant-angled shot at him? Spen wondered. He recalled, with no satisfaction whatever, Carol's original comparison of Flick with himself the day before the wedding, distinctly unflattering to her bridegroom's character.

"Now that I'm here," he said to Owen, "I'd like to see what you've got."

"Right. It's a far cry from Lakeview, though."

"You haven't got quite as much endowment, I expect," smiled Spen.

They rose to the top floor on a slow-moving freight elevator operated by a rheumy-eyed man of sixty.

"There's an interesting case," James said as they walked

down the well-scrubbed hall. "Amnesia. Turned up a few years ago, didn't know who he was or where he came from. Felix has studied him carefully but can't bring back his memory."

"Wouldn't an operation help?" Carol asked.

"Felix says not. He thinks it's a typical case of amnesia for an unpleasant situation. Probably the old man had to live with a daughter or somebody who didn't want him. One day he forgot who he was and turned up in another place. Over-wrought nature's convenient way of shelving responsibilities."

He pushed open the door of a small ward. Cheap hospital beds lined the walls, many of them bolstered with pieces of pipe wired to broken supports. Over one was a rough frame from which was suspended pulleys and weights supporting a bandage-covered leg. "Not quite a Balkan frame such as you would use, Brade," Owen said. "But almost as satisfactory."

"What happened to him?" Carol asked.

"Truck forced his car off the road and went on. They pried him out of the wreckage and brought him here."

"Why here?" Spen asked.

"He had a little accident insurance, enough to keep his family from starving while he's laid up, but not any more. City couldn't take him when he had any money coming in."

"But if he couldn't afford to pay for medical care," Carol said.

"Those are the rules. We try not to have many of them here. He isn't available for charity officially."

In a private room, an almost airless cell with one sagging window, a pale emaciated woman was propped up in bed.

She smiled timidly at them, but the look in her eyes was that of not quite comprehension, so often a characteristic of the mentally unfit.

"Just had her eighth child," said their cicerone as they left the room. "Three are half-wits. This one was born blind but fortunately died a few hours later."

"What's the trouble now?" Spen asked.

"Run down. She had a bad case of secondary anemia."

"But couldn't you teach her birth control?" Carol asked.

"We tried, but her mentality isn't great enough. She needs repair work and sterilization."

"That's no great job, is it?" asked Spen.

"Not if we had a specialist like you at call. We haven't. And Felix thinks we shouldn't tackle such an operation when there's so much objection to the clinic already."

(No, you don't! thought Spen. I'm not going to be caught a second time. You can give me the human-appeal eye all you like, my dear—this to Carol, mentally, who was facing him with faintly raised brows of inquiry—I've done enough for one day.)

As they went through the rest of the inspection, observing many ways in which Owen James was stretching the few loaves and fishes which had been given him to feed and care for the multitude who applied daily at the doors of the rickety building that housed the Owen James Clinic, Spen congratulated himself on not having volunteered to help out. Sterilization was a dangerous procedure, not for the patient, but for the surgeon. There had been many an unpleasant suit following an operation every bit as justified as the one needed by this poor breeder of the unfit. And medical reputations were peculiarly vulnerable to unscrupulous persons who sued or threatened to sue. Carol could keep her beseeching eyes to herself!

Back in the office once more, Spen said: "I suppose you get mostly the dregs here. Local conditions are pretty rotten, aren't they?"

"Not so bad since the new wage scale went into effect. Already there's less trouble from deficiency diseases. I'm looking for a big drop in pellagra. Hookworm is pretty well under control. The worst problems is the housing."

"Shortage of accommodations?"

His host nodded. "The logical result is that the owners can rent, no matter what condition the places are in. So they do nothing and take their profit."

"What you need is a rent strike," suggested Carol. "I'm surprised that you haven't worked one up already, Owen."

James made a wry face. "I'm in bad enough repute in this town right now. If I started advising people not to pay rent they'd brand me as a Red. Some of 'em have been doing that already, I understand."

"I'd say stick to your medicine," Spen advised shortly. "You'll find troubles enough there."

"He's looking for more," said Carol. "He wants to start an insurance scheme now."

"Hospital insurance?"

"It's more than that. It's really a cooperative medical project. All over the country people are joining together into cooperatives and are able to buy things that way that they wouldn't be able to afford otherwise. The average worker who makes just a few cents a week more than it takes for him to live on can't afford to be sick. I hope to fix things so he can afford it without tying up everything he makes for the next ten years."

"You'll have organized medicine on your neck," warned Spen.

"I'm not so sure. I've been working on this thing for months now and I believe I've got it figured where I can make it work without treading on anybody's toes but a few medical scavengers who ought to be thrown out anyway. Any sensible doctor would see what an advantage it would be to enable these people who are mostly a dead weight now to pay their own way." He rummaged in his drawer and took out a broad sheet of cardboard. "Here's the way I've got it organized. The whole thing will operate from one headquarters; that's this hospital. Some of the doctors will be on outside call to take care of patients in the homes. The business end will be handled by selling the idea to the textile unions. I've already done some groundwork on it, and most of the men seem in favor of it. We've got some funds available from the national union, if we get into trouble at the start. They're as anxious to see it work as I am."

"Yes; I can see where they'd be for it," said Spen.

"What I want to do," Owen went on, "is to make it possible for this poorest class to get decent medical treatment. Look at the present system. Could anything be worse? These people won't go to charity clinics at the City Hospital, a lot of them, because they don't like charity. If all of 'em that need it did go the clinics would be swamped. What they do do is call a doctor who tries to take care of them the best he can in the home. If a patient really is ill he can't be treated in the home as successfully as he can in a hospital. Drugs and incidentals eat up the money pretty fast, and before long they can't even afford to pay a doctor, even at the reduced rates that most of them charge the mill people. Then every now and then one of the medical sharks that we have in every city comes along and takes every dime they have, fooling around without really finding what the trouble is and eradicating it. The way it works out is that the poor devil loses everything he's saved and maybe goes in debt for the next five years before his child gets well of pneumonia."

"Those medical sharks will cut your throat," prophesied Spen.

Owen James shook his well-muscled shoulders impatiently. "They'd like to, all right. I'm not worried about them. With a little help we could build a setup to look after these needy cases. We've got the hospital, such as it is. Our clinic has already taken hold pretty well. I can get young men to work with me on low salaries for the experience and cut all the costs to the bone. We can offer people who can't afford doctor bills insurance against getting sick at rock-bottom prices. They'll be protected so that they'll be taken care of when they're sick with the best kind of medicine and surgery we have. At the same time they'll feel like they were paying their own way. As they will be."

The visitors rose to take their leave.

"It's been an experience for me," said Carol. "Not sweetness and light exactly, but I wouldn't have missed it. I have an idea that my husband is *good*, Owen."

"You don't know how good." To the grinning recipient of these bouquets he added, "Come in whenever you feel like it. We'll try not to put you to work next time."

"Why don't you ask him to your heavy-drinking parties, Owen?" suggested Carol.

"What is this? A plot to entrap the unwary?" asked Spen.

"No. All very innocent and social," said Owen. "At ten o'clock every night we blow ourselves recklessly to ale and cheese. Some of the younger fellows drop in occasionally. Terry Martin of the Tyre Clinic, Burling of the City Hospital, and others."

"It'll commit you to nothing, Spen," said his wife in a tone which he did not altogether like.

"I'll be very glad to come sometime, thank you," he said formally.

CHAPTER XI

FOR REASONS OF POLICY Spen became a regular attendant at Medical Academy meetings. So far as improving his technical knowledge was concerned, he might, he soon realized, as well go to the movies. Papers were conventional; discussions, perfunctory. Nevertheless, where opportunity presented he gravely took part in the general aftermath, being careful, before he resumed his seat, to compliment the essayist upon the unusual merit of his treatment. Logrolling, alias professional courtesy! The amiable chicanery served to open up new channels for patients to be referred to him. Why miss any possible tricks?

One hoped-for result was an early invitation to present a paper of his own. For his topic he chose the treatment of periodic disturbances in women by the injection of hormones. There was much to be said for hormones (and he planned to say it) especially in their financial aspect (and he planned to say nothing at all about this). The use of these extracts from the ubiquitous endocrine glands had not been exploited to anything like its full potentialities.

Costing perhaps twenty-five cents an ampoule, the preparation, when administered by a physician in a white coat, with a starched nurse impressively swabbing off the arm with alcohol, was good for a three-dollar office charge any day. Since a long series of injections made up the regulation treatment and a certain percentage of the patients got relief, possibly from the hormones themselves, though quite as probably through the natural course of events, the procedure was usually a success both commerically and from the standpoint of advertising for the practitioner, as proving his astuteness as a specialist.

If this sort of thing was not up to the best standards of

Lakeview, Spen could always argue that if he didn't give the shots someone else would. At least he used legitimate preparations which had the background of a certain amount of laboratory investigation, and he was careful always to sterilize his syringes and needles. Some of his colleagues, he suspected, substituted distilled water, thereby saving the quarter of a dollar. He only hoped they were conscientious about boiling their needles first.

Spen's Medical Academy presentation was an achievement in careful and impressive ambiguities. The subject of hormones was still new enough to be always changing. Anything he said might well be invalidated by new discoveries tomorrow. That made it a safe subject upon which to discourse at length. By reading a few books on disturbances of the endocrine glands, learning a few impressive terms, and presenting his discussion with the correct amount of scientific embellishment, he managed to produce the effect of a scholarly and polished paper about something so complicated that practically none of his listeners had any clear idea what he was talking about. Neither had he. His presentation was a resounding success. Blanton Tyre went out of his way to felicitate him upon it.

Several times he had dropped in on the Tyres for a late-afternoon drink, usually on their specific invitation. When a message was received, asking him to come up before office hours were over, he surmised that there was something special and hoped that he knew what it was.

Kenny Mangan, spruce, imperturbable, was at her desk when he entered. He had had no talk with her since the night she turned him down. Now there was a queer little smile on her pursed lips she bent over her work. Spen walked over and peered across her shoulder. On her pad she had penciled a legend which she was idly framing in diagonal strokes.

Repressing a desire to laugh, Spen said, "A message?"

"Take it or leave it," she murmured.

The outer door opened to admit an overdressed and withered crone. Kenny went to her.

"Which doctor did you wish to see, madame?"

The old lady funneled a hand at her ear. "Haw?" she chirped.

"Deaf as a post," the girl said, motioning the visitor to a seat.

"Then we can talk," Spen said. "Is this *der Tag?*"

"Take it easy." She motioned toward the inner office. He lowered his tone.

He motioned toward the drawing. "You're telling me to be tough?"

She nodded. "Or they'll pick you like a crow."

"You're a good kid. I wonder why you're doing this for me."

Now she looked up with a small, impish smile. "Because I hate your guts, of course. Watch out!"

Footsteps within explained the warning. Castleman Tyre opened the door.

"Why didn't you announce Dr. Brade?" he asked sharply of the secretary, looking from one to the other of them.

She was ready for that. "This other patient came in just as I was going to."

"Come in," said the young man to Spen. Inside the door he added, "There's a patient in my father's office you might be interested to see."

"Consultation?" asked Spen with rising exultation. It was dashed.

"Oh no! I thought you might like to watch the way we handle 'em."

Blanton Tyre, with a sympathetically grave face, was listening to the dolorous recital, punctuated with burpings, of a fat, sluggish, sallow woman whose oversupply of jewelry was sufficient indication of why her case deserved and received special consideration. With only half his mind occupied in what was going on, Spen amused himself by building up an imaginary and soul-satisfying dialogue between himself and the patient, had she applied to him and had been able to afford the luxury of frankness.

THE PATIENT (*at the conclusion of several chapters of self-revelation*)—And so, Doctor, I don't know *what* to do now.

DR. BRADE—Have you a lawn, madame?

THE PATIENT (*aghast*)—But, Doctor——

DR. B.—And a lawn mower?

THE PATIENT—Why—why—why—why, you—you—you—— I

DR. B.—Pick out the heaviest. Hitch yourself to it for an hour every day, rain or shine, and mow, mow, mow.

THE PATIENT (*aghast*)—But, Doctor——

DR. B.—That'll sweat the suet off your bones. That'll cure your bellyaches and your burps. Throw your pills and pellets to your Pomeranian. Follow that lawn mower, and you'll go to the can twice a day and have a breath like a clover-fed cow.

THE PATIENT—Why—why—why—why, you—you—you—— I I never heard such insulting talk in my life!

(Exit in rage, leaving a professional ruin behind her.)

Not a hope! If, he reflected, Mrs. Stannard Shreve, now the object of the Tyre's respectful attentions, were poor she'd have a far better chance of being speedily and effectually cured. But if she were poor she wouldn't have those overlays of fat. Nor would she be in the Tyre Clinic giving ear to the Tyre formula for such profitable cases.

Wrinkling the brow of intensive thought, Dr. Blanton Tyre now turned to the visitor.

"I think there is a condition there, Doctor. Yes; quite definitely we have a condition to deal with. Don't you agree?"

Spen caught his cue. "Unquestionably a condition," he assented.

Mrs. Stannard Shreve sighed importantly.

"Diet is indicated, clearly indicated," the clinic chief resumed. "And a regimen. Not too rigorous, of course." (The patient looked relieved.) "But I think we must go deeper than that." (A phrase which, in Spen's opinion, boded ill for the Shreve bank account.)

With lively interest he took in a low-voiced discussion between father and son—not pitched too low, however, for the subject's attentive ears—in the course of which "disturbance of the function of the gall bladder," "colonic maladjustment," "disregard of basic functional principles" (with an accusatory shake of the head toward the patient), "possible involvement of the pancreas," and other esoteric terms blossomed significantly. Further examination followed, after which the lady waddled forth, convinced of her acumen in having selected experts who

89

understood her complicated, obscure, and important ailments. Nothing was more certain than that she would waddle back and keep on waddling back.

Psychology, thought the admiring visitor. Not Felix Bernitz' brand—Bernie would have no patience with such methods—but a more practical kind. Spen knew something of that type of female. She did not really want to be cured. She wanted to be doctored, coddled, directed, sympathized with, tactfully admonished. It was an old medical axiom that there was nothing a woman liked better than to have her physician scold her kindly—that is, if his standing justified it. The fact that she would have to pay well for it was an added titillation. No one understood better than the Tyres and their ilk this basic law of feminine vanity—the stonger sex is not free from it, either—that the average woman loves to boast how much she paid for her new car, her "exclusive" clothes, her fur coat, her children's smart school, and above all else, her doctor bills.

While his father, having dismissed Mrs. Shreve, was occupied with the deaf ancient from the reception room, Castleman Tyre suggested a drink. Over it he remarked to Spen:

"Nice little setup, that office of yours."

"Not bad."

"Air conditioning was an idea! Patients like it, don't they?"

"They seem to."

"We're putting it in next season." Tyre took several deep inhalations from his cigarette. "We've been watching the way you're building up your practice."

(You would! thought Spen. You'd be more interested in that, than in my knowledge or qualifications.)

"It's slow business at the outset," he said.

"Yes. There are disadvantages in working alone." As Spen offered no comment, Tyre added, "And advantages in being associated with top-notch men."

"No man can cover his whole field," conceded the visitor.

"Our practice is growing so fast we can't keep up with it. In fact, we're considering taking in another man if we can find the right one."

"That shouldn't be so difficult."

"Not on the medical side. But there are other angles. Personality. Connections. Capacity for adjusting oneself to the—uh—social standards of a clinic like ours."

(Pompous ass! thought Spen, cautiously sipping his high-ball.)

The elder Tyre appeared and mixed himself an old fashioned.

"I've been telling Brade that we're thinking of expanding," his son informed him.

"Nothing definite; nothing definite," qualified the elder.

Spen set down his drink, less than half consumed, and put on his most ingenuous smile. "That is, you don't want to raise any false hopes," he suggested.

Father and son blinked at one another. Who was in charge of this conversation, anyway? It was the older man who replied:

"You will understand, Brade, that we have many applicants waiting for an opening here."

"Yes; I can understand that. And I hope you understand that I am not an applicant here or anywhere else."

Castleman Tyre said, "You mean that you would not consider——"

"Just a moment, Castleman," boomed the father, giving Spen his opportunity to say still smiling:

"How can anyone consider anything less than a definite offer?"

(Tough baby, indeed!)

Blanton Tyre's face assumed a formidable scowl. At least he meant it to be formidable.

"Are you trying to force our hand?" he demanded.

"Certainly not," Spen assured him. "I only wanted it clear that I don't consider myself on trial."

A buzzer sounded. Both men got to their feet with alacrity and vanished through the door. The visitor grinned. They would confer outside and probably come back with a definite proposition. His apparent indifference to an opportunity which, in reality, he was aching to seize had, he congratulated himself, taken the play away from them. How right that little Mangan girl was! With a longing look at his drink, he opened a door and poured it down the toilet.

The Tyres were gone eighteen minutes. (He timed them.) When they reappeared Blanton Tyre's large and expansive face had a smile on it that reminded Spen of an alligator he had once met in an abandoned rice field.

"It isn't my way to beat around the bush, Brade," he said. "Would you be interested in coming in with us?"

91

"Yes; I should," said Spen.

"Then that's all right. Shall we have another drink and talk terms?"

"No more drink for me, thank you. I'd be glad to talk terms."

"Quite right. I like your straightforward way, my boy. At first, as you will understand, the salary will not be large."

"Salary?" repeated the other with an inflection of surprise.

"Why, naturally." The other's smile contracted. "Surely you would not expect to come in as a partner. Not at first, though you might come later. On a monthly basis, what would be your idea?"

"I'm afraid I'm not interested," answered Spen gently.

"What did I tell you, Dad?" put in the son in accents of disgust.

Blanton Tyre motioned him to silence. With poisonous sweetness he addressed Spen.

"Doesn't it occur to you, Brade, that your marriage connections may have given you an exaggerated idea of your professional importance?"

(You old son of a bitch! thought Spen. That's going to cost you money before you're through with me.)

"Suppose you leave my family out of it and consider my hospital records," he suggested with undiminished equanimity.

"If you're clearing three hundred a month, net, you're doing better than I think you are at your office work," put in Castleman unpleasantly.

"Whatever I'm making is my own," returned Spen. "It isn't a hired man's wages. And what's more, it isn't hay."

"This isn't getting us anywhere," said the older man, genial again. "What did you have in mind, Brade?"

"Share and share alike," answered Spen coolly.

(Tough baby! Tough baby!)

"No, by God!" shouted Castleman.

"That's hardly reasonable," said his father.

Spen realized perfectly that it was not reasonable; that was why he sprang it on them.

"What is the present office arrangement?" he asked.

"That's our business," grunted the junior.

"Very well. But you sent for me," Spen pointed out. He rose.

"Sit down; sit down," said Blanton Tyre. "I don't know that the question is unreasonable. We split forty-five, thirty-five, and twenty. As the youngest member, Castleman, has the low percentage. I, of course, have the highest, and Carter Hewlett takes the thirty-five per cent."

While the others were out discussing him Spen had done some intensive figuring. He announced himself with an air of careless finality. "I'll accept fifteen per cent of gross for the first year, on a rising scale to be worked out afterward. But I must have a guarantee of four hundred dollars a month, rising to five hundred after six months. If either party isn't satisfied after six months I'm out."

The Tyres exchanged glances of discomfiture. Plainly they had not expected anything but grateful acquiescence. They very much wanted Spen, and they had counted on getting him on their own terms.

"We shall have to consult Dr. Hewlett," said Tyre, Sr. "He is out of town at present."

"No hurry as far as I'm concerned," said Spen jauntily. "Take your time."

"By the way, I hear you've been doing some work at the James Clinic."

"I helped out in an emergency."

"It'll do you no good, being mixed up with that lot," said Castleman.

"I don't see how it can do me any harm."

"James is hardly a desirable associate for a physician identified with the Tyre Clinic," said the head of that organization weightily. "I advise you to drop your activities there."

Spen repressed a surging temptation to tell them both that his outside relations, medical or personal, were exclusively his own business and that they could both go to hell. That could be made clear later. Better go easy now. Tough baby, but not too tough.

"It's a quite casual connection," he said, not committing himself either way. "What's so wrong with James?"

"He's a Red," growled Castleman.

"I've heard that before. But what's the basis for it?"

"Do you know what he's trying to do about housing in the mill section?"

"Clean up some of the worst holes, isn't he?"

"He's trying to destroy property rights," said young Tyre viciously. "That's what he's trying to do."

"You see, Brade," explained the other, "if the housing and health laws were so fanatically applied as to compel modernization of those properties they'd have to raise rentals to a point where the tenants couldn't afford them or else operate practically at a loss—one or two percent on the investment."

"How much do they make now?"

"As high as ten per cent, some of them," answered the younger so chirpily that Spen had a shrewd notion of the ownership of some of those profitable and noisome holdings.

"That's neither here nor there," interposed Blanton Tyre. "The point is that Owen James is alienating our best people by his radicalism, the very kind of people from whom he comes. He's a born troublemaker. Let me fill up your glass, Brade."

"Thank you, Dr. Tyre." Business being concluded, Spen saw no reason for further abstinence. As his elbow crooked he had a thought. "One of your associates is quite a friend of Owen James, isn't he?"

The Tyres looked at one another uncomfortably. "Terry Martin," began Castleman Tyre, when his father broke in:

"Dr. Martin is an employee, not an associate. His is a special case."

"Is he immune to the James contamination?" asked Spen innocently.

"Now, now!" cautioned the elder Tyre. "Contamination is a—a violent term. Quite unjustified. I am sure I have not used it in this connection. To be quite fair, Owen James has exerted a useful influence upon Dr. Martin, who has his—er—peculiarities."

"Drink." The son bluntly supplied the information. "A year ago Terry Martin was headed for the gutter."

"A first-rate pathologist would have been lost to us," added the other.

"Then you do allow some virtues to the man you call a Red," commented Spen with a smile.

"On the spiritual side only. I have nothing to say against James as a spiritual influence," said Blanton Tyre unctuously. "Nothing whatsoever. If he would stick to his religion nobody would wish to criticize him, I am sure. But his social and medical theories—subversive, positively subversive!"

Having finished the highball, Spen rose and shook hands. He felt no misgivings as to the outcome of the interview. The tough-baby formula had worked.

94

Outside Kenny Mangan looked up at him. "I heard them jawing about you. You're set. It's in the bag."

"Thanks to your advice."

"Do you owe me a drink! Or do you owe me two drinks?"

"Say when."

"I'll let you know."

"You seem a pretty wise child. If I come in here I'll need more advice. We might form an alliance."

"If that's what you call it." She laughed. She sketched another design on her pad, covering it with her hand as he craned his neck to see. "We might, at that," she said.

CHAPTER XII

BACK in his own quarters, Spen sat down to consider the developments. The outcome of his cogitations was that he had handled himself so skillfully as to deserve another drink. Not at home, though. Aunt Candace would be hovering with a face of pinched disapproval. He would stop in at the St. Charles bar.

There he was accosted by a slender man with dark hair, hazel eyes, and an angled satyrlike face.

"Better have one with me," said the stranger.

Spen was interested. "Any particular reason why?"

"Two."

"One would be enough."

"Dr. Bernitz is joining me when he gets back from the can. I thought you'd like to make a third."

"Right!"

"The other reason is that we're going to be colleagues, you and I. I'm Terry Martin."

"Of the Tyre Clinic?"

"The same."

"I've been wondering why we haven't met before," he said.

95

"They keep me under cover. I haven't the front-room manner. Here's Bernie. What'll you have?"

"Scotch, thank you," said Spen.

Bernitz shook hands and ordered a ginger ale with lemon and a dash of angostura. "Best hot-weather drink going," he said. "So you're joining the Medical Gold Diggers, Spen."

"Cut it, Bernie," Spen admonished with an uncomfortable look at Martin.

"Oh, Terry has no illusions," said Bernitz. "Have you, Terry?"

"They wither in our hothouse," answered the other. "Make mine a zombie," he directed the barkeeper. "Ever try one?" he asked Spen.

"No. What is it?"

"Three kinds of rum and fixin's, with no dilution but the ice. I can recommend it for what ails you."

"I'll take a chance," said Spen.

When the drink came he observed that it filled the tallest variety of highball glass. However, he was committed, and anyway he felt elated and a bit reckless. He tasted and was agreeably struck by its smoothness.

"You'll have to dope me up on ovarian tumors, Brade," said his new acquaintance. "They're my weak point. I heard your paper on hormones."

"Did you think it was a lot of oil?" Spen was surprised to hear himself say.

"Mostly."

"Still," put in Bernitz, "there's a definite value in the pituitary like hormones."

"And some of these new *corpus lutuem* substitutes seem to be fairly useful," added Martin.

"So's this zombie," said Spen with approval. "Let's have another."

"One's my limit," said Martin, adding, "since I've reformed."

"Sorry, gentlemen," said the barkeep. "Only one zombie to a customer. Rule of the house."

"It's a hell of a rule," said Terry Martin, "but you can beat it by going across the street."

"Me, I'd rather take dynamite," said Bernitz. "Spen, have you actually signed up?"

"No. But I'm going to. Provided the Tyres come across, I mean."

"You're going to be sorry. Isn't he, Terry?"

"A zombie a day keeps repentance away," observed the pathologist with apparent irrelevance.

"If you're not sorry your friends will be," insisted Bernitz.

"My friends aren't running my life," declared Spen. "From now on nobody's running my life but Spencer Brade, M.D. Not even my wi——Not anybody but me."

That was right too. He felt a fine upsurge of independence. Independence of everyone and everything but his own ability. If the Tyre scheme worked out he would be standing on his own feet financially and professionally. No more monthly pay checks for fathering another man's baby. He'd go home now—never mind the other zombie; better off without it—and have it out with his wife.

Driving his car with great care, he told himself that he was perfectly sober; sober and resolute. Carol called to him from the garden as he slowed down. That was well. No Aunt Candace to cramp a conversation which he intended to make definitive. He wasn't going on forever living the life of a eunuch. Not for any woman.

Carol was seated on one of the patterned ironwork garden benches. Her condition was now so apparent that she had stopped going out, except to small and intimate parties. But her face had lost nothing of its piquant beauty. Spen had a grotesque thought: How much simpler the problem would be were she plain and undesirable! He sat opposite her.

"Isn't it too hot out here for you, Carol?"

She smiled. "No. I like the air. And the smell of things growing after rain."

"I've got good news for you."

"Have you? What?"

"From now on I shan't be drawing on you any more."

"What's happened?"

"I'm going to join the Tyre Clinic."

"I'm not so sure that's good news, Spen."

"What have you got against the Tyres? Nobody stands higher professionally."

"Yes; I know. But that Dr. Hewlett of theirs tried to persuade Aunt Candy into a gall-bladder operation when there was nothing wrong with her but a bilious attack."

"Who said so?"

"Dr. Cannaday."

"He may have been mistaken."

"She was all right in three days."

He shrugged. "That's nothing to do with us, you and me. We're the subject of this conference." He tried for a light tone. "Aren't you glad to be rid of your pensioner?"

"I've never thought of you as a pensioner, Spen."

"That's what I've been, though. And I'm never going to be one again. It will take a little while to pay off what I owe you." She made a gesture of dismissal. "So, you see, the whole setup is altered."

"Need it be?"

"From the moment I'm independent I have some rights."

"Haven't you always had?" she murmured. "I've tried not to interfere."

"I think you're avoiding the question. You know what kind of rights I mean. The rights of a husband."

"Are you propositioning me, Spen?" she asked with a nervous little laugh.

There was no response of mirth in his face. "You aren't making it easy for me. To have to ask your own wife to sleep with you—it's awkward. It's humiliating."

She said swiftly, "I hate to have you feel that way. I never want to humiliate you."

"Can't you see that the whole situation does?"

"But—but, Spen, you can't expect anything of me *now*." The hands that fluttered about her swollen figure were eloquent of protest.

He reddened. "I'm not a brute. You're not always going to be that way."

"I hope not!"

"Well—afterwards?"

She looked away from him across the flowering sweetness of the beds.

"I wish you weren't going in with the Tyres, Spen. I'd so much rather it was the James Clinic."

"That wasn't the question before this meeting."

"Perhaps it is, in a way."

"If I go in with Owen James I keep on being dependent on you. Is that the kind of husband you want? Is that your idea?"

"I don't think you're being fair."

"Do you think *you* are?"

"I'm trying to be. Can't you forget the money part? You

made me feel so proud of you when you took over for poor old Dr. Gamble and fixed up that ulcer. How can I be proud of you if you go in with the Tyres? Owen says they're—"

"I don't care what Owen says. I get your point. Either be a goody-goody little Brother or the Helping Hand like James, or continue to sleep in the doghouse."

"If you really think that Owen's a goody-goody——"

"I don't," he interrupted. "I think he's a swell guy. But I never pretended to live on those lofty heights. If he and I changed places he wouldn't be sleeping in the doghouse, I'll bet."

"Are you jealous of Owen?" she said. "That's just silly."

"Leave him out of it. Let's get this straight. If I go in with the Tyres you're off me for life. If I go in with James, okay. That's your price, is it?"

Her eyes were steady upon his lowering face, level beneath down-drawn brows. "I haven't any price. I'm not for sale."

"Unlike your loving husband. Who was it said, 'When you buy a dog you like him. When you buy a man you despise him?' "

"Aren't the Tyres buying you?"

His smile was unpleasant. "You might say they're taking over your bad bargain. After I'm square with you on the money side of this question of you and me is coming up again. Don't think I'm dropping it."

"There'll be another question," she said. "We may as well face it now."

"Divorce? If you want to divorce me now I haven't a word to say. That's part of the deal."

"Not divorce, at present. You're asking me to live with you after this baby. In that case there might be others."

"Why not? Is that an objection?"

"I don't know. Spen, I'm going to ask you something. If it makes you angry I'm sorry. Have you always drunk as much as you've been drinking lately?"

"No. I haven't been too happy lately."

"Is there a tendency to drink in your family?"

"My grandfather, the old general, was a fine old sot, by all accounts. What of it? It isn't hereditary. Or is all this a subterfuge?"

"Don't speak to me that way, Spen," she said with a flash of spirit. "If it's a question of having more children I'd want to know more about their father than I knew about the father of this one."

"I'm not a drunkard," he said angrily. "And it isn't a question of a breeding pen." She winced. "It's a question of whether you're going to live with me when this is over. Yes or no?"

She reflected. "Will you do something for me, Spen? Will you go on the wagon for six months?"

"The hell I will!" The zombie was getting its second wind now, going strong. "Do you think I'm going to let myself be treated like a child? Bargaining again! Haven't we had enough of bargains?"

"I think perhaps we have. You've been drinking now, haven't you?"

"I have. And I'm going to have another right now."

"That's up to you," she said steadily.

"You're right, it's up to me. So is the Tyre hookup. And just to make everything clear, I'm signing on the dotted line tomorrow. Do you know why?"

"Because that's your natural choice, I suppose."

"Because every day that I stay in debt to you chokes me. The Tyre money is my ransom."

"Don't try to make me responsible for your actions," she retorted scornfully. "If there's nothing more, I'm going in."

"I think we're clear to date, all but the money," he said.

Thereafter for a time a new constraint was upon them at mealtimes. Did Aunt Candace notice it? To Spen she seemed more watchful, more suspicious of something not quite comprehended. What did it matter anyway? Why did anything in that alien household matter to him? He might as well accept it as a comfortable, even luxurious abode, a social and hence a professional foothold and nothing more.

Up to now Carol had kept pace with the normal and not too exacting gaieties of her crowd. Though still presentable, she began prudently to slow down. Sometimes she would go to her room shortly after dinner. Whether she felt uncomfortable (which she denied) or preferred solitude to the slightly strained family atmosphere, Spen made no effort to ascertain.

"Why don't you run down to see Owen?" she asked one evening shortly after their inconclusive—or was it all too conclusive?—conversation.

"Not a bad idea," said her husband.

At the clinic office he was introduced to two young local physicians, Brant Murphy and Travis Benton.

"Benton's a laboratory sharp and parasite snooper for the Board of Health," explained Owen James. "He's pretty well ruined the original reputation of Hookworm Flats. Murphy doesn't care anything about *his* reputation, so he takes a busman's holiday every now and again by helping us as a g.p."

Felix Bernitz, dark, lean, and tired, came in. Over the ale Spen asked:

"Have you found anyone to sterilize that half-witted breeder yet?"

"Mrs. Plotzov? No," answered Bernitz.

"Isn't there some legal method of compelling it?"

"Not in this state," said Owen. "Unless she's insane, which, technically, she isn't. But it's just as damaging to let the feeble-minded propagate as the insane."

"I'd like to do that operation for you," said Spen. "And I more than half believe I will, as there's no hurry, I suppose. You know, they're keeping watch on you, some of the crowd that don't like your experiments."

"If they'd watch the medical crooks it'd be more to the purpose," said Murphy. "And that goes for the higher-ups too."

"Brant was telling us about a case he was interested in when you came," Owen explained to Spen.

"It was a little cousin of mine," said the general practitioner.

"A good kid but a touch neurotic. She began to have excess bleeding, nothing bad, something a few shots of theelin would have taken care of any day. I was away at school—I wouldn't have known enough then to prevent it, anyway. Without letting me know, the family sent her down to one of our high-class private clinics——"

"No names," broke in Bernie Bernitz sharply.

The narrator looked up with a grin. "Afraid of being called as witness in a libel suit, Bernie?" He addressed himself to what remained in his stein and held it out for a refill. "Okay. The pious old bastard shall be nameless. What does he do with the kid? Advises a hysterectomy."

"No!" said Spen incredulously. "On a young girl? Unless, of course, he had diagnosed malignancy."

"He had diagnosed money in the family," was the grim response. "Well, he took out the uterus and snooped around to find something else. Because there was a little cyst on one of the

101

ovaries he takes that out too. Then on top of that he makes a slip and cuts the ureter and instead of trying to sew it back together again, as any good surgeon would do, he ties the damn thing off."

"But, good God!" said Spen. "What does he think is going to become of the natural secretions? Why, she'll lose her kidney."

"She has lost it. Damn near lost the other one, too, from infection. Surgical cripple for life."

"That butcher ought to be reported to the local society."

"Try and do it," retorted the g.p. "They'd run you out by the slack of your pants."

Travis Benton set down the cheese sandwich he was eating. "I once got all het up with reform and wrote a paper on 'Surgical Scapegoats.' It was a zizzeroo, if I do say it. I took it to the County Medical, and they politely told me what I could do with it, which was *not* what I had intended it for."

"You'd have been stepping on half the surgical toes of Charlesville," said Murphy.

"Don't I know it! You'd be surprised how many normal organs we get in the pathological lab for study."

"How do they have the brass to send them in?" asked Bernitz.

Benton snickered. "The damn fools don't know what's diseased and what isn't. If all the normal appendices that've been snatched in this town were laid end to end, you'd have all the fish bait you need for the next twenty years."

"Everybody picks on the surgeons. Don't they Brade?" said Owen James.

Something stuck like a burr in Spen's mind after he got home. That case of Brant Murphy's young cousin. Why had Bernie shut up the narrator so sharply? No names. What did that mean? Was it to save his, Spen's susceptibilities? If so, the blundering surgeon's identity was plain enough. Still it might not be. And Murphy's report was not conclusive. He had not been present at the operation on the girl. Besides, there might have been a carcinoma, making removal of the womb imperative. Probably was. Anyway, it wasn't his worry. Better forget it.

CHAPTER XIII

ON THE FIRST OF THE MONTH Spen transferred his equipment to the second floor above and settled into his new work. On one point he was resolved, he would give the best that was in him. There should be no letdown in his professional standards or in his efforts to keep himself abreast of progress in his specialty. He would prove to himself and to Carol that a physician could go out after money without detriment to his scientific virtue.

Also, he would economize. He felt an itching eagerness to be rid of the hair shirt of dependence. At an outside calculation he owed his wife four thousand dollars. There was still eight hundred dollars to pay on his new car, and he could count a couple of hundred in scattered debts. Say five thousand dollars in all. With no household expenses—he would adjust that later so as to pay his own way—he should be able to get along on one hundred and fifty dollars a month and set aside two hundred and fifty dollars for the liquidation of his indebtedness. At that rate he would be clear in less than two years. But before two years were were past he intended to make himself so indispensable to the clinic that he could pretty well dictate terms. If he wasn't worth twelve thousand dollars to fifteen thousand dollars a year to the Tyres he'd quit. And if he was worth it he'd damned well see that he got it!

Of his new associates, Terry Martin, the slender, sardonic director of the laboratory, interested him the most. Terry's relation to the clinic was peculiar. The reserve with which the Tyres treated him was requited by an ill-concealed contempt. Of the man's professional capacity there could be no doubt.

103

Spen had seen the laboratory reports on the charts that passed through the examining rooms every morning, as well as the pathological data on specimens removed from patients by operation. They had enhanced his respect for the clinic.

Martin's working quarters were situated off the main laboratory where the technicians worked. Wandering in there late one afternoon when nothing special demanded his attention, Spen saw that the equipment was modern to the last item. Everywhere was evidence of the presence of a trained laboratory scientist. If Martin was this competent why was he working in an environment comparatively obscure?

The pathologist was bending over a binocular microscope. He looked up and blinked to accustom himself to the light. "Hello, Brade," he said, pushing forward a stool with his foot. "Have a perch. Be with you in a minute." He studied the slide on the stage microscope for perhaps a minute and wrote a short note in a book which the caller could see contained many other entries in his fine script. He closed the book with a snap and tossed it into a cupboard. "I'm doing some work on a more convenient and less expensive test for pregnancy than the Friedman and Ascheim-Zondek tests. Have to grab a few minutes at it when I can."

"If you're busy I can come in later," Spen offered.

"No, no! That old poop Tyre is liable to butt in on us later. Settle down."

He smiled, and Spen appreciated what he had suspected at their first meeting, that this young man with the strange, beady eyes which gave the impression that he was laughing at one could be a specially likable person when he wished.

"I was just about to crack a bottle of beer. How about joining me?" He opened the door of a gleaming electric refrigerator. Spen saw that its shelves were piled high with small rubber-capped bottles; bottles, he knew, which usually contained valuable serums and vaccines.

"We've been doing a lot of vaccine work lately," Terry Martin explained as he reached into the vitals of the refrigerator and fished out two bottles. He snapped the tops off and handed Spen a clean beaker from a shelf by the sink. "It's all right," he explained. "I keep those beakers up there for beer. You can keep beakers when you couldn't keep glasses.

"How do you think you'll like working in the clinic?" he asked.

"Looks like it's going to be swell," Spen replied. "There's certainly enough business for everyone."

"Ever run up against an organization like this before?"

"What do you mean?"

The other man lifted his bottle and poured the remaining contents slowly into his beaker, watching the foam rise to the top. He looked at Spen with a distinctly mocking light in his eyes. "I mean did you ever see such a refined outfit of bloodsuckers as our illustrious associates?"

Spen laughed halfheartedly, as if he thought Martin were merely making a joke. "How long have you been here?" he asked to change the conversation into more pleasant channels.

"Four years. After I got through my research work at Yale."

"Like it?"

"Hell no." Terry Martin's tone was bitter. He was merely stating a fact. "I suppose you've noticed that I'm not exactly *persona grata* with the boys."

"Something of the sort."

"The truth of the matter is that the whole outfit hate my guts, but I deliver the goods, and they know they'd have a hell of a time finding anyone else who could turn out the work that I do. It's quite a job nowadays to find a man who can handle pathological diagnosis, do bacteriology, and prepare serums." He cocked his head to one side, like a perky little bantam. "Did they tell you with tears in their eyes that drink is my curse?"

Spen looked uncomfortable.

"I see they did. Let 'em think it. They were right, until Owen James dragged me out of a booze joint in his pet slum one night last winter and cussed me back to sobriety and sense."

"Cussed you back?" inquired Spen, amused.

"It amounted to that. Not by the letter, maybe, but in spirit. Owen says there are some folks you can pray over and others you have to cuss out. He did a job on me. Oh, I'm no damn teetotaler," he added, interpreting his guest's glance at the beer, "any more than he is. He convinced me that I was man enough to drink like a decent human being, and I guess I've proved he was right."

"That's all to the good," said Spen. "But why do you stick here in a job you don't like?"

"How do I know? Maybe it's because I'm lazy and don't want to get out and hustle for a practice."

"You could work in almost any hospital laboratory," Spen pointed out.

"At five hundred per and all the lab equipment I need?"

"Well, maybe not quite that."

"You're damn tootin'. Show me a hospital that's got a laboratory like this. Or again, maybe I love my dear associates too much to leave. Anyway, they give me a good layout where I have time to work on some things I'm interested in, like this pregnancy test, for instance. Nothing may come of it—I haven't got far enough to tell yet—but if it does it will be worth while."

"I didn't know there was that much value in pregnancy tests," Spen said. "Not that I want to discourage you," he hastened to add.

"At the present stage of development there isn't," Martin admitted. "They don't become positive early enough. The test I'm working on, if it pans out, will be definite within two weeks. And it will be simple. Just a sample of blood, separate the serum and add a reagent or two and compare with a color standard. The whole thing can be done in any doctor's laboratory in fifteen minutes. Think what it will mean to doctors. Every little gal that's been running around and is a few days late will be coming to the doctor for a test. At five or ten dollars a shot the doctors can clean up."

"You'll probably go down in history as one of the great men of the century," Spen told him with a smile.

Heavy footsteps gave signal of Blanton Tyre's expected arrival. He seemed surprised to find Spen there. For a moment his eyes narrowed with what might have been suspicion or displeasure. Then he smiled and set his hand on the younger man's shoulder with a fatherly gesture. "Swapping experiences, eh?" he said genially. "Many a bull session I've sat in on when I was young." He turned to the pathologist. "About the uterus I took out of the Masterson woman yesterday, Terry," he said. "Did they send it over?"

"It's in there." Martin pointed to a jar on the shelf.

"I think you'll find considerable fibroid change there, considerable deviation from the normal. Let me have your report as soon as you read the slides." He lingered a moment, remarking on the state of the market. Spen, wondering if he were waiting for him to go out, nevertheless kept his seat, and Tyre went back through the door alone.

Terry ground his cigarette out in the sink. "Fibroid change! He knows damn well that uterus was normal. That was my cue to give a report of fibroids. And damn my soul for a hypocrite, I'll probably write it up just the way he wants it because I shirk the trouble of fighting the old louse."

Spen's impression that Blanton Tyre was not wholly pleased at finding him with Terry received quick confirmation. The clinic head was waiting in Spen's office for his return.

"How are you and Martin hitting it off?" Tyre asked.

"Fine."

"Brilliant fellow, Terry. Pity he's so erratic. Don't know anyone here who's a better bacteriologist and pathologist, but he's never been stable. Had a good position in a research laboratory in the North. Lost it. Wild as a hawk. We took him in because he's a relative of my wife, a cousin. It's the first job he's ever been able to hold."

"He certainly has plenty of ability," said Spen.

"Ability, yes, but not dependability. You can't believe a thing he says. Why, sometimes he writes pathological reports that I have to destroy. Obviously not accurate at all. I don't know what to do with him. Maybe you could drop him a hint."

"I doubt if Dr. Martin would take kindly to anyone butting in on his clinic relations," said Spen.

"Probably not. He's stubborn. Don't pay too much attention to what he says. He'll tell you some of the wildest tales. And for some reason"—he lowered his voice to a confidential tone although there was no one else there—"for some reason he dislikes me. Oh well"—he laughed—"that's usually the thanks you get when you start doing things for relatives. Can I give you a lift?"

"No, thanks," Spen told him. "My car is in the parking lot."

"By the way," said Tyre, "I have a woman coming in next week whose family doctor thinks she may have a cancer of the uterus. She'll probably have to have a total hysterectomy, and I'm going to try to arrange for you to take the case. He says there may be some difficulties, but I feel certain that you can handle it. These long operations are pretty wearing on me. Getting old, my boy, getting old." He laughed tolerantly at himself, to show that he didn't really mean it.

"I'll do the best I can," Spen assured him.

Nevertheless, he was not altogether comfortable about it. Something a little too hearty, a little overgenial, in the manner of the offer struck him unfavorably. The suspicion shot into his mind that this was a desperate case with an almost surely fatal outcome; that Blanton Tyre chose to keep his own loss percentage low by the clever device of turning over to others operations in which the prognosis was unfavorable. Was he to be the clinic goat? The prospect did not please him.

Remembering some leftover work, Spen set himself to do it. Furious wind and rain were breaking upon his windows when he rose. Going to the anteroom for his coat and umbrella, he found Kenny Mangan still at her desk.

"What a worker!" he jeered. "What keeps you this late?"

"You'd be surprised," she returned, poising her pencil above the pad.

"Go ahead. Surprise me."

"I'm trying to write a poem."

"You? A poem? What for?"

"Money. Same thing you work for here," she replied pertly.

"Do they pay money for amateur poems?"

"Amateur, yourself. Bill Stenson pays me a dollar for every one I land in his Sunday column. And I made the *New Yorker* once."

"Brains!" said Spen admiringly. "What's this one about?"

"It's about a Russian Pink from Minsk who shot a mink from Pinsk."

"People don't shoot minks. They trap 'em."

"How do you know what they do in Russia? Well, I could make it 'trapped' or even 'tamed.' The trouble is with the rhyme. Got a rhyme for Minsk in your date book?"

"Kitchen sinsk," he suggested.

"You're a great help," she said disdainfully. "Do you think this rain is ever going to let up?"

"I'll drive you home, Kenny."

"It seems to take an upheaval of the elements to bring us together, doesn't it?" she reflected.

"Whose fault is that?"

"I've told you how I feel about mixing up office relationships and—and anything else."

"I'll pay for your taxi, if those are your inflexible principles."

"Not so inflexible. I'd rather go with you," she confessed.

"You look like a kid tonight," Spen said as he held the door open for her.

108

"I'll never see twenty-five again. You can learn quite a lot in a quarter of a century."

In the car he asked, "Want to stop on the way for that drink I still owe you?"

"Yes."

"Where shall we go? The St. Charles?"

"Hardly. Your family might be there."

"She won't. And if she were," he added bitterly, "it wouldn't matter to her."

"Yes; I've heard something to that effect," the girl said, "or I wouldn't be here. I'm no husband snatcher."

"What have you heard?" he demanded.

"Common gossip. Are you taking me out to talk about your wife? Let's go to some quiet place."

Kenny asked for sherry and bitters. "Cautious?" he queried teasingly.

"No. I just don't like liquor. It deadens everything inside me."

"Then for heaven's sake, don't take any!" he cried in mock anxiety.

She made a face at him. "Spen, are you blind in one eye?"

"No. Why should I be?"

"You might be better off that way."

"As to what?"

"Certain matters in the office."

"For example?"

"Little irregularities. Lady patients."

"I don't get you," he said uneasily. Was the girl trying to tell him that the Tyres used the office for clandestine affairs?

"You don't look that dumb," said Kenny. "Haven't you ever read the ads in the cheap magazines?"

"Hooey!" he said. "The Tyres don't advertise."

"Heaven give me patience!" prayed the girl. "Advertise? Of course they don't advertise. That sort of thing advertises itself. Quietly. I'm talking of our little private line. Tyre repairing, I call it. We fix flats. For ladies. Only we do it in reverse. We fix 'em so they'll be flat again."

Now he began to get it. "Are you trying to tell me," he said angrily, "that physicians of the standing of the Tyres——"

"Relax," she cut in. "I'm not saying that we're Old Lady-Relief & Co., the Don't-Worry Specialists. Nothing rough and dangerous like that. We don't take all comers, I can tell you!

It's a side issue with us. Emergency stuff, you might say. Only very special personal instances, where it's—er—hem!—medically indicated. If the patient happens to be an unmarried girl, why, that's mere coincidence. I'm only trying to tell you so you won't get a shock later."

"I don't believe it," he said.

Her manner changed instantly. "That's right," she purred. "Save a lot of trouble that way. Don't believe a word of it. I'm only talking through my twelve eighty-seven hat. We didn't come here to talk shop, anyway, did we?"

When they were back in the car she moved close to him. He was conscious of the sweet warmth of the shoulder pressed to his. He slipped his arm around her.

"Better tend to your driving," she said with a little laugh.

"I expect you're right. We don't want any police in this party."

"No. It's a nice party as is. I like it." She drew a little closer.

At the curb before her apartment house he said, "Kenny?"

She lifted her face to him like a child. But it was no child's kiss that thrilled and burned along the current of his blood. She shivered and drew away.

"Someone coming," she murmured.

The front door of the building was opening, giving passage to a woman's figure, shrouded against the weather.

"Kenny?" said a voice. "That you?"

"Yes. Going out, Bertha? It's my roommate," Kenny whispered in Spen's ear.

"I'm on all-night duty," said the figure. "See you in the morning."

"Okay. Good night."

The girl came into Spen's arms again. "Want to come up for a drink?" she asked when that long embrace was over.

"You'll be making me late for dinner," he said unsteadily.

"*No!*" she said in pretended shock. "Wouldn't that be just too terrible!" In the dim light her face was gnomish with mischief and challenge. "I might even make you late to breakfast sometime."

"For instance?" he said. "Tomorrow's breakfast?"

"Why not?" said Kenny.

No explanation was required when he got home early the next morning. He had simply been out on an emergency case.

Toward Carol he felt no special responsibility. He owed her no physical allegiance. If she had been willing to give him a break there never would have been any Kenny Mangan. Hadn't Carol indicated that she would not expect faithfulness from him? How about the reverse angle, though? With his scientific tendency to examine a problem from all sides, Spen asked himself how he would feel if Carol stepped out. Not at all liking that aspect of it, he tried to turn his mind away from it. Anyway, she was the last girl in the world likely to go in for casual amours. Essentially and vigorously feminine though she was, she would always observe the decencies—well, how decent was it in him to be sleeping with Kenny Mangan while living under his wife's roof? Oh, to hell with that! She was a wise little bird.

He was now all the more eager to be rid of the debt to Carol. It was a corrosive in his thoughts.

CHAPTER XIV

THE NEW MEMBER of the Tyre Clinic found the tempo geared much higher than the leisurely pace he had been observing in his own office. This was a medical machine, a sort of slot device that paid off only when coin was inserted, and sometimes a lot of coin had to be inserted before one got much of a return. It almost took his breath away to hear Blanton Tyre speak casually of fees of a thousand dollars for operations he had been doing for a hundred. Yet strangely enough he rarely heard a patient object. They came there knowing the reputation of the clinic for charging high fees, and they paid without murmur. Many of them, in fact, seemed pleased with the privilege.

The setup was simple and remarkably effective. Patients, usually sent in by other patients or by doctors on the outside who patronized the clinic, passed first by Kenny Mangan, who held in the storage of her mind the Dun and Bradstreet rating of everyone worth mentioning for fifty miles around. Without seeming actually to ask, she could learn more in five minutes about a patient's personal and financial history than a corps of census takers could in a day.

It was a lesson in thoroughness to see just how Miss Mangan was able to grade each patient according to monetary and social importance and impart that grade to the record in such a way that he or she would carry the label through all dealings with the clinic. Many things depended on that rating. The time a patient spent with the Tyres, or with Hewlett and, to a less extent, with Spen, who had not yet absorbed the smoothness of the technic of separating people from their money and making them love it, the extensiveness of the diagnostic study that would be made, and the question of whether or not an operation would be "indicated." If one fell in the lower classes his time in the clinic would be short. Barely enough for a rapid history and examination, a minimum of laboratory work, and whatever operation was necessary without any frills. But if one rated A1 under Miss Mangan's softly observant eye there would be a special sign on the chart, a sign that led to pleasant smiles from the clinic nurses and the laboratory technicians, at least an hour with the doctor selected, and, if a man, a cigar and perhaps a drink unless the sufferer were seeking relief from kidney trouble or some other condition that contraindicated alcohol. If a woman, everything bowed before her; the entire personnel of the clinic was at her service, and if the examinations were too long there would be a cup of tea and a wafer appearing like magic in the dressing room when she had finished being overhauled by gentle hands and was permitted to resume her normal raiment. And her operation—there always had to be an operation for the female patients: they came there expecting it and seldom went away disappointed—the operation would be a marvel. The clinic did not have its own hospital, but most of its work went to the Markland Hospital, a privately operated institution that subsisted largely on the Tyre patronage. Spen had heard whispers about the hospital. In many ways it was like a nursing home; in few ways was it like an ordinary hospital. The furniture was more elaborate, the beds softer; the drawsheets of which patients usually complained so much were softest oiled silk instead of rubber. Many of the rooms had private baths, for not all of the Tyre patients by any means had to stay in bed.

Many were there for a study, often merely a way of finding out what the first doctor who had seen them saw at once, that they ate too much for their own good and had too little to do. The first doctor may have made the tactless mistake of telling them that, but the Tyre Clinic never did. There were better ways of handling situations like that, ways that pleased both the patient and the bookeeper of the clinic: days of diagnostic study, reams of X rays, then special diets, special exercises, not too strenuous, starting with single muscles, first contracting, then relaxing. The fat wife of the banker basked in such attention. She hadn't been able to get it for a long time. Her husband was too busy making money and she herself had become such an unromantic object that she could have aroused passion only in the breast of a Turk. She reveled in the contractions of this set of muscles, the caloric content of a piece of whole-wheat toast. She would have been insulted if anyone had told her she could have got as much benefit from scrubbing the kitchen floor and eating off the drainboard of the sink. No one in the Tyre Clinic ever dreamed of telling a patient that, assuming that she could afford to be treated. If she couldn't—well, she got a cheap prescription for her nerves, and that was all.

By no means was all the work done in the clinic needless, Spen saw, for rich as well as poor did fall sick, and the clinic possessed the man power and the equipment to hunt down and treat real illness. Those patients got better treatment on the average then they would have in many places with which he was familiar. They paid a little more for it, perhaps, but they had the certainty of a return for their money. The rich wanted attention, wanted to feel that they were for a time at least the center of their doctor's interest. And the more solicitude was shown, the better they liked it. It wasn't wrong, Spen told his conscience, to pamper these people. They fairly yearned to be pampered; it was only right to give them what they wanted. They expected to pay well for the attentions they received. The more you charged them, the more they appreciated it.

True, there could be little inspiration for a man of Spencer Brade's scientific training in such an environment. Very well; he was not there for inspiration but for hard cash. He could look for his technical satisfactions in his hospital duties and an occasional volunteer job for Owen James. He was keeping up his connection with the City Hospital as a matter of course. All the staff members of the clinic were active on the staff there. It made a good talking point to speak of working in the charity clinics. People were impressed with the magnanimity of these prosperous and busy doctors who were willing to give their own time, time which meant money, so that the poor would receive attention they might not otherwise get. But Spen soon realized that no burning desire to help suffering humanity actuated the Tyres in their charity work. It was merely a bid for reputation and the advantages of piling up long series of case records of this or that unusual condition which they could read before medical societies in the hinterlands, thereby impressing fellow physicians less favored with clinical opportunities. In short, Spen was learning that his hard-boiled commercial attitude was innocence itself, compared with the Tyre brand of "ethical" racketism.

Checking off his observations against what shrewd little Kenny had told him, he summed up to this conclusion: the Tyre outfit, beneath their gloss of high-class practice, were, in essence, arrant quacks. Blanton Tyre was a pompous and dangerous bungler. His son was a self-important ignoramus who had barely scraped through a class-B medical college. Carter Hewlett knew more than both of them put together, but he was unprincipled, a hit-or-miss diagnostician, and given to accepting with indiscriminate enthusiasm any new medical fad emanating from a supposedly reputable source. All three were adroit politicians, and the clinic pretty well controlled the local Academy, as well as wielding influence in the state organization. Of the staff, Terry Martin was first-class, and Palfrey, the roentgenologist, was competent, but they were only salaried employees.

Another phase of office practice which worried him still more than the polite rapacity of the Tyres was the "special" line against which Kenny had warned him the evening when their liaison started. Although he had shut her up, he knew in his heart that she was speaking the truth. Now, testimony was presented to him in such a way that he could not ignore it.

He had dropped in, as had become his habit, at Terry Martin's laboratory.

"Want to see an interesting scientific exhibit?" inquired the pathologist with a significant rasp in his voice.

"Yes," answered Spen, wondering what the eccentric was up to now, and already suspecting that it might have been wiser to say "No."

Terry held up a stained slide containing a section of pathological specimen. There was no name on the slide. He shoved it under the microscope, bent over, and twirled the knobs for a moment. Then he straightened up and motioned Spen to the stool before the instrument. "Tell me what you think of it."

Before applying his eye to the barrel Spen asked, "Who's the patient?"

"*Miss* Maud Heppleton." There was a slight unmistakable emphasis on the title. "Know her?"

"Yes." Spen called to mind the brilliant blonde, a little too soft of voice, a little too hard of surface, a little too obvious of movement and pressure beneath a dinner or a bridge table, whom he had danced with once or twice at the club. Heppleton was an important name in Charlesville.

"Not your diagnosis, was it?"

"No. She was Blanton Tyre's personal patient. I recall seeing the name posted on the bulletin board. Endometrial hypertrophy."

"Endometrial hypertrophy," repeated Terry, embellishing the "per" syllable with a Bronx cheer.

Spen said thoughtfully, "It struck me at the time that she was pretty young to have that develop. Tyre operated, himself."

This was a very common condition, benign, though likely to cause troublesome hemorrhages. It usually responded to simple curettement and could sometimes be successfully treated by the injection of ovarian hormones. Blanton Tyre had naturally chosen the surgical treatment.

"Typical Tyre diagnosis," observed the pathologist. "Now take another look."

Spen did so. He lifted his head after a careful inspection. "Looks to me like syncytial tissue," he said. "Very like."

"No! Does it really?" said the other in exaggerated astonishment. "So what?"

"If that isn't placenta from pregnancy, I'm Elizabeth, the Virgin Queen."

"Why—why!" Terry chided in outrageous parody of the bland Tyre mannerism. "My boy, my *boy!* Look again. How, I ask you, *could* it be that? Perish the unworthy thought! Endometrial——"

"Endo my sphincter!" interpolated Spen. "Plain abortion."

"Tyre abortions I never claim," his colleague rebuked him.

115

"They're very fancy, with all the trimmings. And very, *very* special. None but old and trusted patients of the very highest standing need apply. Then everything moves like oiled machinery. Secluded operating room, discreet anesthetist, reliable nurse. The specimen is whisked to the Tyre Clinic Laboratories where a hand-picked pathologist—me—makes a hand-picked diagnosis—endometrial hypertrophy. The specimen is destroyed. The slide disappears. Nobody could prove anything even if they wanted to."

"What do you really think about it, Terry?" asked the visitor.

Terry shrugged. "It's no skin off my *derrière*. Somebody's got to look after America's pure young womanhood in distress. What's the difference if our dear, good Dr. Tyre does help a society gal out of a scrape once in a blue moon? If he doesn't what happens? The girl goes to a professional abortionist, a quack who won't maybe take the trouble to boil his instruments or do the operation with anything resembling sterile care. She's a damn sight better off having her operation done by someone who knows what he's doing. Our Blanton isn't the only one in good and regular standing. The abortion business needs changing, anyway. It would probably be better to have legal abortions, like they have in Russia. It might increase the number of pelvic infections, though I doubt it. If it did it would merely mean more work for the gynecologists, so where would we have any kick coming?"

"Just the same," said Spen shortly, "they can keep that line of trade in the family. I don't want any part of it."

"Then what are you doing here?" Terry shot back at him. "No; don't answer that. I'll tell you the answer myself one of these days."

On his way out Spen contrived to get a private word with Kenny Mangan. "You were right about the Tyre repairing," he admitted.

"Of course I was. Kenny knows."

"Is Bertha going to be in tonight?"

"Yes; I'm afraid she is."

"Well, we might have dinner together. Haven't we some things to talk over?" he asked smiling.

She smiled back, easy and composed. He had known the other night of course, that she was not a virgin. Now her coolness suggested that she had had a good measure of experience. Yet he knew inwardly that she was no tramp, no

116

pushover. There was too much independence, too much self-respect in her bearing to permit of that easy deduction.

"They'll keep," she said.

"How long?"

The provocative face became serious.

"This is a hot town for gossip. The old hens live on it. That's why we have to be good and careful. I don't mean necessarily that we have to be good." She smiled her impish smile. "Or we shouldn't have to be careful. But it means my job and it might mean yours. At that, it might be the best thing that could happen to you," she added meditatively. "But you don't want any mix-up with the Tyres. They'd naturally raise hell if they knew."

"What right would they have? Didn't you tell me that Castleman Tyre made a pass at you?"

"Several passes," she said cheerfully. "The old man, too, once. It didn't get them anywhere. But how sore they'd be if they knew I'd fallen for you. I did, you know, Spen; the first time I saw you. Yet you're nothing so wonderful to look at. I reckon it must have been your voice and your nice manners. I don't like 'em fresh. As most of the young docs are."

"How about the week end?" he asked hopefully. "Could you get away?"

She nodded. "Why not? Saturday to Monday I'm my own boss. Dr. Martin sent that slide out, I think, Dr. Brade," she added in the briskly neutral tones which she kept for office business, as Blanton Tyre's glossily arrayed form loomed in the entrance.

An emergency, too professionally demanding to be avoided, intervened to spoil the week-end plan.

117

HANDS on his shoulders, shaking him, worrying him out of sleep, woke Spen at dead of night. Carol's face was dim above him. He sat up.

"What's the matter?" he asked dully.

Back of her head the window framed a murky glare.

"Fire in the mill district," she panted. "I'm afraid it's Owen's clinic. Hurry and get dressed."

Quick as he was, she was ready before him. He frowned.

"You ought not to go."

"Please don't try to stop me. Get the car."

On the hill beyond the gates they passed a carriage drawn by a pair of lumbering bays, while a black-clad figure behind the coachman fairly jumped up and down, urging them on.

"Cousin Carrie Carskaddan," said Carol. "She'll break her dear old neck one of these days."

Spreading with savage swiftness through the flimsy shacks of Hookworm Flats, the flames had attacked the James Clinic on the northwest where it was least substantial. Police and firemen made a place for the car with the medical insigne; doctors are welcome and privileged at any catastrophe. Spen looked up a deputy chief.

"Everybody accounted for?"

"We think so. Dr. James is inside with some of our men, checking up."

"Any chance of saving the building?"

"Not a hope."

"I'll get my medical bag," began Spen, when a sizzling oath from the official checked him.

Against a top-floor window, which he was struggling to raise, a man appeared outlined against the glow. Spen recognized him as the nameless victim of amnesia, know as Old Bob. The window flew open, and the man began a metallic, mechanical piping:

"Help, help, help! Help, help, help!"

"Life net here!" bellowed the deputy. As a squad of men rigged it he reached for his trumpet and shouted to the appealing figure:

"Ready to jump! They'll catch you. All set, there?" to his men.

"All set."

"Jump!"

The poor old fellow never paused in his melancholy iteration, now fainter as smoke swirled about him.

"No use!" said the deputy in resigned despair. "I've seen 'em like that before. He'll stick till the fire gets him, unless one of our fellows gets there first. Crazy with fear."

Another figure appeared. It was Owen James. He tried to drag Old Bob away, but the terror-stricken man clung frantically to the sill. The deputy chief trumpeted:

"Don't try to take him back. Throw him out. The net's ready. Throw him!"

"Right!"

Exerting his great strength, Owen broke the insane grip and heaved the struggling body clear. There was a yelp of sheer animal terror. The net surged and strained as the firemen plucked the man out safe.

"Your turn, Doctor. Come on!"

But the clinic head, shouted back something indistinguishable, turned and disappeared.

"The damn fool!" vociferated the official. "Get up there after him, some of you fellows."

Guessing that Owen had gone to the far end to make sure that no patient in that remote ward had been forgotten, Spen remembered seeing a disused staircase at the rear, when Owen had shown him through the plant, which he had assumed to be a makeshift fire escape in the days when the upper floor had been used for meetings. Hurrying around there, he picked up a fireman on the way, and together they made the ascent. Halfway up the third stairway they came upon a crawling object, from which issued a smoke-strangled voice.

119

"Lost my way," it said. "Leg's hurt."

They hustled him to the open where the crowd raised a wild cheer on recognizing their idolized "Doc," smoke-blackened, slightly scorched, but very much allive. Spen examined the injured leg. It was nothing worse than a severely sprained ankle. As the patient absolutely refused to be taken away in one of the ambulances which were transferring the evicted clinic patients to the City Hospital, the surgeon hastily bandaged him and put him in a safe spot.

There the reporters found him, and to them he gave, in his gratitude and nervous exultation, a picturesquely exaggerated account of what was to appear next day as the heroic rescue effected by Dr. Spencer Brade at the imminent risk of his life. The assistant fireman was practically ignored.

As he turned away from his job on Owen, Spen was summoned by a strident call:

"Doc! Hey, Doc! Here's a guy bleedin' to death."

He pushed through the crowd, following the guide. The injured man was thrashing in mingled alcoholic delirium and fear. Blood splurted from his wrist in a regularly recurring fountain. A hastily improvised tourniquet was doing but little to stem the flow of that red, spouting stream. Opening his bag, Spen removed a section of bandage and wound it loosely about the man's arm just above the elbow. Then inserting a wooden tongue depressor into the loop, he began to twist, tightening the loop around the arm until the flow of blood from the severed artery stopped.

"Where's an ambulance?" he asked, looking around him.

All were away, making the transfers.

Afraid to entrust the care of the tourniquet to anyone but him, Spen determined to clamp and tie the artery on the spot.

"Somebody hold this flashlight," he ordered, taking one from his bag.

Rummaging for the artery forceps he always carried, and with the light wavering in the nervous hands of his impromptu assistant, Spen searched for the severed end of the artery. It was not easy to find, for the light was bad, and the vessel had retracted back beneath the cut surface of the skin.

While he was bending every effort to his critical task an urgent voice above him said:

"Spen! Spen!"

He did not even look up. "Not now. I'm busy."

"Spen! It's Carol. You've got to come with me."

"Let me alone. I'll be through presently."

"Presently!" There was an angry sob in her echo. "It's Cousin Carrie. She's terribly hurt."

"All right, all right," he muttered absently, probing among the cut tissues. "Got it," he announced with satisfaction, and clicked the hemostat into place." Be with you in a minute now."

He whipped a tube of catgut from his bag and bound the artery firmly behind the clamp. Looking up and about, he caught sight of a clinic nurse.

"Here! Miss Humphrey! Keep pressure on the wound until the ambulance gets here, will you? He'll be all right." To the fuming Carol he said, "Now, what was that about your Cousin Carrie?"

"The horses ran into a fire truck. I've been trying to tell you that she's desperately hurt. Owen is with her, but he's not fit to do much."

Old Mrs. Carskaddan lay stretched near the tangled wreckage of her brougham on cushions from a near-by car. Her dress was bloody, and there was a large discolored area on her forehead. Her pulse, when he felt it, was fast and thready. Near by old Jim, the coachman, moaned over a broken wrist.

Spen ran expert fingers over the injured woman's body. One finding puzzled him. There was depression in the front of her chest, as if it had been caved in.

"It's serious," he told Carol. "Can't tell how bad yet. We'll have to get her to the hospital.

Miss Humphrey came up to report to Owen James. "There'll be an ambulance back in five minutes."

Carol, very pale, said to her husband between tight lips, "If she dies before it gets here you'll be to blame."

"What's that?" asked Owen James sharply.

"He stayed to tie up a drunken loafer's arm."

"Severed artery," put in the nurse.

"I don't care what it was," began the angry and scared girl, when Owen cut her short with a brusque "Don't be a fool, Carol."

She lifted her eyes to his blackened and haggard face in utter amazement. Never in his long devotion to her had he spoken in that tone.

"Did you expect that he would leave the man to bleed to death?" he went on sternly. A fit of coughing shook him.

Spen spared her the necessity of replying by saying to Owen, "You can't do any good here." The walls, crashing in with a tremendous upburst of flame and sparks, pointed the statement. "Come along in the ambulance. We don't want you developing smoke pneumonia." To Carol he said quietly, "Get someone to drive you to the hospital and bring Jim along. His wrist needs looking to."

"I can drive myself," she answered. "Get in, Jim."

The ambulance was clanging its way to the spot. At the hospital Spen directed the transfer of the still-comatose woman to a private room. The immediate necessity was to bring her out of shock. First he injected plasma, a preparation of the fluid portion of the blood, separated from the cells and put up in sterile containers for just such emergencies as this, with the added advantage over transfusion that it could be given without tedious and time-wasting matching, the purpose being to add strength to the blood stream, to the entire body, and prevent the dangerous cell oxygen lack that goes with profound shock.

A second and more exhaustive examination of the patient puzzled him. She was not entirely unconscious now; there were momentary periods of semilucidity, and once she uttered his name, so he felt safe in assuming that there was no serious head injury. Still her shock did not improve as he would like to have seen it. There were few injuries of note, a bruise here and there, and a few brush burns. On the left side of the chest over the depression that he had already felt. Blood oozed from this wound, but it was not enough to be considered serious. It was her heart action that he did not like, the thready pulse, the low blood pressure. When he explored the chest wound with a sterile clamp it was evident that the inner end of the fourth rib had been driven downward, inward, toward the mediastinum and its complement of great blood vessels and the heart. She had been fortunate; that rib might well have pierced through the heart itself.

Soon it appeared that the plasma, though employed in quantity the equivalent of a full blood transfusion, was not doing the work. To Carol, standing anxiously by, he said:

"We've got to operate."

"Where? On what?"

"There's a depressed and fractured rib interfering with the heart action."

"Is the operation dangerous?"

He shrugged. "There's no choice. She can't go on this way."

"Can I go to the operating room?"

"No." He was thinking of Carol's condition and the emotional strain.

She flushed angrily, was about to speak, but checked herself.

To the waiting nurse he said, "Get the operating room set up and have her blood matched against what you have in the bank. We may need a transfusion." Plasma was effectual for shock and emergency treatment, but if there was a real hemorrhage during the operation he'd want blood lost replaced with blood. Fortunately they had a large bank of stored blood in the big refrigerator downstairs. It would save the time ordinarily spent in searching for a donor and testing his blood.

It was almost an hour, at that, before he stood with scalpel poised, beneath lights focused on a single spot, the rectangle of crimson-stained skin in which was the small wound over the depressed rib. The patient had not improved in that period; if anything her pulse was weaker, her breathing shallower.

He injected novocain carefully into the wound. It would not be safe to give a general anesthetic in her present condition. Local was quite sufficient. All he intended to do was lift up the displaced rib and relieve the pressure upon the vital structures underneath. He could account for her present condition on no other basis than the presence of such pressure. As he did so the possibilities ran through his mind. It must be circulatory disturbance; there were no vital nerves in that area. But just what was the trouble underneath? If there were an opening in the heart itself—it was what he had been fearing—it might be blocked by the end of the rib. Lifting the bone would relieve the plugging action, but it might also turn loose a sudden, flooding hemorrhage which he would perhaps be powerless to control, hampered by small space and the presence of the fracture.

"More novocain." He made a sudden decision. He would treat it as if there were a wound of the heart, turn back a flap of muscles and rib from the chest wall, obtain all the exposure that would be necessary to close a heart wound, before he dislodged the particular rib in question. It was perhaps a dangerous thing to do, but he couldn't afford to take chances with sudden hemorrhage. The assistant looked at him questioningly as he injected novocain in a wider circle.

"I'm going to expose the auricle. This acts like a heart wound."

The interns and nurses drew closer to the table. A heart wound! They all knew what that meant. It would be a rare opportunity to see one, a rarer one to see it closed successfully.

Spen was certain of himself now, since he had decided definitely what should be done. Quickly he completed the incision and surrounded the skin edges with fresh towels.

"Periosteal elevator." It stripped the tough fibrous lining from the ribs above and below the injured rib.

"Costatome." Its broad, guillotinelike blade bit through the ribs. The assistant lifted the removed sections of bone from their beds.

"Clamps." He cut through the muscle bundles between the ribs until there was only the single injured rib holding a flap of the chest in place. The tissues underneath were dark with hemorrhage, he noted, confirming his suspicion that there was a leak of blood inside the chest. Probably the pleura was damaged; there might even be air in the chest, but he had no choice.

The group around the table grew tense. Would the operator be able to get the rib out without fatal damage and then control the hemorrhage which must follow?"

"Periosteal elevator." The surgeon's movements were deliberate and precise as he stripped the lining from the broken bone.

"Costatome." He slipped the protecting base of the instrument beneath the rib, pushing other structures gently away so that the sharp blade might not bite farther than the bone which it was intended to cut, and set the blade until it was tense against the rib.

"Be ready with a pack," he told the assistant. "And clamps," to the nurse.

When they nodded that they were ready he exerted a firm, steady pressure on the instrument.

"Crack!" The sound of metal biting through bone was loud in the silent room.

The bone itself did not move, so careful had been the maneuver. Gently he disengaged the instrument and laid it aside. Now would come the test, to dislodge and remove the bone remnant. Gripping it with a strong, toothed clamp, Spen began to move it gently back and forth, severing muscle connections, pushing away remaining attachments of the periosteum. Then it came away from all its attachments. Lifting it from its bed, he dropped it quickly on the table.

As the rib came up out of the depths of the wound a dark flood poured after it. There had been a wound of the heart, just as he had feared. And he realized, even as he went into speedy action, that it would be almost a surgical miracle if, in the depths of this clot-beclouded fissure, he found the tear in the heart and stopped the deadly leak.

First he must complete his incision and obtain exposure. It was the work of a moment to sever the remaining muscle bundles which had been attached to the injured rib and turn outward the triangular flap of the chest wall that he had been preparing. The upper chambers of the heart, the auricles, were exposed now, together with the great vessels entering and leaving the vital pump. With a practiced hand he removed the accumulated clot and sought for the opening through which the blood was pouring. The stream was not so large now; he could control it with the pressure of his fingers.

"Suture." Quickly he placed guy stitches above and below the opening, enabling him to hold the soft walls of the cavity up for easier access.

He could see the wound now, a small rent through the thin wall of the upper heart chamber, irregular in shape, but not too much, he judged, for satisfactory closure. Turning over the control of the guy sutures to the assistant, he thrust slender needles to which were attached dark strands of silk through both edges of the wound and tied them across the cut edges. Immediately the pulsing flood ceased. A second row of silk sutures reinforced the first.

"How about the transfusion?" he asked an intern who had just come into the room.

"She matched with blood in the bank. We're ready."

"Go ahead, then." Blood would do her much good now with the depressing effect of the heart wound removed, with the hemorrhage no longer seeping its way through the chest, encroaching on vital structures, interfering with the function of those important organs.

The immediate hurry and strain were over. He could take his time washing out the wound thoroughly to remove possibilities of infection having been carried in by the perforating object, which he judged to have been the brass rod that ran across

125

behind the front seat of the carriage. The transfusion was almost finished when he strapped the dressing in place and stepped back from the table. Cousin Carrie looked different now; her pulse was better; her blood pressure was climbing steadily back toward normal, and a tinge of color was beginning to replace the marblelike pallor of the cheeks.

Outside he reported to Carol, "She came through all right."

"Does that mean she will get well?" she asked eagerly.

"The chances are in her favor. With a hole in the heart, it doesn't do to be too sure."

"What will you do now? Go home?"

"No. I'll stick around. It isn't every day I pick up a millionaire patient, you know," he added with a malicious grin.

A cot was found for him. His patient had a satisfactory night. At eight-twenty in the morning a nurse called him. There was a slight heart flurry. He controlled that with morphine and digitalis. While not unforseen or pressingly serious, the development convinced him that he should be on call for at least twenty-four hours.

But today he and Kenny Mangan were to start on their first week end together. Well, that was out. He called up the office and cautiously explained the situation. Kenny made no demur. She understood where perhaps Carol would not have.

In Spen's mind there had been a sharp disappointment but no hesitation or doubt. Once committed to the case, he was incapable of quitting the rich Mrs. Carskaddan, who needed him, as he had been of leaving, in his extremity, drunken Shanahan, who had banged his fist through a windowpane.

CHAPTER XVI

Both of Spen's hospital patients were soon doing well. Of the two, Owen James was the first to make trouble, though not the worst. In the face of Spen's threat to throw up the case unless he obeyed orders, he played hooky at the first opportunity and went prowling about the burned district, conferring on rebuilding with city officials, arranging emergency quarters for the refugees from the destroyed hospital, and rallying the dispirited slum dwellers to the seemingly hopeless task of rehabilitation.

"We can't quit," he said to Spen, who had found and haled him back to his bed. "But where the money is coming from, God knows!"

"How much will it take?"

"To rebuild? That's out of the question for the present. But I've located another old building that could be fixed up temporarily for—well, ten thousand dollars would do it, I think."

"Let someone else worry," said Spen. "If you try to leave again until I prescribe crutches I'll have you locked in."

"Okay, boss; okay," said the older man in pretended humility. "When are you going to do that sterilization job for us? We don't want Mrs. Plotzor turned loose on an over-populated world unless and until."

"I can get around to it almost any time. I'll talk to Bernie."

"Bernie's sunk. By the way, I had a word from your friend Fleming. He's decided to come. I've had to wire him to postpone it." There passed over his face the slight shadow, the almost imperceptible strain and pain that accompanied his thoughts of Carol. "Your wife wants to contribute to the new clinic," he said. "Any objections?"

"It wouldn't do any good if I had," answered Spen. "The money is hers. I've nothing to do with it." In a more generous spirit he went on, "No; of course I wouldn't object. I may not agree with all your theories, but I think the clinic's work is fine."

"She's coming to see me this afternoon," said Owen. He continued hesitantly and gently, "Spen, don't attach too much importance to what she said about your not coming at once to Cousin Carrie. She doesn't quite understand. Why should she? And she was scared and wrought up."

"All right," said Spen. He did not want to discuss that with Owen James.

The subject came to him on the rebound from Carol's talk with Owen.

"I've just come from seeing Owen," she told Spen as they sat outside before dinner. "He's terrible."

127

"Terrible?" said Spen quickly. "What do you mean? He hasn't developed——?"

"Terrible about me," she hastened to amplify. "He hasn't developed anything but a poisonous sense of what he considers justice about you. He called me a willful little scrub. That, from Owen! To me!" she concluded grievously.

"Well, what's your own view?" asked Spen.

"Now don't you go picking on me too. He says I ought to apologize to you. Ought I? Because I won't."

"That seems to settle that." He grinned.

"But I will admit that you were pretty swell when you got going. The whole hospital is ringing with the way you mended up Cousin Carrie's punctured heart. She says now she's going to live to be a hundred."

"She's got spunk and cussedness enough to do it."

"When I saw you going in after Owen I was paralyzed," she continued with a touch of shyness. "I've cut out all the newspaper clippings about it."

"Then, for God's sake, throw 'em away! Of all the unmitigated pot wash! I'd like to bust Owen in the nose for giving it out."

"Don't like being a hero?" she taunted.

"Hero! I'm in more danger every time I cross Main Street in rush hours."

"Well, don't blame it on me. I dislike newspaper notoriety more than you possibly can. But I rather liked those articles. Spen, I want to ask you something."

"Go ahead."

"When it comes time for Baby to be born I'd like to have you with me."

"But, Carol, That's Cannaday's job."

"Yes; I know. But I'd like you there too. If you're there I shan't be too frightened."

"What a gal!" he jeered. "Because I'm a fake hero at a fire you figure that I must be a swell obstetrician." He put his hand over hers for a second. "Of course I'll be there if you want me," he said.

In less than a week Cousin Carrie Carskaddan was sitting up in bed, bullying her nurses, criticizing the food, demanding to be taken home, and making life miserable for the staff. Only Spen could do anything with her, and he not very much. To all representations that effort was bad for her, she turned a deaf ear. She wanted company; she wanted conversation and amusement, and if anyone , whether Spen or another, thought that she could be treated like a damned old mummy, they could damn well take another thought. Thus, Cousin Carrie.

"And don't tell me you're too busy to stay and talk to me," she said to Spen truculently. "I'm paying for your time. Through the nose, too, I daresay. Got any new rough stories for me?"

"Afraid not today. Lie back, now, and I'll stay for a while." It was better to give her a safety valve then to let her nerve pressure mount too high.

"By the way, what am I paying?"

"You'll get the bill in due time."

"I'll bet I will! What's the operation itself going to cost me?"

"How's your heart feeling?" he asked solicitously. "Able to stand a shock?"

"It'll stand anything you can say to me, young man."

"What would you say to ten thousand dollars?"

For a moment he was alarmed lest he had overrated her resistance, so purple did she become.

"Ten thousand *dollars!*" she squawked. "Ten thou— I'll see you in hell and carry you to the United States Supreme Court before you get it!"

"Oh, *I* don't get it."

"You or your associated bloodsuckers. It's all one to me."

"Don't go into an apoplexy or I'll operate again. You see, yours is a peculiar case."

"It isn't that peculiar. Not ten thousand dollars' peculiar."

"In a sense you're not my case at all. Owen James was first to attend you. I came in later."

"Yes; I heard about that," she returned grimly. "You were looking after some drunken bum and wouldn't leave him. Is that right?"

"Yes."

"Isn't my life worth more than a drunken bum's?"

"How do I know?" said Spen mildly. "I'm not God."

The old lady showed signs of choking. "Well, I'll be——"

"If you're asking me for estimates on your life," he pursued, "isn't it worth more than ten thousand dollars?"

"That isn't the point."

"Well, this is. James being first on the ground makes you practically a James Clinic patient. The clinic charges what the

129

patient can afford: five dollars, ten dollars, twenty dollars, nothing at all. Mostly it's nothing at all. Then again it might be ten thousand dollars to someone who could afford it. I suppose you can afford it."

"Never mind what I can afford. Did Owen James put you up to this?"

"Good lord, no! He doesn't know anything about it. This is between you and me. Perhaps I haven't made myself quite clear. If it was a matter of my charging for the operation, it would be, say five hundred dollars."

"Fair enough. I'll pay it."

"I'll take it if you still want to pay after you understand. Look, Cousin Carrie; the one thing that makes life tolerable for a lot of these slum people is Owen James' hospital and clinic. They're gone. You've made a lot of money out of the district—well, your husband did, and it came to you. Ten thousand dollars will enable James to start again. What are you going to do about that?"

"Get out of my room, you—you palaverer! You're taking advantage of a poor, sick woman with your oily talk. Get out!" And as he reached the door she added in tones of still-undiminished exasperation, "And send Owen James down here to see me, damn you!"

• "Cousin Carrie," said Spen solemnly, "if I told you what I really think of you they'd have to set it to music and sing it like a hymn."

Halfway back to Owen's room he remembered something and hurried back to exact a promise from the old lady that, whatever she might do, she would keep his part in it absolutely secret. No sense, he told himself, in stirring up his clinic partners by letting them know that he was helping along the James brand of "medical Bolshevism."

As Carol's time drew nearer indications apparent to Spen's expert eye suggested that she had underestimated the duration of her pregnancy. Either that, or her condition was abnormal.

On Friday evening, when he had returned from a call, tuckered out, and had gone to bed early, he was aroused by an insistent rapping on his door. Half awake, his first resentful thought was that some emergency call had come in.

"Tell 'em to go to hell," he groaned sleepily. "I'm too done up to go out again."

"It's me: Carol," said frightened tones outside.

He sat up hastily. "Come in," he said. "What is it?"

She opened the door. "I feel so queer. Do you think it can be coming?"

He got up and made a swift examination, all his weariness dispelled. "I shouldn't think it was immediate," he said. "Do you want me to call Cannaday?"

"No. It's easier now. I think I'll go to bed. Do you mind if I leave the connecting door open?"

"Of course not." He smiled. "It won't be regarded as establishing a precedent," he said. Going around through her room, he worked over the obstinate bolt. "It's stuck," he said. "Rusted." He got a shoe from the rack and with the heel reduced the recalcitrant metal to submission. "Call me if you feel uneasy, won't you?"

"Yes. But I won't get panicky and stupid again." She smiled at him. "You see, this hasn't happened to me before. I suppose one gets used to it with experience. Go back to bed. Poor boy, you're all in."

He slept uneasily for a time and then deeply. It was nine o'clock when Aunt Candace called him. "I wish you'd come to Carol," she said.

He hurried into the room. Carol's eyes were frightened. "I'm afraid there's something wrong," she said.

There was, indeed, something wrong, as he saw at once. Hemorrhage! He said with an assurance which was far from feeling:

"That's apt to happen when labor starts early."

"This bad?"

"Oh yes. But we'd better get you to the hospital. I'll call Dr. Cannaday."

"There's no pain now. Couldn't I stay home a while longer?" she asked wistfully.

"I'll go with you," he assured her. "Though they'll probably turn me out later. Anxious husbands aren't popular in delivery rooms."

Over the wire he said to the family physician, "Dr. Cannaday, this is Brade. I've just called an ambulance for Carol."

"Anything wrong?" Cannaday's voice was alert. Spen felt his confidence in the older man rising.

"She's just had a slight hemorrhage. I'm a little afraid of a placenta previa."

"Let's hope not," Dr. Cannaday said. "I'll meet you at the hospital. Would you like to have someone called into consultation?"

"Why, I——"

"Don't hesitate," Cannaday said briskly. "I should feel better myself to have someone. I helped raise Carol, you know."

"How about Stanley, then?" Spen asked.

"Excellent. I'll have him there."

In a few minutes the ambulance came. Carol looked at the stretcher and clutched Spen's arm, staring up at him with dilated pupils.

"Is it that bad? Do I have to have an ambulance?"

"You can travel more comfortably this way; that's all. Besides, they don't charge doctors." He laughed to calm her fears.

Spen rode with her. Once or twice he had to hold her tight while spasms of pain made her cry out. Dr. Cannaday met them at the door, and Jeff Stanley came in just as they were putting her to bed, his flaming mop of hair unkempt from hurried combing. Spen felt better now that he had Carol at the hospital and in the hands of men in whom he felt confidence. Stanley and Cannaday went into the room to examine Carol while the husband waited in the little sitting room at the end of the hall. The cushions of the chairs were worn threadbare by the thousands of husbands and relatives who had waited there while nature was going through the inexorable process of birth. There were methods of hastening that process, but in most cases, he knew, things went better without interference. Sedatives did wonders to relieve pain and take away the memory of that period of agony, and once it was over the red-faced little persons whom the mothers cuddled to them took away what memories remained. He was hoping Carol would be able to go on and have a normal labor, have her baby born without complications that he had learned to dread when he had been doing his apprentice work in obstetrics back in Baltimore. But deep in his heart he knew that those strong contractions so early, that telltale dark stain, meant trouble. He only hoped it was not too much trouble.

The two doctors emerged presently. "Everything quiet," said the elder. "I don't look for action for several hours."

"Why don't you go to your office and get your mind off it?" suggested the consultant.

Reluctantly Spen acceded. He could keep in touch from there

Kenny Mangan greeted him. "There's hob to pay inside. I've been combing the city for you."

Castleman Tyre rushed out. "Where the hell have you been, Brade?"

"What the hell is it to you?" retorted Spen. For two cents he would have taken a poke at that pale and smug face. Kenny giggled.

"There's a big smashup on the Gulf & Southeastern," explained the other, calming down. "Father's on his way. He wants you to follow. We're consulting surgeons to the road, you know."

"I can't go. My wife is in labor."

"You've got to," the other urged. "This is vital." He lowered his voice. "We nearly lost the railroad's business last year over a—a misunderstanding. Isn't everything all right with Carol? Isn't it normal?"

"We don't know. They're afraid not. They can't tell yet."

"I'll tell you," said Castleman persuasively. "You get along out to Fenelon—it's just twenty miles—and report to Dad. I'll telephone the hospital. You can call me up in two or three hours, and I'll keep you posted. If anything is wrong you can get back in half an hour. You're needed there more than at the hospital. What could you do, anyway? Just be in the way."

This was sensible enough, as Spen was forced to admit. He got in his car from the parking space and set out at a speed that would have caused his arrest in every block but for the caduceus on the hood.

An express train had smashed into a truck and toppled over a low embankment. Dead and wounded were still being pried out of the wreckage when he arrived. Blanton Tyre welcomed him.

"Keep notes when you can," he instructed him in a half whisper. "There will be damage suits to defend."

So that was part of his duty. He'd be damned if he would! Let old Tyre do the dirty work of the paid medical witness! Until noon he worked without flagging, going from victim to victim, bandaging, ligating, setting broken limbs, now and then reporting on some unfortunate whose pulse had lapsed as he attended him. Blanton Tyre, too, was putting forth his best efforts. Spen touched his arm.

"I've got to telephone," he said. "Back in five minutes. Take a look at that girl on the blanket, will you?"

Over the wire Castleman Tyre reported no news from the hospital. This was, in a sense, true, but not quite honest, since Dr. Stanley, who had talked with the clinic, had said that while there was little progress in the course of labor, symptoms had appeared which were causing worry. At three o'clock Tyre called the hospital again. Dr. Cannaday came to the telephone.

"Where can I reach Dr. Brade?" he asked.

"He's at the Fenelon wreck. Anything wrong?"

"Yes. We have a placenta previa on our hands."

The younger Tyre had seen enough of that condition to appreciate its seriousness. Normally the placenta, the connection between the circulation and the mother, is located on the inside of the uterus, a flat, panlike structure, perhaps six inches in diameter, attached high up on one side. Sometimes, however, it attaches itself across the lower opening of the uterus itself, the cervix through which the head of the child would have to pass. Placenta previa, literally placenta first, in front of the child, usually gave no signs of its presence until labor began, until the cervix began to dilate for the passage of the head. Then the connections between the blood-rich organ and the wall of the uterus would be torn loose, causing bleeding, gradually increasing as labor proceeded. Most dangerous of all was its effect upon the child who was not yet born, who had no chance to breathe the oxygen into its lungs that it would normally receive from the mother's blood which was being gradually cut off from it. Fetal death was an almost certain thing if labor were allowed to go on.

"How about the baby?" Castleman Tyre asked.

"The heart rate is fast," returned the attending physician. "I'm afraid the hemorrhage is burrowing underneath the placenta and cutting off the circulation. We must do a Caesarean section. That is why I am anxious to get hold of Brade."

"He's helping out my father. Is Mrs. Brade in danger?"

"No. I wouldn't say that."

"Then what is there that Brade could do that you and Stanley can't?"

"Nothing, of course. But we think that he should know."

"He'll be calling me up soon. I can tell him then."

But it was Blanton Tyre who called the clinic. His son relayed the message from Cannaday.

"Hm!" said the senior. "We need Brade badly here for the next hour or so. He couldn't do any good at the hospital, could he?"

"No; I suppose not."

"Probably only be in the way," said the older man comfortably. "We'll be cleaned up here by four o'clock. Brade looks like a corpse. Some worker, that boy!"

To Spen his chief reported that there was nothing at the hospital requiring his presence. "Give us another hour here, my boy, and I'll turn you loose. You certainly saved that girl's life, and if the old man pulls through it'll be due to you."

Utterly exhausted, Spen finished his work and dragged himself to his car. He needed a drink. God! How he needed a drink! He stopped at the first decent-looking bar and ordered a big slug of brandy. This was a mistake. The immediate effect was to brace him. He was all right now to go to the hospital. The house wasn't a block out of the way. He'd stop there, wash up, and telephone for the latest news.

On the way up the steps of the house the reaction hit him hard. He staggered into the library where the telephone was, stupid with alcohol and weariness, but mainly weariness. As he lurched into depths of the big overstuffed chair and reached for the instrument he did not see old Miss Candace Grahame stop as she passed along the hall and stare at him. Gathering his faculties, he called what he thought was the hospital. It proved to be the wrong number. When he got the right one from the book the infuriating answer came, "The line is biz-ee." He slumped back, still holding the receiver, and was rudely wakened when it dropped upon his knee. Mustn't go to sleep. Call again. He tried the number. "The line is biz-ee." Hell's damnation! Give it two minutes to be free. He closed his eyes. Sleep utterly engulfed him.

At the hospital Aunt Candace was admitted to the sickroom because her niece had kept calling feebly for her. Carol tried to reach out arms to her.

"Oh, Auntie! Auntie! My baby is dead!"

"I know, dear. I know. Hush, now. You must rest."

"Where was Spen? Why wasn't he here? Perhaps he could have save Baby."

135

"No, dear. Nothing could. Dr. Cannaday told me."

"Where is Spen? I want him. Where is he?"

Candace Grahame's self-control broke. Her face became grim as the face of the dead.

"At home. Drunk," she said.

CHAPTER XVII

ONCE A HERO, always a hero to the newspapers. Spen's exploit at the slum fire had established him in that role. Now the local press played him up as the central figure of the Fenelon wreck, where, indeed, he had been energetic and efficient but had done no more than half a dozen other workers.

The Tyres were delighted. It was the most valuable sort of advertising, in their eyes, and it all redounded to the fame of the Tyre Clinic. This was the sort of thing to swell their practice. Perfectly ethical too. With something resembling nausea Spen perceived that this splurge of printer's ink had advanced him in the Tyre esteem farther than the most difficult skilled technical achievement would have done.

Carol made no mention of it. When she was well enough to see him again she seemed lethargic and indifferent, in significant contrast to her dependence on him when he took her to the hospital. Sore because he was not there for the birth, he surmised. This was natural enough. As soon as she was stronger he would explain it all to her. That she would be reasonable about it he had little doubt. Inwardly he had no sense of guilt in the matter. One drink only. Who would have believed that it could knock a man that way! Of course if he had not been worn out by overstrain of the unremitting hours, aiding the wounded, nothing of the kind would have occurred.

There was something queer about the whole business; about Castleman Tyre not telling him of the Caesarean crisis. But

Spen's memory of the sequence of events after that drink was too fuzzy to permit his following up the thing with assurance. He had to be satisfied with Tyre's explanation. His story was that immediately upon receipt of the message from the hospital he had set out in his car to fetch Spen back with him. He had a minor disabling accident. His attempts to get Spen by telephone were in vain.

There seemed to be no holes in that. And Tyre would back him up in his explanation to Carol if that were necessary. Everything would be all right; they would go away somewhere together, perhaps to Florida. She had hinted at that in one of their increasingly intimate conversations: a delayed honeymoon. After that he would quit drink if she wanted him to. The last experience had given him a jar. He would even quit the Tyre Clinic soon and make his own individual way, if that would bring them closer together. Already he was getting fed up with the Tyre methods and trickeries.

How far he was compromised with Carol he learned only when seated opposite Miss Candace Grahame at the breakfast table the day set for the patient's return from the hospital. Without preliminary she said:

"The next time you come home drunk, Spencer Brade, I hope you will go to your own room."

"I wasn't drunk," he returned sharply.

"The air reeked with whiskey where you passed."

"I'd been working six hours at the wreck," he said, inwardly furious at being compelled to explain himself to this frozen-faced old harpy. "On the way home I took one drink."

"Only one, I suppose!"

"I said one." He did not think it necessary to mention it was a double brandy.

"Simon had to help you upstairs and to bed."

"Did you tell Carol that?"

"I did."

"You want to break up this marriage, don't you?" he said quietly.

"If you call it a marriage," was the old lady's contemptuous retort.

"Perhaps you've got a better one in mind."

She met his look with one even stonier. "I have. I've always had."

"Owen James, I suppose."

137

"She would have married him eventually if she hadn't met you."

He rose from the table "I think you would do well not to interfere," he said with careful politeness. "After all, this is Carol's concern and mine. We're quite capable of handling it ourselves."

She had the last word. "You're not even capable of handling yourself half the time."

To hell with the old harridan! he thought. To hell with all of it! If Carol was going to believe her without giving him a hearing, let her do it. He wouldn't even try to explain. It was up to her now.

For a week after the wife's return the atmosphere of the household was murky with repression and strain. Spen was scrupulously polite to both women; that much was inherent in his breeding. But he made no pacificatory move. He wondered how long it could last. Carol stopped him one morning as he was going to his car.

"Spen, I want to speak to you."

"Yes, Carol?"

"I'm not feeling a bit well. Dr. Cannaday thinks I ought to have a change."

"Very likely he's right."

"Auntie wants to take me to Florida."

So that was it! "Auntie" wanted to take her. Well, "Auntie" was not likely to include him in the invitation. He said:

"How long shall you be gone?"

"That depends. A month. Six weeks. Possibly longer."

"I see. You'll close the house, I suppose."

"Of course not. We expect you to go on living here."

"I'll go on living here on one condition, Carol. You know what it is."

"That condition has become impossible," she said coldly.

"Then I'd better leave."

She raised her eyes to his. "I hope you're not going to do that, Spen."

"Why not?"

"Do you want to advertise to Aunt Candace and all our friends how things stand between us?"

"Whose fault is that?"

She said anxiously, "I agree that the situation can't last. But I'm not strong enough to face it now. If I go to Florida and you

138

leave the house we might as well call in the reporters and give out the news of the divorce."

"Why not now as well as later?" he asked.

"We've gone all over that once. If you insist, there is nothing I can do about it. But I do think you owe me that much consideration."

"Putting on the basis of debt"—she flushed and winced—"I undoubtedly do. Okay, Carol. I'll hold the fort. Tell Auntie to lock up the booze closet."

She regarded him steadily, seemed about to speak, then thought better of it and shook her head. (That hit her, he thought with malign satisfaction.)

"When do you leave?" he asked.

"Dr. Cannaday says I can travel in two weeks. We'll go by car and take Simon with us, if you can get along without him."

"Easily. Dinah can take care of me."

During that fortnight he could feel the alienation of his wife growing daily. Did she expect him to come groveling to her feet for forgiveness? Then she had another guess! If she chose to open the subject in a reasonable spirit he would meet her advance with frankness, and they could have it out and come to a better understanding. As for Aunt Candace, to address her with ordinary courtesy was an effort.

He was coming to hate the atmosphere of the household, false, strained, oppressive. He took to staying at the office after the others had gone, putting in an extra drink or so on top of the one or two of the daily session with his colleagues. That he was overdoing it, he fully realized. It was only temporary, he told himself. As soon as he was rid of the strain caused by Carol's pathetically courageous effort to be cheerful and natural, plus the irritant of Aunt Candace's grim and silent disfavor, he would steady down again.

Meantime there was Kenny Mangan. In her excitant companionship he found release and relief. After the office work he would drive her home, before going back to Grahame Lodge, unless he were taking her out to dinner. Once in that period of their developing association she said to him simply:

"Bertha won't be home tomorrow night."

It brought home to him the fact that in the girl's mind this liaison was becoming a settled relationship. Well, why not? Furthermore, he became conscious of an influence quietly exerted upon him. Once she said to him reflectively:

"Spen I wonder why you picked on me?"

"Did I pick on you?"

"Oh! So I was the one that did the picking."

"No; I don't mean that at all."

"Look, darling. You could get all the women you want. Any doctor can who isn't absolutely a gargoyle."

"You happen to be all the women I want," he answered lightly. "In one small and extremely attractive package," he added.

"Well, it's against all my principles," she mused. "And it ought to be against yours. Office stuff; not so good. Principles don't count much in a case like this, though, do they!"

A few evenings later, when they were dining together, he announced to her, "For the next couple of months I'm likely to have my week ends free."

"Is your wife going away?"

"Yes. To Florida."

"I've got a cousin in Columbia that I could visit," said the girl demurely. "Or, if I haven't, I could invent one."

"Here's to your cousin! She's liable to see a lot of you." Spen reached for his highball glass. It was empty. "Where's that waiter?"

"Look, Spen," said Kenny. "Isn't one bad habit at a time enough?"

"What's the bad habit?" he asked defensively.

"I am. But liquor's worse, for you."

"I don't drink until after office hours."

"You do. You come down in the morning shaky. You come back from lunch with a breath."

"Oh, lay off me, Kenny!"

"Okay, darling. I only don't want to see you gum your own game. And I think Old Fussface has got an eye on you."

From an unexpected source came another jog to his conscience. He had arranged to come to the emergency clinic which Owen James was already running and do the sterilization operation on Mrs. Plotzov. A trying day at the office, followed by an emergency call from Markland Hospital, where Blanton Tyre had painfully though not dangerously mishandled a case and needed his help, left him depleted of energy. One drink failed to restore him. A second helped, and the third and final one made him feel equal to anything.

When he arrived at the gaunt, unsightly building Owen

140

James was outside, consulting with the contractor. Felix Bernitz was waiting for him in the office. Bernitz took one look, then:

"You can't operate, Spen."

"Why can't I operate?"

"You're not in shape to,"

"You make me sick. Certainly I'm in shape to. Look at that hand. Steady as a rock."

Deeply perturbed, the other said, "For God's sake, Spen! Haven't we had enough trouble without you springing this sort of thing on us? Wait till I get Owen."

Spen raised his voice. "Either I operate now or to hell with the whole thing!"

The clinic head entered, limping on his cane. His face was seamed with weariness and worry.

"Hello, Spen," he said. "Everything's ready." His expression altered. "What about you?" he asked slowly.

"I'm all right," returned Spen doggedly. "Bernie's crazy."

"Better go home, Spen," said Owen in the gentle, inflexible tone which had established his authority so firmly in the district that no one ever thought of running counter to it. It, together with the mounting fumes of drink, had the effect of making Spen pity himself.

"I'll go since you don't seem to want me here," he said pathetically.

"We do want you here. We need you. But not this way."

"Good-by, Owen. Good-by, Bernie," said the visitor, and departed with poise and dignity.

At home he had a couple more drinks, called up Kenny, failed to get her, and decided that he was tired out and had better go to bed forthwith. In the morning he privately admitted to remorse. Only two days remained before Carol's departure. In that time he was at pains to be specially considerate of her and helpful to her. He even accepted meekly Miss Grahame's shafts and snubs until his wife protested.

"You're not being fair to Spen, Auntie. I won't have him bulldozed."

On the last morning Spen had an early operation. Carol came to her door, looking fragile and lovely. She said:

"Spen, you don't think I'm doing this to—to be mean, do you?"

"No," he answered. "I know you're not. Don't have me on your mind."

141

"But I do. I know this isn't fair to you. Yet I don't see any way out just now."

"Separation may be a good thing for both of us. We can think it out better apart."

"Very likely," she agreed dubiously.

He had a generous impulse. "There's one thing I want you to know, Carol. I'm terribly sorry about the baby."

Pain twisted her face momentarily. "I'm glad you said that, Spen."

Miss Grahame appeared around the corner.

"Good-by, Spen," his wife said lightly. "Be a good boy."

She kissed him. Spen wondered whether she would have done that except for the presence of the third party. Probably not. He shook hands with the old lady and left.

In the first-of-the-month mail came a check signed "Caroline Carskaddan." It was for five hundred dollars. There was no word with it. He endorsed it over to Carol and mailed it with a friendly note.

That made him feel better.

CHAPTER XVIII

WHATEVER MISGIVINGS Spen might have had as to the ethics of the Tyre Clinic, there was no doubt about its success or that he was contributing to that success. He was busy every day, sometimes operating far into the night. Pressure on his duties kept his medical conscience anesthetized, helped him to ignore the dubious practices of the Tyres, which were still on the safe side of open malpractice. He was not surrendering his own principles, so he told himself stubbornly; he was rigorously determined to maintain his personal standards. Later when he had acquired more standing and influence, he would quietly press for changes, improvements in the methods of the clinic.

Meantime he derived a double satisfaction from his fortnightly checks. They were an earnest of success and a promise of complete independence as they steadily reduced his indebtedness to the wife who refused to be a wife.

By way of maintaining a balance of moral values he had it a rule to go to the James Hospital at least once a week. But several times he had been forced by the demands of the Tyre patronage to turn emergency calls from his charity practice. One such call came direct from Felix Bernitz.

"Can't do it, Bernie," Spen answered over the wire with real reluctance. "I've got an operation at five o'clock."

"Emergency?" asked his friend.

"We—ell, it's an important one."

"This is immediate. It's life or death. You're the man to do it if anybody can. Couldn't you postpone the other for an hour?"

"Afraid not. It's on Mrs. Millinger. You know that neurotic type."

"I know she's the wife of the president of the Second National."

"Oh, go to hell!"

Spen operated efficiently on the neurotic for her insignificant benign tumor. Any other twenty local men would have done as well. It was a routine case. But the two-thousand-dollar fee was distinctly better than routine.

Bernitz called up in the morning. "That surgical case of ours died."

"Is it my fault?" demanded Spen, annoyed.

"Oh no! I just thought you might be interested."

"Well, damn it! I lose some of my cases too," shouted Spen. He was wasting his violence. Bernitz had hung up on him.

How rottenly unfair those idealists were!

As if to carry out his unheard words, bad luck befell him next day. The patient was a big, ruddy, middle-aged fellow named Schultz, the man of all work on Blanton Tyre's place. No special skill was required for the operation; The X ray showed several stones in the gall bladder, easily accessible. Spen had no apprehensions.

Everything went well with the anesthetic. Spen had just opened the peritoneum when he was checked by an urgent word from the anesthetist.

"Something wrong, Dr. Brade."

Setting aside his instruments, Spen came around to the head

143

of the table. The patient's face was suffused and bluish. On the other side of Robbins, the resident surgeon, bent over with an expression of concern.

"Artificial respiration," Spen directed him as he reached for the laryngoscope kept handy on the anesthetist's table in case of obstruction to the respiratory passage by mucus or a swallowed tongue.

"Ampoule of coramine," he said to the nurse in the next breath.

Up to that time Spen had been feeling logy, indifferent, over a purely routine situation. At this challenge every nerve and muscle snapped to attention. It was easy to slide the instrument into place, so relaxed was the throat. In the light of the small bulb at the end the pharynx was clear, the vocal chords separated, with no sign of a mucus plug. He took the rubber tube that a nurse had handed him and slipped it into the trachea before removing the instrument, insuring an open pathway of air to the lungs.

"Any improvement?" he asked the anesthetist. The resident and an intern were pumping regularly on the chest in the movements of artificial respiration.

She shook her head. "I can't get any pulse."

"What happened?"

"The heart started fluttering, then he stopped breathing. Like a coronary attack."

Coronary thrombosis? Blocking of the vital blood vessels that supplied the heart itself? It couldn't be! Carter Hewlett had examined the patient and certified him as safe for general anesthesia.

Placing the metal tips of a stethoscope in his ears, Spen moved the diaphragm at the end of the tube about on the patient's chest. There was nothing, no sound suggestive of a heart even trying automatically to contract.

"He's gone," said Spen, shocked and puzzled.

In the dressing room he racked his wits to account for the abrupt outcome. The man had appeared healthy, a trifle florid, perhaps, but nothing abnormal.

"Do you suppose he had another coronary attack?" Robbins asked from the shower.

The query brought Spen up short. "Another? What do you mean by 'another'?"

"Why, he'd had at least one, hadn't he?" said the intern.

"Where do you get that?" snapped Spen.

"There was an electrocardiogram that came from your clinic on the report. It certainly looked like coronary thrombosis."

The operator pulled himself together. This was a situation for caution. It wouldn't do to involve the clinic.

"Do you remember the approximate date of the cardiogram?" he asked.

Robbins knit his brow. "Let's see. It must have been about four months back. Hadn't you seen it?" he asked curiously.

"If I have it must have slipped my mind," said the other diplomatically. "I knew that he was a questionable case. Still there wasn't much choice, was there? That gall bladder had to come out."

But had it? he thought unhappily as his knotted his tie. It had been an elective operation. Next week, next month, two months from now, it wouldn't make much difference. The stones have been causing no special trouble.

And Carter Hewlett had given assurance that the patient was all right! He'd have something to say to Hewlett.

Finished with the nerve-racking job of explaining to a hysterical wife why her husband had died before the operation had more than begun, Spen carried to his car the damning documentary evidence. Filed upon the chart was a sheet with portions of the electrocardiographic tracing. For any man not a medical ignoramus there was no mistaking the significance of those spidery white lines on the dark surface, representing each phase of the heartbeat as the electric currents from the heart muscle registered themselves on the sensitive string galvanometer of the instrument, no mistaking that abnormal splitting of the QRS complex of sharply peaked lines on the record. Coronary thrombosis: it could be nothing else. That meant a few months ago this man had survived a severely crippling injury to his heart muscle, an injury which if repeated might mean death, in this instance had meant death.

Carter Hewlett was sitting at his desk when Spen entered unceremoniously. He saw the chart beneath the caller's arm, and his pudgy face grew a little pale. "Too bad about Schultz," he said.

"How did you know?"

"The hospital telephoned Blanton."

"Then you know why he died!"

"Anesthesia, they said."

145

Spen set the cardiogram down under the diagnostician's nose. "Why didn't you tell me he'd had a coronary?"

"Why should I? He was completely well."

"How the hell do you or anybody else know when a coronary case is completely well? Yet you let this poor devil in for a general anesthetic for a gall-bladder operation."

"He had to have an operation," blustered Hewlett. "If you know anything, which I'm beginning to doubt, you ought to know that."

"I'm not concerned with your opinion as to my knowledge. Stick to the case. In a healthy person I'd have advocated taking the bladder out as a prophylactic measure. But in a man with coronary disease——"

"What the hell do you know about this case, anyway?" burst out Hewlett, jumping from his seat belligerently. "The man's been cluttering up the office schedule for more than a year. In and out every week. He would and he wouldn't have the operation; couldn't make up his fool mind. There was better than an even chance he'd come through all right. Do you think we can carry a charity patient forever?"

"Charity patient, eh?" said Spen, pale to the lips. "Well, god-damn *you!* I suppose a charity patient has no right to his life, by your standards."

Hewlett backed away from the white fury of the slighter man. "Keep your voice down," he cautioned. "I'm not going to get into a brawl with you. I shall take this up with Blanton Tyre."

Spen laughed aloud at that. Take it up with Tyre, huh? If Blanton Tyre had come in at this moment his junior associate would have thrown the job in his face. Still seething, he stamped out with a view of getting a much-needed drink. Kenny Mangan was standing at the door.

"Next time you goddamn that Hewlett louse," she suggested confidentially, "close the door. You scared one old hen right off the premises."

"Sorry," said Spen. "I'm not in my best temper today."

"You're telling me? Is it that Schultz case?"

Spen nodded.

"Think it would calm you down to take me out to dinner?"

"You're right it would! Anything more?"

She smiled. "Bertha's out of town on a case."

"That's grand."

146

"But I want to talk to you seriously, Spen. No; I mean it."

Over her abstemious one glass of sherry at dinner that evening Kenny said with pretended demureness:

"Darling, you wouldn't take advice from a poor girl who has given you her all, I suppose."

"Advice from the Tyre office generally comes high," he returned.

"This'll be free. And good."

"Let's have it."

"This Tyre business isn't your line of goods, Spen. Get the hell out."

"Trying to get rid of me, Kenny?"

"Not on your life! Listen, Spen. I'm not pretending that this affair of ours is a high and holy love and an undying passion. I've been in love before and got bravely over it. But aside from what I feel for you that way, I think you're a swell guy and a damn good doctor, and I just naturally hate to see you wasted on this high-pressure shyster practice. Besides, you're not happy here. Are you?"

"Well——"

"You see!" she caught him up. "Of course you're not. How could you be?"

"You stay here yourself."

"Quite different. I've got my living to make."

"So have I."

"Nuts! You could be making it right now in private practice. Go back and open your own office."

"And take Miss Kenny Mangan with me as office secretary?" He smiled.

She slowly shook her head. "You think I'm making a play for that. Wrong. It's you I'm thinking of."

"I know, Kenny," he said contrite. "You're a good kid. But I can't get out now. I've got obligations. But I'm not going to stay here forever."

"That's what you think! But you will, unless you do something quick. Kenny knows. Okay, pal. Let's take in a movie."

"Disappointed in me, sweetie?" he asked.

"Yes," she said. A disconcertingly honest little person, this Kenny.

Nothing came of the tiff with Carter Hewlett. Apparently he had swallowed his wrath. Indeed, his position was far too vulnerable in the Schultz case for him to enter a complaint with the clinic head. Spen decided to take no action on his side. But he wanted no more of the Hewlett reports on his cases.

With a grin on his satyr's face Terry Martin accosted Spen. "Understand you've had a run-in with our prize internist."

"Hewlett? Yes; we had a little difference."

"I hope you gave him a good poke in the guts."

"I'd like to have," admitted Spen. "We didn't get that far. He'll probably try to get me out now."

"Fat chance. You're sitting pretty here. Know why?"

Spen pulled a wry face. "They think I'm good advertising for the clinic."

"It's more than that," the pathologist told him with a slant grin. "It's because Blanton's such a rotten surgeon on anything below the navel that patients are beginning to kick. The clinic has to have somebody who's a technical expert on gynecological surgery, and you fill the bill. Haven't they been turning over the real pelvic work to you? Sure they have! Oh, not all of it, of course. Every now and then some flossy little dame will come along who just must have Dr. Tyre do her operation. And you know as well as I do what that operation will be. You won't be asked in on that line till they're surer of you. Don't worry about Hewlett, though. You've got his number."

Encouraged by this, Spen held up the head of the office after the daily ceremonial drink.

"Dr. Tyre, hereafter I'd like to make my own examinations and diagnoses on patients turned over to me for operation."

"Hmm! Any particular reason?"

"Yes."

"The Schultz case?"

"That and others."

"I feel badly about poor Schultz. He'd been with us a long time. He was a good man. You think his death could have been avoided?"

"Absolutely. He could perfectly well have been operated under local anesthesia."

"Then you consider that Dr. Hewlett was at fault?"

"I prefer to let the record speak for itself."

"Very proper. Very proper. Fact is, I've looked up the record. Come down to my office. There is a matter I've had in mind to talk over with you. We may as well do it now."

148

In his quarters, a little too luxurious, a little overfeminized to suit the trade, Blanton Tyre handed his associate a rich-flavored cigar and lighted up his own.

"How do you like your work here?" he began.

"Fine," said Spen mechanically.

"That's good. We're very much pleased with the way you've taken hold, Castleman and I."

Spen grinned. "How about the other member?"

"I'm coming to Hewlett presently. "Yes; we've been watching your work closely. That Fenelon wreck, for instance. That was splendid. A column in one paper and a column and a half in the other on you alone," (Spen winced) "besides the other publicity. Very valuable to the clinic; very valuable. You have the faculty of making what the newspaper boys call good copy."

"Not intentionally," said Spen with distaste.

"No. No; of course not. Perfectly ethical; perfectly ethical. We would not stand for anything else in the Tyre Clinic," he concluded virtuously. He smoked for the space of half a dozen long, deliberative puffs. Spen waited. Tyre shot at him:

"What's your opinion of Hewlett?"

"Essentially commercial."

Tyre seemed taken aback. "That isn't what I had in mind. I'm referring to his qualifications."

Spen debated within himself. He did not want to be unjust, even to a man he despised.

"I think he's a fair, average internist," he said. "He knows his subject, but he's liable to be slipshod. I think he's lazy."

"Fair to average is hardly up to Tyre Clinic standards," said the head. "Spen"—it was the first time he had named him thus familiarly—"Dr. Hewlett's contract is up in a few months. I'm not satisfied with him. We can find a salaried man to replace him for four thousand dollars or at most five thousand dollars. The clinic would be the better for it."

"Frankly, I think it would," said Spen.

"Well, well! We shall see. It isn't a matter of any haste. However, I may tell you this, that any change here will certainly not work to your detriment. Quite the reverse."

"That's very kind of you," said Spen politely.

"It might work out to your devoting more of your time to the work here."

"I hope you don't think that I've been shirking."

"Perhaps I should have put it another way. Say—uh—to your devoting less of your efforts to outside interests."

"No more hospital visits?" asked Spen, purposely misconstruing.

"Oh, bless you, yes! No interference there. That's good advert—— That impresses the profession and to some extent the public. What I had in mind was outside activities." He glanced up and, as it were, around the ash of the fat cigar. "For example, Owen James' hospital.

"But I've done very little there. Mostly at odd hours."

"Too much, my boy. Too much. Association of that kind does a young practitioner no good. Owen James, though I have nothing to say against his personal character, is a dangerous influence in the community. I believe, myself, that he is abnormal. The Messiah complex. And some of his beliefs! Rank socialism. He pretends that disease and poverty are the same thing."

"They pretty well overlap," said Spen.

"Don't let yourself be infected by his nonsense, my boy," warned the other earnestly. "He's plausible, I know. But he's fundamentally unsound. I've heard something of your wife's helping to finance a new hospital and clinic for him. I hope it isn't true."

"That's her own affair," said Spen stiffly.

"Oh, quite, quite! Still, if she understood the full implications of such medical socialism—— You couldn't point it out to her?"

"No, I couldn't."

Blanton Tyre sighed windily. "And that crazy old coot of a Mrs. Carskaddan! She's backing his emergency clinic." (Spen treated himself to a private grin. What would Tyre say if he knew Spen's part in that!) "They say he's working on her to put a hundred thousand dollars into that new venture."

"I don't know a thing about that," Spen was able to say honestly.

"I suppose not. Your wife is away, I understand," the smooth voice continued.

"Yes."

"Are you expecting her back soon?"

"Not very. The baby's death was a shock to her."

"Yes, yes; of course. Too bad! Too bad! Well, a wife is a

great asset to a young physician in a place like Charlesville. Particularly such a girl as Carol Grahame."

(He's heard there's something wrong between us, Spen thought, and he's worried. But he hasn't the nerve to ask right out.)

"One other little matter. You don't mind my speaking plainly?"

"Go ahead," said Spen, wondering what was coming now.

"It's your drinking. I think you should cut down."

"Am I as bad as that?" said Spen, so startled that he put what was meant as a thought into words.

"Oh, I don't imply that you are a drunkard or in danger of becoming one. Here in our own place it is quite all right; a friendly drink or two in private hurts nobody. But in public places—well, people are doubtful about a physician whom they see patronizing a bar. There are also the associations so often connected with drinking."

(What does he mean by that? thought Spen. Does he suspect about Kenny?)

"We'll say no more about it," the smooth voice went on. "Consider the whole matter carefully. Not many men of your age have such an opportunity. I don't want to influence or hurry you, though. Take your time."

By which Spen clearly understood that he had a period of probation in which to prove himself adjustable to the Tyre standards of practice.

CHAPTER XIX

IN SPITE OF WORK and distraction Spen found life unexpectedly lonely. He came to hate the great, quiet mansion with its atmosphere of aloofness and its corps of servents so perfectly trained as to be for him, the alien within the doors, impersonal. More and more he found himself putting in his evenings at the country club, sometimes dancing, more often playing bridge, always to the accompaniment of a few drinks, or many.

To be sure, there was his preoccupation with Kenny Mangan. But Kenny, being shrewd and cautious, was by no means always available. It would not do for either of them, she pointed out, to be seen together in public too often. One or two indications at the office had suggested to her that the Tyres were watchful. Week ends she could manage occasionally, and when Bertha was away he could always come circumspectly to the flat. But not for her the round of roadhouses and expensive restaurants. First, last, and all the time she was a business-woman, efficient in her job and solicitous to keep or improve on it. Her role of mistress was secondary.

For mental stimulus there was the James Clinic where he could sit up half the night, discussing over ale and cheese, medical problems and instances with unflagging zest. He could still do that without too much danger of the Tyres discovering it. But, being by nature neither secretive nor cowardly, he revolted from an association which, for reasons of policy, he must keep under cover. For he was not yet ready to make his final decision. To complicate the situation, James and Bernitz were forever putting up to him technical questions arising from cases which they urged him to see, cases in which there was neither profit nor glory, only trouble in case his furtive, off-hours surgical benefactions came to the attention of his own clinic. It was an irksome taboo. He felt like a bootlegger of his own professional skill.

Restlessness took possession of him. Though he performed his work thoroughly, it was with flagging enthusiasm. An inner urgency, when he was alone, kept impelling him to do something which he could not quite make out. Some threat to himself, to the integrity of his character, seemed impending. There was a subconscious impulse to escape, to protect himself. It intruded on his sleep and left him unrested in the mornings. Sometimes he had to take an after-breakfast drink to brace himself for the office. That was bad. He knew it was bad. But what was a man to do? He needed a rest. No; it wasn't rest he needed; it was change.

The problem clarified itself in an unforseen manner and place. His dreams that night, had been more than ever clouded, troubled. Out of them spoke clearly a testy and revered voice, Old Powsie's.

152

"Why not come back here and talk it over?"

With that Spen came slowly awake. The room, dim in the early light, was strange. He couldn't think where he was for a moment. Good lord! Had last night's liquor hit him as hard as that? Anyway, Powsie's dream suggestion wasn't liquor; it was a message. Spen spoke aloud:

"I'll go."

A voice close to him said sleepily, "Where'll you go?"

He sat up sharply. "Who's that?"

There was a trill of laughter. "Who d'you think you're sleeping with, darling?"

Then it all came back to him. It was Saturday night; Sunday morning, really. He and Kenny had driven a hundred miles to the small-city hotel where there was little likelihood of their being seen by anyone who knew them. Again the girl asked:

"Where is it you're going, Spen?"

"I've been dreaming. About Lakeview. About going back to have a look at the old joint.

"Why not? It might do you good."

He sank back by her side. "It was only a dream."

"Dreams sometimes make sense," said the sage Kenny.

"Do you believe that? Maybe this one does. By God, I will go, at that."

What would the clinic say to his absenting himself for the trip to Baltimore? In his present mood he was almost ready to tell them they could take it or leave it. He had to get into a clearer medical atmosphere for a spell, where he could breathe a different air.

He need not have concerned himself as to any opposition. Blanton Tyre was more than amiable. Why, certainly! Stay a week, if he liked. Doubtless he could pick up some new ideas. When he came back they would have a little conference on future arrangements.

First, however, there was that uterine cancer operation. The patient, a Mrs. Phillips, had been sent in by a prominent physician in Alabama. At first glance Spen saw that it was one of those practically hopeless cases where, nevertheless, an immediate operation might prolong, though it could not save, life. Privately his thought was that euthanasia would be better; put the unhappy woman out of her misery. However, that was not for him to decide. So long as there was a fractional chance it was up to him to take it.

Technically Spen did a brilliant piece of work. For a time it looked as if it might be measurably successful. Then followed shock, collapse, and the end. Tyre came to him with a long face of commiseration.

"Too bad, my boy. Too bad," he purred. "Well, well; a young surgeon is bound to have bad luck with some of his cases."

That was too much for Spen to take. "I don't follow you," he said tartly. "My age has nothing to do with a hopeless case like this." He was powerfully tempted to add, "And you knew how hopeless it was when you shifted it onto me."

As he emerged from Tyre's office, in none too good a temper, Kenny Mangan held him up with her sly and friendly smile, holding out a newspaper for his inspection.

"More publicity for the clinic. You're doing us proud."

The marked paragraph set forth that Dr. Spencer Brade of the Tyre Clinic was leaving for a few days' visit to the world famous Lakeview Hospital where he had been a staff member, with a view to checking up on important advances in his specialty, gynecological surgery.

"Who's our press agent?" he growled.

She put her finger to her lips. "Sshh! Dr. Hewlett handles that end. Very quietly, of course. Don't be gone too long, Spen."

"Not with you here," he answered, his ill-humor dissolved.

"I'll be waiting."

Baltimore was hearteningly familiar from the moment of Spen's stepping off the Pullman. It made him feel good to get back to the Center, though he still considered that he'd had a raw deal there. The first person for whom he asked was Dr. Powers. Old Powsie was at the hospital operating on a buck Negro from the slums. Would he care to attend? the secretary asked. He certainly would!

He looked on with a thrill of sheer professional delight while Power's chubby but amazingly dexterous fingers opened the abdomen, lifted up the cancer of the stomach that was snatching at the patient's life, and began calmly to place clamps for the resection. He watched while those fingers unhurriedly removed the tumor with the tissue around it and made an anastomosis between the remaining portion of the stomach and the small intestine that was a perfect as a textbook illustration.

In the dressing room outside the veteran shook hands with him. There was a perceptible reserve in his greeting, Spen thought.

"Let's see, now. You're at Charlesville, aren't you? How are you getting along?"

"Fine," said Spen with forced gaiety. "Business is booming." The surgeon grunted.

"That was a great job you did just now," Spen continued. "Too bad it had to be charity."

"Why?"

"You ought to have had a thousand dollars at least for it."

Old Powsie went on with his dressing. Having arranged his coat collar to his satisfaction, he commented:

"You men out in practice get a different slant."

"I saw Travers as I was coming in," remarked Spen.

"Travers is doing a competent job." Powers smiled. "I'm not saying that he is as well equipped as you. But he works conscientiously. He's a fellow of genuine ideals."

Wondering whether that last was to his address, Spen said, "He told me of your St. Louis offer."

"Yes. Very flattering. That's an excellent clinic."

"It's a wonderful offer. It ought to be worth fifty thousand a year."

"Forty," corrected the other.

"They're going to miss you terribly here."

"Oh no," returned Old Powsie equably. "They won't miss me. I'm not going."

"Not going!" cried Spen. "You're turning down forty thousand a year for—for—whatever it is here."

"Twelve thousand," supplied the other. "Which is quite all I need or want. If I went out there I'd be busy all day operating on people who could afford to pay for my services. Mind you, they'd be sick people and they'd really need the surgery I'd give them. But I'd be so busy that I wouldn't have time to take a cancer out of the stomach of that poor chap there." He broke off, looking searchingly at his former pupil. "How much of this sort of thing do you do now?"

Spen was glad to be able to answer, "I do it right along."

"That's good. Don't drop it. You need it. I suspect you particularly need it. And I don't mean professionally alone." He jerked his head toward the door. "For me, being able to operate on cases such as the one you've just seen means

155

freedom, independence, a justification of my existence and of what places like this have given me. I'd have to give that up if I went to St. Louis."

"I've joined a pay clinic," said Spen abruptly.

"So I've heard. Well, that's all right. You have your way to make. But I hope you've recovered from"—he smiled to take the sting out of his words—"the temper you were in when you left here. Childish for a man of your potentialities for service. Get money if you must. But never let yourself think of medicine primarily in terms of money. And remember this: the further we separate medicine from the dollar motive, the better the grade of medicine is going to be. Come in and see me, Brade," he concluded, shaking hands.

Leaving the Center, Spen dropped in at his old fraternity quarters where he found several convivial souls who were quite ready to organize a little party in his honor. By midnight they were playing poker and singing "Sweet Adeline."

Morning brought a slight headache but, nonetheless, a feeling of well-being. It had been like old times to get drunk and play poker until 3 A.M. What did it matter if he had lost his shirt? He could afford it now.

After breakfast he went over to the Center and made his way to the surgical division. Powers was not posted for operation this morning, but there was something going on in most of the other operating rooms. That suited him fine. He didn't feel quite up to meeting Powsie again. He had an idea the little man was disappointed in him; certainly there had been hints and warnings of it in yesterday's talk. He was a little depressed and annoyed at himself to discover how much he craved the older man's respect.

Hell, he thought as he put on a gown and tied the strings behind his back, he did enough charity work, what between the hospital and the James Clinic. Every week, practically. Well, he'd had to turn James down a couple of times lately, but it just happened that Tyre needed his help at the time on important cases—well, cases involving important people. He jerked a cap on with an irritated gesture and tied a mask across his mouth and nose.

Everyone in the operating room was intent on the work in hand when he descended the three short steps to the tiny observation balcony at the foot of the table. There were no other observers, and he could not recognize the surgeon whose face was entirely obscured by the mask. It was a delicate job of dissection that was being done. An inflamed gall bladder had to be removed carefully lest it be perforated and spill infection everywhere. Spen could not help admiring the skill of the quick fingers as the surgeon stripped off the peritoneal coat of the turgid red organ and carefully lifted it from its bed. The man was young; his hand was steady and deft.

Spen found himself remembering when he had stood in just this operating room, opening up his first abdomen. Powsie had been with him that day. He hadn't expected to operate, for the assistant residents that early in the game were not usually given anything but minor operations.

He remembered the leap of his heart. His first real operation. His pulse had quickened, but his hand had been steady when he'd picked up the shining knife the nurse had held out for him. This was what he had been working for. It was coming a bit sooner than he'd expected, but he was ready. His nerves were well under control, and there had been no hesitation as he made a quick, sure stroke with the knife, opening the skin and fat until the shiny fibrous surface of the aponeurosis came into view. He'd laid down the knife and taken up the hemostats with which to close the tiny spurting mouths of the bleeders. Watching this young surgeon skillfully remove the diseased gall bladder and begin closing the wound, Spen could almost recapture the mood of that moment, the moment when he'd felt that his career had really begun.

This man, wielding the needle holder with its dark strands of catgut streaming from the eye, looked familiar, but Spen could not recognize the eyes behind the glasses he wore. He made a quick mental calculation. Who would be resident now? Masters, Fleming, Sanders, he couldn't be sure which one. The operator finished closing the wound and stepped back, waiting for the nurse to untie the strings that held his gown together in back. Movie surgeons always stepped back from the table with appropriately grave faces and peeled off their gloves. Real surgeons never did it that way. They had to guard their hands, and there was too much danger of transferring infection from the outside of the glove to the hands. It was simpler to peel off the gown and gloves in one motion so that the contaminated side of the rubber never touched the hand.

The stocky young surgeon with the glasses pulled off his

mask and cap. Flick Fleming! Spen pulled down his own mask, and Fleming grabbed him.

"I had a feeling it was you, Spen," he said, "but I couldn't tell with the mask on."

"Same here. So you're resident now?"

"Masters had a little breakdown," Fleming said. "Had to go to Saranac, so I got kicked upstairs."

"Too bad. Masters was good."

Fleming lowered his voice. "He never will be again. Somebody has to break down every year, you know. Usually the best of us."

Spen did know, for once he was an assistant resident he himself had been forced to take three months off to prevent just such an occurrence. Workers at the Lakeview Center were always under strain. It was the same with the house staff of any large, busy hospital. Those who were intent on going ahead did most of the work; the rest loafed along on a minimum of exertion. All too often a capable man would be halted in his stride by a collapse of overstrained nerves, a mutiny of under-nourished digestive organs, sometimes by worse than that. The beds at Saranac were full of doctors, especially young ones.

"Come on up to my room," Fleming said.

Spen smoked while Fleming changed from the shapeless white suit he wore while operating into crisp white duck. Then they walked through the halls to the intern's quarters. Spen had walked through these halls many times. Then he had been eager, ambitious. Then he, too, had worn crisp white duck, had been cognizant of the respectful glances of the first-year interns and the fourth-year students, the shy smiles of the young nurses. Later he had turned the white duck uniform in for a long white coat, emblem of a teacher. He'd been proud to wear that coat, to pass through these halls, and to think that he was keeping up the traditions of the Center, that he was walking in the footsteps of the great whose feet had helped to wear grooves in the spotlessly scrubbed oak of the floors. Now he felt different: more settled, more assured, more practical. But—how much had he renounced of the things that had once made him proud to be a part of the institution? Thinking those thoughts made him resentful, doubly resentful because he could not get the idea out of his mind.

Fleming opened a door and let Spen in. It was such a room as he himself had lived in; in fact, just around the corner was the actual room. The battered desk, the huge dusty books on the shelf, the Gray's *Anatomy*—he went over to it and sniffed it, almost convinced himself that the smell of the laboratory was still clinging to it. Everything was familiar, even to the picture frame on the dresser, but the girl, of course, was a stranger. Every room had one. They'd promised to wait, those girls. Sometimes they did, but often the years proved too much, years of school, years of internship, years of barely making a living. Too often some bright-haired nurse, her trim beauty more disturbing in the starched whiteness of a uniform than it would be in an evening gown, put the girl back home out of the running. They rarely had a chance, those girls back home. But then, Spen thought cynically, they didn't do so badly. They usually married the young banker and had far more money than they could ever have on the meager income of the average doctor.

"It makes me homesick, Flick," Spen said. "There's nothing else quite like it."

"Yes, it's sweet for a while," said his friend. "But it's an interlude for me. I'm getting out."

"I know you are. Why in hell haven't you written me about coming to Charlesville?"

"I've been meaning to. You know what a louse I am about writing. You know Owen James of course."

"Yes. He's a cousin of Carol's."

"If he's as good as his letters he must be one grand guy."

"He is, in his way."

"What's the matter with his way?"

"Nothing for him. I wouldn't think there was much future in it for you."

"I don't know about that. This cooperative layout he's planning sounds pretty good on the surgical end. Lots of variety."

"Hm! Got some reserve layers of fat on your belly? You may need 'em. He's limiting his membership to the lowest-income group, you know."

"He warned me there wouldn't be much money in it," said Fleming. "That's all right with me. My grandfather left me some money; enough so I won't go hungry. I've done work in mill towns like Charlesville, so I know something of the conditions. All I want is a free hand to do what I think right in the surgical department."

"You'd get that. Anything that Owen James promises you can bank on. You'll also get some trouble, I'm afraid."

"As how?"

"There's liable to be a big fight in medical circles down there. Organized medicine doesn't exactly love these insurance schemes. They're regarded as dangerous and upsetting."

"But this one is different, isn't it? As I get it, it applies only to people who wouldn't be able to pay doctor fees, anyway."

"You've got to remember," said Spen, "that in mill cities there are always a few cheap skates who make their living out of fifty-cent practice among the very poor."

"And what do they give for it? Nothing."

"Or worse," agreed Spen. "But they're members of the medical societies, and their votes count the same as anybody else's. They'll fight like hounds to protect their measly half dollars."

"Oh, I don't mind a fight in a good cause," said Flick cheerily. "I'll be seeing you, then in the course of a month or so. How's the beautiful Carol?"

"Fine," said Spen mechanically. "She's in Florida right now."

"Anything doing?"

"How do you mean? Oh! No. She lost her baby."

"Tough!" said the other sympathetically. "Oh well, you've got lots of time."

Spen suspected Owen James who, with all his idealism did not lack shrewdness, of playing justifiable politics in his attempt to get Fleming as his aid. It was on the cards that he would be involved in a battle with the Academy of Medicine. To have a man with him who was backed by the prestige of Lakeview would be sound strategy. Foster Fleming might well prove to be James's ace in the hole.

Had Fleming been another sort, were he dependent wholly upon his practice, Spen would have warned him more definitively. But, as Flick had said, he liked a good fight. And Spen was by no means averse to helping Owen James out, so long as he was not personally involved.

Inevitably, as between classmates they fell into the what's-become-of-Smith line of talk. Flick had to keep track of most of the men. As the scroll unfolded it seemed to Spen that many of the best prospects had not made the most of their opportunities in a financial sense. There was Alsop, for instance. He had a swell position offered him with a large ethical proprietary firm

160

but had turned it down. And for what? For an underpaid job at Lakeview, out of which he was bounced at the end of a boot for his quixotic honesty.

One day the spoiled and neurotic young wife of old Blanding, who controlled the moneybags that made the Allergy Clinic possible, had come into the hospital. Alsop made the mistake of not rubbing her the smooth way, as Saunders, the professor, always did. Alsop made the mistake of telling her that her precious gas, her frequent "sinking spells," were really due to her own laziness, to too many bridge parties with rich pastries and salads, to too much riding behind a liveried chauffeur when she should be plodding the streets in sensible shoes. He did a good job of telling her earnestly and specifically what the trouble was. Every bit of it was worth thousands of dollars to her, thousands more than the honeyed words, the special massage treatments, and all the rest of the routine that Saunders prescribed for his rich neurotics to keep them satisfied. But she swore that she'd been insulted, and old Blanding had raised all kinds of hell at the special meeting of the Board of Trustees that he'd called. The result was that Alsop went out on his ear, and the Center had lost the best young man it had in medicine.

"I'd have bet he'd be a ten-thousand-dollar-a-year man by now," said Spen.

"Well, he isn't," answered Flick. "And he never will be. But he's doing a valuable job at the public clinic in Springfield."

Then there was Packard, who had graduated up toward the head of the class. What happened to him?

"Dead," said Flick. "Died last week. Hadn't you heard?"

"Good lord, no! What happened?"

"Pretty tricky sort of an accident. He was doing some research with tularemia. You know, rabbit fever."

"Why that? There's very little of it, isn't there?"

"More than you think. It knocks off quite a few people every year. Anyway, he was carrying a culture of the rabbit-fever bugs through the lab one afternoon late. A technician was hurrying out and slammed a door against his hand. It was a pretty messy wound. I fixed it myself."

"And well inoculated with *Bacillus tularense?*"

Fleming nodded. "It didn't take long after that."

"But what was Packard doing in the research lab?" Spen

161

asked. "The last I heard he was headed for a soft berth in his father's practice."

"He tried it a few months and didn't like it. Nothing would do but research, so back he came."

"What was·he getting when he was hurt?"

Fleming looked at him in surprise. "I don't know. Nothing much, I imagine. He was a Voluntary Fellow. Why ask?"

Spen shrugged. "It seems to me the idealists get the worst of it all around."

"Do you still believe as much in medicine for money as you pretended to when you left?" Flick inquired. "Or have you got over the cheap bluff?"

"Bluff? It was no bluff," Spen said harshly. "What the hell else is there to believe in?"

A special-delivery letter came from Blanton Tyre, asking him not to overstay his week. They needed him back. Cynically he interpreted this to mean that other difficult and unfavorable cases were pending which they intended to foist off on him. All right; they'd have to pay for that one of these days.

The talk with Flick Fleming had fortified his faith in the practical side of medicine. He did not go to see Old Powsie again. He did not want those bulwarks of common sense undermined by old-fashioned and impractical idealism.

CHAPTER XX

OWEN JAMES, meeting Spen downtown one morning, said, "Your friend Fleming is due next week."

"I'll be mighty glad to see him here."

"I hope he'll bring you around more often then you've been coming."

Spen mumbled something excusatory about having been pretty busy. Decidely Foster Fleming's arrival was going to complicate matters for him. Or would it? With a competent staff surgeon, James would not be in need of outside services. Still, Flick was just the enthusiastic sort to be calling up for him to hustle over there and look at some patient who presented a new, difficult, or interesting problem. Well, let that decision lie until it came along.

"We've broken ground for the new hospital and clinic," Owen said with satisfaction.

"That's fine," said Spen. "You've got it financed, then."

"I shouldn't have, but for the family. There was a little insurance money, but it didn't amount to much. Cousin Carrie Carskaddan is the one who saved the day. She came through magnificently." He chuckled. "She seems to think I was the one who saved her life, not you."

"That's all right with me."

"Not with me. I've tried to disabuse her on that point. But she wants to show her gratitude, even though misplaced, by backing the new plant, who am I to stop her! Cousin Candace is helping too." He hesitated. "And Carol. But of course you know about that."

Spen nodded.

"We'll have the cooperative clinic offices in the same building. It's the chance I've been waiting for."

"Owen, why don't you let that drop until you're in running order?" suggested Spen.

"Why should I? I thought you were in favor of the plan."

"So I am, in principle. But it's full of T.N.T., that scheme of yours. The old-liners are going to raise the devil."

"I can't help that," said Owen patiently. "Everything I try to do seems to stir up somebody." After a pause he asked, "When is Carol coming back?"

"Soon, I think," Spen answered.

But he did not know. Carol was intruding on his thoughts too often these days. He could not keep her out. Did he really want her back? Was there any possible satisfaction to be had from resuming the anomalous domestic life with its blank spots, its uncertainties, its complications, and its tensions? Obviously not, yet he found that he was impatient to see her again. Grahame Lodge ached with vacancy in her absence. He wanted to hear once more her laughter, to see her vivid face across the table, to get the light of her gay, clear intelligence and commentary upon the everyday occurrences of their existence. If that kind of companionship was not enough, at least it was something. Even Aunt Candace, with her dry, pungent humor, her shrewd, unkindly judgments, would be a welcome relief to the silence. There could be no mental or spiritual stagnation with those two around.

Several letters had come from Florida, light, natural, friendly. He had tried to respond in the same tone but had made a poor fist of it. The last two remained unanswered, except for a hasty post card saying that he was rushed to death, would write in a few days, which he had not done.

Now came her telegram, saying that she and Aunt Candace had decided to return by train and would be there in the morning. Spen deliberately cut out a party at the club, went to bed at ten o'clock without a drink, and rose in the morning feeling virtuous and fit.

The train was on time. Down the Pullman steps came Aunt Candace, followed by Carol, and Spen caught his breath in a pang of longing and regret. Carol was like a young girl, so gay and cool and lovely. She greeted him with a hand wave as he hurried up.

"Hi, Spen!"

"Hello, Carol. Glad to have you back." (Could she not hear in his voice that he was more than glad?)

She kissed him lightly. Aunt Candace said:

"How do you do, Spencer? You're not looking well." She sniffed the air as she shook hands. (Fooled her that time! thought Spen.)

"Haven't you been well, Spen?" asked his wife, scanning him.

"Yes. I'm all right. Working over hours a little."

"You show it. You're thin."

"I'll fatten up with you two to feed me," he said, forcing the note of familiarity. He busied himself giving directions about the baggage. When they were all in car he said to Carol, "By the way, an old friend of yours is in town."

"Who?"

"Foster Fleming."

"How swell for you, Spen! I liked him a lot. Is he here for long?"

"He's joining up with Owen James."

She received this thoughtfully. "Does that mean that you'll be doing less with Owen?"

"Naturally they won't need outside surgery now."

"I'm sorry about that. I think Owen needs you."

Miss Grahame amended grimly, "I think Spencer needs Owen James more than Owen needs him."

"Mutual alliance," said Spen lightly. "What about asking Flick for dinner?"

"Yes; let's do," said Carol. "Sunday, I think. Let's have Owen too."

"If you're going to make it medical," said Spen, "include Terry Martin of the Tyre Clinic."

"Will the Tyre Clinic and the James Clinic mix well?" inquired Aunt Candace.

"Martin will. Wait till you meet him."

As if to make up for time lost, Carol threw herself into the gaieties of the season. She was widely popular. The men of her set swarmed around her. Yet if Spen had been jealous, as he put it to himself, he could have found no ground for complaint. There was no one of her men friends to whom she gave preference over the others. How long would that last? he wondered, attractive as she was and besieged as she was. Only one of the circle was admitted to special intimacy. That was Owen James. After all, they were cousins of a sort.

James came to the dinner, disheveled and awry, as usual; also, as always, exhaling cleanliness and health, physical and moral. Flick Fleming and Terry Martin were very correct in dinner clothes, the latter curiously handsome in his saturnine fashion. Carol's gracious friendliness made everyone at home. The old lady was feeling festive and contributed to the gaiety. Altogether the event was a success from the start. Upon arrival of the coffee, which, in the household tradition, was the signal for departure of the ladies, Aunt Candace rose.

"I'd rather stay," annnounced Carol.

The guests were unanimous in approval.

"It'll be shoptalk," warned Spen.

"I like medical shop," she said.

Aunt Candace sat down. "I'll stay too," she said. (Applause.) She fixed Owen James, whom she adored, with a baleful eye. "One mention of pus and I leave," she said.

"Not a word shall be uttered that could bring the burp of distress to the throat of delicacy," he promised.

"Latin and rose water shall be our speech," added Spen. As an unobjectionable topic, he opened with the new insurance scheme. "Hear you've had to close your lists," he said to Owen.

"Yes; we're overrun already. Fleming will have his work cut out for him."

"All mill hands?" asked Miss Grahame.

"Practically. Those are the people we're after," answered the head of the project.

"Always looking for trouble, Doctor?" said Terry Martin, managing to infuse the cynical observation with an effect of respect and even affection.

"Who? Me?" said Owen. "I'm a timorous fawn. Run a mile any time to escape a row."

"You seem to step on a lot of toes while running."

"I've a one-track mind," confessed Owen. "If the toes are on the track I don't see 'em in time."

"It's a mighty straight track," put in the old lady.

"Leading via Grief Junction to Donnybrook Fair," said Terry. "Fleming, you don't know what you're letting yourself in for."

"Don't let them scare you, Flick," said Carol. "Owen's doing a grand job."

"Oh, I'm sold on the group idea," said Fleming cheerfully. "Even in a small unit like ours you can see that group medicine is ten times more efficient than the old system."

Spen smiled. "That's pretty close to medical heresy around here."

"I don't care," Fleming insisted. "You're in a group yourself. You must know that it's better for a patient to come to a group of doctors and be assigned to a specialist in his particular trouble, instead of fooling around with a man who practices by himself and doesn't have time to keep posted on every line. He can't possibly have the time."

"A lot of them still take a crack at being Jacks-of-all-trades," Spen pointed out.

"And are masters of none, as usual," croaked Terry.

"The best of you are bad enough," snapped the old lady. "I'm sure I don't want every Tom, Dick, and Harry with a diploma framed on his wall to be working on me."

"Certainly you don't," Fleming agreed. "If you're really sick you'll wind up in the hands of a specialist. Or, at least, you ought to. In a clinic you don't have to go through that intermediate period when somebody visits you every day and

166

runs up your temperature and your bill trying to find out what the trouble really is."

"Or opens you up to peek inside in the hope of finding out, before you find out how much he doesn't know," contributed Owen.

"Gentlemen! Gentlemen!" said Spen in mock protest. "Think of our code of ethics. We're not supposed to speak ill of our brothers in Aesculapius. At that, I don't believe we're ready yet to relegate the g.p. to the ash can."

"What's g.p.?" asked Aunt Candace. "Groping physician?"

"Ouch!" said Owen. "General practitioner."

"Don't you think medicine would advance faster if the present system were dropped in favor of one where all treatment was concentrated in hospitals and clinics?" propounded Fleming.

"Maybe it would," Spen admitted. "But change doesn't come that quick. Maybe health insurance is the best thing, but there's bound to be a fight before it comes. Everything worth while in medicine has come only through a fight."

"And look how many people died because the doctors were fighting," Owen James pointed out. "Look at Semmelweiss. He spent his life trying to make obstetricians wash their hands, but they went right on killing women for a long time afterward with infection carried from other people.

"And still do," snarled Terry Martin.

"Look at Pasteur," Owen continued. "He had a long fight before he got recognition. Even so obvious a thing as the use of anesthetics was laughed at and preached against. We've come a long way from the medicine they used a hundred years ago, but our progress is shot through with hypocrisy and dispute. One thing that makes me think health insurance must be a good thing is that so many doctors are against it."

"But surely the local medical association ought to back you up," said Aunt Candace.

Terry gave his short, unpleasant laugh. "You don't know 'em, ma'am. Neither does Fleming yet. He will, God help him! You'll have to join up, Fleming."

"Why should he if he doesn't want to?" demanded Carol.

"Everybody does," said Owen. "It's the open door to the State Medical, and so on."

"They admit on one's record, don't they?" asked Fleming. "I haven't any black spots on mine that I know of."

167

"I should think not!" said Carol warmly. "With your Lakeview service. You'll put him up, or whatever the process is, won't you Owen?"

Owen looked a little embarrassed. "I'm not so popular there, either."

"Why not?" she asked.

"Our insurance plan is cutting into the four-bit pill peddlers, for one thing."

"They don't run your medical society, do they?" asked Aunt Candace.

"No. Our boss does," Terry answered. "Brade's and mine. Blanton Tyre is the power behind the rostrum. Therefore," he went on deliberately, "it looks to me as if Dr. Fleming should be presented by his friend and former associate, Dr. Brade."

Spen shot a quick, startled glance at his associate. What the hell was he up to? Trying to put him, Spen, in a hole? Or testing him out? You never could tell how much Terry knew or what use he would be making of it.

"After all," he said, aware that everyone was looking at him, "I'm only a new member myself. I'd be tickled to death to do it. You know that, Flick. But it seems to me that one of the older men would be more appropriate."

Carol turned her eyes on Owen James, seeking to interpret by his expression what this meant. Owen's expression was uninterpretable. In fact, there seemed to be no expression discernible. His voice was equally neutral as he said:

"That might be better."

For the rest of the evening Spen seemed to Carol depressed and ill at ease. She took Owen aside.

"Is membership in the Academy important?"

"Not per se. But there would be some importance, on the wrong side, in being kept out."

"Surely there isn't any danger of that with a man like Dr. Fleming."

To this he made no reply but said thoughtfully, "Is Martin a particular friend of Spen's?"

"Spen has a great opinion of his ability."

"I don't understand Martin. He came to me just now and offered to stand for Fleming himself. At the same time, he warned me that he would be a poor sponsor for anyone. He's made so many enemies."

168

"I'll bet he's made them in a good cause," commented Carol, who had formed her own estimate of the man.

"That's my belief too."

"Whatever you decide, you know that you'll have Spen's backing," she said confidently.

He nodded. "We may need all the friends we have."

For a week after Carol's return Spen hardly got a word alone with Kenny Mangan. She seemed deliberately elusive, yet he could call to mind nothing that he had done to offend her. Kept overtime one afternoon, he found her at her desk, waiting, so he suspected, for him. Her small face was harried and resolute.

"Am I driving you home, Kenny?" he asked.

"Yes."

In the dimness of the car he put his hand over hers. There was no answering pressure. He said gently:

"What is it, Kenny?"

"Spen, I think it's time you and I quit."

"Why? Tired of me?"

"No; I'm not tired of you," she answered so low that the denial was hardly audible.

"Then why?"

"Your wife is back."

"What of it?"

She made a rather pathetic attempt at humor. "It may not be much of a face, this one of mine, but it's all I've got."

"I've never seen another like it," he said. "I'm rather crazy about it myself."

"Well, I'm not. But I wouldn't want it spoiled with vitriol or something."

Spen frowned. His throat hardened as he said, "You're talking rot. Ladies don't throw vitriol, Kenny."

"How would I know? I'm no lady. Just a tramp. But," she went on with increased strain, "I never did figure to be just one of a harem.

"If it interests you, I'm not living with my wife," Spen said sullenly. He felt humiliated at having to discuss Carol with Kenny, with any other woman.

"That's different," said the girl. "I had to know." She snuggled up to him. "I heard it was that way with you before. Servants talk, you know. But I was afraid maybe she had come back to you. Want to take me to dinner in some quiet place, darling? I've got news for you."

Kenny's news was not entirely new to her hearer. Blanton Tyre, she told him, was working openly toward the presidency of the State Medical Association. Locally there was dissension which might cost him the Academy's support and thus impair, if not ruin, his chances. The issue was Owen James's cooperative medical insurance. A powerful element of the profession was ready to gang up on the James lot, said Kenny.

Spen already knew enough of this to recognize the formidable force of the opposition. Had it centered in the cheap-Jacks of the profession, the half-dollar and dollar-fee drudges and pill pushers, it might have been disregarded as insignificant. But there was a large contingent of conscientious, if overconservative, men who honestly believed that the method threatened the very foundations of medical practice. It probably did, as they saw medical practice. Their position would be strong because it was rooted in principle and prejudice rather than in self-interest. Perhaps from a mixture of both with the latter predominating, Blanton Tyre would, as Spen knew, side with this element. His hostility to Owen James as a socially disruptive factor also entered in.

"I took a letter from Old Puffy to the chief of the State Hospital," Kenny told him. "Our respected Blanton is rounding up the old guard for a fight. Your wife's friend, Owen James, is liable to find a monkey wrench in the wheels, if he doesn't watch his step. I think, myself, he's a grand guy, though I don't know much about this new racket of his. Where do you stand on the thing, darling?"

"I'm hoping to keep out of it."

"Fat chance," said Kenny.

Spen was much of that opinion himself.

CHAPTER XXI

OUT OF A CLEAR SKY Carol Brade said to her husband a few days after her return, "Spen I haven't been fair to you."

"I've had some such thought myself," he answered with a grimness of intention.

She flushed hotly. "I don't mean *that*."

"I do."

"I've been thinking about Baby," she continued with an effort. "I blamed you for that."

"There was nothing I could have done if I'd been there, Carol," he said more gently.

"I know that now. But I held it against you that you weren't there as you'd promised to be. Castleman Tyre tells me it was a misunderstanding, that you didn't get word from the hospital right away."

"How did you happen to talk with Castleman Tyre about it?" he asked, astonished.

"I didn't. He wrote me in Florida."

"Wrote you? Wait a minute. I want to think this over."

Why on earth should Tyre have written Carol without saying anything to him about it? Conscience? Remorse for the trick he had played in not relaying the hospital's message at once. Not likely. In figuring out the Tyres one must seek more practical motivations. The solution presented itself. Rumors of an impending split in the Brade-Grahame ménage must have reached the clinic and been fortified by Carol's long absence. Loss of the Grahame connection might work to the detriment of the firm; hence the Tyre's interest. They would be anxious to see any existing differences patched up.

171

"I think I've got it," Spen said. "So Castleman told you of the delay in the message. Well, he was in a position to know. Go ahead."

Bracing her will, she lifted softly resolute eyes to his. "Spen, were you drunk that evening?"

"You took your aunt Candace's word for it that I was."

"I shouldn't have. Were you?"

Something in her appeal impelled him to be scrupulously, even meticulously honest with her. "In a sense, I suppose I was. I'd been working for hours under a strain. I was all in. On the way home I took a drink. It was a big drink, a double brandy. But ordinarily it would have done nothing to me. In my exhausted condition it knocked me out. Sometimes alcohol works that way. I ought not to have taken the chance. For that matter, though, I'm not sure I could have made the hospital without something. I'm sorry, Carol."

"I'm the one to be sorry," she said. "I ought to have known that you wouldn't deliberately let me down. After all, we'd grown to be pretty good friends. Let's forget it and go back to the old basis, shall we?"

The old basis. Pretty good friends. That was all she had to offer him. The disappointment stung him into saying:

"The old basis of debtor and creditor."

"I didn't mean that, and you ought to know it," she said reproachfully.

"When that's cleared up," he said, "there's going to be a new basis, one way or the other. But all right, Carol. Meantime we'll forget it."

Aftermath of the medical dinner party brought up the name of Foster Fleming in family conversation with a frequency which Spen found irksome. Aunt Candace had taken a fancy to the stubby, earnest redhead and prophesied great things for him.

"That's the sort of man you should have in your Tyre Clinic," she would say with conviction.

"But Spen is their surgeon," Carol protested. "They don't need another."

"You never can tell," said the old lady darkly.

"You don't look for any trouble in getting him into the Academy, do you, Spen?" Carol asked more than once.

"Why do you keep at me about it?" he retorted with an acrimony that surprised her, since he was scrupulously courteous, as a rule. "Anyone would think it was my responsibilty. James brought him down here; I didn't."

"Owen James is a man who stands by his friends," said Aunt Candace with meaning. "It's a family trait. That is why Carol is surprised."

Spen rose and left the table. He had an early appointment, he explained.

At the office the same incubus hovered. Blanton Tyre asked him leading questions about Fleming.

"I hear he's another radical," he said. "James will be raising the Red flag over his plant next.

"Dr. Fleming is no radical," said Spen shortly. "He's a friend of mine and a damned good surgeon."

News which relieved one anxiety for Spen came via Terry Martin, who rambled into Spen's office and slumped down in a chair.

"Owen James has fixed it up to have Dr. Charles Chadbourne present your friend Fleming's name."

Chadbourne was an aged and benign consultant with the position and prestige of a revered emeritus among the local profession. Nothing could be a better solution from Spen's viewpoint. Nonetheless, he felt it incumbent upon him to protest.

"I stood ready to do it, Terry. You know that."

"Oh, sure, I know it," said Terry. "Does Blanton Tyre know it?"

"What's that got to do with it?" said Spen sharply.

"Vulgar curiosity, my boy. Haven't you spotted my defects of breeding yet? I'm not up to the social level of this environment. One of these days I'm going to confess as much to Castleman Tyre. Then I'm going to hand him one soul-satisfying poke in the middle of his fat gut, and if it croaks him I'll go to jail, singing."

"He isn't worth it. Keep out of his way, as I do," advised Spen.

"That's okay for you. But I have to deal with him. Let me tell you what he's just done."

"Shoot. Get it off your laboring chest."

"He knows what I think of him. So he goes out of his way to pick flaws in everything I do. Well, this time he slipped. He's got a kid patient in the hospital that he's been treating for undulant fever. Told the family that's what it was and

173

everything. We've been checking the blood every now and then, and it was positive once for undulant but not any more than anybody's blood is liable to show sometimes. The other day I set up some tests and ran them myself. I got a beautiful Widal reaction for typhoid in a high dilution and wrote it on the report. Castleman never peeped. Probably didn't take the trouble to read the thing. But the boy's father did, and there was hell to pay. One of the nurses told me about it. Papa went to the mat with our respected associate and wanted to know what the hell? If his lad had typhoid why hadn't the doc said so? One guess what Castleman did."

"Claimed your test was wrong?"

"Of course. Said if the boy had typhoid he'd have recognized it long before."

"Why didn't he?"

"There were no rose spots. You know as well as I do that a lot of typhoid doesn't show that symptom, and these cases can't be diagnosed without the Widal test. So Mr. Baby Face Tyre comes and jumps me for getting a false positive. I set up another one this morning and took it in and stuck it under his nose. It was even more positive than the first. He had to back down. Now he's got to admit to the family that he was wrong all the time. And is he sore!"

Spen grinned enjoyably. "I'd like to ask him about it. Still, we all go wrong on diagnosis at times. I know I have."

"Sure. So have I. But we'd be men enough to admit it and take our medicine." The visitor unwrapped an oblong of chewing gum, slid it between his thin lips, and masticated it thoughtfully. "Spen," he said after a few moments, "I'm going to ask you a tough question."

"I'm listening."

"If you found that you were standing still in your work or maybe slipping a little, what would you do about it?"

Spen said sympathetically and honestly, "Don't let that slug Castleman get you down, Terry. I don't believe for a minute that you're slipping."

"Neither do I. But what about you?"

The blunt query brought Spen up in his chair like a jolt under the jaw. "Who's been criticizing my work here?" he demanded angrily.

"Nobody. Not here. You're doing what you're paid for and doing it well, but what about the charity ward?"

174

"You've been listening to nurses' gossip."

"Maybe I have. Nurses' gossip can do damage," returned the imperturbable Terry. "I only asked. If you're satisfied with the job you're doing, who am I to butt in?"

Startled and irritated though he was, Spen could still recognize the other's friendly intent. It impressed him the more in that, as he surmised. Terry Martin seldom went out of his way to concern himself with the interests of others. Spen was glad that he had controlled his first impulse toward throwing Terry out of his office. When his visitor added:

"What about a little drink?" Spen nodded, and they went out together.

Neither then nor thereafter did the pathologist resurrect the subject.

At dinner that evening Spen drank nothing. Perhaps for that reason, after turning in early, he woke up in the middle of the night, pestered by self-questionings that assailed him like a swarm of mental mosquitoes. What had Terry Martin heard? Were the hospital interns who assisted respectively at his operations daring to criticize? Or was it only the idle chatter of the wards? Could it be that he was unconsciously letting down in his technic, his standards?"

If so—while he didn't admit it—he could adduce excuses on the ground of overwork, weariness, strain. But did the strain and weariness come from overwork? There were nights when he had danced or played bridge late at the club during Carol's absence, other nights when he had been with Kenny Mangan, that had left him so spent that he could not face the ordeal of the operating room next morning without a bracer. No hand could be one hundred per cent steady in such circumstances. No judgment could be unremittingly up to par.

His temper too, had suffered. Spencer Brade had always held fast two traditions: the medical tradition of giving the best of himself to every case in his care, the personal tradition of gentle upbringing, imposing on him consideration and courtesy toward all, and particularly toward his inferiors. With a pang of contrition he recalled that big, homely horse of a scrub nurse whom he had found quietly crying to herself in the sterilizing room after an operation in which a dozen small things—if anything is ever small or unimportant over the operating table—had gone awry. He remembered the quick, sensitive flush on the face of that junior intern whom he had so sharply called down for a matter in which the boy may not have been at fault at all.

What about his own technic? That was something he had always prided himself on keeping at the peak of efficiency. Was his procedure becoming less skillful, less sure? Were his surgical scars the fine, narrow lines they ought to be? Did they cause the least permissible damage to the bodies they closed. He had trained himself to be gentle with tissues, handling organs carefully, operating with every faculty addressed to the ultimate combination of skill and speed that he might hold to a minimum the shock to the patient. Was he easing up ever so little on the requirements he had set for himself?

That uterine operation on the backwoods cracker's wife the other morning. Hadn't he left a raw area when he closed over the stump of the uterus? The woman had been complaining of pain. Adhesions might be forming there, adhesions that were liable to tie up a loop of intestine, causing dangerous obstruction.

Then there was the plastic operation he'd done two weeks ago. That suture line shouldn't have broken down; he hadn't expected it to. But it had, and healing had been delayed weeks when it should have taken days. Infection, contamination, had crept in somewhere. Tissues had been crushed, making a fertile field for the infection. Blanton Tyre's wounds often broke down, but Tyre was a bungler, unfit to pick up the knife he was so quick to wield. He'd cut his throat before he'd turn into a butcher, like his chief, thinking not of the way to do the operation but of how much he was going to get for it, how soon he could get it done and be on to the next one.

Spen's restless mind reconsidered that plastic incision. Why had it not healed? Had the nurse erred, or one of the interns? In his heart he knew where the contamination had occurred. He had seen that torn glove but had been in a hurry that morning because he had an early appointment with a patient who had money and influence, a patient who might not need surgery himself but who would have friends, rich like himself, to help boost those checks he deposited on the morning of the first and fifteenth. He hadn't scrubbed quite ten minutes that morning, he remembered now. He hadn't had time for it, and he hadn't had time to change his glove as soon as he discovered the hole. That was where the germs had entered the wound, from his not quite clean fingers. Six months ago he would not have overlooked the

176

presence of that tiny hole in his glove, would not have shaved those two minutes off the scrubbing time.

In those sleepless hours he faced self-conviction. He saw it clearly now. He had let down. What he needed was the bracing effect of cleaner, sterner associations. Owen James project was far from perfection, technically judged, but there could be found the scientific and altruistic spirit in that blend which makes for the highest medical achievement. Men like Flick Fleming and Bernie Bernitz on the technical side, like Owen James on the idealistic side, were the tonic he needed to restore his faith in himself, his fervor for his profession.

He would make it a practice to go there regularly—twice a week, anyway; three times, if possible—to hold himself ready for any emergency call that the understaffed hospital could not meet. If the Tyres didn't like it they could go to hell. No need to tell them that yet, though. The issue need not be met finally until just before Carter Hewlett's contract terminated. Spen was confident of his ability to balance his life satisfactorily between the Tyre Clinic, representing money and success, and the James Hospital, typifying service and altruism.

Carol had once recalled him to a legendary practitioner called Dr. Jekyll who had much the same idea.

One of Blanton Tyre's oldest and best-paying professional connections was with the Folsom family. The Folsoms ran to nerves. Without being precisely hypochondriac, they were definitely introverts on the subject of health, and hence were pay dirt assaying high. One or another of them was always getting out of repair, and there was plenty of money to pay unquestioningly for the more or less expert tinkering of the Tyres. That was a poor week in which at least one of the clan was not to be seen entering the luxurious quarters of the city's most fashionable private clinic. Consequently it was no surprise to Spen to have his senior associate inform him of an impending call from Rogers Folsom, the head of the family. There followed Blanton Tyre's telephone summons.

"Could you come across to my office, Dr. Brade? I have a little problem in which I need your help."

Spen found a slim, fidgety man seated in Tyre's sanctum. He was familiar with the type: a hustler, a go-getter, putting everything he had into whatever he did, wiry and high-strung, an inevitable prey to digestive disorders. He knew also, that Folsom, beneath his brittle exterior, was a useful citizen, progressive and public-spirited, giving his time and money generously to such causes as appealed to him. Blanton Tyre made the introduction:

"You know Mr. Folsom, Dr. Brade. Dr. Brade is Lakeview-trained."

"My wife wants to take me up to Lakeview for examination," said the patient. "I don't quite see it."

"No need; no need," purred Tyre. "We're bringing Lakeview to you."

He clicked on the switch of the X-ray box beside his desk. On the illuminated field Spen saw a stomach filled with opaque barium mixture used to visualize the digestive tract. Just below was the duodenum, the narrowing channel where the intestine begins, with a tiny nick in the smoothness of its outline which might have been passed up by a casual eye.

"What do you think, Doctor?" asked Tyre.

"It looks very like a duodenal ulcer."

"That is my own opinion. Also, I may add, that of our roentgenologist. I'm sorry our good friend Mr. Folsom has an ulcer, but glad there is no disagreement on diagnosis."

The caller grinned weakly. "I read a book once called *When Doctors Disagree*."

Tyre's laugh boomed through the place. "Seldom happens here." He addressed Spen: "There's the matter of treatment."

"Until I have more of the history," began Spen, only to be cut off by his senior's breaking in heavily:

"I have been telling Mr. Folsom about the relative merits of medical and surgical procedure in cases of this type. Of course he could try a period of medication."

"That would be my idea," agreed Spen.

It was in accord with the best Lakeview tradition and teaching: a strict regimen. diet, careful medication for six months at least. If this failed of favorable response it would then be time enough to resort to the knife. But what was wrong with Blanton Tyre? His face had taken on an ominous cast.

"I said that it *could* be tried," he boomed. "Whether it should be is quite a different matter. It would involve a distasteful diet, constant drugging, a long and irksome routine. I fear it would seriously interfere with Mr. Folsom's way of life. He is a very busy man, you understand."

"What's the alternative?" asked Mr. Folsom unhappily.

"Surgery," answered Tyre. "Mind, now, I'm not trying to

rush you into anything, Folsom. That is quite contrary to my principles. I can only tell you what I should consider best in my own case. A gastroenterostomy."

"That means cutting out the ulcer, doesn't it?"

"We-ell, short-circuiting it to let the food pass by the ulcer until it heals. Two weeks in the hospital. Possibly a month's vacation. And there you are!" said the adviser briskly.

Spen hoped that his disgust was not showing in his face. If an operation was necessary at all it must be a radical one, removing the ulcer-bearing area, not any such shoddy makeshift as Tyre advocated. He, Spen, would be elected to do the trick, if operation were decided upon.

Mr. Folsom asked the question which nine out of ten patients propound under surgical threat:

"Can I be sure of complete cure?"

Blanton Tyre spread his plump hands. "Only quacks guarantee cure. Nothing is one hundred per cent sure in surgery. But in this case, practically. Practically certain, I should say. Don't you agree, Dr. Brade?"

"Not unreservedly, I'm afraid," said Spen quietly.

Tyre's jowls tightened over his clamped jaws as the patient turned to the speaker.

"I suppose I'm a coward," he said. "But frankly I dread an operation. I dread everything about it: the anesthesia, the knife, everything."

"Most normal people do," Spen assured him sympathetically.

"Is it dangerous?"

"No." Spen was glad to be able to say so much conscientiously.

"But you don't agree with Dr. Tyre that a cure is practically certain?"

"There are two schools of thought." He was letting his chief down as gently and tactfully as possible. "Many surgeons would agree with Dr. Tyre. At Lakeview we have swung to the other opinion. Our figures indicate that three fourths of all duodenal ulcers yield to medical care."

"And what about surgical, then?" Mr. Folsom pressed the point.

"There is trouble afterward in ten per cent or more of the operative cases."

"And cure in ninety per cent," put in Tyre triumphantly. "So we have ninety per cent surgical success as against only seventy-five per cent medical results."

Spen was itching to point out the speciousness of the argument. He did not need to. Folsom did it for him, directing his shrewd regard upon the elder physician.

"Wait a minute, there! If I've got a seventy-five-per-cent chance of being cured without going on the table, why shouldn't I take that chance first?"

Blanton Tyre shrugged his heavy shoulders. "It's up to you," he replied. "I told you I'm not trying to rush you into anything."

"Will you work out the diet for me?" Folsom asked Spen, patently excluding the senior.

"It's hardly my department," Spen hastened to say. "I'm a surgeon. Dr. Tyre would handle the medical regimen better than I."

"Wait a moment, Folsom," said Tyre as the caller reached for his hat. "I'll walk along with you."

(Is he going to try to scare him into the operation, after all? thought Spen.)

Half an hour later Tyre stood, lowering, in Spen's doorway.

"I've got a thought to leave with you, Brade," he growled. "We're here to sell the public all the surgery we can. Legitimately, of course; legitimately. Surgeons don't make a living by dodging operations—or responsibility."

He was gone before Spen could find words to fit his outraged indignation. Dodging, eh? So that fat, dumb bungler pretended to think that he, Spencer Brade, was evading operative procedure because he was afraid of it. It was a stupid shot in the dark. But it hurt. All right; they'd have it out in the morning.

Next morning Blanton Trye greeted him with the customary geniality. He did not mention their near quarrel. But there was no operation for acute duodenal ulcer posted on the bulletin. Spen made sure of that.

Though Tyre's savage stab rankled, Spen felt pretty well satisfied with the outcome. He had proved to himself and to his superior that, even in the Tyre atmosphere, he could make good without compromising his professional principals. Round one to him. He was inclined to credit himself with a knockout.

Within a week Rogers Folsom called Spen personally on the phone. Preferring to avoid any needless offense to his chief, the junior referred him to Blanton Tyre.

"No, no," said Folsom. "This is your specialty. It's my daughter, Mrs. Mark Ramsay."

"Anything wrong?" Spen asked.

"I'm afraid so. We've wired Mark to come back from Washington. She is having a lot of pain."

Spen called Blanton Tyre, and the two men drove to the Folsom estate up the river. It looked to Spen much like a tubal pregnancy gone wrong. Tyre pursed dubious lips but said nothing in contravention, leaving the diagnosis to the younger man. (Giving me rope to hang myself, thought Spen.) As the evidence became more pronounced he decided upon removal to the Markland Hospital for immediate operation.

The event proved him correct; prompt action alone saved the young wife. Both of the doctors were particularly pleased, since the outcome should go far to eliminate from Folsom's mind any unfortunate impressions caused by the difference of opinion in the Tyre office. Blanton came to Spen's office next afternoon, bland and purring.

"That was an excellent piece of work, my boy. Not too easy a diagnosis, either. A good thing, a most fortunate thing that we hit squarely on the condition."

With amusement Spen noted that "we." He suppressed the amusement. Tyre leaned against the doorjamb, chatting. The telephone rang. Kenny Mangan's voice, crisp and distinct and with the quality of projecting itself clearly from a receiver for all to hear, said:

"Hello. Dr. Brade?"

"Speaking."

"The James Hospital wants you."

Spen glanced at his visitor. Would he leave? With a pleasant smile Tyre lounged over and eased his heavy form into a chair.

"Go right ahead," he said. "Don't mind me."

"Is it Dr. James?" Spen asked.

"No. Dr. Fleming. Just a moment. Here he is."

Flick Fleming's excited voice—he was one of those enthusiasts who are habitually excited over a case until the work was in hand, when they became coolly practical—said:

"Hello, Spen. You busy?"

"Not specially."

"Come on over here, then."

"What's on your mind?"

"I've got a perfectly swell pulmonary embolism."

"Dead yet?"

"No. Almost died, but we stimulated him."

"Who is it?"

"What does that matter?" answered his friend impatiently. "It's a lovely case. Looks to me like we might try an embolectomy. It's ticklish, of course. I want your advice."

"Right," said Spen. "I'll be over."

"Make it snappy, won't you?" Fleming urged. "You know what it would mean if we got away with it."

Spen started putting away his papers when Blanton Tyre interposed:

"That was the James Clinic, wasn't it?"

"Yes. The hospital."

"It's pretty far out of our way, going to the Markland Hospital."

"I'm not due at the Markland this afternoon."

"Didn't I speak to you about it? Dora Ramsay is running rather more temperature than I like. There are other minor symptoms. I called to take you up there with me."

(Then why the hell didn't he say so at first? thought Spen angrily.)

Aloud he said, "It's rather a pressing case of Fleming's."

"I thought it was understood that your—er—casual interest there was not to interfere with your regular duties here," said Tyre suavely.

"I haven't allowed it to," retorted the other.

"At least you will admit that your first obligation is to your own patient."

He had something there! Grabbing his hat, Spen strode into the waiting room. Kenny looked up, impersonal, expressionless, correct as always.

"Call Dr. Fleming back," he directed her. "Tell him that I've had an unexpected call to a critical post-operative development."

"Yes, Dr. Brade."

"I'll come to him later."

"Very well, Dr. Brade. Shall I telephone you at the hospital?"

"Yes. . . .No. Let it go."

He could see Flick's surprise and disappointment; hear him let fly one of his compound comminuted curses. Spen felt like cursing on his own account. Well, there was no way out of it.

Even if Tyre were putting over a fast one there was nothing he could do but accept it. And certainly Flick's operation couldn't wait. Minutes counted on the chances of life in such cases.

At Dora Ramsay's bedside he found an apparently normal patient. Miss Carr, a favorite nurse of Blanton Tyre's, was in charge. Spen studied the chart. True, there was a slight upcurve in the temperature line, but nothing out of the usual, nothing to alarm. His eyes slowly came around to his superior's face. Tyre said to the nurse:

"Any recurrence of that troubled respiration, Miss Carr?"

"Not for the last hour, Dr. Tyre," she answered smoothly.

"No spasmodic symptoms?"

"No sir. She's quite easy now."

"Her color is distinctly better."

"Yes, Dr. Tyre."

It was like a well-practiced rehearsal. Spen put a few questions of his own. Miss Carr's replies were guarded, carefully indefinite.

"There's nothing for me to do here," he said crisply to Tyre. "Have them call a taxi for me, please," he requested the nurse.

"I feel easier about her for having you see the case, my boy," said the senior heartily.

At the James Hospital Spen found Fleming looking depressed.

"I want to see that case," he said.

"What's the matter with my seeing him now?"

"He's gone to glory. How's your patient?"

"Doing all right," said Spen heavily.

So that was Tyre's way of serving notice that the James association would not be allowed to continue indefinitely. Decidedly the second round had gone to Blanton Tyre.

CHAPTER XXII

"Ask kenny," said little Miss Mangan with the pert grin which she kept for unofficial occasions. "Kenny knows."

"Does Kenny know what Kenny looks like?" said Spen somewhat irrelevantly. "A wise and pretty gnome."

"Sure, I'm wise," returned the girl. "I keep my ears open. The Tyres have got loose tongues. What I pick up would surprise a lot of people in this town. They wouldn't sleep so well."

Spen idly watching her mix a highball for him and a lemonade for herself at the icebox in her small kitchen, the roommate being conveniently away. "All-night emergency case," would sufficiently explain his absence from home if any excuse were needed. Carol never asked questions. But at the breakfast table, to which he always returned, since it was expedient for him to be out of Kenny's quarters before the apartment house began to stir, Aunt Candace sometimes regarded him with suspicion or remarked upon his washed-out aspect.

"I'm asking Kenny," Spen now said to her. "What do you know that's so important?"

"It's in the bag for our Blanton."

"You mean the State Medical presidency?"

"Yes. He's going all out against socialized medicine. The James racket is to be his test case and horrible example."

Spen frowned. "It isn't a racket, Kenny."

"You're telling me!" she retorted. "It's the best thing ever happened for the poor in this man's town. That won't stop our Fatty."

"He isn't going to prefer charges against Owen James or anything like that, is he?"

184

"He would if he dared. Dr. James has got too much society pull. He's related to half the big families in town, including yours. Tyre is too smart a politician to go after game of that size."

"What's his game, then? Try to undermine the clinic?"

"Clinic. Hospital. Health insurance. The whole layout."

"He's tried it already. It isn't working."

"This'll work. Anyway, he and Castleman believe it will. They're ganging up to reject Dr. Fleming's application at the fall meeting. If they get away with it by a fair margin they'll cook up something else. I don't know what. Haven't got that far yet."

"The dirty bastards!" Spen burst out. "I beg your pardon, Kenny."

"You needn't to. Diagnosis confirmed. That's what they are. They'll try anything they think they can put over."

"Give me a drink and let's forget it, honey."

Sitting on the kitchen table sipping her lemonade, with her hand on her lover's shoulder, the girl said:

"We won't have many more nights together for a while, darling."

"Why not?"

"My big sister's coming up from Galveston."

"Which sister?"

"Adele. The oldest one. She brought me up."

"She did a swell job," returned Spen with smiling conviction.

"That's as may be. She'd have forty fits if she knew about us. Delly is about as near a saint as they come."

"I'm just as well satisfied *you're* not," Spen said. "How long will she be here?"

"That depends. There's something wrong with her."

"Anything I can do, honey?"

"Yes. That's why I'm getting her up here. I'm worried over what she writes. I don't believe her doctor down there is any good."

"When is she coming?"

"In a week or so. I want you to go over her."

"Of course. Any time. Glad to."

"I've got a lot of faith in you, Spen," said the girl trustfully.

In the early dawn as he was dressing she gave him an additional bit of information which had slipped her memory the night before.

185

"Our blessed internist is getting the boot. Is he sore! Things ought to be shaping up for you pretty soon."

"Do you still think I ought to quit the clinic, Miss Weisenheimer?" he taunted.

On this point Kenny was obstinate. "Nothing's holding you but the money. You'd rather work with the James crowd and you can't deny it."

"I'm still working with James," he retorted with such a rasp that she came back at him with:

"Don't get in a snit over it. And when our Blanton approaches you stand out for your price."

"Thirty pieces of silver?" he asked sardonically.

"Come and kiss me good-by and don't be a simp," she said.

Evidence of Blanton Tyre's slick work became evident to Spen now that Kenny had opened his eyes. Here and there he was hearing depreciatory rumors about the James project. The *Evening Leader* produced an editorial, obviously inspired, deriding the "medical cosseting of the slums." Untraceable derogatory whispers about both Fleming and Bernitz were going the rounds.

The strategy of the attack was plain. In order to join the State Medical and, through it, the all-powerful American Medical Association, Fleming or any other adjunct to the James forces must be first admitted to the local Academy. Membership in all these bodies was essential if he was to receive the official certification of his capacities as a surgeon, which was a prerequisite to recognition in his chosen field. Thus good men could not afford to associate themselves with James at the cost of exclusion. On the other hand, James could ill afford to have his institution staffed by doctors lacking the fundamental credentials of organized medicine. This would deprive hospital and clinic of official recognition. Hence the critical importance of the fight directed upon Foster Fleming.

Spen had expected an approach to the subject on Blanton Tyre's part for some time before it came.

"Want to talk to you a minute, my boy." Tyre motioned the junior to his office. Spen took a seat, declined a cigar, lighted a cigarette of his own.

"It's about this fellow Fleming. I suppose you've heard of his nerve in applying for membership in the Academy."

"I don't quite know what you mean by nerve," said Spen

coolly. "Dr. Fleming is a Lakeview man. That ought to establish his standing."

"Oh, I know, you Lakeview men all stand together," blustered Tyre.

"What are the objections to Fleming?" persisted Spen. "I always assumed that admission to the Academy was a matter of proper qualifications."

"What about ethics? Don't you figure medical ethics as a qualification?"

"I've never heard Fleming's questioned."

"Well, I'm questioning them," returned the other hotly. "He's a partner in that damned communistic project of Owen James'."

Seldom had Spen seen his principal so wrought up. Something must be creaking in the machinery of his strategy.

"Insurance projects have worked out in other parts of the country," Spen pointed out. "Look at the Ross-Loos group in Los Angeles."

"Who cares what they do in Los Angeles or anywhere else!" Tyre shouted, red-faced. "We don't want any of it down here."

"All right," Spen said. "We'll say that any kind of insurance in medicine is bad. But what's going to be gained by hampering an able chap like Fleming in the practice of his profession? If the scheme is wrong why don't you attack it at the source? Why don't you go after Owen James?"

He observed with relish his chief's temple arteries pumping hard over something difficult to follow.

"That infernal hypocrite!" Tyre snorted. "We'll get him yet. The first consideration for us ethical doctors is to defeat this Fleming application. Why, if this idea of James' should spread, it would affect the income of half the doctors in town. It might even affect ours," he added in a tone of profound shock.

"I don't think the Tyre Clinic need worry over that type of competition," said Spen pacifically.

"Well, no; perhaps not," agreed Tyre, mollified. "It is groups like ours that will be expected to maintain the high standards of the profession and to protect the interests of our fellow physicians not so fortunately situated. Well, I merely wanted to be sure that you would be at the meeting. The fourteenth. Put it on your calendar, my boy."

Spen nodded. Apparently it had not occurred to his chief to

doubt that he would vote "right." As he opened the door Tyre fired a parting shot:

"It's wild-eyed, long-haired, socialistic notions like this that pave the way for state medicine and crooked political control. And then where would the decent practitioners be!"

Often enough Spen had heard the specious arguments against any application of cheap medical aid to those unable to pay standard fees. Most of the other practitioners fell for them. The present system of practice must not be changed. Any alteration, any reform, would be disastrous, would bring the government in, would make every doctor an employee of the state and mix politics with medicine.

Spen knew that this needn't be true. A thousand instances could be cited. The United States Public Health Service had never known the taint of politics, there was no possible criticism, except in carping detail, of the work it did wherever the American flag was flown. The army and the navy had built up medical organizations that were the envy of civilian medicine. Spen knew all these things, but he also knew that the average doctor didn't want things different because he was afraid he wouldn't make as much money as he was making before. And sometimes he didn't want change because he knew that in a social medical system there would be some check on a man's ability after he passed the state-board examinations, some requirement so that a doctor not only had to learn in the first place, but that he must go on learning while he worked, keeping up with new things, adopting the new ways of combating disease in the light of modern knowledge. And when such a check was made a lot of them would go by the board, a lot of deadwood would be lopped off, and medicine would be the better for it. Owen James's project had a lot less connection with state medicine than a representative's being able to go to the Naval Hospital in Washington free of charge just because the people elected him to office and paid him a good salary. But because Owen's work smacked of social change he was going to be throttled, politely, by a company of high-minded professional gentlemen. Not with Spen's help!"

Seeking moral support for his position, Spen went on a comparatively easy morning into the laboratory where Terry Martin was busy transferring cultures to new media in order to make up a set of vaccines for a particularly severe case of arthritis that Spen had seen in consultation with Carter

Hewlett a few days before. Terry turned, his lead-platinum wire in one hand, culture tubes in the other, and smiled his satyr's grin.

"Got your voting orders yet?"

"Orders?" repeated the caller, misliking the form of the query.

"Sure. Orders. Vote right, save the honor of the profession and make the world safe for the upright medical money grabbers. Or else."

"That's what I want to talk over with you when you're through. Go ahead and finish."

Terry nodded and lowered his poised wire. Silently Spen looked on while Terry deftly pulled cotton plugs from glass tubes of media, flamed the wire momentarily in the blue point of the Bunsen burner beside him, and transferred a drop of the culture from one tube to another. Tomorrow there would be a cloudiness throughout the entire length of nutrient broth in the tubes as the bacteria multiplied by millions in the new fresh, medium. Terry would then kill these myriads of organisms, and their dead bodies would make a vaccine, harmless when injected into the body, yet tremendously curative because the body would begin to hum with activity, building up protection against these germs, just as if they had been alive. It had to be accurately done, this vaccine making, or some of the bacteria might not be killed, causing disastrous results when injected.

Terry tapped the cotton plug into the last tube and put it in the rack on the table. He shoved the rack into the incubator, already three fourths filled with similar racks, and closed it carefully. Then he washed his hands thoroughly with soap and water and finally alcohol.

Spen stood up. "This isn't a good place to talk."

"I get it," agreed Terry, reaching for his coat. "Castleman is still lurking around. Little pitchers have big ears. Also little sons of pitchers. Let's trip it lightly over to the St. Charles bar."

Over the drinks Spen said, "You're going to the Academy meeting tonight, I suppose."

"Well, I am," said Terry. "Feeling as I do about most of our esteemed brothers in Aesculapius, I hardly ever attend their damn love feasts. But this one time I'll be present."

"Fleming is going to need all the support he can get."

"And then some." Terry looked at him keenly. "I'm not so sure I'll vote for your friend."

"*What?!*"

"Keep your shirt on, Spen. I've been doing some figuring. From our boss's point of view, Fleming doesn't count. The whole business is the opening gun in the campaign against Owen James."

"Of course."

"Who's the more important to the town, James or Fleming?"

"That isn't the question," answered Spen uneasily.

"Maybe it is. Blanton Tyre wouldn't go into a fight like this without an ace in the hole. Isn't that right?"

"Probably."

"I've got it doped out. Here's his ace. The State Insurance Law provides that any concern selling insurance must have a deposit—a big one in this case—placed with the commission before they can operate. James must have overlooked that. Anyway, where would he raise the price? Tyre and his gang can get out an injunction and put a crimp in the scheme any day."

"Then James is ditched," said Spen, aghast.

"Not that easy. It would raise a hell of a stink. James has a strong following. The kickback on Tyre's candidacy wouldn't be so good. So that'll be held for a last resort. Fleming is the other string to the Tyre bow."

"I'm not so sure I get that."

"If he can put his scheme of excluding Fleming through, James can't afford to keep Fleming on his staff."

"You don't know Owen James."

"I know Fleming. Anyway, I know his type. He'll resign rather than compromise the clinic. With him out of the way, Tyre can turn on the heat to keep anybody James hires from getting recognized by organized medicine. Finally he'll find that he can't get any good man to do his surgery. Half of the work of a clinic like theirs is bound to be surgery, and if he can't deliver the goods the whole project has to go under. It's slow death, instead of the quick end by the insurance method."

"If it's slow there's always a chance, medically speaking," Spen said. "Then you're going to vote with Tyres."

"Like hell! Not any more than you are. I couldn't have a hand in blocking a man of Foster Fleming's caliber."

"But your argument just now?" Protested Spen.

"Pretty, ain't it?" Terry flashed his demonish grin. "Sometimes I talk to hear myself talk. All crap. Casuistry. No appeasement is my motto."

"Think there's any chance of pulling Fleming through?"

"Not much," answered Terry sunnily. "But we'll put up a fight, anyhow."

Whatever qualities of the strategist Blanton Tyre possessed, subtlety was not one of them. Otherwise he would hardly have waited until the very day of the medical-society meeting to make his pass at his subordinate. He came into Spen's office, glowing like an obese sunbeam.

"Sign on the dotted line," he burbled.

"What would I be letting myself in for?" asked Spen.

"The best deal any young surgeon ever got in Charlesville, my boy. I spoke to you of a new arrangement sometime back."

"Yes."

"Now I can talk of terms. Dr. Hewlett is leaving us. Good riddance. Poor Schultz' case is not the only blunder he has made. The way is now clear for the office reorganization of which I spoke to you. You may remember."

"Yes," said Spen. (Did he remember!)

"Castleman and I have been working out the plan. The net profits would be divided into three parts. As founder and head of the clinic, I would take fifty per cent. That, you will agree, is fair."

"Yes; I think that's all right," agreed Spen cautiously.

"The remaining fifty per cent would then be divided equally between you and my son."

Castleman Tyre wasn't worth it to the clinic. He wasn't worth anything like it. But Spen could not well say that to the father. Besides, it should mean close to twenty thousand dollars a year for him. His pulses jumped. He could soon be free of all obligation to Carol; quit himself of that humiliating bond which he had so willingly accepted, not forseeing the intrusion of a powerful personal feeling toward his bargain wife. Now he would be in a position to demand a showdown. Not that he had much hope of her. But at least there would be some dignity to his status. He could, at length, meet her, man to woman.

As he was about to express his gratification and gratitude to his chief Terry Martin's warning popped into his mind: that he was practically a necessity to the Tyres. Why, then, be overthankful for a deal out of which they got quite as much as

191

he? Too much enthusiasm would be weak business policy. He thought a moment, then said:

"Would this be a year-to-year contract?"

"Hewlett's was. We should prefer yours to be a longer term. I was thinking of five years."

Incontinently Old Powsie's keen and severe face rose before Spen. What would the old boy say? That five years devoted to pure commercialism, at his time of life, would permanently set his professional character. All right; why not? Since it would set it in the mold that he had, himself, chosen. He said:

"That is an interesting proposal, Dr. Tyre. I should like time to think it over."

Tyre seemed taken aback. Evidently he had expected the young man to jump at the offer. "How much time?" he asked.

"I can't tie myself down. There are other considerations."

The other played his final card. "There is another proviso that we had in mind. If you are prepared to give us all your time, all your efforts, to the exclusion of all outside professional activities, you can doubtless enlarge our practice on the surgical side where we have been wea—er—where we have not been making the same progress as on the medical. In that case we might be prepared to credit you on our books with, say, ten per cent of the fees on such new surgical business brought in by you for operations."

For a startled moment Spen saw this as the tabooed though frequently (and secretly) practiced evil of fee splitting. Why, no! How could it be? It was all in the same clinic. Nevertheless, he had a shrewd notion that the bonus would be found charged up against the patient's account. Well, what was the matter with that? Most of the Tyre clientele could well afford the extra.

"Well?" said Blanton Tyre persuasively.

"I might be prepared to consider such an offer when, as, and if you are prepared to make it," said the young man.

"Very well," barked Tyre. "It's made. Is it a deal?"

A palpably double-edged deal, designed, on the one hand, to detach him wholly from the James activities; on the other, to stimulate him to perform all the operations possible, Spen perceived. It ought to run close to twenty-five thousand dollars a year. He could pay Carol off quickly. He was going to be a rich man. . . . Why couldn't he feel more exultant?

"It certainly sounds all right," he said. "Give me overnight to think about it."

Blanton Tyre expatiated, prophesying great successes. After all the old boy wasn't so bad. He had his points. Certainly he knew how to appreciate sound work on the part of his subordinates.

To a proposal that they run out to the Tyre estate and have a drink on it, Spen assented with pleasure. Tyre produced a bottle of his very special reserve stock. They had a drink, and a second. Then Castleman appeared, which involved another. Blanton Tyre was talking again, talking of the meeting tonight, of how much the future of local medicine was bound up in the outcome, of what a threat to the profession an enterprise like that of the James co-op constituted.

As he elucidated a great illumination came to Spen. He caught and interpreted the undertones of the Tyre exegesis: the imminent threat against James, himself. Terry Martin had been right; how right! He had been one hundred per cent right in the theory which he had, himself, repudiated as casuistry. It wasn't casuistry. It was logic. In the long view the only hope for the James enterprises prescribed that James's real friends should play along, for the present, with the Tyre faction to turn down Flick Fleming, distasteful though that would be.

Yes; it was crystal-clear. If Fleming were passed it meant immediate trouble for Owen James. If Fleming were kept out James would be allowed to operate a few months longer, anyway. And much might happen in that period of respite. Just what, Spen did not pause to inquire. He was happily sure that the important consideration was to gain time.

The things Owen stood for, Spen realized, now meant more than just the success or failure of this particular scheme of his. It meant the chance of the little man to make himself a bit bigger, to give his children a chance to go farther than he had. That was what Owen meant to those poor devils down there in the mill section; that's what the things Owen stood for meant to people like them everywhere. Between Flick Fleming and Owen James there could be no doubt to an open-minded man. Spen won his own argument with himself, hands down. . . . What was this that Blanton Tyre was putting up to him?

"Speak?" repeated Spen. "No; I'm not much of a speaker."

"We may not need you," said his chief. "But you'd better be ready to say a few words if the situation tightens up."

"Against Fleming?" said Spen, shocked. "Good God! I couldn't do that. Why, he's my friend. He was my best man. You can't ask me to do that."

"No, no; of course not," soothed the other. "No need to make it personal. You can confine yourself to opposition to the principle of socialized medicine."

"I'd much rather you'd leave me out altogether," insisted Spen.

"It doesn't seem likely that we shall have any difficulty," Tyre said. "What about staying to dine with us?"

It being already quite late, Spen called up Carol and told her not to expect him.

"Owen James has been trying to get you," Carol told him.

"What did he want?

"Something about tonight's meeting. He seemed worried. Almost depressed, for Owen."

"Is he going to be there?"

"No. He and Dr. Bernitz have to go over to Millersville on a case. He doesn't think they can get back in time."

"Tell him not to worry if he calls again. Everything is going to work out eventually."

"He's heard rumors that they may cite him or something for expulsion."

"Over my dead body!" said Spen magnificently.

"That's the way I love to hear you talk." Her voice was soft and thrilled; it stirred its hearer to sudden hopes. He almost thought that he had heard a final and whispered "dear."

One after-dinner brandy, and the three doctors set out for the meeting which was set for eight o'clock. Spen was feeling fine. He was set for life. Everything was working in mesh like a smooth engine. His apparent yielding to the Tyres was only temporary. Soon he would be strong enough to assert his independence. Then he would devote a regular part of his time to unpaid work in the James Clinic. Nothing in the form of a promise had been given to Blanton Tyre; there is where he had been clever.

When the time came he could explain it all to Carol. She would understand that his decision as regarded Flick Fleming was no more than a strategical compromise to achieve a more important end, the saving of Owen James's enterprises. Look at it any way one might, Flick was done for, anyway. But Owen and his works might still be salvaged. Put that way, with perfect honesty and frankness, it could not fail to convince Carol, who was fundamentally fair-minded. Spen had succeeded in convincing himself, one hundred per cent. . . .

Well, ninety-nine.

CHAPTER XXIII

THE ACADEMY OF MEDICINE regularly met in the auditorium of the City Hospital. Having ridden out with Blanton Tyre, Spen dropped off at the parking lot downtown to pick up his car. Thus he arrived at the hospital a few minutes later than the Tyres. Although it was still ten minutes short of the appointed hour there was already an abnormally heavy attendance. Spen inferred that the Tyres had been beating the bushes for support, and how successfully!

The men were gathered in little knots, talking earnestly. Now and again as he moved through the crowd Spen heard references to "contract practice" and "state medicine." Blanton himself he saw moving from group to group, like a general encouraging his men before the battle, speaking a smiling word here, slapping someone on the back jovially there. He was a past master at this sort of thing, a natural politician.

Terry Martin came up to Spen, his face ironic. "The hosts of Midian," he said. "On the prowl."

Spen nodded. "There are some here that haven't been to a medical meeting since I've been a member of the Academy."

He moved away before Terry could ask any embarrassing questions. Later on would be time enough for explanations.

The president, a portly practitioner of the old school, called the meeting to order, banging on the table with his gavel to attract the attention of the crowd still talking in the hall outside. They filed in slowly and took seats. Looking over the assemblage, Spen thought how little effect a professional education really had on most men. All of them had been through at least two years of college, that is, all of them except one or two white-haired oldsters who had come up through the dark ages, so to speak, of medical education. Then all of them had attended medical school for four years, and many of them had served internships. Still, taken as a body, they were little different from any other group of men who might be gathered together at a Rotary Club or a convention. There was about the same amount of intelligence reflected in their faces. Some were well dressed; some used good English. Others were as sloppy in their apparel as they were in their speech. He wondered what Hippocrates would have thought, looking over this group. Certainly here was no aggregation of outstanding men, credits to a noble profession, followers in the footsteps so carefully marked out by Hippocrates. Rather, it was a hodgepodge collection, some intelligent, some so dense mentally that one wondered how they had ever gone through even a diploma mill. What a bunch to pass on the life and work of a man like Owen James; to decide whether or not a surgeon of the caliber of Foster Fleming should be allowed to practice his profession in the way he chose!

Spen relaxed in the seat which he had selected, well to the rear of the room, while the preliminaries preparatory to the main bout went on. The secretary read the minutes of the previous meeting. There was a paper on heart disease which should theoretically have interested a number but actually appeared to afflict all with acute boredom. Polite applause died without an echo.

The president pushed his glasses up on his nose and selected a paper from the table before him. He cleared his throat.

"First on the order of business tonight," he began, "we will consider the application of Dr. Foster Fleming for membership in this Academy." He read a record of Fleming's education, training, and experience, finishing with, "now engaged in the practice of surgery in the Cooperative Medical Clinic." he stopped and placed the application on the table. "Is there any discussion before we proceed to the voting?"

This was not the usual procedure in considering applications for membership, as Spen knew. Presentments were usually voted on merely as a formality since the Committee on

Membership would not ordinarily let an application come before the Academy unless objection to it was unlikely.

Down near the rostrum old "Cholly" Chadbourne rose and propped himself on his cane. His expression was one of surprise and displeasure.

"I had the honor of sponsoring Dr. Fleming's candidacy," he said in the florid manner of his period. "The Committee on Membership has passed it with no dissenting voice. That should determine the matter once and for all."

There was an uncomfortable stir. The doctors looked at one another or at the Chair or at nothing. The Chair announced:

"Dr. Blanton Tyre."

The head of the Tyre Clinic walked slowly forward to the foot of the dais. His large head hung low, as if weighted with responsible thought. By the serious cast of his countenance all might read that he found himself confronted by a painful and necessary duty, which he would carry out at whatever cost of laceration to his sensibilities.

"Mr. President, and gentlemen of the Academy of Medicine," he began in his rotund tones. "Reluctant though I am to differ with Dr. Chadbourne, than whom no member of our body commands more affection and reverence, my professional responsibility constrains me to speak. Against Dr. Fleming's professional competence I have nothing to adduce. Unhappily there are other considerations which we dare not evade. The difficult and honorable profession of medicine, gentlemen, has come down to us through the ages as a carefully limited guild, membership in which is a sacred trust. With participation come certain high traditions and responsibilities. We should be untrue to the illustrious example set by Hippocrates more than two thousand years ago if we did not uphold those traditions and the honor of our ancient calling." Here he lifted his eyes to the framed copy of the Hippocratic Oath on the wall. Spen found himself wondering how many of the men there remembered anything of its contents.

"It is our duty to protect our calling from influences which might cheapen or degrade it, from influences which might take away from us the right to say how we shall conduct ourselves. First among our duties is that of nurturing always the welfare of those who put their trust in us, those who come to us in their infirmity, trusting that we shall make them well. It is an axiom that the sick shall always be free to choose among us who he

197

thinks may best treat his sickness. It is an axiom that we will in no wise try to influence that choice. Now and again there comes into question in these meetings the subject of contract practice, of insurance practice, of any system whereby the patient, thinking perhaps that he may thereby save money, may receive treatment for his illness for less than the niggardly sum which we consider our just due for the great work to which we have dedicated our lives. Experience has shown us that such schemes do not work out to the best interest of the sick; we would be the first to admit it if they did, for is not our first duty toward those who are ill in body or in mind?" He paused and poured himself a glass of water. The room was still. There were no shuffling feet, no muffled whispers. Silence and attention paid tribute to Tyre's undeniable appeal as orator.

"The young who have not had the weight of experience to stabilize them do not always realize the dangers of new ideas, do not realize that this thing they call social medicine is not new, do not realize that down through the ages attempts have been made to take from us some of the privileges and duties that go with our honored profession. It is the duty of those who are older, those of us who have fought through similar battles before, to guide them in their steps. Sometimes the hardest blow is the kindliest blow, if it turns one away from danger and destruction.

"Gentlemen, I have nothing against the young doctor who has applied for the right to be one of us tonight. I have nothing against him either on the grounds of character, for I understand him to be of excellent moral stature, nor on the grounds of ability for he was trained in an institution for which I have every respect and by a man whom I am proud to call my friend. On this ground alone it would pain me to have to vote against his application for membership tonight. But I feel that it is a duty both to my own conscience and to organized medicine. Dr. Fleming has chosen to follow a way of practice which we can but condemn. It violates every tradition of our calling, first because it destroys the intimate relationship between the doctor and patient, the right of choice upon which our code of ethics is built, and second because in some instances—mind you, I do not say in this particular instance—but in some instances it might be possible, in such an insurance scheme to which Dr. Fleming has chosen to lend his undeniable talents, for unscrupulous organizers to exploit young men for their own gain. Gentlemen, we must not let such things soil the honor we have kept bright through the ages."

He bowed his head. "That is why I have no choice but to vote against the application of Dr. Foster Fleming for membership in this Academy." He sat down, and a wave of applause swept over the crowd.

It was well done; Spen could not but admit that. He looked over at Terry Martin and saw by the wry smile on his face that he too, recognized the power of an oration like that upon minds already fertile for the seed which had just been sowed.

In the back of the room a stubby, dull-eyed man popped up, whom Spen remembered vaguely as one of the mill-town half-dollar semiquacks, a flourishing parasite on the earnings of the slum populace. He had seen some of the results of the treatment men like that gave out in the City Hospital, and he had nothing but contempt for his clan.

"Dr. Torpie," the Chair acknowledged.

"Members of the Academy." The man's voice was shrill with excitement, his words tumbling over each other in his anger. "Dr. Tyre has said a mouthful, but he ain't said it all. The very existence of all of us is at stake. This thing they call a Cooperative Medical Clinic is a communist nest, a bunch of Reds. They're out to poison the people against the medical profession, and you know who we'll find behind the whole thing when we get through—the government. This here project is nothing but state medicine disguised to look like something else. I say throw this young doctor out; throw them all out. We don't want no damn Yankees coming down here telling us what to do. Who have they got in it?—a preacher, a damn Yankee and a Jew. You don't have to go no farther to see what it is." He sat down and mopped his brow.

There was scattered applause and laughter and here and there admiring cries of "That's tellin' 'em, Torp!" and "Good going, boy." The speaker settled back in his chair, looking pleased at himself.

So this was the type of individual who was to pass on whether or not Foster Fleming, Felix Bernitz, and Owen James were qualified to treat the sick. And what was he, Spencer Brade of Lakeview, doing in that galley with maggots like Torpie?

From the audience came cries of "Let's vote" and "Question! Question!"

"I appoint as teller for the voting Dr. Castleman Tyre and Dr. John Torpie," the chairman announced. Slips of white papers were passed out. Spen took his and hurriedly wrote "against" on it.

There was a smirk on Castleman Tyre's round face as he collected the slips of paper. Spen saw him drop one and pick it up. He recognized it as his own vote and knew that his colleague had read it.

There was no doubt in Spen's mind as to the outcome of the ballot. The announcement, "Seventy-five against, thirty-five for," was about what he would have guessed.

"Gentlemen," the president announced, "the application of Dr. Foster Fleming has been rejected. Is there any other business?"

Another "four-bit-doctor" from the slums, a competitor and congener of Torpie, named Galliani, got up. "Why not make a clean sweep of it? Why not run all them Reds out of the medical society?" he demanded. "We got one, but he ain't the only one. Let's break up this cooperative communistic Medical Clinic. Let's show them government sharks they can't put nothing over on the medical profession." He sat down. The chairman asked:

"Are you making a motion, Dr. Galliani?"

"You're right I want to make a motion," said Galliani, looking around for approval. "I move that we black-list that hospital they got out there."

Torpie was on his feet again. "I second that motion. I claim those folks are doing an insurance practice which is against the rules of this Academy. I claim they're Reds. I claim they're takin' money from them poor, ignorant mill people and are not giving them the medical care they're entitled to in return. I claim they're putting a lot of fool notions in people's heads with all that social-service business. We have enough trouble now, makin' a livin', without putting more Red ideas in people's heads."

Dr. Cannaday, chairman of the Committee on Laws and Legislation, interposed:

"Mr. President, does this gentleman want to get us indicted by a Federal grand jury? Is he ignorant of what happened in Washington because of an abortive boycott of this kind?"

"The motion is out of order," the Chair decided. "We may proceed against individuals. Hardly against the institution."

From the corner of his eye Spen saw Castleman Tyre moving purposefully toward him. This would not do; he wasn't going to be mixed up in it. He was feeling slightly sick. That last brandy had perhaps been a mistake. Or was it a spiritual nausea inspired by Torpie, Galliani & Company? Before he could squeeze through to the aisle Castleman had him by the sleeve.

"What's the name of that other fellow Owen James has with him?" he asked urgently.

"Felix Bernitz," answered Spen before he thought. Then, in alarm, "See here, Tyre, you're certainly not going——"

"But the other was gone. Spen saw him speaking in the ear of a young henchman and picker-up of medical crumbs from the clinic, named Cranston. Now the latter was on his feet.

"I agree with the gentleman who offered the motion. Let's clean out the nest. I move that Dr. Felix Bernitz of the communist cooperative clinic be hereby removed from the membership rolls of this body."

"Second it," shouted a voice, followed by another, "Second it twice."

"Any discussion?" asked the Chair.

"There ought not to be. It ought to be defeated without discussion." The harsh, strident voice was Carter Hewlett's. He directed a venomous glance at the two Tyres who were now conferring in excited whispers. "I do not think that this Academy is prepared to take orders blindly from the heads of private clinics from which I am thankfully dissociating myself."

Spen, who had reached the exit, paused. So Hewlett had got his notice. And did he look savage!

"Who conferred upon the Tyres the power to bless or ban in this organization, I should like to inquire?" pursued the acidulous tones. "May I call to their attention and particularly to that of the Chair a bylaw of this Academy which has never, as far as I am aware, been revoked, providing that no member may be deprived of his fellowship without the process of a suspension pending investigation of the charge against him, with full opportunity of being heard in his own behalf?"

"The point is well taken," pronounced the president.

"Then I move the suspension of Dr. Bernitz," snapped Cranston.

"Does any member wish to be heard on the subject?" asked the Chair after several had seconded the motion.

"Mr. Chairman!" Terry Martin was advancing upon the platform. His face was drawn with controlled fury. His voice rasped like the warning of an angry hornet.

"Dr. Martin, will you come up on the platform?"

"I will not. What I have to say I can say from the floor. I had no intention of speaking when I came in here. But I'm not going to sit still and hear decent men attacked by a bunch of four-bit, nit-wit quacks and their high-priced stooges." (Cries of "Order! Order!" "Go to it, Terry." "Sit down." "Throw him out"—"Who the hell is going to throw me out?" inquired the little pathologist, to which pertinent query there was no answer—"Give me a chance," and similar interjections, punctuated by the rhythmic fall of the presidential gavel.) "All right. I'll be parliamentary. I'll be orderly as all hell. This is what I've got to say to you. I know the kind of work they're doing in the James Clinic, and damned good work it is. The city of Charlesville ought to be grateful for it, and this Academy ought to be proud of it. Every man here who isn't blinded by mean prejudices or out for every cheap dollar he can squeeze out of his pitiful pillmongering—— All right, all right, Mr. President; I'll confine myself to the question. Every man here ought to realize that there is a definite need for a method whereby people with very low incomes can finance their own medical care. The cooperative is not treading on anybody's toes in treating these people. They could not afford anything like the best medical care." This was a slam at Torpie and his crowd. "In fact, in most instances they are forced to go on to the City Hospital. Most of these people work for a living; they like to feel that they are responsible citizens, able, with a little help, to pay their own way. Are we prepared to go on record as opposing a system which will help a man keep his own self-respect, save him from the galling knowledge that he must accept charity or see his wife and children suffer and perhaps die? Yet the best that a certain type of shyster mind can do is to call these people Reds and Communists, when they are only trying to do a necessary piece of work in the best way they know."

There was a spontaneous round of applause. Spen had slipped through the doorway to escape the impending vote. At least he would not humiliate himself to the extent of supporting so shameful a move. But what a surprise Terry Martin had been! Who would have suspected such evangelistic fervor from the sardonic laboratory scientist! From his place opposite the door he could hear the speaker's voice, now tempered, continue:

"As for Dr. Bernitz' personal and professional status, others are better qualified to speak than I. I wish the Chair would call on his close friend and loyal admirer, Dr. Spencer Brade."

God damn Terry! What right had he to drag him, Spen, into it! Panic chilled his blood. No; he couldn't do it. It wasn't fair. To back Terry up meant the abandonment of the success for which he had worked so hard and which was on the eve of consummation. If there were any hope of success he might have taken a chance and joined Terry. But it was a lost cause, hopeless, foreordained. Any fool could see that the Tyres had the meeting absolutely sewed up. For him to take a stand against them would only involve him in personal disaster without in any way helping Bernie. As if by propulsion outside his will, he moved in flight along the hallway. Behind him he could hear impatient calls:

"Question! Question! Let's vote."

So much for Felix Bernitz. So much for Foster Fleming. What would come next? Whatever it was, he couldn't help it. Turning his mind from such undermining considerations, he made his way to the car. As he climbed in another car slowed to a stop in the parking space. Two men got out. One of them looked liked Bernie Bernitz. Spen hastily leaned back. He did not want to be recognized.

He needed a drink. In that vicinity there were no decent bars. But the country club was only a few blocks distant. He drove there. One of his familiars of the bridge table hailed him:

"Hi, Doc! What's the matter? You look as if you'd met a ghost."

"I'm all right," answered Spen dully. "It's this damned heat."

No one was in the bar. That was a relief. He wouldn't have to chatter. He ordered a long brandy and soda and sat sipping it.

The liquor set him right. He was cold sober after it. Miserably sober. Well, he would need all his faculties to explain to Carol. As to Flick Fleming, that was all right. He had his defense—hell, no! Not defense. He didn't need to defend a position that was perfectly sound. He had his argument, Terry Martin's argument, pat. That covered the Fleming rejection. But what about Bernitz? He could plead that it caught him

203

unprepared; that he wasn't even in the hall. That was true too. It was all over before he could realize what was going on. . . . Or maybe he could go quietly to bed without Carol hearing him and explain in the morning. No explanations through that damn bolted door.

He meditated another drink and decided against it. But he didn't feel like going home yet. Give Carol time to be asleep before he got there. Finding a dark and quiet corner of the veranda, he hunched down into a chair and tried to doze. It wouldn't do. He was too fidgety. After an hour he went back to the car.

Light glowed brilliantly through Carol's windows when he drove in. She was still awake. Naturally. She would be. Waiting to get his account of the meeting. He half expected her to come down to him. He put up the car, let himself into the front hallway, stood there listening. No sound. Now that he was nerved up to it he hoped to have it over with. Then perhaps he could sleep. He had not been sleeping too well lately. If he could justify himself to Carol, if he could persuade her that he had acted wisely, kindly, and in the spirit of ultimate loyalty, whatever appearance of surrender his immediate course may have had, why, then his mind would be at peace again. He needed her absolution.

As he passed along the upper hall he could discern no thread of radiance from beneath her door. Doubtless she had heard him come in and switched off her light. Pondering that, he undressed and refreshed his weary body with a cold shower.

Then, having slipped into his pajamas, he listened at the connecting and forbidding door. He heard her cough. He knocked. Her voice called:

"Come in."

He laughed embarrassedly. "How can I? The door's bolted."

"Try it." There was a soft mirth in the voice now.

He turned the knob. The hinges creaked in protest as the door opened to his pressure. Carol was propped up on her pillows. Beside her shone the soft glow of a shaded bed lamp. Now she dropped the book she had been holding. There was a faint smile on her lips.

Spen moved toward her loveliness like a man entranced. Thoughts rushed, torrential, through his mind, matching the tumult in his blood. If this meant what his throbbing hopes interpreted it to mean, if that kindness in her eyes meant the welcome for which he had yearned, the end of long separation and deprivation, there was nothing he would not give up for her—Kenny, the Tyres, every ignoble tie and ambition; nothing that he would not do to prove himself in her eyes. He said hoarsely:

"Carol!"

"Did you beat them, Spen? Did you win?"

"No."

A shade dimmed her face. "Oh, poor Flick!" she said. "And poor Spen!" she added under her breath. "Was it very bad? You look so done up."

"Yes; it was bad. They had us beaten from the start."

"Never mind. As long as you put up a fight. That's all I wanted of you, dear—my dear."

He stumbled forward. "Carol?" he breathed. All the suppressed longing of the impatient months was in the appeal and the question that he put into her whispered name.

"Yes," she said softly and clearly.

He bent to her waiting body, her waiting lips. There was a rush of wheels below in the drive. A horn blared blatantly, without cessation. Carol wrenched her mouth from his.

"What is it?" she whispered.

"Wait." He switched off the dim light, went to the open window.

"Get out of here, whoever you are."

The raucous summons died away. A voice called monotonously:

"Spencer Brade! Spencer Brade! *Doct*-or Spencer Brade! You are wanted."

"What for? Who are you?"

"You're wanted. You're wanted. You're wanted. What for? For high treason."

Recognizing the voice now, Spen leaned out, shaking with fury. "Is that you, Terry? Damn you, you're drunk!"

"Drunk," echoed the voice below. "I'm drunk. You're right, I'm drunk. First time in one hell of a while. Who did it? Dr. Brade. Paging Dr. Spencer Brade."

"Go home. I'll talk to you in the morning."

"I'll talk to *you* now."

"What is it, Spen? What does he want?" Carol asked from her bed.

"Nothing," he answered shortly. "A drunken fool. I'll go down and get rid of him."

"No don't. He might be dangerous. He sounds so queer."

Terry's voice steadier now, said almost sadly, "Do you know what happened after you ran away?"

"Ran away?" The echo came in Carol's frightened whisper. *"Spen!* What does he mean?"

"Nothing. It's Terry Martin. He's crazy. Liquor does that to him."

The scornful accents went on, "I'll tell you what happened I'll tell the world what happened. They kicked out Bernie Bernitz. Then they turned around and kicked out Owen James Get that? Owen James, the finest——" The voice faltered. "Never mind. That's why I'm drunk. That's why I've come here before I'm too drunk to tell you what I think of you." The voice hiccuped once, then resumed with deadly deliberation, "And you, you treacherous, double-crossing son of a bitch, what did you do about it? Sneaked out and left him flat. . . . Good night."

The car ground its gears like teeth, gave one contemptuous snort, sped away amid a rattle of spurned gravel.

From the bedside came the slow glow of the small lights as Carol's fingers fumbled for the button. She sat up, her eyes affrighted.

"Is it true, Spen?" she asked quivering.

"Not as that drunken fool put it."

"Is it true?" she persisted. "Did they put Owen out?"

"Only a suspension. He'll get his hearing when——"

"Didn't you defend him?"

"Listen, Carol. There was no chance. The meeting was packed. I wasn't even there. But if I had been——"

" 'Over your dead body,' " she said in a gasping laugh. "It isn't your body that's dead, Spen. It's worse than that."

Suddenly she wailed aloud and twisted, burying her head in the sheet. He set his hands on her shoulders, striving to lift her. She cried out as if in terror of him then gave herself over to racking sobs.

Spen turned and stumbled back into his own room.

Neither Carol nor her aunt was at breakfast the next morning. Very well, he thought sullenly; if that was the way they wanted it, that was the way it would be. He couldn't stand much more.

He came late to the office. On his desk was a small parcel,

wrapped in tissue paper. He undid it. A toy yellow dog looked out at him from beady eyes. Pinned under its tail, a strip of paper bore this message in the small neat writing which he associated with the clinic's laboratory reports.

> Hang yourself, brave Crillon. We fought at
> Arques—and where were you?

White-faced, Spen shot down the passageway to Terry Martin's quarters. The place was empty. He went to the reception room. Kenny Mangan looked up and waited, her face set in the mask of professional impenetrability.

"Where's Ter——? Where is Dr. Martin?" Spen demanded.

"Dr. Martin has left, Dr. Brade."

"Left?"

"Yes. Resigned." She added after a moment, "Dr. Castleman Tyre has also left for the day. He has a nasal hemmorrhage and superficial facial contusions. Anything else, Dr. Brade?"

"Thank you, no. I am going to the hospital and may not be back today. Tell Dr. Tyre, Sr., please."

Instead of the hospital, Spen went home. Neither of the women was there. He set mechanically to the work of packing his belongings. While he was still at it he looked up to see his wife in the doorway.

"Come in," he said shortly "Sit down." He pushed a chair toward her. She shook her head, remained standing there, her eyes fixed on his stony face.

"Are you going away?" she asked.

"Yes."

"Where to?"

"I've taken a room at the St. Charles for the present."

She answered listlessly, "It had to come. I suppose it's just as well."

He said in a tone of intense bitterness, "I've been your pimp long enough." Her hand went to her breast. "Without even a pimp's privileges."

"Is that how you think of it?"

"What other way is there to think?"

"I couldn't have believed that you'd look at it that way."

Her stunned eyes and grievous mouth almost weakened him. But he was punishing himself now and taking a sour, perverse satisfaction in the reflex upon her.

"How much do I owe you now?" he demanded.

"How should I know?"

"I've got the figures. I want to make sure they agree with yours. It'll be paid, every damned cent. Just as soon as I can get the money. And I want to tell you I'm not going to be too particular how I get it."

At that a faint color came to the still face below him. "Oh no, Spen!" she said clearly. "That I won't let you say. You shan't make me responsible for what you do. If you go to the devil you go on your own. Pay me or not; it makes no difference. Money is pretty unimportant compared with what has happened to us two."

"I tell you," he cried with sudden violence, "the debt is poison to me. Can't you understand that?"

"Yes; I can understand. It was a bad bargain from the start. I blame myself for that. But not for what you've made of yourself since."

He laughed harshly. "Watch me! See what I'm going to make of myself. From now on I'm concentrating. I've been a silly, weak fool, setting out to make good and thinking I could mix in my pink-ribbon idealism. Maybe I idealized you a little too. No more of that for me. Do you want a divorce?"

"Do you?"

"It's all one to me. But it seems the logical thing."

She reflected. "You don't have to answer this one, Spen. Is it true about you and that girl in your office?"

"What if it were?" he said brutally.

"Do you want a divorce to marry her?"

"No."

"I'll be frank with you, Spen. I think divorce is the best thing. But I have a horror of the publicity, of having our name smeared all over the newspapers. Any scandal would just about kill Aunt Candace."

"There needn't be any scandal, unless you make one."

"No. I suppose there are ways. Let me talk to my lawyer."

"Certainly. Anything he fixes up I'll agree to. He grinned bitterly "I'll promise not to ask for alimony, Carol."

"Still harping on the money side of it, Spen!"

"Well, it's been a money deal. You've shown me plainly enough that I mustn't expect it to be anything else. At that, I don't think I've been such a hot investment for you."

"You might have been."

"More idealism," he jeered. "No thank you. Say good-by to your aunt for me and thank her for her liberal hospitality. I'll pay that off, too, when I get ahead enough. Good-by, Carol."

"Good luck, Spen. I'm sorry it had to turn out this way." Throughout the long night in his new quarters his resolution hardened. In the morning he went straight to Blanton Tyre's office. The chief was in high spirits.

"We certainly showed up that bunch of radicals," he bragged.

"Yes," agreed Spen. "You did a job there, Dr. Tyre. I decided to sign the contract."

"I knew I wasn't mistaken in my estimate of you, my boy," chirruped the clinic head with a smile.

That smile turned Spen slightly sick.

CHAPTER XXIV

"THEY set the bait," said Kenny Mangan. "They pulled in the line. And what was wriggling on the hook? You, darling."

"The best thing I ever did for myself," asserted Spen. "Wait till you hear what terms I made. This time next year I'll be buying you a mink coat."

"Not me. I don't take that kind of money."

They were in the living room of her flat, having dined together in the small restaurant which they frequented nowadays.

"You take Tyre money," he pointed out.

"For legitimate services rendered."

"My services will be legitimate," he retorted warmly. "Don't you think anything different."

"Maybe," she returned. "On the other hand, maybe you'll be helping girls to preserve their girlish figures. Tyre repairing."

"Kenny, you're a malevolent little liar. Come over here and kiss me."

"Well, I might. But it commits me to nothing. Bertha'll be coming in on us any minute."

After a silence she moved away and said, "Just the same, Spen, I wish you hadn't tied yourself up."

"I don't have to do anything I don't want to do."

"That's what you think. You don't know the Tyres yet. I wouldn't be too sure that you know yourself."

"Do I give the impression of an abortionist, Kenny?"

"Neither does Blanton Tyre," she retorted. "I've nothing against abortion, in case of need. It's got its uses. But that's a layman's point of view. Medically it's something else again."

He contemplated her meditatively. "You don't think much of me, do you, little Kenny?"

"As a lover, you're swell," she replied frankly. "I'm crazy about you. And I think you could be absolute tops in your specialty, if you wanted to be. Haven't I always told you that? But not with the Tyre bunch."

"I'm going to be tops," he asserted earnestly. "The Tyres can't stop me. Why would they want to? The better I am, the better for them."

The piquant face was obstinate. "Okay, Spen. Argue yourself into it. But I wish you were on your own." She paused before asking, "What happened between you and Terry Martin?"

The line of Spen's mouth hardened. "Among other things he called me a crook and a son of a bitch."

"Maybe he thought you were," she said quietly.

He flushed. "Do *you* think I am?"

Without answering she asked, "Was it the Academy-meeting business?"

"Yes. I suppose you know all about that," he said sullenly.

"Something. Terry lost his temper at it, didn't he?"

"Terry made a damned fool of himself."

"I like a man to make a damned fool of himself for his friends."

"Christ!" said Spen unhappily. "Do you suppose for a minute I wouldn't have spoken out if I'd known what they were going to do to Owen James? Or I could have helped Bernie Bernitz? I was on a spot, Kenny." He appealed to her. "Can't you understand that?"

"Yes. Who put you there? The Tyres." She answered her own query.

"Oh, what's the use?" Why should I ruin my future over something I couldn't have helped, anyway?"

"Terry Martin had such an admiration for you," she said in a tone of musing regret.

"I won't have to see anything of him, anyway."

"You will, for a while."

"How's that?" cried Spen. "I thought he was out."

"Blanton Tyre is holding him to his contract. Two months left to go. Besides, he's got some unfinished work on his serums that he's crazy to finish. So they fixed it up."

Spen grinned. "Did he apologize to Castleman Tyre for busting his sweet face?"

"I doubt whether Terry ever apologized to anybody for anything, right or wrong, in his life." The girl lifted her head. "Here comes Bertha. Let's go to a movie."

Taking her home after the picture, Spen asked, "What about your sister?"

Her face clouded. "Adele? Some faith-healing faker got hold of her and talked her into putting off the operation."

"But that's dangerous?"

"You're telling me!"

"Can't you tell her? Get her up here."

"I can't. Her husband has been sent to Mexico on a six month job. She's gone with him."

"That's bad. You're terribly fond of her, aren't you, Kenny?"

Tears flushed to the bright eyes. "Delly's just the finest, cleanest, *holiest* person I've ever known in my life. If anything happened to her—let's not talk about it. Good night, darling."

Walking down the clinic hallway two mornings later, Spen met Terry Martin face to face. Terry stopped.

"I was drunk," he said.

"So I assumed," Spen returned coldly.

"If I hadn't been I wouldn't have gone to your wife's house—I've written her to apologize—or said what I did say."

"Well?"

The little man moved a step nearer. His eyes were both somber and fierce. "That doesn't mean that I didn't think it."

Spen smiled without friendliness. "Where does that leave us?"

Terry looked relieved. "As long as I'm here we have to work together more or less." He hesitated. "You probably don't care what I think about you."

"Not one single goddamn," confirmed Spen, hoping that his voice did not betray the falsehood.

"That's all right, then. We'll get along—professionally."

"We will, provided you get this," said the other, speaking with slow emphasis. "I'm not interested in your judgement on my actions and I don't want to hear any more about it."

"Right," agreed Terry Martin cheerfully. "Every man to his own hell by his own path. I'll even buy you a drink."

"No, you won't. Not till you've apologized."

Terry laughed. "There'll be ice on said path when I do that," he stated and went on about his business.

When next they met the pathologist was natural and easy. That was his way, Spen guessed. He had spoken his mind; he had retracted nothing; each knew exactly where the other stood—now go on as before. Very sensible too.

One of Blanton Tyre's occasional patients was a rather colorless young widow named De Long, with whom Spen had once played a rubber of bridge at the club. He knew little about her except that she was not quite in Carol's set. Tyre had never said anything about her case, but this was not unusual, as the clinic chief had a number of "pets"—generally very good-paying ones—whom he kept jealously to himself.

At an hour when Spen was immersed in an intricate problem of diagnosis Blanton Tyre entered his office. The worker looked up briefly and nodded in acknowledgment of his superior's greeting.

"Sorry to interrupt," the chief apologized, "but did you get any samples of that new synthetic ovarian preparation?"

"What was that?" Spen asked, trying to smother his impatience.

"The formula that new company's putting out."

"Oh, that," said Spen vaguely. "Yes; I believe they did send in a few samples. Do you mind looking in that lower compartment? I can't drop this just now."

"Of course. Stick to your work, my boy," approved his senior. "Here they are. Mind if I take 'em along?"

"No. Go ahead."

"I want to try it out in a case of amenorrhea. Girl hasn't any money. Can't afford expensive preparations. It's a good place to use this lot that doesn't cost us anything."

Spen nodded. "Yes; of course." He was too deeply absorbed in writing up his chart to be surprised at Tyre's unusual concern over an impecunious and presumably non-paying patient; later it struck him.

212

Later in the afternoon, as he was passing along the little hall at the rear which connected the offices and afforded a way of quiet exit to certain patients who might not wish to court the glances of a crowded waiting room, he saw Blanton Tyre ushering out Mrs. de Long. The treatment room was empty. He stepped in and looked about him.

Six of the special ampoules lay empty on the table with an intravenous syringe beside them. Spen whistled softly. So Mrs. de Long, who lived in a smart apartment and drove a high-class car, was the moneyless victim of amenorrhea. But—six ampoules at once! He went to Terry Martin's laboratory.

"Have a seat," said Terry with suspicious politeness.

Spen shook his head. "What do you know about this new sex hormone?"

"Why do you ask?"

"You're a hormone shark, aren't you?"

"You're the one that's supposed to be."

"Oh no! I'm just the dispenser with the charming manner," said Spen dryly.

Terry looked over at the door to make sure it was closed before he answered.

"The dope is that it's the most powerful stuff yet. It soups up the female mechanism like a shot of ether does your gas tank."

"Blanton Tyre just gave six ampoules intravenously to a smart young widow."

"Six ampoules! Not all at once?"

"Must have been, I think."

"The old bastard! That's powerful stuff. Nobody knows yet just how potent. I hope it don't take the coroner to find out."

"Tyre said it was for amenorrhea."

Terry rubbed his chin. "Uh-huh. Well, it's rumored around that a healthy shot of it in the circulation fixes up all the little gal's troubles. Of course the manufacturers don't say so. They wouldn't dare."

"My God! I *am* dumb. Just like that, eh?"

"Just like that. No fuss. No worry. Now you have it and now you don't."

Spen said more to himself than to his companion, "And that's the sort of thing we're supposed to stand for."

"Listen," said Terry Martin. His grin had no mirth in it, only a cynical ruthlessness that rasped Spen's nerves. "Listen, young

213

Dr. Brade. You stick around here and before you're a year older you'll be doing things that would have made you cut your throat when you came out of Lakeview."

"You're a damned liar," Spen said hoarsely.

"All right. I'm a damned liar. Tell me that next spring."

Living at the hotel, Spen promptly discovered, was quite a different matter from the costless luxury of the Grahame ménage. Never inured to petty economies, even at Lakeview where he had exhausted the last of his patrimony, he now found that his stated income was dribbling away through countless leaks and that after deducting the sum which he conscientiously set aside for Carol, his margin of living was scanty to the point of embarrassment. At the close of the fiscal year, when the profits of the clinic were apportioned, he would have plenty. But that was a long way off. Of course he might let the debt to Carol wait until then. No; it was a fierce and constant irritant, for which the only relief to his morbid conscience was that regular payment. To ask for grace now would be too humiliating. Other obligations could wait. That one must be met.

He resigned from the country club and cut his personal expenditures to the bone. It was not enough. He fell steadily behind. In his desperation he had figured out a scheme which he thought might work on Blanton Tyre—who was tough in money matters—and was waiting for a favorable opportunity to present itself when his chief gave him an opening.

"Spen, I've got a patient I'd like you to look over."

"Hospital?"

"No. Home. I don't want to hospitalize her unless it's necessary. It's a Mrs. de Long."

"Oh!" said the junior with deliberate intent. "Wasn't she the one you treated with the sample sex hormones?"

Tyre blinked and scowled. "How did you know that?"

"I saw the empty ampoules. You gave her a pretty heavy shot."

"I followed the directions faithfully," said his chief fretfully. "She may be supersusceptible. She's developed a temperature. I don't like it."

Together they went to the De Long apartment.

The patient was evidently in great pain; her lips were pinched, and her eyes showed that dull look that comes with the administration of a narcotic. The pupils were small, almost pin-point.

"How much morphia?" Spen asked.

"Two quarters. She's having powerful contractions."

Spen laid his hand upon the woman's abdomen. Momentarily her muscles contracted like boards beneath his sensitive touch, and she cried out.

"Can't you stop the pain?" she begged. "It was never like this before."

(One of Blanton's regulars, Spen thought as he made a brief examination.)

"What do you think?" Blanton Tyre asked. "Infection?"

Spen shook his head. "Simple mechanics, I'd say. Your heroic treatment with the needle was enough to stir up trouble but not enough to carry through."

"Do you think a D & C would help?"

"Not only help. It's indicated."

Blanton Tyre breathed more easily. "I'll have them send over the instruments from the hospital. You'll do it, of course?"

Spen considered. Technically he was within his rights. An abortion had been begun by another person; there was danger that serious complications might develop, unless he operated. But in the home!

"Why not take her to the hospital?"

"Oh, I can't go to the hospital," Mrs. de Long cried. "I just couldn't!"

"I think we'll be perfectly safe here," Blanton Tyre said. His certainty of the outcome told Spen that this was not the first such occasion that had arisen.

"Oh, all right," he said. "The pioneers operated on kitchen tables, so why not us? You can give her a whiff of vinyl ether."

Blanton Tyre nodded eagerly and went to the telephone.

Pioneer surgery wasn't half bad at that, Spen decided when he had finished.

"So that's all right," said Blanton Tyre with a sigh of relief as they left.

"Yes; but it might have been a lot worse," said Spen. "Do you think it's wise to experiment with this new stuff before it's been proved up clinically?"

"Maybe not; maybe not," sighed the elder. "I should have preferred a standard D & C in the first place. But this patient is a neurotic type, abnormally afraid of operation."

215

"Which she didn't escape, as it was," Spen pointed out. "There's always the element of uncertainty, of danger in these hormone treatments. The only clean, sure way is the knife."

Tyre's head jerked up. He peered at Spen excitedly. "I agree," he said. "I quite agree. You're the gynecologist here. Properly these cases come within your department."

(If I should speak the word "abortion," thought Spen with bitter amusement, he'd probably throw a fit. What a dreary bluff!)

"Not your personal and private patients," he said urbanely. "They would always feel more confidence with you. But it might be as well to let me see them after treatment."

"An excellent idea, my boy. Very excellent. I shall always be glad to have your opinion."

(And we'll all be glad, reflected Spen, to lessen the chances of a death from peritonitis which might be awkward to explain.)

"There's a matter I've wanted to speak to you about, Dr. Tyre," he said. "I'm running on a pretty close margin financially."

The Tyre mouth puffed out; the Tyre eye became cold and glassy. "I consider our arrangement very liberal to you, Brade."

"So do I," assented Spen. "I'm not asking any change in terms. But my drawing account doesn't cover my living costs. This is my idea. On surgical cases which I bring in personally I'd like my ten per cent when the bill is paid."

The general swelling of the features before him mitigated. "Means complications of bookkeeping," Tyre grumbled. "Still, it might be managed. Yes; that's not unreasonable. I'll see what can be done, my boy, if it's a matter of convenience to you." He chuckled flatly. "You remember, Spen, I once told you that surgeons don't make money by dodging operations."

Thus far all was well. The drawback to Spen's deal was that long-deferred payments are the rule in medical practice, and the more fashionable and expensive the practice, the slower the cash. In an establishment such as the Tyres' there is practically no spot business, very little first-of-the-month squaring of accounts, and a loss of above twenty percent on bad bills. Possibly that is why Tyre had fallen in with his junior's suggestion so readily.

For the first month Spen did not take in an extra dollar. He was behind on his hotel bill and had to borrow the money for the installment on his car. Nevertheless, he sent Carol her check on the dot.

It was up to him he perceived, to create a type of medical trade new to the Tyre Clinic, a quick-payment line. His first chance to test it out arrived with a young woman whose kind was familiar to him through his Lakeview experience. She was thin, nervous, undernourished, and probably got no exercise unless someone invited her out to dance. Not much money there, he estimated; most likely a secretary. Her personal history thoroughly confirmed his guess.

"How did you happen to come to me, Miss Dorner?" he asked.

"I heard you were from Lakeview," she answered in the slow, dulled tones of the undervitalized. "I've got a cousin who's a nurse there. She says the Lakeview training is the best in the world."

Spen smiled. "That's something to live up to."

"I've tried other doctors. They tell me so many things; I don't know what to think."

"Suppose you tell me," Spen said kindly.

"Well, I have a lot of trouble all the time: backache, and my right side is sore. I never seem to feel right well."

Though he went on eliciting her further history with well-placed questions he could have set it down almost as accurately at first sight of her. Also, he could have deduced in advance with equal ease what he presently learned from examination.

"Dr. Cranch says I have chronic appendicitis and a cyst on one ovary," she recited wearily, "and that my uterus is out of place. He wanted to operate."

Spen nodded. He knew Cranch for a pretentious third-rater. That kind would want to operate whether or not surgical intervention was indicated. How many such cases had he, Spen, seen with Old Powsie at Lakeview, usually after they had been operated on, after some bungler had removed the appendix and stitched up the uterus, probably at the same time removing an ovary that at the most contained nothing but the *corpus luteum* cyst that came every month and disappeared the same way before the next month was out. He'd heard Powers curse under his breath at the men who'd done these things, who'd taken good money for unnecessary surgery, who'd operated to cure a stomach-ache that came from lack of exercise, improper diet, and the strain and competition of city life.

"Go back to the country," he'd heard Powers advise the patient. "Eat three good meals a day, get plenty of exercise. Marry some healthy boy and have a lot of children. That's the only thing that will cure you.

"I've saved up a little money." The girl's voice recalled his wandering attention. "The office will hold my job for me if you think an operation is necessary. I simply can't go on feeling this way."

"No; you can't," Spen said soothingly. "You don't have to."

"Can you give me an idea how much it will cost me?"

Spen did some fast thinking. How much would the traffic bear? He and Kenny had planned a week end in the country. Kenny was an inexpensive traveling companion, adjusting herself happily to the simplest living conditions; but even so, he couldn't get by on less than twenty dollars—which he didn't have on hand.

"Did you want to pay in advance?" he asked.

She looked surprised. "Would it make any difference?"

"Yes. It would be cheaper. On that basis I can perform the operation for two hundred dollars."

"All right," said the patient. "I don't think that's so bad. And I won't be afraid with you."

Spen reached for the telephone. "Get me the hospital, please."

"Yes, Dr. Brade." Kenny's most officialish accents. What would she say if she knew where the money for their outing was coming from? She wouldn't like it. Spen didn't think too well of it, himself. But if he hadn't undertaken to do the operation Dr. Cranch would. Surgeons didn't make money, certainly by turning patients over to others and less skillful operators. At least he was saving this patient from a bungler. When the hospital connection was completed he said:

"I should like to post a patient for operation tomorrow. Appendectomy and suspension. Thank you."

"Now you've nothing to worry over," he told the Dorner girl. "No danger at all. We'll have you back at work in three weeks."

"I'll go to the bank and bring back the money," she said.

Turning in the two hundred dollars to Blanton Tyre, Spen received back his twenty dollars' commission.

"Cash in advance, uh?" commented Tyre, eying him curiously. "Something new for us. Well, it has its advantages; it has its advantages."

That evening Spen assuaged his loneliness with fewer drinks then had been his recent habit. He was resolved to give the Dorner girl the best he had for her two hundred dollars. To that extent he could appease his conscience.

Everything looked normal when he opened up the abdomen. The appendix was not diseased; he had not expected that it would be. Still she was better off without it. Nor was there a cyst on the ovary, as that fool of a Cranch had made her believe. As for the uterus, the displacement was so slight as to be unimportant. But in his exploration he noted something out of the usual and, to his surprise, located a small mass, hardly more than a nodule, in the cervix. Too small yet to have caused the patient's symptoms, it was definitely ominous.

"Tenaculum," he said to the instrument nurse, and, fixing the body of the uterus firmly in the strong-jawed instrument, he began to examine the nodule more closely.

"What is it?" asked the assistant. "A fibroid?"

Spen shook his head. "Too hard. An early carcinoma, I'd say." He pondered for a moment, while his hand moved rapidly over the entire back wall of the uterus. Should he take a chance and remove the uterus entirely? It didn't feel like the sort of thing that should be treated with radium. He was afraid to cut into the growth; it might cause spreading. It was bad enough to do a needless suspension; it would be nothing less then criminal to remove the entire uterus because of a benign nodule. But his surgical judgment was one thing upon which he felt he could depend.

"Large Kelly," he said. "We'll do a total hysterectomy."

It was a neat job; he had to hand that much to himself. The ligaments clamped, cut, and ligated, the uterine arteries safely secured by double ties of catgut, the entire uterus, cervix and all, removed *in toto* without disturbing the growth that he was certain must be malignant. He could see the approval in the eyes of the assistant when he called for the closing sutures.

The growth was in the receptacle, the wound neatly sewed up.

"Send that specimen down to the laboratory for microscopic examination, please," he directed.

In the morning he had the report: "Tissue unmistakably carcinomatous."

An incipient cancer! Hidden, unsuspected, potentially deadly. Sheer luck for the surgeon; sheer luck for the patient, who would never know from what she had been saved now, since there was no need to give her that worry. Ten to one the hideous growth, eradicated in its first stage, would not return. Instead of a weight of guilt, Spen felt richly, righteously, gloriously justified for an operation which, Old Powsie would have sternly told him, should never have been undertaken on the evidence.

CHAPTER XXV

ECONOMY was not the only reason for Spen's resignation from the country club. He shrank from encountering Carol. Not that he felt any guilt, he angrily told himself; rather, frustration. For that one, thrilling moment she had turned human. Then, because of a drunken fool's version of something that she knew nothing about, she had put him out of her life. Therefore she was responsible for what followed. He had stood all that any man could be expected to stand. Often, after a few drinks, he felt that he would like to explain his attitude to her, coldly and in convincing detail. But would it convince her? Probably not.

In a city as small as Charlesville it was inevitable that they should meet. The rencontre, when it occurred, opened on a note of commonplace conventionality. He was coming through a gate on Grove Avenue after visiting a patient, when Carol rounded the corner close upon him.

"Why, hello, Spen."

"Hello, Carol."

Her manner was neither friendly nor unfriendly; merely

casual. She was as vivid and lovely as an early flower. Her mouth smiled faintly; her regard was cool and almost quizzical.

"Are you all right?" she asked with polite interest.

"Quite, thank you. Can I take you somewhere?"

"No, thank you. I'm only going to the next block." She laughed a little. "You won't believe it, Spen, but Aunt Candy actually misses you."

"I suspect she's the only one of the household who does."

She passed this over without change of expression. "Poor Auntie! She has no one to be stern and disapproving with in the mornings. I'm no good to her because I don't answer back."

"No. You never quarrel, do you? It's part of that natural indifference of yours."

She ignored the personality. "Spen, have you seen Owen James lately?"

He flushed painfully. "No. Why should I?"

"I think he's good for you."

"Thanks for your continued interest."

"There's no need to be bitter about it. You're still my husband legally. I'd hate to see you—I mean, I shouldn't want to have you——" She hesitated again.

"You don't want to see me go completely to hell," he interpreted. "I can see that it might hurt your pride. Make your mind easy. I'm not going to fall victim to unrequited passion."

Carol was not without a healthy equipment of temper. "So I understand," she flashed back at him. The reference was obviously to Kenny Mangan. "Not that it's any of my business," she went on. "But Owen asked about you."

"What am I supposed to do? Grovel at his feet and ask pardon?"

"If you did he'd probably kick you. I hope he'd kick you," she stated with vivacity. "No; he doesn't hold it against you what you did—what you didn't do at the Academy meeting. He says you couldn't have stopped them, anyway. He makes allowances for you, more charitably than I do."

"I'm not asking anybody to make allowances for me."

"Is that a boast?" Her eyes had turned scornful. "If it is I think it's a pretty cheap one."

"So do I," he admitted, suddenly depressed.

Her hand made a quick, involuntary movement, which she immediately controlled.

"One of these days we've got to have a talk," she said.

"What is there to talk about?"

"A number of things. We're civilized people. There's no need for us to deal with each other through lawyers, is there?"

He said obstinately, "Until the slate is clear there is no question of anything else."

"Oh, Spen!" she exclaimed impatiently. "Why must you make the money part so important?"

"Perhaps its the only self-respect I've got left," he said harshly.

"Don't say that. I won't let you say that. Owen says——"

"Always Owen," he broke in. "That's all right, though. That's as it should be, I suppose. Owen will have to wait, though. I'm not going to owe money to any other man's wife."

"I think you're childish," she said.

"Very likely. Good-by, Carol."

"Good-by, Spen. Good luck."

For a man to leave his wife's house and take up quarters conspicuously in the town's leading hotel admits of but one interpretation. Charlesville buzzed and hummed with discussion of the Brades. Family friends, attempting the indirect approach of hints or the direct assault of questions, were met with chill rebuffs from Miss Grahame and with a blank and smiling silence from Carol. No one spoke of it to Spen. He had a way of being dangerously unapproachable when he chose. Sometimes he wondered whether the tongues were busy with Kenny Mangan too. If they were and she knew it, she never let fall any hint. The little office girl could be very closemouthed.

Kenny was an anodyne to Spen's senses. But she was more than that. In some peculiar and indefinable way she was a brake on his growing laxity. Her cynical prophecies of what the Tyre association and influence would do to him operated as a warning and a deterrent. Exactly what her feeling for him was, apart from their physical relation, puzzled him. It was contrary to all the rules that a mistress should be an influence for good. Yet she discouraged his drinking as far as she could without rousing him to resentment, and in a hundred subtle ways, ranging from warning to ridicule, sought to conteract the undermining Tyre pressure. Once, in the lonely dimness of early dawn, he woke up laughing consumedly. He had been dreaming of Owen James and Kenny Mangan, teamed as his guardian angels, in full panoply of halo, robe, and harp, blockading his *facilis descensus* into yawning Avernus of quackdom.

More and more of his leisure was spent with the girl, on week-end trips when they could manage it, occasional stolen nights at her apartment in the absence of her flat mate, and always on Thursday evenings when Bertha was on regular duty up to midnight. On one of these Thursdays they were lying side by side, the girl reading to him by the light of the bed lamp a short-story manuscript, the scene of which was laid in a consultation room, now in the process of being revised for the fourth time. Spen suggested a technical change or two, then put the typed sheets aside and propped himself on his elbow, looking down on the small, intent face.

"Kenny, why don't you get rid of Bertha?"

"How?" she smiled up at him. "Poison?"

"No. Get her out of here. Tell her your sister's coming and you want the place to yourself."

"She'd know why."

"She knows already, doesn't she?"

"About us? Probably. Too many people do. And now you want to make it still more apparent. Don't you think we're together enough as it is?"

"No. Do you?"

"No." She snuggled closer to him. "But I couldn't afford to run this place without Bertha. She pays half the rent."

"That's my affair. I'll look after the rent."

She reached up and cupped his chin in her two hands. "You want to make a kept woman of me?"

"What does that mean? Just words."

"Your kept woman," she went on. "I'm your woman as much as I could ever be anybody's. But I don't want to be kept by you. You wouldn't get that, would you, darling? You don't understand much about what goes on inside me, anyway. Spen, why didn't you tell me you'd left the Grahame home?"

"I didn't tell anybody. I just left."

"Is it final?"

"Absolutely."

"Spen, I didn't have anything to do with it, did I?"

"You? No."

"It isn't too flattering, the way you said that. Does your wife know about us?"

"Yes. I think so. Suspects, anyway."

223

"You dirty hound," she said with no particular heat.

"You don't suppose for a moment that I told her, do you, Kenny? I can't imagine where she heard."

"If I get dragged into a divorce-court scandal, darling, I'll buy me a gun and shoot your lofty brow full of holes."

"Don't shoot. Better marry me."

Now she was contemplating him meditatively and with a touch of sadness. "I don't know about that," she said. "I'm not so sure I'd want to marry you, even if you meant what you just said."

His hand clamped down on her bare shoulder. He shook the slight body. "If you don't love me why are we here this way?"

"I do love you. But I don't trust you. Not yet."

"That's nice," he said, aggrieved. "That's charming. A fine thing to tell a man for a bedtime story. . . . What's *that?*" Something was buzzing in his ear.

Kenny laughed softly and nuzzled his throat with her chin. "Alarm clock. Eleven-thirty. Bertha'll be here a little after twelve." She reached out and switched out the light. "Debate postponed," she whispered.

No suggestion of their intimacy was ever manifested at the office. Kenny was prudence personified. "Yes, Dr. Brade." "No, Dr. Brade." "I have a note of it, Dr. Brade." Never a side glance of the eye, a quiver of the mobile lips. Consequently Spen was the more surprised when she came into his office and shut the door behind her.

"Spen, there was a man here to see you while you were at lunch."

"Well, why not, Kenny?" he asked, smiling.

"He wasn't a patient."

"Who was he?"

"I don't know. He wouldn't give any name. He said he'd be back. Shall I send him in?"

"Why not?" he repeated.

"I don't know. There's something queer about him. I think he's a foreigner."

"Maybe you're allergic to foreigners. My conscience is clear. So far as I recall I haven't any injured husbands on my list looking for my blood. And my debts aren't in the sheriff's hands yet. You might frisk him for guns or bills, though, if it will ease your mind. Also you might come over here and kiss me before becoming your strictly official self again."

"Certainly not!" she whispered indignantly. Then, in fuller volume, "Very well, Dr. Brade."

The stranger was announced at four o'clock. "He says he's a connection of yours, Dr. Brade," said Kenny's skeptical tones over the wire. Spen deemed it more likely that he was one of those "private-disease" cases who dislike to give their names, though this was distinctly not the Tyre line of practice.

The man who entered was not much older than Spen in appearance, lightly and firmly built, with the grace of perfect coordination in every movement. An athlete of some sort, Spen guessed. Not a boxer, probably; perhaps a fencer. His color was high; the large eyes, dark, soft, somber were belied by an expression inimitably blithe and frank. He was beautifully dressed in every last minute particular. So engaging a personality Spen seldom met with.

"Dr. Spencer Brade?" he said with just the faintest Roughening of the "ence" to a z sound.

"Yes. Sit down. You wished to consult me?" This was as good an opening as any.

"Not professionally." The visitor smiled, showing teeth as perfect as a dentifrice advertisement. "This is personal."

"I don't think I know you, do I?"

"I am Antony d'Zaril." As the other looked politely puzzled he leaned forward and added with confidential amiability, "Your wife's husband."

Spen said coldly, "I don't care for the assumption. As an ex-husband you are definitely out of place here."

"Ah! But I am not an ex-husband, if you will pardon me. That is your role."

"What's this rot?" demanded Spen.

"The police were quite wrong, as I am now able to prove, through advices from Europe. My former wife died six weeks previous to my marriage with Miss Grahame."

"I think you're lying," said Spen hoarsely.

"That I shall pass over in view of your natural disturbance of mind. You can verify the record in Washington."

"Have you seen Carol?"

"No. She is out of town. You did not know that?" he added with a swift, shrewd glance. "Perhaps all is not well between you. That should make the readjustment easier."

A fury of protectiveness swept over Spen. The notion of Carol, with her morbid hatred of publicity, shamed, humiliated,

225

pilloried in the newspapers by a scandal in which there would be the added venom of absurdity, was intolerable.

"There will not be any readjustment," he said.

"There you are in error," was the calm response. "I shall wait for her return."

Spen gripped the arms of his chair, his face tense and white. "Do you want to get yourself killed?" he said.

The other shrugged. "It has been tried before," he replied sunnily. "Never with success. I fight well."

"There won't be any fight," retorted Spen grimly. "I'm perfectly ready and willing to shoot you like a dog."

"And then what a scandal! No, no, my friend." He shook his head. "I give you credit for your honorable intention to kill me. It is what I should wish to do, myself. But it counts for nothing here. Because, you see, I am not afraid."

Obviously this was true. Spen sat back.

"Very well, Mr. d'Zaril——"

"Count d'Zaril, as a matter of record," corrected the other. "And quite genuine if you have any doubts."

Spen bowed. "Count d'Zaril. Why have you come to see me?"

"A visit of courtesy."

"It wouldn't perhaps be blackmail?" suggested Spen on an insinuating inflection.

"Now we shall be serious," said the claimant. "The term blackmail is inadmissible. I am in need of money; I admit it. Your wi—my wife is a very rich woman. *Admettons*-pardon, let us admit for the argument that I could establish my status legally only after difficulty and delay. It can be done—make no doubt of that, my friend—and with unpleasing consequences of publicity if I were legally challenged. But it would perhaps take time. Six months. A year. In a year I may be dead."

Spen stared into the other's eyes. "I think it more than likely," he said.

"Are you trying to be insolent?" asked D'Zaril coldly.

"No. Only professional. If I were your physician——"

"Which you are not." The visitor recovered his smiling aplomb. "I ask your pardon, Dr. Brade. You startled me for the moment. The Orientals say that one's fate is written on his forehead. Are you, then, a prophet?"

"I should not venture to prophesy without further data."

"Ah well! We are never dead till we die."

226

The man turned suddenly white, stretched out a groping hand toward Spen, half rose, and toppled forward as the other jumped for him. He caught the lax body in time to ease it to the floor. Instantly the trained medical mind concentrated upon what was now a technical problem.

D'Zaril was completely unconscious. Breathing and pulse were slow and regular. The color, while pale, was not the bluish tint of oxygen shortage which would indicate a heart attack. Expertly Spen loosened the clothes and ran his hand over the body while he reached with his foot for the concealed switch beneath his desk which would bring Kenny Mangan in with a pretended emergency call, a device to get rid of unwelcome callers.

In front of the left elbow his fingers encountered a curious lump. A small fibroma? An enlarged epitrochlear lymph node? He couldn't tell, but as he continued his brief examination the evidence accumulated in orderly sequence. Lumps in the armpits, in front of the other elbow, in both groins, behind both knees in the depressions that were labeled "popliteal fossae" in the anatomy books. Enlarged lymph nodes everywhere, probably within the abdomen, too, and in the chest. General glandular enlargement. It went with a number of things, but particularly at this age with that strange disease that nobody knew much about except that it sometimes affected the entire lymphatic system of the body and that it was characterized by those peculiar giant cells under the microscope which went under the deceptively innocent name of Dorothy Reed cells. They meant death as certainly as if they had been branded with the death's-head itself.

Kenny Mangan opened the door. "You're wanted in the opera——" she began. "Oh! What happened?"

"Passed out. Get the ammonia."

She returned almost immediately with the bottle.

"I can manage now, thanks," Spen told her. "Don't let anyone come in."

D'Zaril coughed and opened his eyes. "Pardon that I derange you," he murmured.

Spen half lifted him to a chair and brought him a glass of water. "Do that often?" he inquired casually.

"Too often. More often lately." He eyed Spen narrowly. "That surprises you?"

"Not in the least."

The sick man looked down at the disarray of his clothing. "You observed the—the symptoms?"

Spen nodded. "How long have you had them?"

"Oh, a year. More. More." He summoned a pale smile. "We become professional, eh? What would you say?"

"There is considerable glandular involvement," said the surgeon cautiously. "Was there a biopsy?"

"They took out a gland at the hospital for their microscope. It appeared to satisfy them. They were not optimistic. You agree?"

"I should like to make a more thorough examination. Suppose we move into the examination room."

"I see. A medical survey."

"Yes. It won't cost you anything."

"It would be an opportunity," said D'Zaril politely. "For you, also, an opportunity," he added with his slow smile.

"For me?" Spen was puzzled.

"Doubtless. People die under examination, do they not?"

Spen laughed aloud. "I see. But I don't kill my patients. Not intentionally. From the moment you enter that room you are my patient. No more; no less. However, if you are uneasy, I will have in a colleague to safeguard you. Would that relieve your mind?"

The foreigner scrutinized him for a long moment, then made a gesture. "There is no need," he said. "I have made a study of men. I place myself in your hands unreservedly."

Though he went over his subject with scrupulous care, Spen felt that he would be better satisfied to have another opinion. He called in Dr. Sewall, the internist who had taken Carter Hewlett's place, and asked him to make an independent diagnosis. When it was over D'Zaril, once more clad in his impeccable elegance and smoking a cigarette, said quietly:

"And the verdict, if you please?"

"You're not in very good shape."

"They said at the hospital Hodgman's disease."

"Hodgkins," corrected Spen.

"Hodgman, Hodgkin, what does it matter! That those gentleman should have the disease of their own invention instead of me!" said the other with his imperturbable good humor. He drew a deep inhalation of smoke and let it trickle out with obvious enjoyment. "How long would you say?" he inquired in the manner of an impartial observer.

"With reasonable care——"

The visitor stopped him a gesture. "I cannot remember the time when I have lived with rizzonable care."

"I'm afraid you'll have to now."

The handsome head moved from side to side in vigorous negation. "To wrap myself in cotton wool? To go softly all my days? To deny myself this and abjure myself from that? Ah no, I thank you! Life is different to that. I shall live while I live. *Dum vivimus, vivamus.*"

"Not long then."

"And if I take to the cotton wool? What, then, is the bright promise?"

"No promise, bright or otherwise. You might go out to-morrow. You might live six months. Hardly more, I should think. I assume that you want me to be frank with you."

"I thank you," said D'Zaril. "You are kind. You are honest. One feels that you know what to say. I shall then dedicate myself to the life merry. For that money is required."

"How much?"

"A thousand dollars a month," replied the Count. "You would not consider that exorbitant for a rich woman. And it will not last long."

"I do consider it exorbitant," said Spen. "Car—Mrs. Brade. is not rich enough to carry such a burden in addition to her normal expenses."

"The Countess d'Zaril," corrected the other with his fine smile, "must have twice that income. Surely she would be ready to share."

Spen stood up. "I'll get in touch with her," he said, having no such intention in mind. "Come in at this time tomorrow. There will be a full diagnostic and laboratory report for you. Does anyone know you're in town?"

"I'm incognito. It seemed more prudent. Au revoir, Dr. Brade."

Spen got out of a dinner date with Kenny Mangan that evening. He wanted to be alone, the better to think. The upshot of his cogitation was that he cursed himself roundly for a quixotic fool. How was he to get the money, hard-pressed as he was to keep up his payments to Carol? Let her go back to her Tony. . . . No, by God! He wouldn't stand for that. The thought of it made everything within him writhe. And if she elected to deny D'Zaril and fight it out, there would be the scandal, the smearing ink, the insatiable publicity.

Incongruously there flashed into his brain the picture of her as he had left her that night when he passed out of her life, the tousled head buried in the pillow, the gracious, slender figure beneath the filmy nightdress convulsed with sobs—and with it came a hot and angry chivalrous pity. He had caused her enough trouble. She had played fair with him. It wasn't her fault if she couldn't give him all that he wanted of her at first, if she had turned to him too late. Here was his chance to square himself with her—no, with himself. He would keep this new trouble off her; she need never even know of it. He would deal with D'Zaril.

At least it was fortunate for Carol, in view of this development, that she had not lived with Spen. Yet, except for her inner emotions, that would be little help. So far as Charlesville knew, they had been man and wife in the usual relation; the scandal of their supposed cohabitation while she was, in fact, the wife of another man, would be just as morbid, just as destructive to her self-respect. No; he must shield her from that knowledge and dread. That involved meeting D'Zaril's demands. Well, at worst, he could intermit his payments to Carol, thereby showing himself up as a quitter in her eyes, after his haughty and noble gesture. A nice mess for a thin-skinned man.

Count d'Zaril faced a quietly impersonal consultant on the following day.

"On the medical side," Spen told him, "I have to insist upon this: no alcohol, no tobacco, a limited diet, and preferably a month in a sanitarium."

"Advice rejected, my dear Doctor," the patient said gaily.

"You won't last many weeks, then."

"At least they will be lively weeks. I have had few that were not. And the terms?"

"Five hundred dolllars a month. Not a cent more. And only on condition that you leave town and do not try to see or communicate with Mrs. Brade."

To Spen's astonishment a fleeting expression of pain passed over the attractive face before him.

"Is that her wish?" asked D'Zaril in a low voice.

"Yes, explicitly."

"I am sorry. You will tell her that I am sorry, please." Spen nodded. "I have no mind to trouble her. I accept her terms. I shall need one hundred dollars on account to get out of town."

"I'll get it for you," agreed Spen.

"Thank you." He put a card on the desk. "This is my address. Shall we now go to the hotel and have a little drink on it?" As Spen hesitated he added, "Every little drink shortens the time doesn't it?"

Spen laughed. "I can see why women fall for you." He said. The charming blackmailer's last, smiling word as he waved a good-by at the station whither Spen had driven him as a precautionary measure against his changing mind about departure was:

"You are a hard-boiled egg, my friend. That kind one may trust. Perhaps I shall yet return to die in your arms."

"Don't," advised Spen.

CHAPTER XXVI

PUBLIC OPINION is frequently stupid, often rooted in prejudice and guided by unreasoning emotion. But this is to be said for it: convince it that the spirit of fair play has been denied and it revolts. Blanton Tyre's campaign against the James Clinic, which had gone farther than he originally intended, backfired.

Notice was served in uncompromising terms upon the Tyre medical clique that if Owen James and Felix Bernitz were expelled from the Academy, Blanton Tyre's medico-political ambitions would be relegated to the ash can. The Committee on Membership, after a stormy session in which formidable support for the two accused physicians developed, recommended that the suspension be abrogated. At the full meeting of the Academy the report was adopted by a whacking majority, the Tyre forces preserving the silence of intimidation.

"We pulled some power politics on 'em," Owen James

chuckled, reporting to Carol. "The churches got in back of us and the labor unions. My democratic district boss threatened to stir up an inquiry in Council. Cousin Carrie Carksaddan drove down in all her majesty to the *Leader* office and read the riot act to the awed staff. She owns a big block of stock, you know. A couple of the civil organizations passed red-hot resolutions. Old Charley Chadbourne got really mad for the first time since twenty-five years ago, when he punched the Mayor in the nose for trying to bully the Board of Health, and threatened to go to the State Medical Society convention and show up Blanton Tyre. The Tyres quit. They couldn't do anything else."

"Did Flick Fleming get in?" asked Carol eagerly.

Owen's satisfaction dimmed. "No. We couldn't quite put that over yet. Later, I hope."

Carol hesitated before asking, "How did Spen vote?"

"He wasn't at the meeting. He doesn't attend any more."

The morning after his defeat on the James issue Blanton arrived at the office looking deflated.

"Everything is going wrong these days," he said plaintively to Spen.

"What's the matter?" asked his junior, not unsympathetically.

"I'm having a lot of trouble with some of the patients," confessed the clinic head. "They don't seem to have the confidence in me that they used to. It might be age. Some say a surgeon ought to drop the knife at sixty. Yet I feel as vigorous and husky as I did twenty years ago," he declared. At once he drooped. "Sometimes I get to worrying over my technic, that it isn't what it used to be."

"Oh, I wouldn't say that!" returned Spen, reflecting sardonically that said technic probably never had been anything to rely on heavily. "Anything special that's bothering you?"

"Several minor operations that should be mere routine have developed complications," complained his chief. "Nothing serious, but—well, I don't know." He sighed.

(He'd like to have me take over his very private cases, thought Spen. Only he hasn't got the guts to open the subject. It would be a damn sight safer, at that. Wonder what he pulls down for those little relief measures. There must be more of it going on than I thought. Dangerous, too, in hands like his. Something will go really wrong one of these days, and the whole Tyre Clinic will be blown to hell, and my chances with it. Pleasant thought!)

232

"I'm here to pick up any loose ends," said Spen amiably. "Any of them you specially want me to look at?"

Tyre shook a lugubrious head. "Some women are so fussy! They get so they have confidence in one man, and they don't want any others prowling around their insides." Which meant, as Spen readily perceived, that the Tyre "special" patients did not wish to entrust their peculiar feminine secrets to more than one person. "It complicates matters," concluded the other.

Spen gravely agreed that it was unwarranted prudishness.

"You might check up once more on Mrs. de Long," said the other.

Spen found the young widow still languid and weak. All was clearing up satisfactorily, however. After giving her a local treatment he told her that she would need no further attention.

"I like to keep up to date on my bills, Dr. Brade," she said. "Shall I write you a check now?"

"No. Better mail it to the office."

"Very well. You can tell me, I suppose. Does the thousand dollars cover these extra visits?"

He controlled his surprise to answer, "I'm pretty sure it covers everything, Mrs. de Long. You might wait until the first, when you get the bill."

A thousand dollars! So that was what the old boy charged for his "private" cases. That sort of thing certainly paid well. Something popped into his mind which set him to an effort of memory. How would this kind of entry appear on the clinic's books? D & C, probably. And the usual charge for this was one hundred dollars. He could not recall having heard of any larger figure.

"Holding out, is he?" said Spen to himself as he walked to the elevator. "The old bastard!"

He made a mental note to look up the bill against Mrs. de Long, as posted. There was no question of his ever taking a hand in that sort of dirty work, he told himself, beyond clearing up the mess and making all safe after Tyre; but if there were fancy fees going, he'd see to it that he got his proper percentage at the close of the year. Moreover, if he could substantiate his suspicions as to the juggling of the figures, he would have a gun to put to Blanton Tyre's head, at need.

Up to now Dr. Spencer Brade would have indignantly repudiated any slackening of his ethical principles. In the Dorner case there might have seemed to be a letdown, but

233

pragmatically he could justify his course, since his timely intervention had doubtless saved the patient's life. As for Blanton Tyre's peculiar practices, Spen did not *know* but that the treatments were perfectly proper. Therapeutic abortion where the mother's life might be seriously endangered by the ordeal of birth was recognized medical procedure. He himself had not examined any of those cases; certainly no responsibility could attach to him.

Spen was clinging to the letter of his medical virtue like a maid to her technical virginity.

Only the sore pressure of his money needs could have weakened him to his first deliberate concession. The local traction magnate, Rogers Folsom, who had conceived a high opinion of Spen since the young doctor's diagnosis of his stomach trouble, brought in his second daughter, Mrs. Chris Farr. Selena Farr, heavy with child, was a husky, healthy, handsome, generously built woman who played number two on the local golf team and now resented the interruption to her favorite game. Spen knew her to be a patient of Dr. Samuel Pendergast, a capable and conservative obstetrician, who was often associated with the Grahame family physician, Dr. Cannaday.

Mrs. Farr explained that she wanted a Caesarean delivery. Examination showed her to be quite normal.

"Why a Caesarean?" Spen asked.

"My last kid kept me off the course for two months," she answered. "Besides, I want to be sterilized at the same time. This'll be my third. I've done my duty by the country. Enough is enough. No more for me."

"What does Dr. Pendergast say about it?"

"Oh, he's against it, of course, the old sissy. He thinks a girl ought to go on having chain children till she drops."

Spen smiled. "You look able to."

"Well, I'm not. I was just getting back onto my game when this one came along."

"Get your clothes on," he directed. "I'll talk to your father."

He was sweating lightly when he went out to tackle Rogers Folsom. This was going to be touchy business. But the want of immediate cash drove him.

"Is it all right?" Folsom asked.

Spen had already set him down as a hard man but a doting father. "Why, yes," he answered with calculated hesitancy.

"The method is one which physicians don't like to adopt in ordinary cases."

"My daughter is not an ordinary case," returned the arrogant old man.

"No; she isn't," allowed Spen.

"Would there be any danger?"

"Practically none. Though normal birth is—well, more normal."

Folsom turned upon him the impatient glance of the man of affairs, accustomed to getting his own way without demur. "Well, what's the hitch?"

"It's a delicate matter, Mr. Folsom. While I don't like to bring in the financial——"

"Charge what you like within reason," said the other curtly.

"The charge will be the usual thousand dollars. But there is the matter of time. For special reasons, it would be a convenience if you could see your way to——"

The visitor's eyebrows went up, but he said, "Give you a check now, if you like."

"That will not be necessary." Spen breathed a sigh of relief. That hundred, his commision, would save his life for the present, though there would have to be other hundreds to follow. "If you will make it out to the clinic and mail it in. It's very kind of you. Mrs. Farr had better be at the hospital Friday afternoon."

And what about Dr. Pendergast? Spen knew him slightly, enough to estimate him as a positive and potentially troublesome customer. Ten to one he would be around.

The forecast was correct. The obstetrician was a small rolypoly man with a merry eye and a firm mouth. The latter was the more in evidence when he appeared in Spen's doorway, confronting him with a cold stare.

"I hear that a patient of mine has been consulting you, Dr. Brade," he began.

"Mrs. Farr? Yes. Sit down, Dr. Pendergast."

"I can say what I have to say standing," was the uncompromising response.

"Very well; stand then," said Spen pleasantly.

"You agreed to do a Caesarean section on her."

"I did."

"Do you happen to know that she has had two children without difficulty?"

"I am in the habit of getting histories on my patients, Dr. Pendergast."

"And that her pelvic measurements are normal, even oversize?" The little man was controlling himself with an obvious effort.

"I noted the fact."

"Then in the name of hell, why do a Caesarean?"

"Because she wishes it," returned Spen blandly. "Also she wishes to be sterilized."

"Great God! And when did that become an indication for a section in normal pregnancy? Don't you know that section carries a heavy mortality through the country?"

"Not in my hands."

"Damn your hands!" The visitor was letting himself go now. "I'm putting it to you as a matter of principle, if you can understand that. Why not do it after she's had the baby normally? You can't deny there's less chance of trouble that way."

"I might argue about that," said Spen with the full knowledge that no argument would stand up for a minute.

"Then you're still going to do the section?"

"I am."

Pendergast said nothing more until he reached the door. Then he fired back, "Then to hell with your arguments and you. You're a fit partner for Blanton Tyre. I can't think of anything worse to say."

His voice rang along the hallway. In a few moments Blanton Tyre appeared. Spen thought that there was a tinge of apprehension in his smile.

"What was Sam Pendergast sounding off about?"

"I'm doing a Caesarean on Mrs. Farr."

Tyre nodded approvingly. "And you'll do a good one, my boy. Funny thing about Pendergast. He always raises hell when anybody does a Caesarean on one of his patients. He hates the sight of me, since I had a bit of bad luck several years ago and lost one of them."

When Tyre had departed Brade went to the shelf and took down his worn copy of Williams' *Obstetrics*, which had been the Bible of obstetrical procedure at Lakeview. Under "Indications" he read once more the words he had remembered hearing from the lips of the great one himself:

"At the present time I consider that the operation is being

abused and that not a few patients are sacrificed to the *furor operativus* of obstetricians and general surgeons, who are ignorant of the fundamental principles of the obstetric art. This being the case, the conscientious obstetrician should be particularly careful in the recognition of indications for Caesarean section."

He dropped the book and lighted a cigarette. "Just the same, the patient has *some* rights of decision," he argued with himself.

He did an expert job on Selena Farr. There were no complications. There would be no more pregnancies to impair her golf scores. Rogers Folsom not only sent in his check overnight but when his daughter was discharged from the hospital handed Spen two hundred-dollar bills as a personal recognition. The money went into the D'Zaril fund.

On the pretense of checking up the records, preliminary to putting in his ten-per-cent claim, Spen got his chance to see the De Long entry.

Mrs. Carol S. de Long; D & C and aftercare......$150.00

So Blanton Tyre had held out the extra eight hundred and fifty.

The old skate must be up against it to have taken such a chance. Rumors had reached Spen that both the Tyres had been plunging in the stock market unsuccessfully. With a sour grin he reflected that they, too, had reason for working the medical money racket overtime. All in the same boat.

He carefully copied the line from the ledger.

Scrimping, borrowing as he could, and holding out on all but the most pressing of his bills, he was able to cover his three-hundred-dollar-payment to Carol on the first of the month and to send D'Zaril his promised check. The one to Carol came back by return mail with a cool little note, one sentence of which worried him.

"I am sure," she wrote, "that you must be in special need of the money these days."

"Special need." What could that mean? Had D'Zaril double-crossed him and seen Carol after all? He had to know that. He called up Grahame Lodge.

"When can I see you, Carol?"

"What about?"

"I can't tell you over the wire."

"Well—any time, I suppose."

237

"This afternoon?"

"If you like. But I don't think you'd better come here."

"Aunt Candace?" he interpreted.

"Yes. You're not right popular with her. What about meeting me at the club?"

"I've resigned."

"Oh! Well, the Green Bay Tree then. Five o'clock all right? . . . Good-by."

He was first at the rendezvous. Carol arrived five minutes late, nodded brightly as to a casual acquaintance, and sat down opposite him.

"Martini, please," she said.

He ordered two. "What's the idea, sending back my check?" he queried.

"You wouldn't have resigned from the country club unless you were hard up."

"You didn't know that when you wrote," he pointed out. " 'Special need'; that was the phrase. What did you mean by it?"

Her eyes, raised to his, were a cold challenge. "You won't like it."

"Shoot," he said.

"When you have to do operations like that on Selena Farr, you must be pretty desperate. I don't want any part of that money, Spen."

"I suppose that damned old tittle-tattle, Cannaday, has been shooting off his mouth," he said angrily. "What business is it of his? She is my patient, and that was recognized surgical procedure."

"Would you have done it before you married me?" she demanded.

"Where it was indicated, I certainly would."

"Oh, Spen!" she said wearily.

He tried to switch back to the money issue. "You know how I feel about my debt to you," he said.

She disregarded this. "What makes it so rotten for me," she said bitterly, "is that it's partly my fault. If I hadn't bribed you to marry me you might have been all right. I'm responsible."

He had an impulse of generosity. "That's not true, Carol. It would have been just the same without you. That dirty deal they gave me at Lakeview settled it for me; after that I was out for the dollars, anyway. You only made it a little easier for me to get them."

"Yes; but you were going to get them legitimately. A thing like this Farr operation makes me feel degraded for you."

He flushed darkly. "I might point out to you that it is none of your business."

"Aunt Candace has always said there was nothing the Tyres won't do for money. But you—even after you went in with them, I hoped you'd be different."

"You don't know what you're talking about," he snapped. "If I'd followed your wishes and your aunt's I'd be working my head off for Owen James' amateur Utopia and living on your money. I'm all through with charity. I'm sending back that check to you, and I want you to cash it."

"Oh, all right, Spen," said she dispiritedly. "Let's not quarrel over it. I hate quarreling, except in good cause."

He could not resist one more shot in his own defense. "Don't you think that you're just a little bit miscast as a defender of medical ethics? You seem to have swallowed whole everything that stuffed shirt of a Cannaday told you."

"Very likely," was the listless reply. "Let's talk of something else."

They chatted at random for a while, until he found an opening in her reference to the girlhood escapade in Miami.

"By the way," he said with an effect of complete casualness, "have you ever heard any more of your ex-husband?"

"No," she answered indifferently. "Why should I?"

"No reason," he admitted with a lightened mind. "If he ever should turn up I hope you'll let me know at once."

"I don't think Tony's the sort to make any trouble," she said. She rose. "I've some shopping to do before the stores close."

CHAPTER XXVII

UNTIL he met Blanton Tyre coming out of church that Sunday morning Spen never realized how poisonously he hated his chief. The fat jowls shone with unctuous self-righteousness. The Sabbath voice which issued from them in greeting was rich in the carry-over of pious intonations. Plainly the old crook had made his peace, or more likely his bargain, with heaven to his entire satisfaction. To hell with him!

Back of him a few paces Owen James walked with old Mrs. Carskaddan. He nodded to Spen with smiling friendliness. More than I'd have done in his shoes, thought Spen. Lifting his hat, the non-churchgoer passed on, reflecting sourly on the contrast between the two medical types, the go-getter and the humanitarian. Well, he had made his choice. No regrets, he told himself.

Having no special destination or object other than exercise in his stroll, he found his feet steering him by subconscious direction toward Hookworm Flats. Nearing the James Clinic, on the opposite sidewalk, he saw a familiar figure emerge. He remembered hearing that Terry Martin, whose contractual term with the Tyres had been completed, had joined the James forces. The little pathologist saw him and fairly ran across the street.

"By God, you're my man!"

Spen wrenched his arm loose from the hard grasp. "Drunk again, Terry?"

"No, damn your eyes! Come in here. I've got a case I can't handle."

"This is my day off," returned the other coldly.

"No; it isn't. I'm in a hell of a hole. These goddamn emergency cases are always popping up when there's no one to handle them. Flick Fleming's out of town until evening. I can't find Owen. I've called up four fellows, and every last one of the sons of bitches has ducked. The man's dying before my eyes, Spen, and I don't dare touch him. I don't know enough."

Spen hesitated. Reading his expression, as he thought, the little man said slowly, "I see. Of course it's a charity case. Not a cent in it. Okay; I'll pay you, myself."

"To hell with your money!" retorted Spen angrily.

Terry's face cleared. "That's the talk! You'll come, then?"

At any other time Spen might have refused. He had practically promised that he would have no further dealings with the James enterprise. But Blanton Tyre's smug, Sunday visage rose before him, inspiring rebellion.

"Yes; I'll come. What's the case?"

"Strangulated hernia. Brought in with scalp wounds after a barroom fight and almost died while we were getting him to the operating room. I'll get you some instruments."

At first sight Spen saw that it was touch-and-go. Probably the effort of the fight had brought on the crisis. Speed and precision would count here. So he must race against death for a prize that was worthless to him.

Never had he worked better. When at the end of an hour he took off his gloves and gown he met Owen James's smile.

"I got in for the finish. That was a swell job, Spen."

"He ought to pull through."

"If he doesn't it won't be your fault. I'd have been too late and probably too slow."

"What'll Old Puffgut say when he finds you've been out of bounds?" inquired the irrepressible Terry.

"I see no reason why he should find out," put in Owen quickly. "Spen, why don't you drop in for cheese and ale this evening?"

Spen changed color. He could face Owen James, with his broad and understanding tolerance, or Terry Martin's waspish cynicism, but not the possible contempt of Bernie Bernitz or the hurt friendship of Flick Fleming.

"I'm afraid I'm all tied up this evening," he lied awkwardly.

"So we're social outcasts as well as medical," jeered Terry. "Hey! Don't swing on me. I take it back. I'd like to take a lot

241

more back if I weren't so honest," he added with a wistful directness which hurt the listener. "Why don't you quit that bunch, Spen?"

"Why don't you mind your own business, Terry?"

"Okay; okay. Question withdrawn. Thanks, anyway, boy. I've never seen a neater job."

After he had gone Terry said regretfully, "There's a fine ruin, Owen."

The other shook his head. "I won't believe he's ruined yet. Only warped."

"God! What a waste! Did you ever see a slicker bit of surgery in your life?"

"That wasn't wasted, was it?" countered Owen with his slow smile.

Waiting on his desk when he entered his office in the morning, Spen found an envelope. Within was a one-paragraph item, clipped from the morning daily, reporting the injury of John Marrabout in a saloon brawl and the operation "by Dr. Spencer Brade. The injured man is expected to recover."

"Please see me about this at once. B. T." was penciled on the margin. (Every inch the schoolmaster, Spen thought. It's about time I had it out with Dr. Blanton Tyre.)

No Sabbath beatitude mollified the severe countenance which the chief turned upon his erring subordinate. Instead there was a magisterial scowl, intended to intimidate and awe. It missed fire. Spen smiled cheerfully. He had decided upon cool courtesy as his best play.

"Is this item in the *Leader* correct?" Tyre began formidably.

"Substantially."

"What is your explanation?"

"No explanation."

"I insist upon one."

"My Sundays are my own," Spen pointed out. "Any of my working hours, insofar as they are connected with the clinic, I shall be glad to account for."

"Not your own to employ for the benefit of the James rabble," retorted the chief with rising choler.

"This was an emergency case. The man would have died."

"I don't give a damn."

"Nor I," agreed Spen with provocative amiability. "From that point we start even."

"You have no excuse for violating our agreement?"

242

"I might refer you to the code," answered Spen. "As I told you, the man was on the point of death."

The old man's breath puffed violently. "I shall see my lawyers about this at once. Your usefulness here is ended." He reached for his gold-headed cane, presented by the local society.

"Just a moment, Dr. Tyre." Spen's voice and manner were smooth. "If this goes to the lawyers they might be interested in an item of bookkeeping that I have noticed."

"Bookkeeping?" repeated the other irresolutely.

"What is your regular charge for an abortion?"

"Why you—— Abort—— What do you mean by this insolence?" spluttered Tyre.

"A thousand dollars, isn't it?" pursued the relentless questioner.

Tyre cast an affrighted glance at the door. "Keep your voice down," he pleaded. "I don't know what——"

"Oh, I think you know quite well. You entered the De Long D & C on the books as one hundred and fifty dollars. Mrs. de Long's check was for one thousand dollars. I saw it." This was stretching the truth, but Spen was in no mind to be meticulous about details.

The chief's shaking hand went to his lips. "That was a private arrangement," he managed to get out.

"I don't doubt it. And I don't doubt that you have plenty of others. The point is that you are withholding fees from the clinic."

Tyre flapped his hands in feeble protest. There was no more fight in him. "You don't understand the situation," he protested.

"Oh, thoroughly!" his junior assured him. "Not only that, but I consider that it is growing too risky. I happen to know that the Sigmund girl came within a short inch of dying last month."

"That was a therapeutic abortion," protested Tyre, beginning to sweat between the eyes.

"Queer, isn't it, how many therapeutics are found necessary among widows and supposed virgins?" observed Spen. "That class of case seems to develop the most troublesome symptoms, too, I've noticed."

Tyre's plump countenance seemed to be disintegrating before Spen's eyes. He almost whimpered. "I know it's dangerous. But what am I to do? I'd lose some of my best families if I turned them down when cases of this sort come up."

Spen knew by frequent hearsay that often the severest kind of pressure was brought to bear by influential patients, which only rigid rectitude on the part of the physician could withstand. It was so easy to yield and save a desperate situation, involving scandal and disgrace, "just this once." More than likely this consideration, quite as much as the money involved, had first overpersuaded Blanton Tyre to embark on the shameful and perilous course of irregular medicine.

"What am I to do?" repeated Tyre wretchedly.

"Refer the cases to me," answered Spen bluntly.

The other turned incredulous eyes upon him. "I didn't suppose you'd touch that sort of thing."

"I didn't say I would. But at least I could be at hand to see that it's properly done and that nothing goes wrong."

"It would be the heaviest kind of weight off my mind," admitted his chief.

"I'm only willing to go that far because I need the money," said Spen bitterly. "I've got to have it. Here is my proposition; take it or leave it; I don't care a damn which. Hereafter we are going to be more careful about these cases; take only those that are absolutely trustworthy and, of course, can pay the price. And we divide the fees fifty-fifty."

"Fifty-fifty!" squawked Tyre. "When I do all the work?"

"And with what results? What about the De Long aftermath? And the Sigmund peritonitis?"

Indignation turned to sadness in the other's voice. "What about my son?" he inquired in virtuous protest. "He is entitled to his twenty-five per cent."

"Pay it out of your share, then," replied Spen, unmoved by this paternal solicitude. "No; this is going to be quite separate from the regular clinic work. It won't appear on the books. Those are the conditions, and I'm not going to argue them. If I'm going to be a medical whore I'll get my price for it," he concluded firmly.

Tyre's opposition collapsed. "Have it your own way," he yielded. "I never want to go through the same anxieties that I've been having with some of those patients."

Triumph and nausea were mingled in Spen's heart as he walked out of his superior's office. All right; he'd sold out deliberately; let himself in for a moral responsibility, even though he did not actually perform the illegal act. But only for a special purpose and a limited time. As soon as his debts were settled, Carol paid off, and the D'Zaril threat lifted from his shoulders—and he figured a few months at the most for this—he was forever through with anything but strictly ethical practice.

That there was a twofold risk in the racket to which he had committed himself as a participant, though not as a principal, he fully realized. His technical skill would minimize surgical danger. Even so, women and particularly inexperienced girls were prone to reckless disregard of directions and thus to disastrous aftereffects. At Lakeview he had seen deaths due wholly to the carelessness of the patient. Then, too, women were apt to be loose-tongued; even where their own reputations were involved. Medical circles in Charlesville still gossiped about the brilliant young obstetrician who had left town because a high-school girl got drunk and babbled.

Such were the hazards of the game. Spen reckoned them coolly. If Blanton Tyre could get away with it for years, with no worse penalty than vague suspicions and suppressed whispers, surely he, Spencer Brade, was taking only the shortest chances in the few months to which he meant to limit his unhallowed specialization. He would see to it that every precaution was taken. He would insist on the right of veto. On any reasonable theory of chances, it ought to come through all right. If it shouldn't . . . To relieve that grisly speculation Spen got so thoroughly drunk that he had to cancel two hospital operations on the plea of illness next morning.

Blanton Tyre now kept exerting pressure upon him to participate in whatever "special" cases came into the clinic.

Several of these Spen peremptorily rejected, once where the physical condition of the applicant involved special risk, and more than once where the reliability of the patient was dubious. In two instances, after stormy argument, Tyre took matters into his own inefficient hands and proceeded without his assistant's aid. Disaster followed.

It was on a Monday morning that the chief was waiting for Spen in the door of his own office, which he had left open. His habitually ruddy face was pale, his usually urbane composure lacking.

"I'd like to talk to you a minute, Brade," he said.

"Sure, said Spen. He went in. Tyre closed the door.

"I need your help on a case."

"All right. What is it?"

"Well, it's sort of an infection."

"What kind of infection?"

"After a curettement."

Spen's face grew grim. "I see. Where is she?"

"Markland Hospital."

"Let's go."

As he stood beside the bed of the flashy blonde woman a short twenty minutes later Spen saw that Blanton Tyre was indeed badly in need of help. The hectic flush on cheeks normally pallid, the overbright eyes, the restless movements, all these spelled infection to trained eyes. He made a brief examination that covered all important points, then followed Tyre from the room.

"How long has this been going on?" he asked when the door closed behind them.

"Shh!" Tyre looked up and down the hall. "Come into the next room; it's empty." With the door closing them in, he wiped perspiration from his broad forehead. "I operated on her a week ago."

"Where?"

"At the office."

"Why didn't I know about it?"

"You were away on one of your week ends," returned his chief with a touch of malice. "It was after hours Saturday."

"And you let her come to the office!"

"It looked easy. I've done them there before," protested Tyre.

Spen curbed his angry disgust. "Well, what happened then?"

"She went home. Two days later she had a hemorrhage which was controlled with ergot and pituitrin. I thought she was all right then." He wiped his brow with a large silk handkerchief. "Day before yesterday she had a chill, and I sent her to the hospital."

"Temperature?"

"Hundred and four yesterday. She had another chill."

"What did you do?"

"I gave her some aspirin. It reduced the fever."

"What has reducing the fever got to do with it?" Spen burst out. "What did you give her to control the infection?"

"I gave her some more ergot."

"While she went ahead and got septicemia!"

Tyre bleated like a fat sheep. "How did I know it wasn't a

246

sapremia, that there wasn't some placenta there that was causing the trouble?"

"How did you know anything? Well, this isn't getting us anywhere. Let's get busy."

It was a familiar battle that Spen began to fight now, a battle against infection that was swiftly attacking the vital structures in its path. Threatening to destroy the whole community of organs and systems that made up the body. Years before he had learned how to fight this battle when he had been a white-suited intern back at Lakeview. Then there had been no wonder-working sulfannilamide drugs to use in the blitzkrieg against bacteria, but they had fought a good fight, nevertheless. Transfusions, alcohol sponges for fever, morphia to relieve pain, even antiseptic drugs injected directly into the blood stream, all had been weapons with which his skilled hands were familiar. But sometimes every effort had been useless, every defense against infection too late to prevent its going on to other structures.

And in spite of the new wonder drugs, this was one of those cases where nothing seemed to avail. One whole night he stayed at the bedside of the woman who was dying of Blanton Tyre's carelessness. One whole night he injected the drug carefully at regular intervals, helped the nurse with alcohol sponges, the cold packs that seemed to make no headway against the invader who could not be seen, yet whose presence was nevertheless so definite. And toward morning he knew what he had intuitively known all along, that he was not to succeed. As dawn broke into the east windows he drew the sheet up to cover the face.

Blanton Tyre was pacing nervously up and down the hall outside when Spen came from the room. He hastened toward him.

"She's gone," Spen said.

Tyre staggered against the wall. "My God! My God! The death certificate! What shall we say?"

Spen looked at him with eyes too tired to show contempt. "I'm thinking of that," he said. "I'll certify that death was from endometritis and metritis from a cervical infection."

"Can you get away with it?"

"I don't know. I think so." He smiled mirthlessly. "Who's going to make trouble? After all, nobody suspects me of doing abortions—yet."

The choice now presented itself in plain terms. No longer was Blanton Tyre to be trusted. Spen must either definitely break his ties with the clinic and get out, which he could not afford to do with D'Zaril on his hands and the debt to Carol unsatisfied, or he must, himself, assume responsibility for such "private" cases as could not be avoided. For a time he tried to cozen himself into thinking that he might continue his halfway measure of acting as non-participating consultant. Even so, he could not insure the aging surgeon's keeping his methods clean of such infection as had carried death to young Mrs. Parry. No; he must either go the whole hog or quit.

Then the decision obtruded in simple form.

No inkling of what impended had entered his mind when Selena Farr came into his office that morning. The big, gay, careless woman athlete slumped into a chair, fished a cigarette from her bag, lighted it with shaking fingers, and turned an anxiety-furrowed face to the physician.

"Can I talk to you, man to man?"

"Certainly."

"I'm in a hell of a jam."

"Have you been having any more trouble?" asked Spen, concerned. That superfluous Caesarean!

"Not that. No; I'm fine. Broke eighty twice last week. Do you know my older sister Clarice?"

"That's Mrs. Manning, isn't it? Only slightly."

"She's very pious and correct and strait-laced and all that. Everything that I'm not. And she's tried to bring up Mariette on those lines."

"Mariette is her daughter?"

His visitor nodded. "My goddaughter. She's a darling kid. Only eighteen. Lovely and happy and innocent. Too damned innocent. With logical results."

Spen whispered softly. "Won't the man marry her?"

"He happens to be married, the bastard! He doesn't even know. Mariette came to me. I'm the only one she isn't afraid of. She's desperate, poor kitten! Dr. Brade, will you help us out?"

"Why do you come here?"

"Don't try to bluff me." There was more of entreaty than rudeness in the speech. "That old harpy of a Blanton Tyre has been in that line for years. You won't pretend you don't know it."

"Then I refer you to him," returned Spen sourly.

"Don't be that way," she pleaded. "I wouldn't let him touch the child with a ten-foot pole. Doctor, let me bring her here to see you."

"No. Not here. Where is she?"

"At our house. My husband doesn't know anything about it."

"Who does?"

"Not a soul in the world except me and my father. I had to go to him for the money. He's a grand old guy. He's given me a signed check in blank. I'll turn it over to you." Reading his face, she got up, ran to him, seized his arm in her strong grip. "I know the money wouldn't do it with you," she said tensely. "But think of that poor kid. I swear to God, I believe she'll kill herself unless I can get her out of this. Anyway, you can't refuse to see her."

"Very well. I'll come to your house at five o'clock," said Spen. "But mind you, Mrs. Farr, it commits me to nothing."

The girl came into the darkened room, pitifully young and frightened, pitifully shamed, cowering like some small, scared wild creature. She was incoherent, could hardly answer Spen's gentle questions. It was not hard for him to believe that she might kill herself or even wear herself down into a collapse from sheer nervous terror and apprehension. This being so, would he not be saving a life by surgical intervention? No; that wouldn't do. That slippery subterfuge, "therapeutic abortion," was all very well for a pious fraud like Blanton Tyre. Such easy self-deceptions were not for Spencer Brade. An abortion was an abortion—and he was going through with this one.

Yet he could honestly plead to his own judgment that it was not wholly the money consideration. The element of human pity and of helpfulness in distress entered into it too.

"Have everything ready here at five o'clock tomorrow," he bade Selena Farr.

"Bless you!" she said and, to his astonished distress, burst into tears.

When it was over he gave his directions to Mrs. Farr. "Keep her in bed and absolutely quiet for three days."

"What shall I fill in the check for?"

"A thousand dollars."

"Father would stand for more. He's been almost crazy about this. Mariette is his favorite grandchild."

Spen shook his head. Conscience might be lax in one department; it would not permit him to cheat.

249

Back in his office he made an entry in the page-a-day book which contained his personal record.

Performed my first pay abortion today. Very successful. Evidently I am a natural for this kind of practice. Brilliant future for rising young specialist.

He read the lines over with a rancid smile, then tore out the page and chewed it to a pulp. After that he went to the St. Charles bar.

He slept that night in alcoholic heaviness and woke with the foul taste of self-contempt in his throat. One drink did not wash it out, but the second helped. Several more brought him through the day. Happily he had no operations posted which could not be postponed. On succeeding days he thought Blanton Tyre regarded him queerly. Let the old bird make one crack and he, Spen, would jump down his throat. Over the week end he would get away and steady down. He got a private word with Kenny.

"Let's run down to the seashore over Sunday, hon."

"I don't know, Spen," she returned with a troubled little pucker between the level eyes.

"What's the matter? Not off me, are you?" He smiled confidently.

"I'm worried. Do you know, there hasn't been a day this week that you haven't had liquor on your breath?"

"Bunk!" he said impatiently. "When a man works as hard as I do he needs something once in a while."

"I'll tell you," she said persuasively. "Let's go somewhere where there aren't any drinks."

"Is it as bad as that?" he laughed. "Okay, guardian angel. You're all the stimulant I need. Pick your place."

In a distant, quiet mountain resort he got a good rest and a sober view of himself. On the drive back early Monday morning he said to the girl:

"Kenny, I'm thinking of going on the water wagon."

"It's a grand idea," she said with enthusiasm.

"For a month."

"If it was a year it wouldn't hurt my feelings."

"Oh well; it's only an experiment. To prove how easy it is."

"Of course it'll be easy for you, darling," she said with a confidence which was half hope, half pretense.

250

WITH the end of the fiscal year now approaching, Spen calculated that he should draw down nearly ten thousand dollars as his share of the clinic's profits, after deducting his monthly allowance. The figures presented to him in the accountant's neat schedule fell some two thousand dollars short of his estimate. At first he angrily believed that the Tyres had gypped him. Reflection convinced him that the "D & C specials" which, for obvious reasons did not appear on the books, accounted for the discrepancy. It was equally patent that he could not insist upon a checkup. What composition Blanton Tyre had made with his son on the specials, Spen had no way of knowing. Quite possibly the whole matter had been concealed from that rather obtuse and undiscerning young man. However, that was no concern of Spen's.

What did concern him was the disposition of the fund now at his disposal. A horde of small bills ate up nearly a thousand dollars of it. After careful calculation he sent to Aunt Candace a check for eighteen hundred dollars to cover his share of the household expenses during his stay at Grahame Lodge. Her reply by return mail was characteristic.

DEAR SPENCER,

I have your check for eighteen hundred dollars, for which my acknowledgments. Presumably you expected me to return it with a haughty note. Instead I have turned it over to Owen James for the work of his clinic.

I bear you no ill will. But I hope you will see your way to

cooperating in setting Carol free to rebuild her life on a basis of reality, with the least possible delay, trouble, and publicity.

Yours faithfully,

CANDACE M. GRAHAME.

"Free to rebuild her life." That meant marriage with Owen James. Illogically Spen revolted from surrendering what little claim he had upon Carol. Another consideration swayed him. Carol's marriage to Owen would be a genuine union. She would live with him; have children by him presumably, a thought which caused Spen a sick qualm. Assuming D'Zaril's statement to be true, those children would be illegitimate. He must protect her against that.

If now he yielded to his uneasy impulse to be free of financial obligation to her, what excuse would he have for not agreeing to a divorce? Legal action would surely get into the papers. There was always the risk of its reaching D'Zaril's eye. What would be his course if he saw Spen's financial responsibility toward him dissolving with the dissolution of the supposed marriage tie? No; that was too great a chance to take. He must hold off; dribble the monthly installments along; perhaps decrease or even omit them until D'Zaril was obliging enough to die. Meantime he should be able, with his enhanced means, to lay aside something from month to month.

Once he had broken over and taken pay for the forbidden medical practice, Spen had no longer an adequate defense against Blanton Tyre's increasing insistence that he do the actual work in this class of surgery. Indeed, it was much safer so. And, after all, the number of applicants was small, the accepted ones smaller still. Spen's rigid censorship held it down. He got an unpleasant intimation, however, of how widely the "grapevine," always operative in a city like Charlesville, had spread information of the clinic's secret side, when Blanton Tyre called him in consultation upon a Northern visitor who appeared at the clinic.

Miss Ethelreda Cassilis was a Detroit belle who was spending several months with the Arbuthnots, relatives of Carol and old patients of Blanton Tyre's. So self-possessed was she as she answered Spen's interrogation that he at once suspected former experience, an assumption which later proved correct.

"Who sent you to Dr. Tyre?" he asked.

252

"I asked for the most reliable doctor in town, and they referred me here," was the bland reply.

"Then you've been through this before?"

"Oh yes; I've always been irregular."

Repressing a sardonic impulse to ask whether the irregularity was moral or functional, Spen inquired:

"When were you exposed?"

She made her eyes wide and innocent. "I don't know what you mean, Dr. Brade. I only want a treatment."

Spen said sternly, "Unless you are honest with us it is quite useless to come here."

Still she would not give in. "There's been something queer for just over two months. It's nothing new. I've never been quite normal."

"I'm sure this is entirely normal, Miss Cassilis," said he grimly.

"Dr. Tyre said the condition was easily relieved," insisted the girl.

Spen drew his principal aside. "I don't like this. She knows too much."

"That's the safest kind," argued Tyre.

"She didn't just walk in on us. Somebody told her."

"Sally Arbuthnot telephoned me. We can't afford to turn her down."

"Are the Arbuthnots paying for this?" asked Spen with distaste.

"No indeed. The girl has millions back of her. They're the Cassilis Gear people, you know."

"She's a spoiled beauty. I know the type. They're not to be depended on to follow orders."

"I'll take all the responsibility," declared his chief pompously.

"Very well," said Spen, though still reluctant. "Have her come back at five-thirty." The clinic would officially be closed then.

The girl went through the nerve-racking process with perfect composure.

"Thank you both very much," she said with casual politeness when it was over. "I'll send you a check the first of the month. I'm a little short just now."

"What would you bet we ever get it?" said Blanton Tyre with a face of discomposure as the door closed behind her.

"The money isn't what worries me," answered Spen. "It's the girl. Absolutely irresponsible. I'm afraid of that kind."

"She promised me solemnly to stay in bed for three days and keep quiet the rest of the week. She's supposed to have had a superficial growth on the thigh removed. I'm to dress it once a day, so I shall be keeping track of her."

Spen shook his head. "I don't like it."

Passing the lobby entrance to the St. Charles restaurant two evenings later, he heard a clear laughing voice, familiar in its intonations, announcing:

"But I *want* to sing. I sing very well."

He advanced to the doorway. Ethelreda Cassilis was seated with a group of young married people and post-debs. She caught sight of him.

"There's my handsome young doctor. Sit down and have a drink."

Scrutinizing her in dismay and wrath, he thought better of his first instinct to refuse. Something had to be done about this. Her face flamed with danger signals: the too-brilliant eyes, the fiercely flushed cheeks, the throbbing vein in the slender throat. She gave him her hand. It was dry and hot. Taking the chair brought by the waiter, he accepted the offer of a highball, which he barely touched.

"Will you dance?" he asked Sally Arbuthnot, who was next to him, as the music resumed.

"I think you might have asked *me*," pouted the beauty.

"That leg of yours ought to be quiet," he warned her with all emphasis he dared express.

She made a face at him. "Sour puss!"

On the floor he said to Sally, "Can you get her out of here?"

"Why, she's all right," protested the other.

"Get her home," insisted the physician. "Can't you see she's ill?"

"It's only that she's been drinking. She says she feels grand."

"She's burning with fever. Do I have to argue it with you?"

Impressed at last, Sally said, "Will you come with us?"

"No. But I'll phone Dr. Tyre to come to your house at once."

Only after vehement argument could the guest of honor be prevailed upon to leave. Then she insisted that "the handsome doctor" accompany her.

"I like the handsome doctor," she kept repeating pathetically. "Don't part two loving hearts."

Sorely against his inclination, Spen was forced to go along in the car. They met Blanton Tyre's car at the entrance to the Arbuthnot place, and the junior managed to get away.

Going to Blanton Tyre's room in the morning, Spen got a shock. The man looked unbelievably old and shattered. At sight of his associate he began to rock himself to and fro. Tears ran down his puffed cheeks.

"What is it?" demanded Spen.

"The Cassilis girl."

"Is she dead?"

"Not yet. I've been up all night with her at the hospital. General peritonitis."

"Great God! Why didn't you call me?"

"I thought she was going to die in my hands. I didn't want to involve you, Spen."

Moved by the first decent impulse Spen had ever known the old boy to exhibit, Spen went over and laid a hand on his shoulder. "Get hold of yourself. We're in this together. Take over for me here. I'm going to the hospital."

Spen left him still crying helplessly.

A nurse was holding Ethelreda Cassilis in bed when Spen arrived. The girl kept repeating in the bitter persistency of delirium:

"I won't go through with it. I tell you, I won't. You can't argue with me. I won't! I won't!"

It wasn't a pretty clinical picture; these things never were. The flushed cheeks, the roving brilliant eyes that recognized nothing, the constant picking at the bedcovers as if they were alive with vermin, the continually reiterated pharases which were meaningless but always insistent—all those were things that anyone could see. The real story was there for the trained hand and eye to discover, the tense rigid abdomen, the red spots on toes and fingers that could be nothing but secondary abscesses from a blood stream rotten with infection of pyemia, the spiking lines of the temperature and pulse chart. Blanton Tyre, damn his craven soul, had ordered no laboratory work, but Spen could visualize the report, the elevated white blood count, the red plates of the blood culture with the pale spottings of bacterial colonies surrounded by the clear zone of hemolysis. He could even picture the streptococci under the microscope in long purple chains. He prayed that it was the hemolytic form, for that would respond to drug therapy, not the other anerobic, oxygen-hating bugs that swept on their path, unhindered by any treatment yet known.

Wearily he braced himself for the fight.

"Sulfathiazole, one gram every four hours. Cold sponge for elevated temperature," he wrote in the order book.

Even as he left the picture had changed again. The girl was shivering beneath heavy bedcovers in the rigor of a chill, shivering while the fire within her burned unceasingly.

Disaster was hanging over him, like a Damoclean sword, by the slender threat of a girl's life.

The next twenty-four hours Spen passed in a frozen hell of apprehension. Little change was apparent, for better or worse. Tyre was of no use; the old man had collapsed, did not even appear at the hospital. Castleman Tyre was surly and fearful. Plainly he suspected what was going on but wished to know no more about it. Thus the whole burden fell upon Spen. He called Percy Sewell, the internist, in consultation, and they decided upon the heroic measure of fighting the deadly bacteria with intravenous injections of sodium sulfathiazole.

On the third day a wire from the girl's father was brought to the hospital by Sally Arbuthnot.

Do not understand about E.'s illness. Am sending my old friend, Dr. Robert Powers of Lakeview Medical College, to consult with physicians on case. Please arrange it. Do you advise my coming down?

RICHARD N. CASSILIS.

Dread and relief divided Spen's mind. In all the world of medicine he could think of no one whose counsel he would rather have than Old Powsie. On the other hand, there would be awkward questions to answer. . . . Let that take care of itself later. He wired back to Cassilis:

Will advise you if desirable that you should come. Condition unchanged.

SPENCER BRADE, M.D.

What use could the father be there? It was wiser on all counts to keep him away.

Old Powsie arrived that afternoon, quite off schedule. He

had chartered a plane. He shook hands gravely with Spen, took one look at the patient, another at the chart, and asked to have her taken to the examination room. When he came out Dr. Sewell, whose presence he had requested, was waiting for him. He made his inquiries and his decision with Powsian conciseness

"What dosage of sulfathiazole have you been giving?"

Spen stated the amount. "All that we dared," he added.

"Is that your opinion also, Dr. Sewell?"

"Yes sir."

"Increase the dosage by twenty five per cent."

"Isn't that extremely dangerous, Dr. Powers?" protested Spen.

"It is. But she won't live through the night, as matters are going. It may save her. She is a powerful woman."

With strength draining out of him every hour spent in vigil, the wretched Spen watched over his patient. He resented the time necessary for other duties; he begrudged the few hours claimed by exhaustion. He observed the ebb and flow of vitality in that burning young body with an absorption far beyond any professional interest. Hidden, in the impenetrable depths of physique, the battle progressed, indicated dimly by the code signals of temperature, pulse, respiration.

Old Powsie went in and out, studied the chart, grunted, gave his clear, curt directions, spoke his quiet encouragement to the girl in her lucid intervals, consulted more with Sewell than with Spen. On the fourth day he met his former pupil in the hallway.

"She's coming through," he said. Spen staggered and reached out a groping hand toward the support of the wall. "Go home and get some sleep.

The panorama of disaster so narrowly eluded swept past Spen's closed eyes as he sat in his car, too nerveless to drive: the girl's death, the inquest, the inquiry, Blanton Tyre and himself in the stocks of public disgrace, the probable indictment, the irretrievable ruin. He roused himself to drive to the hotel. He needed a drink; something strong: brandy. The barkeep set it out for him—and he could not so much as lift it to his lips.

"Take it away, Jim," he said. "I reckon I don't want it."

"You sick Doc?" asked the man solicituously.

"No. I'm all right. Tired out; that's all."

He went to his room and threw himself on the bed with coat

257

discarded and collar loosened, and fell into deep slumber. The telephone woke him.

"Hello. . . . Dr. Brade? . . . This is Dr. Powers. I am leaving in half an hour. I should like to see you before I go. Room 709."

Just like the old days at Lakeview, thought Spen. But this time there was a sick dread within him. He freshened his face with cold water and walked down to 709.

Powsie, plumper, pinker, puffier than ever, and with the same old innate, indestructible dignity and force, motioned him to a chair.

"I want to know more about the Cassilis girl."

"Yes, sir."

"It was a miscarriage, of course."

"Yes."

"Induced?"

"Yes."

"Who performed the operation?"

"I did."

"Medically necessary?"

"No, sir."

A long silence followed. The great teacher lighted a cigar. Spen saw the delicate hand which had brought near miracles of surgery tremble; it gave him a prickling back of his eyelids. Finally the other spoke.

"At least you did not lie about it."

"I couldn't. Not to you. I meant to when I came in. But I couldn't.

"It wouldn't have been any use. I knew." Another pause. Spen waited, inert. Powsie stood up. His voice was somber as he said:

"Brade, I have some advice to give you."

"Yes sir."

"I shall expect you to follow it. I advise you to quit."

"Quit this case?" asked Spen stupidly.

"Quit medical practice. You're unfit. I am sorry to have to say so to you. Good-by."

He did not offer to shake hands. Spen returned to his room in a daze.

Waking in the morning, he spurred himself to weak indignation. Quit medicine? Give up his whole career? Why the hell should he? What else could he find to do? It was like asking a man to commit suicide. Old Powsie could go to hell!

One thing, though, he would quit, finally and forever, the sort of practice he had slipped downward into, step by facile step. Never again, so help him God! He meant the oath to the very depths of his humbled and affrighted soul.

He stated his determination to Blanton Tyre, ready to resign on the instant if there was any objection. The old man said in shaking tones:

"You needn't tell me, Spen. I'm done with it forever. Go through with what we've had this last week? Not for all the money in America."

Richard Cassilis' check for one thousand dollars came by mail. Spen cashed his half, made a packet of the bills, and sent them to the James Clinic "from a well-wisher." It was his penance.

CHAPTER XXIX

Take me to dinner. Important.

K.

SPEN found the note on his desk the day after the shattering Powers interview. He got word to Kenny to meet him at their habitual restaurant. Her first word was:

"You look terrible, darling."

"I've been worked to a frazzle."

She looked skeptical. "How about the drink?"

"Lost my taste for it. I'm all right, Kenny."

"You'd better be," she assured him. "It's Adele. She gets here this afternoon. I just had a wire."

"Adele? Oh yes; your sister. When do you want me to see her?"

"Could you come up this evening?"

"Of course. What's my cue?"

"Cue?"

259

"She doesn't know anything about us, I suppose."

"Good lord, no! She mustn't suspect. It would wreck her. I'm just a kid to her still. Watch your step. You're Dr. Brade. I'm Miss Mangan. You're taking her on out of the goodness of your heart, because I'm an employee of the clinic. Have you got a good heart, darling?"

"You'd be positively amazed at its goodness. In fact, I don't believe you've ever appreciated it. Look for me at eight, then."

No sooner had he set eyes on Adele Harrow than he recognized the justness of Kenny's characterization, "a sort of holiness about her." Though she must have passed her fortieth year, there radiated from her a quality of spiritual loveliness, both serene and gay. The appeal in her eyes went straight to Spen's heart.

"You will tell me the truth, won't you, Dr. Brade? I'm not scared."

"I'm sure you're not. You can stand the truth. But it isn't going to be bad, I hope."

Half an hour later he was able to make positive his forecast.

"It's what we call an ovarian cyst. Ken—your sister will tell you that there is nothing dangerous about it. It's got a pretty long start on us, but there shouldn't be any difficuly. Could you pack up and go to the hospital now?"

"If you think best."

"I'll telephone for a room. We'll have that little obstruction out in the morning, and you'll feel fine again, just like your old self."

While the patient was packing Kenny came to him and slipped an arm around his neck, putting her lips close to his ear.

"Is it true, what you told Delly about herself?"

"Absolutely, as far as the indications go."

"Not malignant?"

"No sign of it."

She pressed a tremulous mouth to his. "Darling, I know you'll do your best. I couldn't stand it if anything were to happen to Delly. Isn't she a wonderful person?"

Spen smiled indulgently at her fervor. "From a long and intimate acquaintanceship of nearly an hour, I should unhesitatingly say that you are right."

In normal tones she said, for the benefit of her sister who was coming out of the bedroom, grip in hand, "It's awfully good of you, Dr. Brade. We certainly appreciate it, don't we, Delly?"

"It's a kind world," said the soft, rich voice of the other. "And you're a kind man, Dr. Brade."

"It's nothing, Mrs. Harrow. We think a lot of Miss Mangan at the clinic."

"She says you're a wonderful surgeon. I couldn't feel safer with anyone."

After depositing his charge in a private room and trying to assuage Kenny's nervous apprehensions as he drove her back home, Spen was glad to get to bed for a good night's rest. Sleep would not come to him. His insomnia had no connection with the morrow's operation; that was standardized procedure. It had its roots in the long-drawn-out crisis of the Cassilis abortion, and through it rang Old Powsie's somber contempt. "Unfit" was his word. It worked like a rodent ulcer in Spen's consciousness.

He got up out of bed, went to his closet where he kept a bottle of bourbon in reserve, and took a two-finger drink. An hour later he followed this with a four-finger potion. That did the trick. He slept.

Everything went wrong in the morning. His nerves were taut. He managed to cut himself shaving and lost a few minutes in a profane search for the stypic. His breakfast was savorless and set ill on his stomach. In consequence he reached the hospital a few minutes late, a very rare occurrence for him, as he prided himself upon a precise punctuality. It upset him.

Already there had grown up about young Dr. Brade a hospital tradition. If all the appurtenances were in place he was the easiest of operators to work with, accurate in every motion, considerate with assistants and nurses. But everything must go off like clockwork, the patient anesthetized on the table, the scalpel exactly on the stroke of the hour. His operations normally were models of mechanical perfection and efficiency.

This morning when he wanted to be at his best for Kenny's sister an evil influence was in control. The patient had not been properly prepared with sedatives—some intern had forgotten to leave the right orders—and she was taking the anesthetic badly, straining and coughing as the ether went into her lungs for the last preparatory breaths before she would be sufficiently relaxed. There was a green nurse on the instrument table. She dropped an enameled basin on the tiled floor just as Spen was preparing to make the incision, causing a clangor that seared through his tense nervous system. He whirled about on her.

"Goddamn it!" he barked.

The unfortunate girl gasped. He heard about him the hissing, indrawn breath of shock. Physicians did not curse their subordinates in the hospitals of Charlesville.

"Sorry," he muttered.

But temper still commanded his nerves. He steadied himself to make the incision, surrounding it with spotless white sterilized towels before cutting deeper, to prevent any access of bacteria from the skin to the underlying, more vulnerable structures. He picked up a fresh knife and completed the incision through the thin, paperlike layer of peritoneum. The cyst was there all right, just as he had diagnosed it, a bluish globular structure the size of a grapefruit, lying to one side of the pelvic organs. He slid his hand around it. Adhesions, of course! Just his luck, he thought, to have the thing tied down. Any other morning it would have delivered through the incision easily. He began to dissect loose the bonds with rising irritation, to expose the pedicle upon which the tumor grew. Finally the tumor came loose, and there was the pedicle, a narrow stalk whose pulsing blood vessels were clearly visible.

"Ligature!"

The dark strand of chromicized catgut came into his outthrust hand. He clamped the pedicle to crush the tissues and tied it with the catgut strand.

"Scalpel!"

It came into his hand with a smart slap, and he cut the pedicle between the cyst and the ligature and dropped the tumor into the waiting basin.

"Closing suture." The appendix had already been removed in this case.

"Dr. Brade," Burling, the resident surgeon, spoke hesitantly across the table, "don't you think it might be better to tie that pedicle again? Or maybe put a suture through it?"

Ordinarily Spen would have given this suggestion of safeguard due consideration. Now his cumulative irritation dictated his reply.

"Is there anything wrong with the quality of catgut supplied to this hospital?" he snapped.

"No. But——"

"Then my suture will do the business. Why prolong the operation unnecessarily?" He laid an unpleasant stress on the final word.

The young physician reddened. "Very well," he said.

Spen began sewing together the walls of the abdomen with smooth movements. The assistant said no more; Spen's tone had warned him it was better not to push the matter further. Having finished, Spen went into the dressing room. He'd have to get better control of his temper. There was no need to be rough with the resident just because he wanted to be doubly sure that the pedicile wouldn't come loose and cause a dangerous hemorrhage. Those had been pretty large blood vessels. Maybe he should have sutured them after all, tied off the stalk with a needle thrust through it, so there would be no chance of it slipping off. Well, it was done now, but back in his mind was the nagging thought that in Baltimore at the Center, when time hadn't meant money to him, he would have doubly ligated that pedicile just as a matter of course. Oh well; that suture was a good, firm job. Not a chance in a thousand of it slipping.

It was ten o'clock when Spen arrived at his office. Kenny, who had already had word from the hospital, asked tremulously:

"How is she now?"

"Fine. I've just seen her. She's out of the ether. Very little nausea."

"I'll never know how to thank you."

Spen looked over his shoulder. There was no one else within hearing. "Oh yes; you will," he said.

She answered his smile. "Well—perhaps I will."

Castleman Tyre appeared.

"Father won't be down today," he announced. "He still isn't feeling well. Someone has been trying to get you on long-distance, Brade. He was switched onto me, but I couldn't make anything of it."

"Oh yes!" put in Kenny. "I'm sorry, Dr. Brade. I meant to tell you. The call is from Sasawatchie Plantation."

The plantation, about one hundred miles east, was, as Spen knew, one of the show places of the coast, now engulfed in the southward sweep of Yankee multimillionaires.

"I don't know anyone there," he said. "Who was it?"

"He wouldn't give his name," said Castleman as he went out. Kenny said, "You know that attractive foreigner who came here to see you two or three months ago?"

263

"Yes."

"It sounded like his queer accent."

Tony d'Zaril! What could that mean? Further blackmail?

"Get the plantation and see if you can locate the call," directed Spen.

"What name?"

"No name. Just ask if anyone called me."

Within half an hour she had called him back. "Here he is."

The voice, for all it's lilt and smoothness, sounded weak. "Dr. Brade? This is a friend. Tony. *Compris?*"

"Yes."

"Could you drive over here to see me?"

"Hardly. I'm very busy."

"This, is also business."

"What kind? A holdup?" snapped Spen.

"No. No holdup, my friend. I think you would better come."

"Is that a threat, then? It has that sound."

"I am in no position to threaten." Spen could hear the panting breath over the wire. "I beg that you come. It is important to you as well as to me—to another, also."

"I'll be there within two hours," promised Spen.

From the spacious suite which he occupied Count d'Zaril was evidently an honored guest. He was also, Spen judged, scanning the face against the pillow of the chaise lounge, a very ill one. But he summoned up his flashing smile to greet the caller.

"This is, indeed, kind of you, Dr. Brade."

"What have you to say to me?"

"I should like to say it to your wife, too, if it were possible."

"There is no hope of more money there," Spen informed him flatly.

The sick man closed his eyes in lassitude and opened them again, as if weights were upon them. "You mistake me. What further use is money to me?" he said in lifeless tones.

"I suppose you can always find some use for it."

"You think I married her for that?"

"Of course."

"You are a fool, my friend," he said feebly. "You pay her a poor compliment. Is it, then, beyond your conception that I loved her?" Again he closed his eyes. When he reopened them they burned with strange fires. "That I still love her?" he went

264

on. "One does not so easily get over her kind of woman. Do I need to tell you this?"

Shaken, Spen said, "I will ask her, when I go back, whether she will come."

"Perhaps she will not. Perhaps it is better so. She never loved me. She was carried away. Perhaps in time she might have. Does she love you?"

Startled by the abruptness of the question, Spen blurted out, "No."

"Then I am sorry for you, my friend. For you must love her. How could one help it? So gay, so beautiful, so trusting."

"She trusted you," retorted Spen harshly. "But did you bring me over here to tell me this?"

"No. Matters of more—more practical concern. Will you so kindly fetch me the large envelope in my brief case?"

Spen brought him an official-appearing document, which he held in both hands, speaking with an effort.

"Much speech is not good for me. I shall be brief. You recall I told you that I could produce proof of the death of the Countess d'Zaril previous to my marriage with Miss Grahame?"

"Yes."

"That is true. But it was a *soi-disant* Countess d'Zaril. I employed this subterfuge for reasons of—shall we say financial pressure?"

"A very good term," said Spen grimly.

"There was, however, a former marriage, never dissolved, still legally binding. I have"—he smiled faintly—"as you Americans say, got around places. These papers establish the fact of the real Countess d'Zaril being alive and in Buenos Aires."

"And they are for sale, I suppose, at a price?" inquired Spen.

"Cannot I make you comprehend that money no longer interests me?" asked D'Zaril patiently. "You are welcome to the proof. It establishes you as the legal husband. I envy you, my friend." He put the document into the other's hand.

"Why are you telling me this?"

"Because of Carol. Because—a little—of you; that I like you. . . . You do not look happy."

"Because my wife is divorcing me, and this makes it all easy," burst out Spen. "But you would not understand that."

"No. But I am sorry for you, I who also have lost her." He

265

considered Spen's somber face. "You must have been very stupid. Or worse."

"Worse."

"Then you are in no position to speak to her for me?" he asked wistfully.

A surge of pity rose in Spen's heart. "Yes. We are not on unfriendly terms. I'll go to her and tell her. I'm sure she will come to you."

"I have no right to expect it. But she is kind and generous. Perhaps even now I can make her understand that it was not her money; that it was herself. I should like her to know that." He smiled again. "But there is not a great time left. Look at me again with the eye of the physician and you will comprehend that."

"Is there anything I can do?"

"Nothing but what I have asked. Good-by."

Spen found himself shaking hands, which had not been at all his intention. "You'll pull out of this yet, D'Zaril."

The other shook his head. The smile still lurked at the turn of the mobile mouth. "It has been a good life," he said, "and part of it beautiful."

On his way back Spen meditated on D'Zaril's final words. "A good life." What makes life so good to live? For the man whom he had left dying bravely, it had been the pursuit of excitement, adventure, glamour. For Spen himself, the grail, faithfully sought and afterward abandoned in anger and disillusion, had been achievement and service. Later is was success; material success, it is true, but dignified by the intention of hard and honorable work. Now he had abandoned that. His professional career was committed to the cajoling of rich patients, to dollar chasing; his personal life—time wasting, casual amusements, drink, Kenny—was feverish, restless, unstable. Unfair to put Kenny in that category, though. She was better than he; truer to her own character and standards. Would not it be wisest for him to marry her and settle down? She was clear-visioned, courageous, loyal. She would be good for him. She might even pull him out of the slough into which he saw himself helplessly descending.

"Part of it beautiful"—D'Zaril's wistful phrase. Had any part of Spen's life been beautiful? It might have been, with Carol. It so nearly had been, he reflected, and a stab of pain and longing shot through his heart. . . . Someone shouted frantically at him,

266

and he plucked at the steering wheel barely in time to swerve away from the approaching farm wagon. It was unwise to think of Carol while traveling at sixty miles an hour. . . . It was unwise to think about Carol at all.

Very soon D'Zaril would be dead. That burden would be off his shoulders. There was enough money in the bank to pay off Carol. He would be free. He could quit the Tyres—to hell with his contract!—taking Kenny with him and start out for himself again, but this time with a growing reputation. He was good still, as good as he had ever been; he knew that he was good. . . . The quiet, stern voice of Old Powsie said in his brain, "Unfit."

Now he had reached the outskirts of Charlesville. From the bridge he could look down into Hookworm Flats and see the plain, rectangular solidity of the new James Hospital in the process of building. Idly he wondered whether Owen James had found life beautiful. He, too, was in love with Carol. . . . Carol again! Must every thought lead his mind back to Carol?

Should he return to the office late as it was? All at once he felt very tired. He decided to go to the hotel and lie down; have a drink first, perhaps, to pry him out of his depression. He could telephone the office from there.

The bartender had a message for him. Significant, he thought bitterly, that the hotel should relay his messages to the bar; showed how regular a patron he had unwittingly become. This one was from the hospital; would he please call up immediately and ask for Dr. Sewell? Sewell! What was Sewell doing at the hospital? Probably some emergency case that had come into the clinic and been rushed over to the Markland. He went to the booth. Sewell's voice on the wire said:

"That you, Brade? Get up here as soon as you can."

"What's the matter?"

"The cyst case you operated this morning. She's hemorrhaging. They tried to get you, and Burling was so insistent that I went up."

"Hemorrhage?" said Spen stupidly.

"Yes. Don't stop to talk. Step on it."

Rather than waste time getting his car from the garage, Spen jumped into a waiting taxi.

"Emergency," he told the driver. "Hit it up. I'll take care of the police."

Hemorrhage! Then the single ligature to which he had trusted must have slipped off the pedicle of the tumor. With a qualm he remembered the size of the blood vessels in that narrow stalk. He knew how swiftly they might cause a fatal flow. Thank God Sewell was a capable man. The first question that Spen put to him was:

"Who's with you on the case?"

"Nobody but the resident. I was afraid there might be talk if I called anyone else in."

"Right."

"We've got the interns matching up donors for transfusion. She's going to need blood as quick as we can get it into her."

At the bedside Spen found young Burling, the resident, leaning over with a blood-pressure instrument in his hand. There was a flask with a brownish-yellow solution in it hanging from a stand by the bed with a rubber tube running down from it to a needle in the patient's arm vein.

"I'm giving her plasma," he said. "They haven't finished matching blood yet."

Sewell glanced at his wrist watch. "It'll be another half-hour before we can read the blood-matching tests."

"We can't wait that long," said Spen decisively. A glance had told him that Adele Harrow was losing blood rapidly. That pale face with drops of sweat beading on the forehead almost faster than the nurse could wipe them away, the rapid, thready pulse, the constant panting appeal, "Why can't I get air?" all went with hemorrhage, internal hemorrhage that could go on increasing, concealed within the abdomen, until the heart would stop pumping, stop because there was no longer any blood in the vessels to pump. The plasma she was getting through the vein would provide a fluid nearly like blood to give the heart something to work upon. It had saved lives before in temporary emergencies and surgical shock, but Spen knew that it was not enough to save this one. Nothing could save her but stopping that hemorrhage and replacing some of the blood she had lost.

"Get the operating room ready," he told the supervisor at his elbow. "Move her carefully. Keep that needle in the vein. We'll probably give her an autotransfusion."

Autotransfusion was the best hope, he thought, as he tore at his necktie in the dressing room, pulled off the rest of his clothes, and stepped into one of the operating suits hanging on a rack in the corner. They wouldn't have time to get the blood from anyone else right now. Perhaps later they could.

"Get a technician up here," he called through a crack in the door to a passing nurse. "They can be matching my blood while we're operating." He came into the operating room, tying the strings of his mask behind his ears. There was a bustle of smoothly efficient activity in the room; a nurse was laying out sterile drapings on one table, and another was arranging instruments in shining rows.

"Get some sodium citrate solution up," he directed the operating-room supervisor. "Have a couple of enameled basins ready to ladle out the blood from the abdominal cavity."

The supervisor nodded and hurried off. An intern came in breathless from hurrying, tying his mask with inexpert fingers. Spen began to scrub his hands.

The anesthetist was at his elbow. "Shall I start the anesthetic, Dr. Brade?"

"Wait until I get her draped and ready. She can't stand much anesthetic; no more than a little gas."

The anesthetist nodded and went back to her shining machine with its silvered tanks and valves. The operating table rolled into the brightly lighted space beneath the big lamps. The resident was at the left side, holding aloft a flask of acacia solution. Sewell put the twin tips of a stethoscope into his ears and squeezed the bulb of a blood-pressure apparatus.

"Intravenous going all right, Dr. Burling?" Spen asked.

He nodded. Sewell raised his head and took the tips out of his ears. Spen waited expectantly for the report.

"Eighty over forty. Sounds pretty weak."

Spen nodded. They'd have to work fast. Perhaps it was already too late, but he put that thought out of his mind. He had, of course, lost patients, some of them cases which he had not expected to die, but this was the first time he had ever had a case which was likely to die because of his own bungling. He mustn't think of that now. Every thought must be concentrated on getting the bleeding stopped and the blood pressure built up to a safe level.

Working quickly, he painted the abdomen with brilliant crimson antiseptic. The incision which before he had closed with neat sutures of jet-black silk looked odd now against the pallid skin. He would reopen the old incision. It was quicker and safer, for there would be no bleeding in the abdominal wall. Every drop saved would count now.

"You can go ahead now." He nodded to the anesthetist, who

269

twirled several dials on her machine and adjusted the mask over the woman's face. She stirred faintly as the pungent gas reached her lungs.

"Cyclopropane?" Spen asked, and the anesthetist nodded. It was the best anesthetic for such a crisis, since large amounts of oxygen were used with it. This patient could not stand even partial asphyxiation; there were too few red blood cells in her circulation now, barely enough to carry the oxygen that was keeping her alive.

Working swiftly, Spen removed the black silk stitches from the skin and clipped the strands of catgut that held each layer together as he opened deeper and deeper into the woman's body. The peritoneum was dark blue in color, not its usual parchment appearance. That meant a large amount of free blood inside the abdomen.

"Citrate ready?"

The instrument nurse held out an enameled basin with a small amount of clear solution in the bottom. She had an enameled cup in the other hand which would be used to dip the blood from the abdominal cavity. The citrate would keep the blood from clotting, would keep it fluid so that it could be pumped through the rubber tube and into the arm vein and the circulation.

Spen slit the peritoneum. Blood gushed out immediately, but he made no attempt to catch this, leaving the intern to wield basins as best he could. It was more important now to put a clamp on those bleeding vessels; there would be plenty of blood in the pelvic cavity that would not spill out. He thrust his gloved hand deep into the pelvis, seeking the cut stump of the pedicle. For an anxious moment his fingers encountered only slithering loops of intestine, then they reached the top of the uterus and moved outward toward where he remembered clamping the slender stalk. He felt a faintly pulsing jet of blood beat against his finger, and he knew it was the artery from the pedicle, its cut end partly open, spilling blood into the abdominal cavity in a spurting stream. His fingers closed over the stump now, and he could feel the beat of the artery against his fingers, trying vainly to push blood past them.

"I've got it," he anounced. There was an audible sigh of relief in the room. "Kelly clamp."

The device came smartly into his waiting left hand. Shifting it to give a better grip, he slid it slowly down inside his right hand until he could open the jaws and clamp them around the stump of the pedicle he was holding. It was ticklish business, for if he clamped in any vital structure such as a loop of the intestine, there would be trouble. Finally he could be sure that only the pedicle was in grip. He tightened it slowly. There was a satisfying something about that click-click-click as the ratchet tightened and held.

"That's got it," he announced. "Now let's get this blood into her veins as fast as possible." Tying the pedicle could wait until the autotransfusion was begun. Carefully they ladled the dark pool of blood out of the woman's body and poured it into the basin containing the citrate solution. One nurse stirred the contents slowly while another surrounded it with hot towels from the electrically heated basin at her side. Soon there were almost two quarts in the basin, mixed with a few clots. Sewell was carefully pouring out the remainder of the plasma solution in the flask which was still connected to a vein. He held the empty flask up now while the supervisor lifted a glass funnel from a near-by table with sterile clamps and dropped it carefully into the mouth of the flask. She picked up a pad of sterile gauze and placed it across the top of the funnel.

"That's it," Spen said approvingly. "We'll have to strain this rather carefully. Don't want to inject any clots into her system." He lifted a basin of the blood and poured it carefully into the funnel. It ran through the funnel in a steady stream, filling the flask. At the same time Sewell opened a clamp on the tube below the flask and allowed the blood to begin to flow into the vein.

"Going okay," he announced.

It was a tricky procedure, that autotransfusion, but a lifesaver sometimes when other blood was not available. Of course a lot of blood had been lost irretrievably, but that made little difference. Injecting the blood which had been removed from the abdominal cavity back into the vein would remove the immediate danger of complete exsanguination. It would relieve shock, too, and air hunger, raise the blood pressure to a safer level. Later it would be simple to give her a transfusion from another person whose blood matched her own.

"Blood pressure's rising. Pulse slowing down," Sewell reported in a tone of satisfaction.

That was welcome music to Spen's ears, but there was still work to do. He could see the stump of the pedicle now that the blood had been removed, could even see the pulsations of the artery that had been causing the trouble. The catgut ligature he had put on first was still in place, but somehow, he had no time to conjecture by what process, the artery had slipped out of the restraining leash. With a needle from which streamed another dark-colored strand he transfixed the stump of the pedicle behind the clamp and tied it securely. There would be little chance of anything slipping when the strand of catgut went right through the stalk that it was holding, but just to be certain he ligated it once more, tying the last knot with the grim certainty that there would be no more hemorrhage from that blood vessel.

"Still going all right?" he asked the anesthetist as he reached for a long suture to begin closing the incision he had made in the peritoneum.

"Pressure rising and pulse slowing all the time," she reported.

Spen glanced questioningly at the resident beside the transfusion flask.

"She's had seven hundred," Burling reported. "A little over a thousand cubic centimeters of blood yet to go."

Spen nodded approvingly. "That ought to do her a lot of good," he said.

He began to close the abdominal wall, replacing the sutures which he had put in first but which he'd had to cut out now in his hurried passage toward the source of the hemorrhage. He was conscious now of release of tension that had carried him thus far through the operation. His muscles were suddenly weak. He had to push each needle through with a forced effort. He'd be glad to be done with it, now that everything was safely under control, to satisfy his craving nerves with scalding black coffee and hot food.

"That was a swell job, Brade," Sewell said from the head of the table.

Spen's smile of weary relief was wiped out by the anesthetist's voice, now tight with alarm: "Dr. Brade! She's stopped breathing."

Spen jumped from the table, stripping off his gloves.

"Was she getting any anesthetic?"

"No, I stopped it several minutes ago. She was all right and then she suddenly stopped breathing."

"Pulse?" he snapped.

"Still strong. Her blood pressure a moment ago was one-ten."

"Get some adrenalin."

He began tearing away the sterile drapings, preparatory to artificial respiration.

The nurse was at his elbow with the syringe almost before he finished speaking. He could feel the pulse now, a little rapid but full and strong. There was no discernible breath, however. The lips were beginning to turn blue. He lifted an eyelid and allowed the light to reach the pupil. It did not change. There was no reassuring contraction.

"Let's get going," he said urgently to Sewell, who had come up to the other side of the table and was releasing an arm from the drawsheet that held it. Hardly ten seconds had elapsed since the anesthetist had given warning before they were lifting the arms and pressing them down against the chest with a rhythmic pumping motion that alternately pressed air out of the lungs and allowed them to expand and fill up again. The anesthetist was holding a maskful of oxygen over the face, trying to encourage as much of it as possible to enter the circulation. There was no sign of effect from the injected adrenalin.

"How's the pulse?" Spen asked hoarsely.

"Still beating. A little weaker."

"Color any better?"

"She's very cyanotic, but it doesn't seem to be increasing."

Surely this couldn't be, Spen thought, while he and Sewell continued the artificial respiration in regular rhythm. To lose a patient after the hemorrhage had been stopped, after the blood was once more circulating in the vessels. But he *was* losing her, he realized as they pumped on at her chest with still no sign that she was able to take up the task of breathing for herself. Losing her from respiratory failure. Why? Why? There had been little anesthetic. She had plenty of oxygen all the way through. She was even getting no anesthetic when the trouble had occurred. The operation had been finished.

He looked at Sewell who smiled a puzzled, painful smile; at Burling who would not meet his eyes.

"I can't get the pulse," the anesthetist reported. Spen's heart contracted. But he wasn't giving up yet, wouldn't give up until there was no hope.

273

"Take my place here, Burling," he told the resident. "Have you got a syringe and a long needle?" he asked the supervisor.

She held out a tray, having anticipated his wants. "Intracardiac?" Sewell asked, and Spen nodded as he filled the syringe with adrenalin. An intracardiac injection of adrenalin, the most powerful stimulant to the circulation that was known, would sometimes start a heart that had practically or actually stopped beating.

Spen sponged off an area on the chest over the heart with alcohol and thrust the long needle deep between the ribs and down through the pericardium, the membrane surrounding the heart, through the myocardium, the muscle of the heart itself and into the blood-filled cavity. He pulled at the plunger of the syringe, and dark blood jetted into the clear solution, telling him the needle had reached the cavity of the heart. He injected the adrenalin, a large dose, swiftly and removed the needle. If that didn't do it, nothing would.

Again he set himself to the movements of artificial respiration. How long he had kept at it he did not know—five minutes?—ten minutes?—when he was conscious of the intern, with his stethoscope against the quiet chest, shaking his head.

"No use; she's gone," he heard Burling say.

"Tough luck, old man," said Sewell sympathetically. "You certainly did everything that anybody could do. Pulmonary embolism, I expect. You couldn't prevent a thing like that. Nobody could." He looked the other over. "Here! You'd better let me send down to the dispensary for a shot of brandy. You look all in."

"I'm all right," said Spen dully. "Let me out of here."

At the door he saw a taxi discharge two passengers, Kenny and her flat mate, Bertha May. Kenny's small face was a tight mask of agony. As they approached Spen cowered into an angle. They passed without seeing him.

He looked around for his car, remembered with an effort that that it was not there. He set out to walk.

CHAPTER XXX

Two PROBATIONARY NURSES stood on the front steps of the Markland Hospital. Gossip is the spice of a probe's life. The taller one said:

"I told you he was slipping."

And the shorter one, "Just the same, if anything went wrong with my private works, I'd rather have Spencer Brade than anyone else who comes here."

"That's because you're stuck on him, like half the goops in this hospital," returned the other with an unpleasant cackle. "He certainly loused up that ovarian-cyst case."

"What d'you mean, loused up? Every surgeon loses out sometimes."

"Not that way. Haven't you heard? Burling warned him that a single ligature wasn't safe. He as good as told Burling to go take a suppository and closed up the wound without putting a suture in the pedicle. That's why she bled to death."

"I don't believe it," said the defender stoutly. "He's the most careful operator I ever watched."

"Don't be silly. Billie Springer told me. She was on operating-room duty that day. They say he's been drinking a lot lately. And his wife has ditched him. She was that Miss Grahame, the society beauty, you know. Gobs of money. . . . Oh, Bertha! Come over here a minute."

Bertha May answering the summons, said, "What's on your mind, Caroline? I'm in a rush."

"Just a sec. You knew that ovarian-cyst case, didn't you? Brade's patient?"

275

"Yes. She was my roommate's sister."

"I was just telling Clara here how Brade bitched the operation."

"What's that?" said Bertha sharply.

The probe repeated her account with embellishments. Bertha May's sharp face grew more and more pinched as the words rolled forth.

"Listen, you!" she broke in. "Button up that loose mouth. I don't want this to get back to Kenny Mangan; not yet awhile, anyway. She's about at her limit right now, poor kid! If she hears that Adele's death was unnecessary it'll just crash her."

"She'll hear, all right," returned the probe sourly. "It's all over the hospital."

"Okay. But I'm going to keep it from her till she can stand it better."

All next day Bertha was busy with preparations for getting the body off on the morning train. Kenny stayed at home with her grief. Once she said:

"Hasn't there been any word from Spen?"

"No."

"Are you sure he hasn't called up?"

"I don't believe so. Probably he's been called out of town."

The small face quivered. "I thought he'd call. Or, anyway, send some word. Are you sure, Bertha?"

Bertha was pretty sure. There were flowers from the Tyres, with a kind note from the senior; more flowers from Terry Martin and Drs. Sewell and Palfrey, for Kenny was well liked at the clinic. Nothing from Dr. Brade.

"You'd better forget him," said her friend harshly.

On their way to the 8:30 A.M. train Kenny remembered some papers, left in her office desk, which she wanted with her and held the taxi while she went up. Letting herself in with her private key, she saw a muddied and draggled raincoat drooping across one of the waiting-room chairs. With a catch in her throat she hurried into Spen's office. He was sprawled forward across his desk, his eyes closed, his face darkly flushed. She gripped his shoulder.

"Spen! Spen! Wake up!"

He only shook himself and grumbled. Running to the water cooler, she filled a glass and poured the water, first over the back of his neck, then over his forehead. Stirring uneasily, he opened his eyes. Recognition drained slowly into them.

"Kenny," he muttered. "Black. All in black."

For the moment she put aside her own sorrow in her protective solicitude for him. "Get up, Spen. You must leave here. They'll be back in a few minutes."

"All in black. She *is* dead, then."

"Oh, Spen!"

"I couldn't help it, Kenny. I swear to God I couldn't help it."

"I know you couldn't, darling. Dr. Sewell said you were wonderful. Try to stand up now." She got him to his feet. "Shall I take you back to the hotel?"

He pulled himself together with a mighty effort. "No I can make it now." He regarded her with a sort of dim horror. "You know how it happened?" he whispered.

"Don't tell me. I know you did your best. They all did their best. Oh, Spen, don't let me cry again! Come, now."

She got him into the elevator and out to the street. He said that he would walk, promised to go straight to the hotel and to bed. Kenny watched him disappear around the corner with forebodings.

Savoring a moment's rare leisure in that busy place, Terry Martin and Owen James sat in the James Clinic office, smoking companionably. Terry, with a glance out of the window, said lazily:

"Do we take d.t.s, boss?"

"We take anything that comes along."

"Well, here comes an incipient case, if I'm any judge, and under its own power." He bounded out of his chair. "Holy Mike!" he ejaculated and bolted from the room.

Beyond the range of vision from the window he intercepted the newcomer, who was painfully removing two large leaves from his path, lest he trip and come to grief over them.

"Well, you're a fine son of a bitch, ain't you!" was Terry's welcome.

Spencer Brade, M.D., looked up. His face was a mask of twitching gray. His speech was slow and effortfully exact, as he replied:

"I am, as you say, a fine son of a bitch. In case you are interested, I am also a murderer."

"Hey!" said Terry, momentarily at a loss. "What kind of talk is that?"

"I wish to see Owen James," said Spen carefully.

277

"He's busy. Better get some sleep first."

"I can't sleep. Her face won't let me. So peaceful; so beautiful."

"Oh! Woman stuff, huh?"

"The woman I killed."

"What's that?" snapped the other.

"On the operating table." Terry drew easier breath. For the moment he had feared that the drunken fool really might have killed someone. "I wish to confess to Owen James."

"No; you don't," returned Terry with vigor. "Owen's got troubles enough of his own. You come along with me and let me give you a little shot in the arm."

With the new patient safely drugged in an upper room, Terry reported to his boss.

"What do you figure he means by this murder stuff?"

Although he never gossiped, himself, or perhaps because of that fact, Owen was the repository of all kinds of information; he seemed at times to absorb it effortlessly out of the teeming air.

"He made a slip," he said. "All of us do. It was his bad luck that this one turned out fatally."

"It's got him down. I gather he's quit the Tyres. Swears he'll never touch a scalpel again."

"It's a sick soul. But he'll snap out of it."

Over the evening refection of ale and cheese the staff held council on the case referred to them by their chief. After hearing what he and Terry had to give out, Flick Fleming, who cherished no resentment for the Academy episode, said:

"I remember Old Powsie's telling a Lakeview graduating class, 'Gentlemen, I don't suppose there is a really first-class surgeon in the world who hasn't waked at night in a cold sweat to tell himself that if he'd done or not done so-and-so on such-and-such an occasion, the patient might still be alive.'"

"That would be an error of judgment, though, wouldn't it?" pointed out Felix Bernitz. "This seems to have been close to egoistic negligence."

"I'm not an expert enough to pass judgment," said Owen. "But here's the point. The man is a good surgeon."

"None better in his own department," confirmed Fleming.

"Then he'd be a loss to society. That's what we have to consider."

"Rescuing neatly done at lowest rates; apply to the James

Clinic," put in the irrepressible Terry. "What's the prescription?"

"You say he thinks he'll never operate again?"

"That's what he said. Then he cried."

"We've got to overcome that somehow."

"We have emergency operations every day," said Flick. "Couldn't we cook up an excuse to ring him in on one, as Terry did before? What do you think, Bernie?"

"Dangerous ground," objected the psychiatrist. "The scheme might work. But if it didn't you'd get an unfavorable reaction that would be permanent. Then, no more surgery forever."

"What's the alternative, then?" asked Terry.

"Let him rest up awhile. When he approaches normality we can sound him out."

For a week Spen lay abed, ambitionless to move or make any effort more pronounced than reading fluff magazines and detective novels. Well-meant attempts to beguile his mind with recent reports of surgical interest met with blank unresponsiveness. While vaguely grateful for what was being done for him, he seemed otherwise to be insulating himself from life. On the third day of his stay he said to Terry Martin:

"Terry, is my mind going?"

"Nuts!" said Terry. "Get the hell out of that bed and come to the ball game with me."

"No; I mean it," insisted the patient. "I hear things. Voices. Repeatedly."

"For instance."

"My wife's voice. In the corridor."

Terry cackled. "Why not? She does volunteer work here two days a week. She's damned good too."

"Terry, do you think I could see her?"

"That's up to her, I expect."

He relayed the conversation to Owen, who sent for Carol.

"Carol, do you want to save a man's soul?"

"That's your specialty, isn't it? I wouldn't want to butt in."

"Not this one. We've got Spencer Brade here, mending him up."

"Accident?" she asked quickly.

"No. . . . Yes. To his mind."

Her fingers went to her mouth. "You mean he's—insane?"

"We don't use that term any longer. In any case, it wouldn't be applicable to him. You'll find him perfectly normal, to all

279

outward appearances. But his mind is sick. It goes even deeper than the mind."

"Then you want me to see him?"

"I think it might help. But don't let him go tragic on you."

Room No. 38's occupant was sitting listlessly beside the window in his dressing gown, when there was a knock at the door and Carol entered.

"Spen!" she gasped with the quick indrawn breath of shock.

His smile, painful and compressed, crooked the corner of his mouth. "Am I as bad as that?"

"No," she answered, regaining her poise. "It's several weeks since I've seen you, you know."

"I have a message for you that I ought to have delivered earlier, but it got away from me. Everything got away from me for a time. Tony d'Zaril is in Savannah. He's very ill. He wants to see you very much."

"Tony is dead. Didn't you see it in the newspapers?"

"No. Your name didn't appear, did it?" he asked anxiously.

"Of course not."

"Hard luck on you, Carol, to have married two crooks."

"Is that the way you think of yourself, Spen?"

He shrugged. "It doesn't matter. I'm done for."

"I don't believe it. Owen doesn't believe it."

"Therefore, you don't. You ought to have married Owen. I expect you will, yet. There's nothing to prevent our divorce now."

"You were protecting me before," she said in a gentler voice. "Tony wrote and told me all about it. I'm sorry I misjudged you, Spen. I ought to have known you better."

"I owed you that much."

"You better come back home, Spen," she suggested quietly. "Now that you've paid Aunt Candace your board bill," she added with a twinkle.

"On old terms, I suppose," he said somberly.

"Do you think you have a right to expect any others from me?"

"No rights at all. But let's have this clear, Carol; I'll never accept that status again."

"Why not?"

"It ignores one important factor. You see, I happen unfortunately to have been and to be in love with you, though I've fought against admitting it to myself."

280

Her eyes grow hard. "And that girl in your office? What about her?"

"She was a palliative, an anodyne. I was trying to forget you, to fool myself."

"Nice for her!"

"I'm not boasting of my part. I told you you'd married a crook. I might add a rotter too. But I'm not going to have Kenny blamed for her part in it. She played straight enough. I wish I could say the same for myself. She was much too good for me as you are. Only *she* didn't think so." Carol flushed angrily. "And she tried to do more for me than you ever did."

"Yes. I daresay. In one way."

"It's a very important way. There were others too. Well, that's all over with. She'll never want to see me again when she knows."

"Knows what?"

"That was a slip. Never mind. Owen will tell you the story if you want to hear it. I think you'd better. Then you wouldn't want me to come back on any terms."

"Then I don't want to hear it," she said with spirit. "I think you're morbid, Spen."

He straightened in his chair, speaking with suddenly acquired vigor. "Get this, Carol. I'm not accepting any missionary endeavor from you. Don't let Owen James get around you to try and pull any rescue stuff on me. If there's any rescuing to be done I'll do it myself. But it isn't likely. On a dispassionate prognosis of the case of Spencer Brade, M.D., I should say that he was definitely done for. No more surgery for him."

"You can't give up your work that way," she cried. "What will you do?"

"I don't know. Don't have it on your mind. There's only one way in which I want you to be interested in me, and that way is impossible. You'd be a fool even to consider it."

She took her chin in her hand and leaned forward, the long, lustrous eyes contemplating him between the heavy lashes.

"There was a time when I was ready to be in love with you," she said slowly. "You know that."

"Yes; I know that," he replied with bitterness.

"I might be again. But not with the man you are now."

"I'll never be different."

"Oh, don't be a quitter!" she flashed. "Aren't you going to

281

make any effort? Aren't you worth that much to yourself? What's happened to you?"

He rose, turned to the window, stared out into the revealing glare of sunshine. Old Powsie's words bored into his brain. "Unfit." Like the "unclean" that doomed the leper to lingering futility and slow death. He turned back to look with a fierce concentration into her eyes.

"What do you want me to do?"

She was prepared for that. Owen James had given his directions. "Go into the operating room and help with their cases."

He shivered. "I couldn't hold a knife."

"Then look on. But go, anyway. Every day."

After a long silence he said, "I'll try it."

When this was reported via Owen James to Felix Bernitz the psychiatrist was pleased.

"It's the start of reconstruction," he said. "Now we have a foundation to build on."

"What if he can't stand it?" asked Flick Fleming.

"The fact that he's summoned up nerve to try is the first essential," Bernie returned.

It was an insignificant operation that was selected for the soul-sick man to attend: a small wen on the nape of a girl's neck, which threatened to become inflamed and might develop malignancy. At the preliminary examination Spen showed a normal interest and made a suggestion or two. He appeared, on the dot of time, in the operating room, clad in the whites and mask set aside for him. Flick Fleming was operating, with Bernie Bernitz as assistant, the latter having been rung in to observe Spen's reactions.

As the anesthetist busied herself with the cone and the ether fumes began to spread their sickish-sweet aroma, the operating nurse said in Dr. Bernitz ear:

"Look out for Dr. Brade. I think he's going to faint."

Spen did not faint. But he was sharply and disgracefully sick. One of the nurses led him out, and an orderly, hastily summoned, got him into bed. After the operation Bernie Bernitz went to the upper story and tiptoed along to listen at Spen's door. He returned, grinning.

"What's he doing?" asked the disgusted Terry Martin. "Crying himself to sleep?"

"No. He's goddamning himself all over the map for a yellow-

282

bellied quitter. Don't say a word to him, anybody. One dollar gets you three, he shows up for tomorrow's session."

Nobody took him; Bernie was a notoriously shrewd better. In this instance he would have borne out his reputation. Spen appeared in the operating room on the stroke of eight the next morning, a little white about the gills, but with a grim jaw. This was a longer process, the amputation of a gangrening foot.

"Two or three gulps and a series of burps from him," Flick reported to Owen after it was over, "and that was all. He stuck it out."

On the following day he was nauseated again but not until he had seen the operation through. From then on he had no trouble and volunteered to assist at several minor operations.

The real test was yet to come. Owen and Bernie held anxious consultations, with Flick and Terry sitting in. A case of carcinoma of the uterus was coming in. It was a bad case. Fear of what she might learn had caused the woman to put off consulting the clinic until the malignant growth was far advanced. Now it was a question whether the life could be saved. Flick and Spen went over her together. There was instant agreement; the knife afforded the only chance.

"This is your job, Spen," said Flick.

"Why mine?"

The other smiled. "I wouldn't admit on oath that you're a better man than I am, but uteri are your special line of country in the female geography. You're elected."

"You wouldn't be trying to pass an extra risk on to a soft mark, would you?" demanded Spen with a grin. That friendly insult was a mark of how much ground he had gained since his arrival.

"Sure, I would," retorted Flick genially. "How else can a surgeon keep his mortality percentages down?"

"Just for that I'll take it and fatten up my batting average by pulling Mrs. McDall through."

Having seen Spen early to bed, the staff held council on him. Three to one, they were agreed on the desirability of the test, Terry Martin dissenting.

"It's a risk," he kept repeating obstinately.

"Everything's a risk when you're dealing with a situation like this, Terry," said Owen James.

"I don't like it," insisted the pathologist. "If anything should go wrong——"

"If anything goes wrong," cut in Bernie, "we'll pull him out by the slack of his pants and try again."

"You're a hell of a good syke, Bernie," said Terry. "But were you ever a souse?"

"Not that I can recall."

"Well, I was. And Spen has been tending that way. I'm telling you if he should get another bad jar he's liable to go promptly to hell via the Old Booze Road."

Being overruled, he stamped off to bed, muttering dire prophecies. Later a messenger from the St. Charles Hotel brought in a special-delivery letter for Dr. Spencer Brade. Rather than wake him up, Owen directed that it be slipped beneath his door.

The operation on Mrs. McDall was set for 8 A.M. Spen did not appear for early breakfast. Through the locked door, when Terry Martin knocked, his voice came, muffled.

"Have a cup of coffee sent up to me, will you, Terry? And my whites. I'll dress here."

Terry descended, shaking his head.

In the hall outside the operating room Bernie Bernitz stopped Spen. The surgeon's face was set and colorless. He seemed to be in command of himself.

"All right, Spen?"

"All right as I ever shall be."

Bernie hesitated. "Well, I guess that's good enough." He left to see a critical mental case.

Spen's hand, as he took up the knife, was steady. The very feel of the implement gave him assurance. This was his business, for which the best training in the surgical world had fitted him. He made the first long, sure incision. At that moment the penetrating voice of the head nurse, addressing the instrument nurse, forced its way to his attention.

"Is that the old catgut, Miss Gray?"

"I don't know, Miss Potter. It's what the office sent down."

"Well, be sure," returned the head nurse sharply. "We don't want any ligatures slipping in this case."

Spen's fingers relaxed nervelessly on the haft. The knife, released, slithered along the curve of the naked abdomen and so to the floor where it landed on its point and stuck, quivering, like an omen of catastrophe.

Spen shivered from head to foot. "Take over, please, Dr. Fleming," he said in a lifeless monotone.

Violating the unwritten law of the operating theater, Terry Martin who was asssisting, hurried after him.

"Let me alone, Terry," Spen said, still in that dull, devitalized voice. "You can't do anything for me. I'm through. Get back in there. You're needed."

At eight twenty-five, so the desk nurse reported after the operation was over, Dr. Brade left the building, dressed in his street clothes and carrying his overcoat, but nothing else. She spoke to him but got no reply. Upon receiving this information, Terry hurried to Room 38. Everything was in place. An opened letter lay on the bed. This was no time for the niceties of etiquette. The worried Terry glanced at the signature, "Kenny," and read:

Bertha has told me the whole thing. I am never coming back to Charlesville now. There is nothing for me to say to you nor for you to say to me. But how can you hope to hold a knife again without her face coming between you and the next patient you may kill?

Terry jumped for the telephone. The St. Charles answered: yes, Dr. Brade had come to the hotel, packed a grip, settled his account to date, and left. One after another, the canny inquirer tried the barrooms which the missing man frequented. Two of them had had a visit from him. At nine, the opening hour, Terry learned, Dr. Brade had been to the Second National Bank and cashed a check. He appeared very nervous. The garage reported him taking out his car at nine-twenty.

There the trail ended. Nothing further could be ascertained about Spencer Brade, M.D.

CHAPTER XXXI

EARLY-MORNING MIST shrouded the water front of New Orleans. Uneasy in the current, the dingy freighter, *Parson Reuben,* nudged her pier as if anxious to be on her way. A spare, smartly dressed figure, holding itself rigidly erect, made its way among the sweating stevedores and ascended the gangplank. At the deck level the considerable bulk of First Officer Olsen intercepted it.

"What do *you* want, mister?"

"Passage."

"Where to?"

"The war."

The large Swede chuckled. "What do you want with the war?"

"I want to be a goddamn hero."

The seaman guffawed. "Now ain't that somethin'! Want to be a goddamn hero, huh? And get yourself bumped off mebbe."

"Why not? I'm no good for anything else."

"Well, we're keepin' the *Parson Reuben* as far away from this war as we can. So you better step ashore."

"Where are you bound?"

"South American ports."

"That'll do."

Olsen eyed him intently. "Drunk, ain't you, mister?"

"Yes. Where's the bar?"

"Lissen, buddy. This ain't no luxury liner. My advice to you, beat it before the Old Man sees you and boots you overside. He's rough, the Old Man is."

"I'll pay," said the applicant. "I'll pay one hundred dollars—two—three; whatever the price is. I'll give you twenty dollars cash if you'll help me."

"Sure, I'll help you," said the other, now favorably impressed. "But we ain't licensed for passengers. I don't believe the Old Man'll touch it. You can ask him. Here he comes."

A small, square, hard, brisk Yankee stamped up and glowered at the stranger. "Who are you?"

"He wants a passage, sir," explained Olsen.

"No passengers," snapped the captain.

By this time the mind of the newcomer had wrapped itself around the captain's query. "Spencer Brade, M.D.," he said.

"He's got money," put in Olsen hopefully.

"What's this M.D. bilge?" demanded the captain.

"Never mind that," was the hasty reply. "I'll give you three hundred dollars to take me where you're going."

"Means you're a doctor, don't it?" pursued the captain.

"I was."

"Can't take passengers. But I can log a ship's doctor. Show me three hundred."

The other produced a roll from which he counted the amount. The captain eyed the impressive show of greenbacks.

"Better stow that in the ship's safe," he advised. "We're honest folks here."

"Looks like bank money," suggested Olsen. "The police wouldn't be wantin' you, would they now, mister?"

"Nobody wants me. How long will we be at sea, Captain?"

"Six months or so. Maybe ten days before we make port."

"Could I buy a few cases of bourbon and have them sent aboard?"

"Sure. Give Mr. Olsen the money. But if you get disorderly I'll stick you in the brig."

The passenger nodded. "I'd like to get some sleep now."

"Just a minute. You say you're a doctor. That don't prove anything. One of my men's got a smashed foot. Come and have a look."

With catlike attentiveness he watched the stranger as he dressed and bound the injured member.

"Drunk or not, I guess you know your business," he conceded. "Got any dunnage?"

"Only what I have on."

"Two hours left. You can pick up some slops. I'll send a boy

287

along to see you don't get lost. Report to me at ten o'clock, Dr. Brade."

He turned his back and marched off to enter the new officer in the log.

The *Parson Reuben* made its leisurely way through the Gulf and the Canal and, in due time, was off the coast of South America, shoving its prow deep into the chilly waters of the Humboldt Current, breasting the long rollers from across the Pacific, now and again taking a big one over the bow, for she was heavily loaded. The second mate was taking over the watch from First Officer Olsen one blowy evening.

"How's Doc?" Olsen inquired.

"Lickerin' up, as usual."

"Funny guy. Don't know as I ever saw a man so set on drinkin' himself to death."

"Yeah. Woman in it somewhere. I wouldn't wonder," opined the second, who was young.

"Worse'n that," said the other. "One night when I had to take the stuff away from him for fear he was gettin' the heebie-jeebies, he kept mumblin' something about a face that was dead and wouldn't leave him be."

"Maybe he killed somebody in an operation. I read a story like that once."

First Officer Olsen went down the companionway to the tiny dining room, where he found the ship's doctor with a three-day beard and a half-empty bottle on the table before him. Taking off his sou'wester, Olsen wiped the salt spray from his face with a large green handkerchief.

"Have a drink?" Spen asked as the other dropped into a chair.

"Don't mind if I do. It's cold out there."

He poured a liberal portion into a glass and drank slowly, letting the warmth and comfort seep through his grateful system.

"Listen, Doc," he said, leaning foward. "You're young. You're brainy. You got money. You're a hell of a nice guy when you're even half sober. What's all this gettin' you?"

Spen regarded him sardonically. "Temperance lecture?" he inquired.

"No," protested the mate. "I'm no sissy about the stuff. But the way you're lettin' yourself slip, it makes me kinda sorry."

Spen sat for a long time, not speaking, intent upon his glass and the amber fluid that half filled it. When he answered his voice had lost its truculence.

"You're a good chap, Nils. But it's no use."

"Look," persisted the other with squarehead doggedness. "You was goin' to transship to London. And what happens? We touch at Guayaquil and you're in your bunk, stewed to the gills. We make Valparaiso, and you never sober up enough to go ashore. We lay three days at La Concepcion, but do you make a move? Only to reach for another drink. Here we are, ten weeks out, and you still with us. And they tell me they need good doctors in London; need 'em like hell. They could use you."

"Now, *you* listen," said Spen with savage intensity. "I was a surgeon. A good one. I'm through. Never mind why; I'm through. All washed up. Unfit. Kaput. Have another."

"Then what the hell were you goin' to London for?" demanded Olsen.

"Because I'm good for nothing else," was the weary reply. "I thought I might volunteer as an ambulance driver, or stretcher-bearer, or a hospital orderly, and if a bomb got me, there goes nothing! What else is there, except drink?"

"Well, I'm not feelin' too good," said the mate, putting aside the bottle which Spen invitingly shoved toward him. "Guess I'll turn in."

"Here's to a good night's rest," said Spen politely, refilling his own glass.

It was eight bells in the dogwatch when Spen felt himself being violently shaken in his bunk. Captain Harker's face loomed darkly above him.

"Get up."

"What's the matter?" Spen's head, as he raised it, was thick with fumes.

"Get up. I've got a case for you."

He dropped back. "Let me alone. I'm no good."

The captain soaked a towel in cold water and flicked the drunken man's face with it. "I know goddamn well you're no good. But maybe you can doctor a pain in the belly that's tearing a man apart."

"Give him castor oil, then, damn you," returned Spen, shivering.

"Listen, you!" said Harker violently. "You're the ship's

289

doctor, signed on as such, and by living God, if you don't come out of there and look at Olsen I'll——"

"What's that? Olsen?"

"Yes; Olsen. He's doubled up like a jackknife. Like he'd been poisoned."

Sometimes a sheer effort of the will can go far toward overcoming drunkenness. Spen twitched his shoulder from the other's angry grip, rolled out, and hustled into his clothes, sobering every second as the significance of the words penetrated to his brain. "Pain in the belly—doubled up like a jackknife." Definitely a danger signal to the surgical intelligence. It might not mean anything more than a slight upset from food idiosyncrasy, but then again it might mean an acute appendix, or a perforated ulcer, eating its way through the wall of the stomach until there was a tiny hole through which the acid stomach juice poured to set up a devastating peritonitis.

The first mate was tossing in his bunk. "Hiya, Doc!" he gasped with a ghastly effort at gameness. "That booze of yours didn't do me no particular good."

"All right, Nils. Let's have your wrist."

He pressed his finger over the course of the artery that pulsed there. The beat was fast but fairly strong. The forehead was hot; fever was already there.

"Where does it hurt?"

"Right here. The sick man placed the palm of his hand gingerly, as if the mere pressure hurt him, over the upper part of the abdomen. "It started in bad two hours ago, but I thought it would wear off."

"Had anything like this before?"

"Not like this. I've had little pains. Usually right before I ate."

"Eating make the pain better?"

Olsen gasped with another paroxysm. "Y-yes."

Gently Spen pushed up the man's shirt until his abdomen and lower chest were exposed. His breathing was shallow, and he seemed to catch his breath with each respiratory motion, as if it caused intolerable pain. The abdominal wall was as hard as a board, the muscles beneath the skin in a tight spasm, trying to protect the tender organs beneath them from danger. It was somewhat less rigid in the lower part, and in the region of the appendix. All that fitted in with the diagnosis which had come to mind the moment Spen's hand had felt that stiff rigidity of the abdominal muscles.

His mind went back to one of Powers' clinics, an operative clinic this time, when he had been a student back at the Center in Baltimore. The patient was on the table, waiting for the anesthetic, and Powers had called several of the students down from the rows of seats around the operating amphitheater, Spen among them. He had placed his hand on that abdomen and had felt the unyielding rigidity of the muscles, even though the man was under the influence of a hypodermic.

"Don't ever forget that sign, gentlemen," Dr. Powers had said. "Boardlike rigidity of the abdomen. It can mean only one thing. A perforated ulcer."

He had watched the operation and had seen Powers locate the place where the ulcer had eaten its way through, perforated, the wall of the stomach. He had seen the cloudy fluid of the gastric juice free in the peritoneal cavity. He had seen Powers' short, incredibly deft hands wield the needle which had closed the perforation, blocking any further leak. And a week later he had seen the patient in the ward, as well and happy as if nothing had happened to him. But that had been in a modern hospital operating room. He himself had operated upon a number of perforations, but always with a nurse and interns handy, a trained anesthetist at the head of the table, glittering instruments on the table, everything he needed to hand.

This was different. This was a plunging bunk in the fo'c'sle of a dirty tramp steamer with a sea raging.

Captain Harker, who had gone out, returned with three seamen. "Take him to my cabin, boys," he directed.

"Let him alone." Spen's voice snapped with authority.

The men stopped in their tracks. The captain's hard jaw dropped. "Who gives orders here?" he demanded.

"I do, in this sickroom."

"The hell you do!"

Spen met his angry stare. "Very well," he said quietly. "Then I quit right here, and you take the responsibility for this man's death."

"Death?" repeated the other in altered tones. "Is it as bad as that?"

"Yes."

"Appendix?"

"No. I wish it were anything as simple."

For an appendix would be relatively easy to handle. It might form an abscess if he let it alone, an abscess which could be drained at the hospital in the next port they reached, or he might be able to freeze it out with ice packs. At worst he could perform a simple appendectomy. This was different. Waiting here meant death.

Quite humbly for him the captain asked, "What is it, Doctor?"

"Perforated ulcer of the duodenum, just below the stomach."

"Can't you do something for him?"

"Of course. But it's a major operation. I've no instruments. And this old tub is bucking like a mule."

"We could ease her off some by heading into the wind. Might even broach a barrel of oil and make a slick."

"That's a good idea. The best place to operate is in the galley, I suppose. What have you got in your medicine chest?"

"I'll have it fetched right down."

At first sight of the disorderly equipment Spen's heart sank. But the discovery of two cans of ether cheered him vastly. To go through such an ordeal without the alleviation of an anesthetic would have been too much for him, he feared. Further investigation brought forth some morphine tablets, a few rusty instruments, and a bottle of mercury cyanide, which was more than he had any right to expect. The cyanide would assure antisepsis. There was also a spool of linen thread, which would have to serve as suture material and to tie off blood vessels which were sure to spurt.

"No needles, I suppose," he said, half to himself.

"Ought to be, somewhere," answered Harker. "I sewed up the boy's hand a few months ago when he cut it in the galley."

They found them under some bandages, half a dozen curved needles, their blades rusted and dull.

"I don't suppose there'd be a pair of rubber gloves aboard?"

"Not a chance."

"Well, we'll just do the best we can. Captain, I'll have to depend on you to help me."

"Yes sir," said Captain Harker, and corrected himself sharply, "Yes."

"While I get the hypo fixed you'd better call in whichever one of the other officers you think will be handiest."

"That'll be Evans," said the captain, naming the young second mate.

"I'll need a dozen clean towels. We can wring them out of boiling water and make sterile drapes and sponges with them."

While Harker was transmitting his directions Spen mixed a stiff dose of morphine, drew it up into the syringe, went to the sick man, and shot it into him. That done, he stepped into the small room where the officers had their meals. His own cabin opened off this. He went in. The light in the room was still burning. There was a bottle of whiskey set in a rack at the end of the cabin.

Every nerve in his body was crying out for drink. The prospect of the approaching test made the craving more acute. Just one drink. It would do wonders to steady him.

Some new-found strength checked him, something which had come to him first when he learned that his friend was in peril, and again in increased power when he laid hand on that convulsed abdomen and made sure that the man's life depended upon him and him alone. With a great upsurge of spirit to meet the crisis imposed on him, he knew now that he was not going to shirk or falter or be afraid.

In the galley the second officer, Evans, was waiting, and with him a tough hulk of a bos'n named McBride who, as he stated without reservation, had served as orderly in penitentiary hospitals during two separate terms.

The long, narrow table which the cook used was fairly suitable, and the hanging light over it afforded excellent vision. The bos'n was already heating water. Spen mentally put him down for a bottle of whiskey as reward when it was over. Taking a large dishpan from an overhead shelf, he filled it almost full of water and dropped in a handful of the cyanide tablets. There would be no way of measuring accurately the strength of the antiseptic solution thus prepared; he'd have to take a chance that the patient wouldn't absorb enough of it from the instruments and towels to poison him. In one of the bos'n's kettles he put the instruments he had found in the cabinet; in the other he put the towels.

"Get your shirt off, McBride," ordered Spen. "You're my assistant. We've got some scrubbing to do."

"Yes sir."

"Captain Harker, I was going to ask you to give the ether. But Mr. Evans tells me he has done it once before."

293

"I'd do better on my bridge, Doctor," said the captain obviously relieved.

Spen nodded. Already the motion of the ship was easing perceptibly.

When they had finished scrubbing Spen and the bos'n soaked their hands and arms for several minutes in the cyanide solution. He'd probably have a skin rash tomorrow, Spen thought. Cyanide always did that to him. Then as the third mate and several sailors came in carrying Olsen, he ordered the instruments dumped out of the kettle into the large pan of antiseptic to cool them. Then with a clamp in each hand he lifted the steaming towels from the other boiler and wrung them out. Not the best sterile drapes in the world, it was true, but still probably pretty effective. As he surveyed the setup of his emergency operating room he thought that even these primitive accessories were much better than doctors had had a hundred years ago. And they had saved many a patient by their courage and skill in an emergency.

Evans proved steady and reliable with the ether cone, directing coolly the stream of drops upon the folded towel that had to serve as a mask. Olsen squirmed and fought for a few minutes as the pungent fumes entered his lungs, but soon he quieted down. When his breathing was strong and regular Spen motioned the bos'n to open the eyelids so that he could look at the pupil. The eyeball was moving slowly from side to side in nystagmic movements.

"He's almost ready," he said. "Keep the ether going at about that rate. He won't be getting too much."

With the end of a towel moistened in cyanide solution he scrubbed the abdomen thoroughly. Waving the steaming towels in the air to cool them, he draped them over the body, leaving exposed only the small area just above the navel where he would make the incision. He looked up at the tough bos'n. The man was a little pale, but he met the other's eyes and conjured up a reassuring grin.

"Stand across the table from me," Spen directed. "Cut one of the hot towels up into strips with those scissors I boiled and use the strips to mop with when I start." He picked up the knife. It was dull compared with the razorlike sharpness of the scalpels he had been used to working with, but that couldn't be helped now. He had to press hard to make the blade cut through the tough skin, but after that the going was better.

294

It was some twenty minutes later when Spen lifted the abdominal wall gently away from the stomach and disclosed the ulcer. It was there, about where he had figured it would be, just beyond the stomach in the first part of the small intestine, the duodenum, a tiny hole in the center of a reddened and thickened area of the intestinal wall. A tiny hole through which poured the acid gastric juice to sear the sensitive peritoneum. The strange audience stared with fascinated eyes.

They had got it in time, he knew that, if he were only able to close the hole with the primitive sutures at his command. Perforations operated upon within six to eight hours after the leak occurred usually got well, provided there were no complications from the operation. If there was none from this one, he knew it would be a miracle.

With McBride giving him exposure as best he could with untrained hands, Spen began the difficult task of closing the opening. Once or twice the dull needles tore through the outside layers of the wall when he tried to stitch it together over the ulcer. His forehead was wet with sweat when finally he tied the last stitch, closing effectively the tiny opening through which death had almost made a successful attack. Even then he was not satisfied, and he pulled a layer of omentum, the fatty apron that hangs down in front of the abdominal organs and frequently acts as a policeman to wall off dangerous infection of the appendix and other organs, across the top of his crude sutures and held it there with a last stitch.

The rest was easy. In some twenty minutes Olsen was ready to leave the table.

He would need nursing, would need large doses of sedatives to keep him quiet until nature could successfully supplement the job he had done with her own vastly more powerful healing power. But barring accidents, all should be well.

All that day and through the following night Spen watched by the bedside of the sick man, at first keeping him in a stupor with the morphine from the medicine cabinet, later, after the first dangerous twelve hours had passed, giving him sips of the water he begged for, with a spoon. Not too much at first, just enough to allay a little the tormenting thirst and supply the fluid needed by the body. In a hospital he would have had flasks of sterile salt solution and glucose, food which could be given intravenously through a needle; here he had to do as best he might. Toward morning of the second day Olsen dropped off into a natural sleep. The battle was won. Utterly spent for lack of sleep, the surgeon called the second mate, who was off watch, to come and sit with the patient and staggered on deck for a breath of air. There the captain sighted him and lugged him off to bed. The next day Spen was informed that his passage money would be returned to him. Amused and touched, he figured this was the deep-sea method of apology on the captain's part.

The *Parson Reuben*, having rounded the Horn, plugged northward along the east coast toward warmth and sunshine. Spen's supply of liquor was gone now, except for a small amount which he had turned in for medical emergencies. For a time his nerves craved it. Soon that wore off. He settled himself into the ship's routine. He was not happy, but he had found a measure of peace.

Confidence, however, was not to be won back thus. In the emergency, when it was a question of life or death for a man of whom he had grown fond, he could summon courage to fight off his obsession and meet the crisis. To do as much in cold blood and without the pressure of necessity was another matter. Adele Harrow's saintlike face still came back to him in dreams. Old Powsie's "unfit" echoed in his brain. Kenny's letter was a searing acid in his memory.

No; when the trembling wreck of Spencer Brade, M.D., walked out of the James Clinic into the protracted alcoholic daze which had ended on the *Parson Reuben*, he had left hope and ambition behind. After the voyage was over he would go back to Charlesville, settle his affairs, and then, if he could find a place on the map where he could be useful without assuming any responsibility either at home or abroad, he would do what he could. But not anything connected with the actual practice of surgery.

He doubted whether he could ever endure to enter an operating room again.

CHAPTER XXXII

SPRING was flooding the countryside with gold of jasmine and purple of the judas tree when Carol Brade, back from a visit at the shore, got a wire call from Owen James.

"Carol, Spen will be in town tomorrow."

There was no answer for so long that he asked, "Did you hear me, Carol?"

"Yes," she replied then, a little breathlessly. "It—it rather knocked me off my feet."

"I had a letter this morning."

"In nearly ten months he's never sent me a word."

"He's been out of the world. And I think he's been a sick man. From his letter I judge that he's well now. Or on the way to be."

As if to herself she said, "And what am I expected to do about that?"

"Help, if you can."

"But can I?"

"That I can't tell until I've seen him. If you come to the clinic you're pretty sure to run into him. That's what I called up to tell you."

There was stress in her voice as she said, "Then I'd better not come? Is that what you mean?"

"In your heart you want to see him again, don't you?" he said, unable to keep the sadness from his voice.

Once more there was a pause. At length, "Yes; I suppose I do. But I'm afraid. I don't want to see a wreck," she added with an effort. "Or a shadow."

"No; I don't want you to. So we'd better wait."

"But, Owen! Tomorrow's my day on duty. And I've been away for a week." Carol had been giving eight days a month to the work of the clinic.

"See if you can't get Virginia Teale to take over for you. We'll talk it over after I've see Spen."

The first word after "hello" that Owen said over the early-morning telephone call from the fugitive was, "Your old room is ready for you, Spen."

"That's kind, after the way I left it. But—I don't know," answered Spen haltingly.

"What's on your mind?"

"Carol. Owen, are you going to marry Carol?"

"Carol is not a free woman," returned the other stiffly.

"I thought—I was afraid—— You see, I left word for her that I wouldn't contest any action she wanted to take."

"That can wait. When are you coming up?"

"Why, I thought I'd lay off today; get acclimated to being in Charlesville again."

"Not a bad idea. I'll tell you, Spen. Why not come around for the evening spread at ten?"

"Gee, I'd love to!" It sounded like his old boyish self.

Terry Martin was the first to greet the wanderer at the hospital. "Hi, Spen! You look as hard as a steel spike. And about as thin."

"Hello, Terry." They shook hands. "I'm feeling fine."

"Where have you been mostly?"

"All over the map. By land and by sea. I put in three months knocking around in the car, trying to forget I was alive. Then I found myself on a tramp steamer, pretending to be a ship's doctor."

"Just wandering?"

"*And* drinking."

"You don't look it. Not the last part. How long since you had one?"

Spen grinned. "Last night."

"How many?"

"Just the one."

"Didn't the one call for another?"

"Wouldn't have done it any good if it had."

"Think you've got it licked, then."

"I know I have."

"Well, damn you!" said the little pathologist. "I bet Bernie Bernitz a ten-spot that the booze had got you and you'd never come back."

"Sorry to lose you money, Terry." Spen went on with a visible effort, "About my quitting on you all the way I did——"

"Ah, shut up," said Terry rudely. "Nobody wants to hear about that."

"Well, God knows I don't want to talk about it."

"Well, nobody else is going to if you don't. Hi, Bernie!" He hailed a figure passing across the corridor. "Look what's here."

Bernitz greeted the returned wayfarer as simply and warmly as if there had never been the ugly episode of the Academy of Medicine meeting. Terry said:

"See you in a few minutes," and went on.

The psychiatrist scanned Spen's face. "How much weight have you lost?" he inquired after the first exchange.

"Twenty pounds or so."

"That's too much."

"Tramp steamers don't carry a Ritz café," said Spen.

"Was the food the only trouble?" asked the other keenly.

"Do you mean drink? I quit making a fool of myself several months since."

"I wasn't thinking of drink. How about the sleep?"

"Not too good. That is, not too certain."

"Spen, you're holding yourself in by main force, aren't you?"

"It isn't easy, coming back here."

"Harder than you thought?"

"Yes. But I don't have to stay here."

"I think you do," returned the other quietly. "This is your place. I think you ought to stick. I'm sure of it, Spen."

"There are things I'll never get away from, if I do."

"You haven't got to get away from them. You've got to lick 'em on their own ground. Spen, I know about that operation on the woman at the Markland. The one that died of hemorrhage."

"I expect everybody knows it by this time," said the other bitterly.

"That's what on your mind, isn't it? The loss of that patient?"

"Mostly. It's the sort of thing one doesn't forget."

"Because it was your fault?"

Spen winced. "Yes."

"Suppose it wasn't your fault?"

"Ask Burling. He warned me about that ligature."

"Suppose it was the ligature that was defective, the catgut below par so that it gave way?"

A painful grin broke up the lines that had drawn Spen's face when the psychiatrist opened the subject. His hand fell heavily on the other's shoulder.

"Bernie, you're a good friend and a swell syke, but you're a damn punk liar. I hoped that, myself, about the catgut. So I had what was left over tested. It was as tough as a cable. No, Bernie; that won't do. But thank you, just the same."

They walked down to the office where Owen James and Flick Fleming joined them. The newcomers listened with absorption to Spen's narrative of his deep-seas experience.

"Then you've been operating again," said Fleming hopefully.

"In another world," answered Spen.

"We've got plenty for you to do here," said the chief. "Flick's been worked to a frazzle lately. When can you start in?"

Slowly the color drained out of the lean face. "Have you forgotten my last appearance in your operating room, you fellows? I haven't."

"Let's not talk shop," said Bernie quickly. Thereafter, until Spen left, the conversation was held to a scientific and impersonal basis.

"I thought, from his looks and his talk, that he'd got it all out of his system," said Flick after the visitor's departure.

"Maybe he has. I can't tell. But if he doesn't show up tomorrow you can just go hunt him," said Bernitz.

Spen did show up, bag and baggage, on the following morning. On the psychiatrist's suggestion, he was put in his former room, No. 38.

"Now," said Bernie to his associates, "pray for a good, critical emergency patient."

"We get plenty," said Terry. "What's the idea?"

"To force it on Spen. It's his best chance for a comeback."

"But he has come back," objected Flick Fleming. "How could he have pulled that first mate through if he hadn't?"

The other shook his head. "It isn't the same thing at all. Operating in a dingy ship's galley with no decent equipment and a bunch of ignorant sailors to help is absolutely different psychologically from going through the familiar, instinctive processes of an operating room. Environment—that's what I fear for him. It's liable to recall the whole disastrous business: the woman for whose death he blames himself, his collapse here, everything. Did you notice his face when he came in the other day and got his first whiff of the hospital smell?"

"Then why try it on him?" demanded Terry.

"If he doesn't go through with it now and here he never will. Men don't outgrow this kind of inhibition; it grows in on them. Now, if one of you fellows would obligingly take a club and fracture Terry's skull we'd have the build-up we need."

"Thanks," said Terry. "If I'm going to be treated for fractured skull I'll take a chance under Flick."

"There's a difficulty right there," said Owen. "If the emergency we're looking for should come in Flick is the logical man to operate. Is it your idea, Bernie, to get Spen to assist Flick?"

"Not good enough. Spen's got to have the whole responsibility thrown on him."

"I'd be willing to fracture Flick's skull in a good cause," offered Terry magnanimously.

"There's a thought," said Owen. "Flick can have a timely accident."

"Very kind of you," the surgeon made the acknowledgment. "What sort of accident would you recommend?"

"Fall downstairs," said Bernie. "Anybody can fall downstairs. Colles fracture, maybe. No; that's too troublesome. Just a good, sound sprain."

"Very ingenious. But we haven't got our emergency case yet," Terry grumbled.

Mill and slum mishaps, large and small, normally averaged better than one per day at the clinic. Now, for a space, everybody in the district seemed to be avoiding all but minor troubles with discouraging persistency. It would be hardly feasible, as Bernie pointed out, to risk Spen's future on a lacerated scalp or an infected toenail. Yet nothing better was coming in.

Spen settled quietly into the routine of the place, avoiding only the operating floor. Six months of separation from medical news had given him a ravenous appetite for the technical journals. He read insatiably. At the evening talkfests he drank his mug of ale, smoked his one cigar, and for the most part, listened.

"Isn't as cocky as he used to be," observed Terry. "Good thing too."

"Bad thing," contradicted Bernie. "He's going to need all his self-confidence. He's still brooding over something. Is it still Mrs. Harrow's death, do you think?"

Privately Owen suspected that it was more than that, but he answered only, "Very likely."

It was only a question of time, Owen knew, when husband and wife must meet. Presumably Spen, too, recognized this. But after those first few questions put to Owen he had not reverted to the subject. He went out little, and downtown not at all, except once to see Blanton Tyre, whom he found aged, discouraged, and plaintive. Both the Tyres besought him to come back. Matters were not going well at the clinic. Spen declined; he wouldn't be of any use to them, he said. Hesitantly he asked about Kenny Mangan. He had no longer any particular feeling about her except kindliness and that ineradicable sense of guilt for Adele's death.

Yes; they had heard from Kenny through the new office girl who was a friend of hers. She was working in Beaumont and was going to be married to a Texan, an oilman, much older than herself and more than well to do. Spen reflected with entire sincerity that the unknown groom was going to get a good and loyal wife.

Walking along Main Street after leaving the Medical Arts Building, Spen was surprised to find how many people stopped to greet him and tell him how glad they were to see him back. Then as he turned away from one of them he faced Aunt Candace Grahame getting out of her car to intercept him.

"*Well!*" she said. "How do you do, Spencer Brade?"

"Hello, Miss Grahame," he answered.

"What's happened to you?" demanded the old lady. "You look like you were a man again."

"Sea air," he explained. "I've been on a voyage."

"So we hear. Where are you going now?"

"Back to the James Clinic."

"Get into the car and I'll take you. Carol's there."

There was no escape. Aunt Candace herded him forward. Carol held out her hand.

"Hello, Spen," she said.

"Hello, Carol." He took the extended hand. "You're looking quite wonderful."

"Did you expect her to pine away?" asked Miss Grahame with asperity. "Why haven't you been to see us?"

"I've only just got here."

"That's a lie, isn't it?" said the old lady, and Spen grinned and said, "Yes."

"Well, come and dine with us tonight." Spen hesitated. "What's the matter? Don't like the board?"

"I'd probably stuff myself to death on it. You should have seen my bill of fare for the last six months."

"You certainly paid me a good price for your board and lodging," continued Aunt Candace. "Though I daresay the lodgings weren't all that might be desired," she added maliciously.

Both Carol and Spen reddened.

"You were a good-money boarder, though," Aunt Candace continued. "I might consider taking you back."

"Can't afford it," said Spen good-humoredly. "I'm out of a job."

"The dinner tonight won't cost you a cent," she assured him. "You may consider it as a bid for your trade."

"Sorry, but I've got some work to do for Owen James on his accounts."

"I don't believe you for a minute. But it's all right. My feelings aren't easily hurt."

At the hospital Carol got out with Spen. "I want to see Owen for a minute," was her excuse. Then, "Do you mind if I ask you something, Spen?"

"No. Go ahead. Anything."

"You've got a hold of yourself again, haven't you?"

"Yes." He smiled at her. "I've even shucked off the Midas complex. Money doesn't seem so important any more."

"Are you going to stay in Charlesville?"

"I don't think so."

"Why not?"

"Various reasons."

"Am I one of them, Spen?"

"Why—yes; I suppose you are."

She crinkled her brows at him. "Don't you think you ought to stick around and live me down?"

"You aren't so easy to live down, Carol. Six months of salt air hasn't washed you out of my system."

She said nothing to that. But as they parted at Owen's office door she remarked, "Auntie will ask you to dinner again. Better come."

Owen, after hearing her account of the talk, told her of the plan to try Spen out.

"It's rather frightening," she said. "Could I come, Owen?"

"We could sneak you into the gallery. Sure you want to?"

"Yes; I'm sure—I've got an interest in that test."

In the car again, Carol was confronted by her aunt's sardonic smile.

"You're a crazy little fool, aren't you, Carol?"

"Am I? Why?"

"You've never really got over your yen for that lad, have you?"

Carol's nose was elevated. "I think that's a very low and vulgar way of putting it, quite unworthy of a lady, let alone a Grahame," she said loftily. "Oh, Auntie!" She came down abruptly from her high horse. "I'm so sorry for him."

"Pooh! He isn't sorry for himself any more."

"No; he isn't. But there's something deep down there yet. Can't you see there is?"

Miss Grahame contemplated her niece with a sort of reluctant respect. "Sometimes, my dear, I think you aren't as much of a moron as you're entitled to be, with that pretty face of yours," she allowed. "Well, if there's something there, get it out of him. Make him tell you. You can."

"I don't know," said the girl unhappily. "I can't put him on the stand and cross-examine him."

Accidents have a habit of occurring at the most inconvenient hours. Delbert Green, a worthy truckman, having gone sleepless all the way around the clock, took a short involuntary nap at the wheel while passing through Charlesville at 1:30 A.M. and woke up in a ditch with most of the truck leaning on him. Skilled engineering by the police extracted him, and he was hustled to the James Hospital. Terry Martin, on duty, after a hasty examination roused his chief.

"Looks like the case we've been hoping for. Internal injuries. Critical, I'd say."

"Get Spen," said Owen. "I'll call Flick." On the way he instructed the night operator to call Mrs. Spencer Brade and tell her she was wanted at the hospital immediately. Returning to finish dressing, he was accosted by Terry.

"How did he take it?" Owen asked anxiously.

"I told him we'd need his help. He looked rattled but said

he'd do what he could if Flick needed him. Great Cripes! What's that?"

"That," said Owen, cocking an ear toward the upper hall, "should be Dr. Foster Fleming giving a realistic imitation of a sleepy surgeon falling downstairs."

Flick limped in. "Get me a splint and a sling, quick, for the arm," he demanded. "Damn and blast me if I didn't overdo it and nearly bust my kneecap."

Convincingly rigged out, he met Spen on the operating floor. Spen turned white at the sight of the supported arm.

"What's the matter with you, Flick?"

"Fell down those blasted stairs."

"Can't you operate?"

"Not a chance."

"Who will you get?"

"No time to get anyone," put in Terry, coming up. "You can't put a ruptured spleen on ice. And that's what it looks like."

Spen struggled for command of himself. "Bring him into the office," he directed. "Owen," he explained with appeal ir his voice, "you know I can't trust myself in that operating room; not to take charge."

"You've got to. The man'll die on our hands. You've got to, Spen."

Spen shut his eyes for a moment. "God help me!" he said, and Owen, moved, thought that he had never heard a prayer of more agonized sincerity.

Both Spen's hands were trembling as he forced himself toward the table on which was stretched the great hulk of the injured truckman.

"Hello, Doc," the man said with pitiful jauntiness. "What about me?"

The animal-like appeal in the bloodshot eyes was a steadying influence.

"You're going to be all right," said Spen with the kindly assurance that gives courage. "Let's have a look."

It took only a moment to make examination and diagnosis. There was no doubt about those ominous signs, the shallow breathing, the rapid, small pulse, the beading of sweat on pallid forehead and cheeks, the splinting of the lower chest, the reiterated complaint of left-shoulder pain from pressure beneath the diaphragm—it all fitted in with Terry's surmise, rupture of the spleen, that strange, reddish organ that lies high on the left side, not often seen at operation, not often considered unless enlarged to the point where it can be felt, or until burst under the pressure of external force, filling the upper abdomen with blood, exsanguinating the injured person into his own body cavity, knocking down every defense mechanism of the body with the paralyzing influence of surgical shock.

"Better prod up the lab on a blood donor," Spen said to Fleming.

"I'll go down, myself."

"Terry drew Spen aside. "Was I right?"

"There's very little doubt of it."

"Not much chance for him, uh?"

"If we get in there quickly I'd give him a pretty near even break."

Bernie Bernitz caught him by the arm. "Then what are you dawdling for, goddamn it!" he demanded with calculated brutality.

Spen gave a great start. He had not realized that he was hanging back.

"I'll get ready."

Outside Owen James was explaining to Carol, who had just driven in.

"It's one of the toughest operations. If he can pull this he ought to be fit for anything. Go into the far corner of the gallery. He won't be likely to see you there. I don't want anything to divert him now."

The operation was just starting as she seated herself in the narrow observation post that ran halfway around the operating room, well above the workers below. Leaning forward to gaze down through the glass shield, she could see and hear everything that went on, while not, herself, visible unless someone on the floor craned a neck in that direction. She watched with an intense concentration.

Down there a fight was in progress for a helpless life, a fight that had been repeated in one form or another millions of times, yet one that could never lose its poignant thrill for those who fought or those who watched and hoped. So much, so terribly much depended upon one man's skill and resource. In this instance, she knew, his fate too, might hang upon the outcome. One slip, one uncertainty or hesitancy at the critical moment . . . She would not let herself think of that.

The incision was through the peritoneum now, that

glistening membrane lining the abdominal cavity. Here it was darkly discolored by the infiltration of blood spurting from the opened cavity

"Ruptured, all right."

There was no huskiness or uncertainty in the voice now. It was the old Spen speaking with the quiet steadiness of authority and command. Carol, bending forward with parted lips, could feel her heart quicken.

"Pedicle clamp." The operator reached into the clot-filled space which he had just opened, searching for something with his left hand while his right stretched backward for the long instrument with its sharply curved end. For a moment he groped blindly. She saw him shake his head.

"Badly torn," he said. "I'll have to ligate the blood vessels."

Catching Fleming's frown, Carol sensed that this increased the gravity of the procedure. With fascinated eyes she saw Spen's fingers move searchingly along the upper border of the stomach until they stopped and pressed firmly down in one spot. Immediately the flow of blood from the wound ceased.

"Got the splenic," he said. "If I can just get a tie around it. Here, Terry." He guided the pathologist's fingers to the same spot. "Keep pressure there."

Carol was lost now. Her amateur knowledge of anatomy could not follow his movements further.

"Clamps." He clicked the instruments into place and cut between them. Even the spectator's untrained eyes could appreciate the size of the blood vessels which he shortly delivered from the opening through the fat-filled veil attaching to the lower border of the stomach.

"Good work!" This was Flick Fleming. "Never saw the splenic artery and vein exposed more smoothly."

Nodding acknowledgment, the surgeon slipped a dark strand of catgut about each of the vessels and tied it tightly, slipping it back, when made secure, into the opening he had cut beneath the stomach.

"Release your pressure," he directed Terry. "I think we've got it."

No spurt of blood followed when Terry's fingers lifted. The rest was smoothly and swiftly accomplished. With no dark flood welling up into the wound the operator was able to expose and isolate the spleen. It was dark and swollen, with a deep clot-filled rent in its substance. Once again he slipped loops about

307

the smaller blood vessels, tying them also. When he finally cut along the edge of the organ and removed it there was no hemorrhage. The wound was clean. To close the incision was but a few minutes' work. He stepped away from the table.

"That ought to do it," he said.

"A fine job, Spen." Bernie Bernitz, stopping him on the far side of the door, spoke quietly. He did not want to suggest by his manner that there was anything out of the ordinary routine of a surgeon's duties in what had just taken place. It was no more than a job well done; different only in kind from many more that Spen would be expected to do. This was the implication.

"I'd like to slip him a shot of morphine," he said to Terry as Spen went on. "So much depends on how he comes through the night."

Owen James intercepted Spen. "Come into my office when you've cleaned up, will you, Spen?"

Ten minutes later Spen opened the door. Carol, seated at the chief's desk, smiled up at him with shining eyes. She was alone.

"That was marvelous, Spen."

"You saw it?"

"All but the very start."

"I never thought I could go through with it." The light that had come into his face at sight of her dimmed out.

"Why?" she demanded.

"Don't you know?" he asked morosely. "I thought everyone knew."

She shook her head. "I knew there was something."

"Ask Owen. He knows all about it. He'll tell you."

"If I'm going to be told I'd rather you'd tell me."

His face paled and hardened. "All right. If you want it that way. I killed a woman. On the operating table."

"One?" she said.

He stared at her. "What's that?" he asked uncertainly. "What did you say?"

"I asked if there was only one that you've killed."

"Are you crazy?" he cried.

"No. I'm the sane one. How many lives have you saved on the operating table? Like that poor fellow just now. Set all those against the one case that you lost, and does it seem so important?"

"Lost!" he repeated bitterly. "I've lost plenty. But this one died because I was criminally careless and wouldn't admit that I might be wrong. Morally that death is on my shoulders."

Leaning forward, she cupped her chin in her hand and looked up at him between her lashes, in the old contemplative, unforgotten posture that made his heart jump and ache.

"That's childish and morbid," she said calmly. "Shall I give you a parallel case? If it hadn't been for you I might have had an illegitimate baby. Does that make me morally an adulteress?"

With a thrill she saw the taut lines around his mouth relax. "No. Of course it doesn't. But the cases aren't the same," he argued, tightening up again. "You were tricked. It wasn't your fault."

"I was headstrong and egotistical and stupid. Just as you were. One bad break. We've both paid for it. Does that convict us for life?"

The breath came from him in a long sigh. "You're a pretty wonderful person, Carol. I've always known that. But I've never known quite all of it."

She rose, glancing at the clock which pointed to three-twenty. "Pretty late for a respectable matron to be out."

"I'll go out to the car with you," he said.

"Yes; do."

In the murk of the night as they crossed the yard she thought, What if I asked him to go home with me now? It would not be hard to do. For this was not the wreck or the shadow she had shrunk from seeing. This was the husband to whom she had so nearly surrendered herself with all the old, sure charm, but finer, firmer, more of a man, more to be trusted.

Why not?

He was speaking now. "There's some money still due me from the Tyre Clinic. Just how much I don't know. Almost enough, I should think, to——"

"I won't touch it," she said harshly. The glow had died from her eyes.

"Neither would I," was the quiet response, "except that I want to pay you off. I'm afraid you've got to let me do that, Carol."

Chilled, she said with resigned lassitude, "Oh, I suppose so! Since it seems to be on your conscience."

She was at the wheel of her car now. He put his hand lightly over hers which rested on the window ledge.

"About the other thing," he said. "You've helped me a lot. More than I can tell you. The powers of darkness—they're hard to stave off, once you've let them get you."

"They've never got you, Spen," she said quickly. "Don't think it."

If she left him now, she thought with sorrowful dread, all the old morbid thoughts that preyed upon him would come thronging back and take possession of his mind.

"Look, Spen," she said with resolution. "Want to talk it out?"

"With you?"

"Why not? We'll go back to Owen's office. Maybe there's some ale left in the icebox. We'll make a night of it."

"Oh no!" he said gently. "I'm not going to burden you with my troubles."

"I seem to remember that I once burdened you with mine," she reminded him.

"You go home," he said obdurately. "I think I can get some sleep now."

"You don't sleep?" she asked quickly.

"Not always. There are times when I'm afraid to sleep." He checked himself. "I'll be all right tonight," he concluded.

"Why are you afraid to sleep?" she persisted.

"It's childish," he answered, "but—well, sometimes I find myself back in the operating room and I see faces."

"What faces?" she demanded.

"A woman that Tyre and I lost between us, and—and the woman I told you about. And others."

Carol had an inspiration. "Did you see them when you operated tonight?"

"No, thank God! I was too absorbed after I got started."

"There's your answer."

"But that was because everything I had was concentrated on the work. It's different at night. Then is when the faces get their chance."

Carol had another inspiration. "I've got the cure for those faces." The old impudently gay voice brought an involuntary smile to his lips.

"You have? What is it?"

"Think of my face instead, of course," she prescribed. She was laughing at him as she let the clutch slip in. "Good night, Spen, and pleasant dreams."

310

TRAFFIC was congested along the Main Street as Spencer Brade came out of the Medical Arts Building. There was much exasperated blaring of horns as two perspiring policemen strove to accelerate the unacceleratable in the person of Mrs. Caroline Carskaddan, imperial in the rear seat of her old-fashioned carriage, whence she issued her orders to her ancient black coachman Jim. One such order was:

"Stop."

"Whoa!" said Jim.

The impatient cars lined up; the officers argued and importuned; pedestrians chuckled as the old lady rose and summoned Spen with an authoritative wave of her black parasol.

"Get in," she directed. "Sit down. Go on, Jim."

The parade resumed motion. Feeling like a cross between a guest of the city and a prospective victim of mob violence, Spen ventured the suggestion that they turn into a quieter thoroughfare.

"Linden Avenue, Jim," said Cousin Carrie. "I'll drive you back to Owen James' place, young man, if that's where you're going."

"Thank you. I am," said Spen.

"And why? Why are you living there?"

"Where else should I be living?"

"With your wife."

He made no answer.

"Why haven't you been to see me?" she demanded.

311

"There wasn't any occasion for it, was there?"

"Not professionally. But I'm a member of the family. Are you cutting out the family?"

"Certainly not."

"Spencer Brade, I once told you that you wouldn't get a cent of my money by marrying Carol. You said you didn't give a damn."

"Aren't you misquoting me slightly?" he murmured.

"Well, maybe you only told me to go to hell," she qualified. "I didn't blame you. I'd stuck my neck out. Now I might change my mind about the money."

Spen grinned in her face. "What's this, Cousin Carrie? Bribery?"

"Don't be impudent. You know, I always say what I think."

"So I've understood."

"And I know more about what's going on than some people give me credit for."

"I'm ready to believe that too."

"Well, what are you going to do about it?"

"About your knowing more of what's going on than people think?" he asked innocently.

"About the present situation," she snapped.

"What would you advise?" he asked cautiously.

"Now you're being sensible," she approved. "Spen, what about the Mangan girl?"

He had not expected an attack from that angle. "She's gone away," he said after a moment.

"I know she has. Is it all over between you?"

"She's going to be married."

"That's good. I know all about you and her. If that were all that's wrong between you and Carol——"

"Have you been talking to Carol?" he broke in.

"Yes. But I didn't have to tell her about that. There's lots of ways in which Carol isn't as big a fool as she is in other ways," said Cousin Carrie generously. "About you, for instance. I don't blame you, myself, one damn bit. If I were a man and had a wife who bolted the door on me I'd probably do the same."

"You seem exceptionally well informed about my domestic affairs," said Spen grimly.

"Oh, I get around! But it was Candace Grahame that told Carol about the office girl. That dried up old virgin! What does she know about the man-and-woman business! I got Carol

312

straightened out as to that. Told her it was all her own fool fault."

Spen suppressed an untimely desire to laugh. "You apparently have pretty definite theories, yourself."

"So I have. Candace has had a change of heart about you. She's given up hope of marrying Carol to Owen James. I never was for that. Owen's too good for her. Don't try to contradict me. Now, you're not; maybe not quite good enough. That's as it should be. Only don't let her know it."

"Where is all this getting us?" inquired Spen.

"I'm coming to that. We're going to drive to the clinic and I'm going to wait while you pack your duds, and then I'm going to move you back to the Grahame Lodge."

"Is that a message from Carol?" he asked quickly.

"If I hadn't more conscience than I have sense I'd lie and say yes. It isn't a message. But it's my best advice, and you'd better follow it.

"I'm sorry. I can't do that."

"Why can't you?"

"Cousin Carrie, ever since I came to Charlesville I've been living on the Grahames. I've paid off Aunt Candace. I'm still in debt to my wife. Now do you understand?"

"Does that mean you won't go back?"

"Just that."

"You've got a mean, ugly, pigheaded mouth when you set it that way, Spencer Brade. I don't know which of you two I think is the biggest fool. When I find out I'll let you both know."

"I'll be waiting anxiously to hear," said Spen.

"Umph!" snorted Cousin Carrie, and for the rest of the drive confined herself to local gossip.

Spen's visit to the Tyre Clinic had been less productive financially than he had expected. The balance due him was nearly twelve hundred dollars short of clearing him with his wife. He endorsed their check over to Carol with a note in which he thanked her for her help in dispelling his obsession. He had been definitely better since their talk, he wrote.

Her reply was cool, non-friendly, with a hint of resentment. It was always that way when the question of money came between them. Well, there was nothing to be done about that now. As her volunteer work for the James Clinic took her mainly outside, through the Flats, he saw her occasionally and

313

casually. Meanwhile he had settled into the routine and was operating or assisting Flick Fleming every day.

Cheese and ale were on the office table one stormy night when the operator called for Dr. Brade.

"Hello, hello," said Carol's strained voice. "Is that you, Spen?"

"Yes. What is it, Carol?"

"It's Cousin Carrie Carskaddan. She's had a heart attack."

"Where is she? At home?"

"No. Here with me. She had dinner with us. Aunt Candace has gone out to a meeting. I got Cousin Carrie upstairs, and she asked me to send for you."

"Be there in five minutes."

"Wait a minute. She's calling me."

Spen held the receiver. Presently Carol was back on the wire.

"She seems stronger. She says to tell you to bring a toothbrush because she might have another attack in the night and wants you on hand. I'll have your roo—the red room ready for you."

"All right," said Spen. "Keep her quiet if you can."

At first sight of the old lady, curled up like a locust shell in the big bed, Spen was surprised. She did not look like a heart case. Indeed, there was no reason why her heart should go back on her other than her age. The operation after the fire had, so far as any evidence showed, left a perfectly healed wound. Yet she lay there, apparently semicomatose, and breathing stertorously. Nevertheless, her color was good; there was none of the blue cyanosis in lips or fingernails; no weakness of pulse. Nor, when he set the stethoscope to her chest, could he detect anything abnormal in the cardiac rhythm.

As he lifted his head the patient opened one languid eye, then the other. She said:

"Hello, young man. You took your time getting here."

"Ten minutes at most," returned Spen. "What did you expect?"

"Lean over," she directed. He put his ear close to the firm old lips.

"Ten minutes, my glass eye!" she murmured. "Three weeks. That's how long you've been living with Owen James instead of here."

"Get me a hot-water bag, Carol," he said in his best

314

professional manner. When she was out of the room he turned a stern eye upon his patient.

"Now, then, what's this, Cousin Carrie?"

"What's what?"

"You wouldn't be malingering on an innocent and trusting young consultant, would you?"

"Don't you use any of your rough medical talk on me, young man. I'm a sick woman, a very sick old woman."

"There is something quite unusual about your breathing," conceded Spen.

"Is there? What is it?"

"It doesn't run true to form," he replied with a grin. "When I arrived you were putting on a fine, convincing show. It almost got me. Now your respiration is as regular as——"

"Shut up!" snapped Cousin Carrie as returning footsteps sounded in the hall. She resumed her effortful exhalations with admirable realism and lay passive again.

Carol stood over her, anxiety dimming the vividness of her young face. She plucked at Spen's sleeve.

"Can you leave her a moment?" she whispered.

He nodded.

"Come across into my room. I want to talk with you." Half closing the door, she asked, "How is she, really, Spen?"

"Nothing to worry over for the present," he answered conservatively. "When did this hit her?"

"Less than an hour ago."

By this time Spen was well satisfied that he knew all that was necessary about Cousin Carrie's heart; what had happened within that lively old maid was something else again.

"Did anything happen to excite her?" he inquired, still maintaining his professional manner.

"We did have rather a snappy discussion after dinner, just before Aunt Candace went out."

"What about?"

The corners of her mouth flickered. "Is that a medical question?"

"Strictly."

"We-ell, about you. Cousin Carrie was arguing that you were an obstinate, wrong-minded, muddle-headed young fool, and I was another. Then Aunt Candace chipped in, and I was just taking a hand when Cousin Carrie said she was sick of both of us and wanted to lie down and forget our nonsense. After I got

315

Aunt Candace into the car I came back and found her shaking all over. I asked her what she was laughing at, and she said she wasn't laughing; it was her breathing, and—" She broke off to regard him with mounting suspicion. "And now *you're* laughing," she said, aggrieved. "If it's a family joke why am I on the outside looking in? What's the matter with you people, anyway?"

"Not a thing in the world," said Spen. "Particularly Cousin Carrie. Except that she's got illusions of grandeur about herself as a strategist. She's trying to prove that she was right and Aunt Candace was wrong in this evening's debate."

"How do you know which side they took?" she demanded.

"I can guess. I'd be more interested to know where you stood."

"I didn't commit myself," she murmured.

He wandered restlessly over to the window and looked out. "Here comes a car," he said. A car had come the last time he was in that room. He wondered whether Carol, too, was thinking of that.

"It's Aunt Candace," she said. "I'll tell her that everything is all right and she can go to bed. Shall I?"

"Yes."

He was still at the window when Carol came back. There was a smile on her lips now, and color had risen in her face as she stood facing him.

"You're not very observing, are you, Spen?" she said.

"Probably not. What have I missed?"

"Don't you notice any change in the room since you last were here?"

His eyes followed hers to the connecting door between the rooms, his and hers. The bolt was gone.

"Don't you think it's an improvement?" she said lightly.

"*Carol!*" he said.

"Well," she whispered a moment later in his arms, "you did bring your toothbrush, didn't you?"

After a long pause he said, "There's Cousin Carrie. We mustn't forget her. Don't come in with me."

"What are you going to do?"

"Give that grand old faker my eternal blessing and a sleeping tablet that'll hold her till at least nine o'clock tomorrow morning."

Carol laughed softly and happily. "I always knew that I was cut out to be a surgeon's wife," she said.

316